Curious to see how the Grandmaster had visualized the three beautiful goddesses, I turned away from him towards the interior of the cave. The chill deepened as I stepped away from the entrance. The tunnel appeared to descend into an infinite darkness; another illusion perhaps, a bend, a false perspective . . . unless there were really an opening into some labyrinthine underworld.

The goddesses were not finished yet. Two had no faces. The third – Hera, goddess of marital fidelity and orthodoxy – had the face of Molly Danzig.

S. P. SOMTOW

THE PAVILION OF FROZEN WOMEN

VISTA

To the Caceks, my eccentric Denver family:
Joe, the shootist; Trish, the gipsy;
Mike, the jester; and Peter, my godchild

First published in Great Britain 1996
by Victor Gollancz

This Vista edition published 1997
Vista is an imprint of the Cassell Group
Wellington House, 125 Strand, London WC2R 0BB

© Somtow Sucharitkul 1996

The right of S. P. Somtow to be identified as author of
this work has been asserted by him in accordance with
the Copyright, Designs and Patents Act, 1988.

A catalogue record for this book is
available from the British Library.

ISBN 0 575 60074 8

Printed and bound in Great Britain
by Cox & Wyman Ltd, Reading, Berks

97 98 99   10 9 8 7 6 5 4 3 2 1

Contents

Acknowledgements

'The Pavilion of Frozen Women' © 1991 by Somtow Sucharitkul first appeared in *Cold Shocks*, ed. Tim Sullivan

'Fish are Jumping, and the Cotton is High' © 1992 by Somtow Sucharitkul first appeared in *Monsters in Our Midst*, ed. Robert Bloch

'Fire from the Wine-dark Sea' © 1979 by Somtow Sucharitkul first appeared in *Other Worlds*, ed. Roy Torgeson

'Chui Chai' © 1991 by Somtow Sucharitkul first appeared in *The Ultimate Frankenstein*, ed. Byron Preiss and John Betancourt

'Though I Walk through the Valley' © 1992 by Somtow Sucharitkul first appeared in *The Ultimate Zombie*, ed. Byron Preiss and John Betancourt

'Hunting the Lion' © 1992 by Terminus Publishing first appeared in *Weird Tales*, copyright reassigned to author

'Mr Death's Blue-eyed Boy' © 1991 by Somtow Sucharitkul first appeared in *Phobias*, ed. Wendy Webb, Richard Gilliam, Edward Kramer, and Martin Greenberg

'The Steel American' © 1992 by Somtow Sucharitkul first appeared in *Grails*, ed. Richard Gilliam, Martin Greenberg, and Edward E. Kramer

'Gingerbread' © 1992 by Somtow Sucharitkul first appeared in *The Ultimate Witch*, ed. Byron Preiss and John Betancourt

'Darker Angels' © 1994 by Somtow Sucharitkul first appeared in *Confederacy of the Dead*, ed. Edward E. Kramer and Richard Gilliam

The Pavilion of Frozen Women

1

Alles Vergängliche
Ist nur ein Gleichnis . . .
Faust

She was draped against the veined boulder that jutted up from the snow and gravel in the rock garden of Dr Mayuzumi's estate. One hand had been placed demurely over her pubes – the Japanese have a horror of pubic hair that has caused it to become the last taboo of their pornography – the other was flung against her forehead. A trickle of blood ran from the side of her lip down her slender neck, past one breast, to a puddle beside her left thigh.

When I got there with my notebook and my camera, they were milling about in the cloister that ran all the way around the rectangular rock garden. Their breath hung in the still cold air, and no one had touched the body yet, not even the police.

I hadn't come to Sapporo to cover a slasher; I'd come there for the Snow Festival. I'd only been in town for a couple of hours. I'd just started unpacking when I got the phone call from the Tokyo office and had to grab a taxi to this estate just outside town. I didn't even have time to put on a coat.

To say that it was cold doesn't begin to describe it. But I'd been feeling this cold since I was just a *winchinchala* back at the Pine Ridge Reservation in South Dakota. I stood there in my Benetton sweatshirt and my Reeboks and looked out of place. I ignored the cold.

A police officer was addressing the press. They weren't like

Stateside reporters; there was a pecking order – the Yomiuri and Asahi Shimbun people got the best places, the tabloids hunched down low in the back and spoke only when spoken to – gravely, taking turns, scribbling solemnly in notebooks. They all wore dark suits.

I'd had Japanese at Berkeley, but I couldn't follow much, so I just stood there staring at the corpse. There wasn't a strand of that stringy blonde hair that was out of place. It was the work of an artist.

It was the hair that jolted me into remembering who she was. So this wasn't just another newspaper story after all.

The snow was beginning to obliterate the artist's handiwork – powdering down her hair, whitening away her freckles. She'd been laughing all the way from San Francisco to Narita Airport. I still had her card in my purse.

I snapped a picture. When the flash went off they all froze and turned towards me all at once, like a many-headed monster. It's uncanny the way they can do that. Then they all smiled that strained, belittling smile that I'd been experiencing ever since I'd arrived in Japan a week before.

'Look,' I said at last, 'I'm with the Oakland *Tribune*.' Suddenly I realized that there wasn't a single woman among those ranked reporters. In fact, there were no other women there at all. I felt even more self-conscious. No one spoke to me at all. It didn't matter that what I was wearing stood out against the black-white-and-grey like a peacock in a hen coop. I was a woman; I was a *gaijin*; I wasn't there.

Presently the police officer murmured something. They all laughed in unison and turned back to their note-taking. One reporter, perhaps taking pity on me, said, 'American consulate will be here soon. You talk to *them*.'

'Yeah, right,' I said. I wasn't in the mood for bullshit. 'Listen, folks, I *know* this woman. I can *i-den-ti-fy* her, *wakarimashita*?'

The many-headed monster swivelled around again. There was consternation behind the soldered-on smiles. I had the distinct impression they didn't feel it was my place to say anything at all.

At that moment, the people from the consulate arrived. There was a self-important bald man with a briefcase, and a slender black woman. A few flashbulbs went off. The woman, like me, hadn't planned on a visit to the Mayuzumi estate on a snowy afternoon. She was dressed to the gills, probably about to hit one of those diplomatic receptions.

'I'm Esmeralda O'Neil,' she said to the police officer. 'I understand that an American citizen's been—' She stopped when she saw the corpse.

The policeman spoke directly to the bald man. The bald man deferred to the black woman. The policeman couldn't seem to grasp that Esmeralda O'Neil was the bald man's boss.

'Look here—' I said. 'I can tell you who she is.'

This time I got more attention. More flashes went off. Esmeralda turned to me. 'You're Marie, aren't you? Marie Wounded Bird. They told us you were coming, and to take care of you,' she said. 'I was hoping to meet you at the reception tonight.'

'I didn't get invited,' I said testily.

'Who is she?' she said. She was a woman who recovered quickly – a real diplomat, I decided.

'Her name's Molly Danzig. She's a dancer. She sat next to me on the flight from San Francisco. She works – worked – at a karaoke bar here in Sapporo – the rooftop lounge at the Otani Prince Towers . . .'

'You know anything else about her, darlin'?'

'Not really.'

She looked at the corpse again. 'Jesus fucking Christ.' She turned to the police officer and began talking to him in rapid Japanese. Then she turned back to me. 'Look, hon,' she said, 'All hell's gonna break loose in no time flat; CNN's already on their way. Why don't you come to the reception with us?' Then, taking me by the arm so that her aide couldn't hear her, she added, 'You don't know what it's like here, hon. Machismo up the wazoo. I'd give anything for an hour of plain old down home girl talk. So – reception?'

'I'm not sure . . . I'd feel a bit like trespassing . . .'

'Why darlin', you've already gone and done *that*! This is the Mayuzumi estate we're standing in now ... and the reception is Dr Mayuzumi's bash to welcome the foreign dignitaries to the Snow Festival...' I had heard of this Mayuzumi vaguely. Textiles, beer, personal computers. Finger in every pie.

The Japanese reporters were already starting to leave. They filed out in rows, starting with the upscale newspapers and ending with the tabloids. It was only then that I noticed the man with the sketchpad.

At first I thought he must be an American. Even from the other side of the rock garden I could see that he had the most piercing blue eyes. He was kneeling by the railing of the cloister. In spite of the cold he was just wearing jeans and a T-shirt. He had long black hair and a thick beard. He was hairy ... bearlike, almost ... Asians are hardly ever hairy.

The policeman barked an order at him. He backed off. But there was something in his body language, something simultaneously deferential and defiant, something that identified him as a member of a conquered people, a kind of hopelessness. It was so achingly familiar it made me lose my cool and just gape at him. That was how my mother always behaved when the social worker came around. Or the priest from the St Francis Mission. Or whenever they'd come around to haul my dad off to jail for the weekend because he'd guzzled down too much *mniwakan* and made himself a nuisance. All my aunts and uncles acted that way towards white people. The only one who never did was Grandpa Mahtowashté. And that was because he was too busy communicating with the bears to pay any attention to the real world.

My grandfather had taken me to my first communion. Nobody else came. He knelt beside me and shouted out loud: 'These damned priests don't know what this ritual really means.' They made him wait outside the church.

God, I hated my childhood. I hated South Dakota.

The man stared back at me with naked interest. I hadn't seen that here before either. People never looked you in the eye here.

I had become an invisible woman. It occurred to me then that we were invisible together, he and I.

I stopped listening to Esmeralda, who was babbling on about the social life of the city of Sapporo – explaining that it wasn't all beer, that the shiny-modern office buildings and squeaky-clean avenues were no more than a veneer – and just stared at the man. Although he was looking straight at me, he never stopped sketching.

'Anyway, hon, I'll give you my card ... and ... here's where the reception's going to be ... the Otani Prince Towers ... rooftop, with a mind-boggling view of the snow sculptures being finished up.' Esmeralda made to leave, and I said something perfunctory about seeing her again soon.

Then I added, 'Do you know who that man is?'

'That's Ishii, the snow sculptor. Aren't you here to interview him?'

It showed how confused I'd become after seeing my fellow traveller lying dead in the snow. Aki Ishii was one of the Grandmasters on my list of people to see; I had his photograph in my files. It had been black and white, though. I couldn't have expected those eyes.

And he was already walking towards me, taking the long way around the cloister.

He said to me: 'Transience and beauty ...' He was a soft-spoken man. 'Transience and beauty are the cornerstones of my art. It was Goethe, I think, who said that all transient things are only metaphors ... should we seize this moment, Miss Wounded Bird? Or is the time not yet ripe for an interview?'

'You know me?' I said. I had suddenly, unaccountably, become afraid. Perhaps it was because there were only the two of us now ... even the corpse had been carried off, and the Americans had tramped away down the cloister.

The temperature fell even more. At last I started to shiver.

'I know you, Miss Wounded Bird – perhaps you will let me call you Marie – because the *Tribune* was kind enough to send me a letter. I knew who you were at once. Something about your body language, your sense of displacement; you were that way even with your fellow countrymen. I understand that, you see, because I am Ainu.'

The Ainu ... it began to make sense. The Ainu were the aboriginal inhabitants of this island – blue-eyed neolithic nomads pushed into the cold by the manifest destiny of the Japanese conquerors. There were only 15,000 pureblooded Ainu left. They were like the Lakota – like my people. We were both strangers in our own land.

It occurred to me that I was on the trail of a great story, an important story. Oh, covering the Festival would have been interesting enough – there's nothing quite like the Sapporo Snow Festival in all the world, acres and acres of snow being built up into vast edifices that dissolve at the first thaw. It's all some Zenlike affirmation of beauty and transience, I had been told ... and now I was hearing the Grandmaster himself utter those words over the site of a sex murder ... hearing them applied with equal aptness to both art and reality.

'Perhaps I could escort you to the reception, Marie?' he said. Behind his Japanese accent there was a hint of some other language, perhaps German. I seemed to remember from his dossier that he had, in his youth, studied in Heidelberg under a scholarship from the Goethe-Institut. It was quaint but kind of attractive. I started to like him.

We left the rock garden together. He had an American car – a Mustang – parked by the gate. 'I know the steering wheel is on the wrong side,' he said apologetically, 'but I'll drive carefully, I promise.'

He didn't. The thirty kilometres back into downtown Sapporo were terrifying. We lurched, we hydroplaned, we skidded, past tiny temples enveloped in snow, past ugly postmodernist apartments, past rowhouses with walls of rice paper crammed along alleyways. Snow bent the branches of the trees to breaking. The sunset glittered on roofs of glossy tile, orange-green or cobalt blue. I was glad he was driving with such abandon. It made me think less of Molly Danzig, laughing over how she'd been fleecing the rubes at the karaoke bar, trading raunchy stories about men she had known, wolfing down airline food in between giggles ... Molly Danzig, who in death had become part of an ordered elegance she had never evinced in the twelve hours I had sat beside her on the plane from San Francisco.

★

The reception was, of course, a massive spectacle. These people really knew how to lay on a spread. The top floor of the hotel had been converted into a styrofoam and plastic replica of the winter wonderland outside. Three chefs worked like maniacs behind an eighty-foot sushi bar. Elsewhere, cooks in silly pseudo-French uniforms sliced patisserie, carved roasts and ladled soup out of swan-shaped tureens. Chandeliers sparkled. Plastic snowflakes rained down from a device in the ceiling. You could have financed a feature film by hocking the clothes on these people's backs – Guccis, Armanis, Diors – a few of those $5,000 kimonos. Although Aki had thrown on a stylish black leather duster, I found myself hopelessly underdressed for this shindig. It didn't help that everyone was studiously ignoring us. Aki and I seemed to be walking around in a private bubble of indifference.

One wall was all glass. You could see down into Odori Park, on the other side of Sapporo's three-hundred-foot-wide main drag. The snow sculptures were taking shape. Once the Festival started they would be floodlit. Now they were ghostly hulks haunching up towards the moon. This year's theme was *Ancient Times*; there was a half-formed Parthenon at one end of the park, a Colosseum in the foreground, an Egyptian temple complete with Sphinx, a Babylonian ziggurat ... all snow.

A huge proscenium filled one end of the lounge and on it stood a corpulent man who was crooning drunkenly into a microphone. The song appeared to be a disco version of 'Strangers in the Night.' There was no band.

'Jesus!' I said. 'They should shoot the singer.'

'That would hardly be wise,' Aki said. 'That man is Dr Mayuzumi himself.'

'Karaoke?' I said. There's only one karaoke bar in Oakland and I'd never been to it. This fit the description all right. As Dr

Mayuzumi left the stage to desultory applause, someone else was pushed up on to the stage amid gales of laughter. It turned out to be Esmeralda O'Neil. She began singing a Japanese pop song, complete with ersatz Motown gestures and dance steps.

'Oh,' Aki said, 'but this is the club where your ... friend ... used to work. Miss ... Danzig.' He pronounced her name *Danjigu*.

'Let's get a stiff drink,' I said at last.

We went and sat at the sushi bar. We had some hot saké, and then Aki ordered food. The chef pulled a pair of live jumbo shrimp out of a tank, made a few lightning passes with his knife and placed two headless shrimp on the plate. Their tails wiggled.

'It's called *odori*,' Aki said, 'dancing shrimp ... hard to find in the States.'

I watched the shrimp tails pulsing. Surely they could not feel pain. Surely it was just a reflex. A lizard's tail goes on jerking after you pull it off the lizard.

Aki murmured something.

'What did you say?'

'I'm apologizing to the shrimp for taking its life,' he said. He looked around shiftily as he said it. 'It's an Ainu thing. The Japs wouldn't understand.' It was the kind of thing my grandfather did.

'Eat it,' Aki said. His eyes sparkled. He was irresistible.

I picked up one of them with my chopsticks, swished it through the soy sauce dish, popped it in my mouth.

'What do you feel?' he said.

'It's hard to describe.' It had squirmed as it went down my throat. But the way all the tastes exploded at once, the soy sauce, the horseradish, the undead shrimp with its toothpaste-like texture and its exquisite flavour ... there'd been something almost synaesthetic about it ... something joyous ... something obscene.

'It's a peculiarly Japanese thing,' said the Ainu snow sculptor, 'this almost erotic need to suck out a creature's life force ... I have been studying it, Marie. Not being Japanese, I cannot intuit it; I can only listen in the shadows, pick up their leavings as I slink past them with downcast eyes. But you, Marie, you I can look full in the face.'

And he did. The way he said my name held the promise of dark intimacy. I couldn't look away. Once again this man's body language evoked something out of my childhood. It was my father, reaching for me in the winter night, in the bedroom with the broken window, with his liquor breath hanging in the moonlit air. And me with my eyes squeezed tight, calling on the Great Mystery. Jesus, I hated my father. Although I hadn't thought of him in ten years, he was the only man in my life. I felt resentful, vulnerable and violated, all at once. And still I couldn't look away. Then Esmeralda breezed over and came to my rescue.

'You never stop working for a moment, do you, hon?' she said, and ordered a couple of *odori* for herself.

I said, 'What about Molly Danzig? Any word about—'

'Darlin', that girl's just vanished from the universe as far as anyone can see. The press aren't talking. Nothing on TV. Even CNN's been put on hold for a few days. Total blackout . . . even the consulate's being asked to wait on informing the next of kin . . . it's that Festival, you know. It's a question of face.'

'Doesn't it make you mad?'

'Hell no! I'm a career diplomat, darlin'; this girl doesn't rock any boats.' She bit down on the wriggling crustacean with relish. 'Mm-mm, good.' No squeamishness, no regret.

I looked around. The partygoers were still giving us a wide berth, but now and then I thought I could see stares and hear titters. Was I paranoid? 'Everyone knows about it, don't they?' I said.

'It?' said Esmeralda ingenuously.

'It! The murder that no one can talk about! That's why they're all avoiding me like yesterday's fish; they know that I knew her. I stink of that girl's death.'

'It's nothing, hon.' She took a slug of saké.

Aki tugged at my elbow. 'I can see you're getting uncomfortable here,' he whispered. 'Would you care to blow this joint, I believe that's how you Americans call it?'

I could see where this was leading. I was attracted to him. I was afraid of him. I had a story to write and I knew that a good story sometimes demands a piece of your soul. How big a piece? I didn't want to give in yet, so I said, 'I'd love to see the snow sculptures. Now, when the park's deserted, in the middle of the night.'

'Your wish is my command,' he said, but somehow I felt that it was I who had been commanded. Like a vampire, Aki had to be invited before he could strike.

★

In the moonlight, we walked past the Clock Tower, the only Russian building left on Hokkaido, towards the TV tower which dominated the east end of Odori-Koen. The park was long and narrow. Mountains of snow were piled along the walkways.

They had brought in extra snow by the truckload. There were a few men working overtime shovelling paths and patting down banks of snow. A man on a ladder was shaping the entablature of a Corinthian column with his hands. Fog roiled and tendrilled about our feet. I didn't ask Aki why the park and the zombie shrimp had the same name; I had a feeling the answer would unnerve me too much.

We walked slowly up the mile-long park towards the tableau that was Aki's personal creation – I knew from my notes that this was to be the centrepiece of the Festival, a classical representation of the Judgment of Paris.

'What do you think of Sapporo?' Aki asked me abruptly.

'It's—'

'You don't have to tell me. It's an ugly town. It's all clean and shopping-mall-ridden and polished till it shines, but still it's a brand-new city desperately looking for something to call a soul.'

'Well, the Snow Festival—'

'Founded in 1950. Instant ancient culture. A Disneyland of the Japanese sensibility.'

It was not what I'd come to hear. I'd had the article half written before I'd even boarded the plane. I'd wanted to talk about tradition, the old reflected in the new. We walked on.

People go to bed early in Japan. You could hardly hear any traffic. A long line of trucks piled high with snow stretched the length of the park and turned north at the Sosei River end. It took three hundred truckloads of snow for the average snow sculpture. The snow came from the mountains.

Most of the sculptures had been cordoned off. Now and then we passed artisans who would turn from their work, bow smartly, and bark out the word 'sensei'. Aki walked ahead. We did not touch. Public displays between the sexes are frowned on here. I had been relieved to learn that.

'It was a shame about that Danjigu girl,' Aki said. 'I have seen her many times, at the karaoke club; Mayuzumi rather liked her, I think.'

Molly had said something about fat rich businessmen. I wished he would change the subject. I said, 'Tell me something about your art, Aki.'

'Is this the interview?' Our footsteps echoed. Ice tinkled on the trees. 'But I have already talked about beauty and transience.'

'Is that why you were sketching Molly's corpse? I thought it was kind of . . . macabre.'

He smiled. No one was watching us. His hand brushed against mine for a fleeting second. It burned me. I walked ahead a few steps.

'So what are you looking for in your art, Mr Ishii?' I asked him in my best girl-reporter voice.

'Redemption,' he said. 'Aren't you?'

I did not want to think about what I was looking for.

'I feel a bit like Faust sometimes,' he said, 'snatching a few momentary fragments of beauty out of the void, and in return giving up . . . everything.'

'Your soul for beauty?' I said. 'Kind of romantic.'

'Oh, it's all those damned Germans, Goethe, Schiller: death, transfiguration, redemption, *weltschmerz* – going to school there can really fill you with Teutonic portentousness.'

I had to laugh. 'But what about being Ainu?' I said. 'Doesn't that contribute to your artistic vision too?'

'I don't want to talk about that.'

So we were alike, always running away from who we were. He strode purposefully ahead now, his shadow huge and wavery in the light of the full moon.

A wall of snow towered ahead of us. Here and there I could see carved steps. 'I'll help you up,' he said. He was already climbing the embankment. My Reeboks dug into the snow steps. 'Don't worry,' he said, 'my students will smooth them out in the morning. Come.'

The steps were steep. Once or twice he had to pull me up. 'There will be a ramp,' he said, 'so the spectators can cluster around the other side.'

We were standing on a ledge of snow now, looking down on to the tableau he had created. Here, at the highest point in the park, there was a bitter breeze. It had stopped snowing and the air was clear, but the sky was too bright from the city lights to see many stars. The artificial mountain wrapped around us on three sides; the fourth was the half-built viewers' ramp; the area formed a kind of open-air pavilion.

Aki said, 'Look around you. It's 1200 BC. We're on the slopes of Mt Ida, in the mythological dawn. Look – over there – past the edge of the park – the topless towers of Ilium.' It was the Otani Prince Towers, glittering with neon, peering up through twin peaks. It was an optical illusion – the embankment no more than thirty feet high, a weird forced perspective, the moonlight, the fog swirling – that somehow drew the whole city into the fantasy world. 'Come on,' he said, taking my hand as we descended into the valley. A ruined rotunda rose out of a mound of rubble. A satyr played the panpipes and a centaur lay sleeping against a broken wall. It was hard to believe it was all made of snow. On the wall, sculpted in bas-relief, was the famous judgment: Paris, a teenaged version of Rodin's *Thinker*, leaning forwards as he sat on a boulder; the three goddesses preening; the golden apple in the boy's hand.

'Now look behind the wall,' Aki said.

I saw a cave hollowed out of the side of the embankment. At its entrance, sitting in the same attitude as the bas-relief, was a three-dimensional Paris; beyond, inside the cave, you could make out three figures, their faces turned away.

'But—' I said. 'You can't see the tableau from the spectators' ramp! At best, you'd see the back of Paris's head, the crook of Athena's arm. You can only see the relief on the ruined wall.'

'But that is what this sculpture is all about, Marie,' Aki said. He was talking faster now, gesticulating. 'I hold the mirror up to nature and within the mirror there's another mirror that mirrors the mirrored nature I've created ... reflections within reflections ... art within art ... the truth only agonizingly, momentarily glimpsed ... and that which is most beautiful is that which remains unseen ... come on, Marie. You will get to see my hidden world. Come. Come.'

He seized my hand. I climbed down beside him. A system of planks, concealed by snowy ridges, led to the grotto. Like a boy with an ant farm, Aki became more intense, more nervous as we neared the centre of his universe. When he reached the sculpture of Paris, he became fidgety. He disregarded me completely and went up to the statue, reshaping a wrinkle in the boy's cloak, fussing with his hair. Paris had no face yet.

Curious to see how the Grandmaster had visualized the three beautiful goddesses, I turned away from him towards the interior of the cave. The chill deepened as I stepped away from the entrance. The tunnel appeared to descend into an infinite darkness; another illusion perhaps, a bend, a false perspective ... unless there were really an opening into some labyrinthine underworld.

The goddesses were not finished yet. Two had no faces. The third – Hera, goddess of marital fidelity and orthodoxy – had the face of Molly Danzig.

I thought it must be some trick of the moonlight or my frazzled nerves. But it was unmistakable. I went up close. The likeness was uncanny. If the snow had started to breathe I would not have been more startled. And the eyes ... what were they? ... some kind of polished gemstone embedded in the snow ... snow-moistened eyes that seemed to weep ... I could feel my heart pounding.

I backed away. Into Aki's arms. 'Jesus,' I said, 'this is sick, this is morbid—'

'But I have already explained to you about beauty and transience,' Aki said softly. 'I have been watching this girl ever since she started at the karaoke club; her death by violence is, how would you say it, synchronicity. Perhaps a sacrifice for giving my art the breath of life.'

Molly Danzig shook her head. I think. Her eyes shone. Or maybe caught the moonlight. She breathed. Or maybe the wind breathed into her. Or my fear. I was too scared to move for a moment and then—

'Kiss me,' he whispered. 'Don't you understand that we are both bear people? You are the first I have met.'

'No!' I twisted free from him and ran. Down the icy pathway, with the moist wind whipping at my face, past the Parthenon and the Colosseum and the Sphinx. Past the piled-up snow. Snow seeping into my sneakers and running down my neck. It was snowing again. I crossed the street. I was shivering. It was from terror, not from cold.

Jesus, I'm getting spooked by illusions, I told myself when I reached the façade of the Otani. I took a deep breath. Objectivity. Objectivity. I looked around. There was no one in sight. I stood on the steps for a moment, wondering where to get a taxi at one in the morning.

At that moment, Esmeralda and her portly aide swept through the revolving doors and glided down the steps. She was wearing a fur stole, the kind where you'd be mugged by conservationists if you tried to wear it on the street in California. She saw me and called out, 'Marie, darlin', you need a ride to your hotel?'

I nodded dumbly. A limousine pulled up. We piled in.

As we started to move down the street, I saw him again.

Standing at the edge of the park. Staring intently at us. Sketching. Sketching.

2

Das Unzulängliche
Hier wird's Ereignis.
Faust

Bear people—

When I was a child I saw my grandfather speaking to bears.

The hotel I was staying at was a second-class *ryokan*, a traditional-style hotel, because I wanted to get the real flavour of the Japanese way of life. The smell of tatami. The masochistic voyeurism of communal bathing. I tossed and turned on the futon and wished for a waterbed in San Mateo. And the roar of the distant surf. But my dreams were not of California.

In my dream I was a *winchinchala* again. In my dream was my father's shack. Midnight and the chill wind whining through the broken pane. I'm twisting on the pee-stained mattress on the floor. Maybe there's a baby crying somewhere. A damp hand covers my mouth.

'Gotta see to the baby, *até*,' I'm whispering.

'*Igmu yelo*,' says my father. *It's only a cat*. The baby's shrieking at the top of his lungs. Dad crushes me between his thighs. Even his sweat is turning to ice. I ooze through his fingers. I run down stairs that lead down down down down caverns down down to—

'*Don't!*'

From the dirt road that runs alongside the frozen creek next to the outhouse you can see a twisted mountain just past the edge of the Badlands. The top is sheared off. I wish myself up to the ledge where I'm going to stand naked in the wind and I'm going to see visions and know everything that's to come and I'm going to stand and become a frozen woman like the other women who have stood there and dreamed until they dreamed themselves into pillars of red and yellow stone.

'*Tunkashila!*' I'm screaming. 'Grandpa!'

I'm running from the wind that's my dad's breath reeking of *mniwakan*.

Suddenly I know that the man who's chasing me is a bear. I don't look back but I can feel his shadow pressing down on me, on the snow. I'm running to my grandfather because I know I'll be safe with him, he'll draw a circle in the ground and inside everything will be warm and far from danger and he'll put down his pipe inside the sacred circle and say to the bear: *Be still, my son, be still.*

I'm running from the cold but I might as well run from myself. I'm going to be frozen right into the mountain like all the other women from now back to the beginning of the universe, women dancing in a slow circle around the dying fire. I'm running through the tunnel that becomes—

The tunnel beneath the sea. I'm riding the bullet train, crossing to Hokkaido Island, to the Japan no one knows, the Japan of wide open spaces and desolate snowy peaks and spanking-new cities that have no souls. I'm staring out as the train shrieks, staring at the concrete cavern. I see Molly Danzig's eyes and I wonder if they're real, I wonder if Aki has plucked them from the corpse and buried them in the snow woman's face.

The frozen woman shakes her head. Her eyes are deep circles drawn in blood. 'No, *até*, no, *até*,' I whisper.

Be still, my son, my grandfather says to the bear who rears up over the pavilion of frozen women. My grandfather gives me honey from a wooden spoon. He puts his pipe back in his mouth and blows smoke rings at the bear, who growls a little and then slinks, cowed, back into the snowy forest.

Circles. Circles. I'm running in circles. There's no way out. The tunnel has twisted back on itself. I will turn to snow.

★

Molly Danzig's card: an apartment building a few blocks west of the Sapporo Brewery. It was about a fifteen-minute ride on the subway from my *ryokan*. The air was permeated with the smell of hops. Snow piled against a coke machine with those slender Japanese coke cans. At the corner, a robocop directed traffic. Its metal arms were heaped with snow. The first time I'd seen one of those things I'd thought it must be a joke; my Tokyo guide told me, self-importantly, that they'd had them for twenty years.

The afternoon was grey. The sky and the apartment building were the same dead shade, grey grey grey.

I took the elevator to the tenth floor. I don't know what I expected to find. I told myself, Hey, sister, you're a reporter, maybe there *is* a gag order on this story now but it won't last out the week. I had my little Sure Shot in my purse just in case.

The hall: shag carpet, dull modern art by the elevator. This apartment building could be anywhere. The colour scheme was nouveau *Miami Vice*. I followed the apartment numbers down the corridor. Hers, 17A, should be at the end. There it was with the door ajar. An old man in overalls was painting the door.

Painting out the apartment number. Painting out Molly's name. A brushstroke could obliterate a life.

I pushed my way past him into the apartment. I'd had a notion of what Molly's place would look like. Molly was always laughing so I imagined there'd be outrageous posters or funky furniture. She loved to talk about men – I don't – so I imagined some huge and blatant phallic statue standing in the middle of the room. It wasn't like that at all. It was utterly still.

The windows were wide open. It was chillier here than outside. A wind was sighing through the living room and the tatami floor was peppered with snow. No furniture. No Chippendales pin-ups on the walls. The wind picked up a little. Snowflakes flecked my face.

The kitchen: two bowls of cold tea on the counter. The stove was still lit. I turned it off. A half-eaten piece of sushi lay in a blue-and-white plate. I took a few snapshots. I wondered if the police had come by to dust the teabowls for prints.

I heard a sound. At first I thought it must be the wind. The wind blew harder now and behind the sighing I could hear someone humming. A woman.

I stepped into the living room. Snow seeped through my sneakers. I was shivering. It was a contralto voice, eerie, erotic. I could hear water dripping too. It came from behind a *shoji* screen door. A bedroom, I supposed.

I knew I was going to have to go in. I steeled myself and slid the *shoji* open.

Snowflakes whirled. The wind was really howling here. Through a picture window I could see the Sapporo Brewery and the grid of the city, regular as graph paper, and snowy mountains far beyond it. I smelled stale beer on the snow that settled on my cheeks.

The humming grew louder. A bathroom door was ajar. Water dripped.

'Molly?'

I could feel my heart pounding. I flung the bathroom door wide open.

'Why – Marie darlin' – sure wasn't expecting *you*.' Esmeralda looked up at me from the bathtub, soaping herself lazily.

'You knew who she was the whole time,' I said.

'It's my business to know that, hon,' she said. 'Not too many American citizens in Sapporo, as you might have noticed, but I keep tabs on 'em all. Hand me that washcloth? Pretty please?'

I did so numbly. Why had she asked me who the dead woman was if she already knew her? 'You tricked me!'

'In diplomacy school, Marie, they teach you to let the other person do all the talking. Oftentimes they end up digging their own grave that way.'

'But what are you doing here—?'

'This is my apartment. Molly Danzig used to sublet. I've got a suite in the consulate I usually end up crashing out in, but the hot water in our building never works right.'

She reached for a towel and slid out of the tub. She steamed; she was firm and magnificent and had a way of looking fully clothed even when she was naked; I guessed it was her diplomatic comportment. The Lakota are a modest people. I was embarrassed.

'Believe me, this ain't St Louis. I mean, girl,' she said,

reaching for the hair dryer, 'here's me, on a GS salary with
perks up the wazoo, housing allowance, no mouths to feed . . .
but if it weren't for all those receptions with all that free food,
I'd be lining up at a fucking soup kitchen. Let's forget this and
just go shopping somewhere, Marie.'

'All right.' I couldn't see where I could go with the story at
this point. I had three or four pieces, but they didn't seem to fit
together – maybe they didn't even belong in the same puzzle.
Perhaps I just needed to spend a mindless afternoon buying
souvenirs.

★

Esmeralda drove me to the Tanuki-koji arcade, a labyrinthine
underground mall that starts somewhere in the middle of town
and snakes over and under, taking in the train station and the
basement of the Otani Prince. She parked in a loading zone
('*Gaimusho* tags, darlin' – they're not going to tow any of us
diplomats, no way!') and, although it was afternoon, we
descended into a world of neon night.

When you're confused and pushed to the limits of your
endurance and you think you're going to crack up, sometimes
shopping is the only cure. I never went shopping when I was a
kid. Yes, sometimes we'd take the pickup and lurch towards
Belvidere or Wall, where at least you could watch the mechanical jackalopes for 25¢ or gaze at the eighty-foot fake dinosaur
as it reared up from the knee-high snow. Shopping was a vice I
learned from JAPs and WASPs in Berkeley. But I had learned
well. I could shop with passion. So could Esmeralda. It was an
hour or two before I realized that, for her as well as me, the
ability to shop effusively was little more than a defence
mechanism. As we warmed to each other a little, I could see
that she spoke two different languages, with separate lexicons
of gesture and facial expression; they were as different as
English and Lakota were for my parents, except they were both
English, and she could slide back and forth between them with
ease.

We moved from corridor to corridor, past little noodle stands with their glass cases of plastic food in front, past *I Love Kitty* emporia and kimono rental stores and toy stores guarded by mechanical Godzillas, past vending machines that dispensed slender cans of Sapporo beer and iced coffee. People shuffled purposefully by. The concrete alleyways were slick with mush from aboveground. Glaring neons blended into chiaroscuro.

By six or so we were laden down with shopping bags. Junk mostly – fans, hats, coats, orientalia for my apartment in Oakland, postcards showing the Ainu in their native costume, with ritual tattoos and fur and beads – not that there were any to be seen in the antiseptic environs of Sapporo.

'What do you know about the Ainu?' I asked Esmeralda.

'They're wild people. Snow people, kind of like Eskimos maybe – they worship bears, have shamanistic rituals – only for tourists – the Japanese forced them all to take Japanese names and they can't speak Ainu any more.'

It was a story I knew well. My grandfather Mahtowashté had told me the same story. 'I can speak to bears,' he said, 'because once, when I was a boy, a bear came to me in a dream and gave me my name.' And he'd give me a piece of bread dipped in honey and I'd say, '*Tunkashila*, make it so I can get out of here . . . make it all go away.'

'There're more Ainu around than you might think. A lot of them have interbred with the Japanese. They don't *look* Ainu any more, but . . . people still feel prejudiced. They don't advertise, not like your friend Aki. Most of them just try to blend in. They'd lose their social standing, their credit rating, their influence . . .'

I knew all about that. I'd spent my whole life escaping, blending.

'Come on,' Esmeralda said, 'time for coffee.'

We stopped at a coffee shop and squeezed ourselves into tiny armchairs and we each ordered a cup of Blue Mountain at ¥750 a pop. Tiny cups of coffee and tall glasses of spring water.

'Help me, Esmeralda,' I said. 'Jesus, I'm lost.'

'This isn't the place you thought it would be.' A neon blue-and-pink reproduction of Hokusai's *Wave* flashed on and off in the window. The alley beyond was in shadow. You could hear the whoosh of the subway trains above the New Age muzak and the murmur of conversation. I wondered whether the sun had already set in the world above. 'You're thinking dainty little geishas, tea ceremonies, samurai swords ... cute gadgets ... crowds. And you're on Hokkaido which isn't really Japan at all, which looks more like Idaho in January, where the cities are new and the people are searching for new souls ...'

'You sound like that sculptor sometimes, Esmeralda.'

'Oh, Aki ... did you fuck him yet, honey? He's a good lay.'

'I'm not easy,' I said testily. Actually, in a way, I was a virgin.

Oh God, I remembered the two of us in the cavern, I remembered the eyes of Molly Danzig, I remembered how he'd stared straight into my eyes, as though he were stalking me. A hairy beast of a man. Lumbering. A grizzly bear tracking me through the snow.

'Marie? Are you all right?' She sipped her coffee. 'They don't give refills either – five bucks and no fucking refill.' She drained it. 'But you know, you should get to know him. You know how hard it is for a red-blooded American girl to get laid here? These people don't even know you're there – oh, they're polite and all, but they know we're not human. Blacks, Indians, whites, Ainu, we all look alike to them ... we *all* niggers together. Besides, everyone here *knows* that all Americans have AIDS.'

'AIDS?' I said.

'Stick around here, hon, and you'll know how a Haitian feels back home. Hey, I screwed Mayuzumi once – but I might as well have been one of those inflatable dolls.' She laughed, a bit too loudly. A schoolgirl at the next table tittered and covered her mouth with her hand. 'Molly Danzig now ... he liked her a lot ... actually he was paying her rent you know ... he liked to have her around whenever he needed to indulge his secret vice ... I guess he thought it was kind of like bestiality.'

'Molly was—'

'Shit, darlin', we all whores, one way or another!' she added. I felt I was being backed into a corner.

'Aki frightens me.'

'Don't he! But he's the only man in this whole godforsaken country who has the common decency not to roll over and fall asleep right after they come.'

The neon wave flashed on and off. Suddenly *he* was there. In the window. The blue and pink light playing over his animal features. 'It's him!' I whispered.

Aki's eyes sparkled. He had his sketchpad. His hand was constantly moving in tiny meticulous strokes.

'What does he want?' I said. 'Let's get out of here before—'

'What do you mean, hon? I told him to meet us here.' Aki was closing his sketchpad and moving into the coffee shop. A waitress hopped to attention and bowed and rapped out a ceremonial greeting like a robot. His gaze had not once left my face.

'But – he *knew* her, don't you see? He knows you – he knows me – and she's *dead* and one of the three goddesses in his sculpture has her face . . . and the other two are blank . . .'

Esmeralda laughed. It was the first time I had ever voiced this suspicion . . . or even admitted to myself that I *had* a suspicion . . . I realized how preposterous it must sound.

I felt ashamed. I looked away. Stared into the brown circle of my coffee cup as though I could hypnotize myself into the phantom zone. I could hear his footsteps though. Careful, stalking footsteps.

He stood above me. I could feel his breath. It smelled of honey and cigarettes. He said, 'I understand, Marie. It's spooky there in the moonlight. You are in the middle of a city of a million people, yet inside my snow pavilion you are also inside my art, a sculpted creation. It's frightening.' He touched my neck. Its warmth shot through me. I tingled.

'It was nothing to do with you,' I found myself saying. 'It's something else – out of my past – that I thought I'd forgotten.'

'Ah,' he said. Instead of moving his hand, he began to caress my neck in a slow, circular motion. I had a momentary vision of him snapping off my head. I wanted to panic but instead I found myself relaxing under his gentle pressure ... sinking into a well of dark eroticism ... I was trembling all over.

'Culture tonight!' Aki said. 'A special performance of a new *bunraku* play, *Sarome-sama*, put on by the Mayuzumi foundation for the edification of the ... foreign dignitaries.'

'*Bunraku?*' The last thing I wanted was to go to a puppet show with him and Esmeralda. I had heard of *bunraku* in my Japanese culture class at Berkeley – it was all yodelling and twanging and wooden figures in expensive costumes strutting across the stage with excruciating elegance.

But she wouldn't hear of it. 'Darlin', *everyone* will be there. And this is a really *weird* new show ... it's the traditional puppet theatre, sure, but the script's adapted from Oscar Wilde's *Salome* – translated into a Mediaeval Japanese setting – oh, honey, you'll never see anything like it.'

'But my clothes—' I said. I felt like a puppet myself.

'And what,' she said, putting her hands on her hips, 'are credit cards for, girl?'

*

Weird did not begin to describe the performance we witnessed at the Bunka Kaikan cultural centre. The weirdness began with the opening speeches, one by Dr Mayuzumi, the other by a cultural attaché of the German Embassy, which belaboured endlessly the concept of cultural syncretism and the union of East and West. What more fitting place than Hokkaido, an island so rich in cross-cultural resonances, whose population was in equal parts influenced by the primitive culture of the enigmatic Ainu, by Japan, by Russia, and – in this modern world – by – ah – the 'Makudonarudo Hambaga' chain ...

Polite laughter; I had a vision of Ronald McDonald prancing around with a samurai sword.

I thought the preamble would end soon; it turned out to be interminable. But they had promised a vast buffet afterwards at the expense of the Mayuzumi Foundation. I saw Mayuzumi himself, sitting alone in a box on the upper tier, like royalty. Esmeralda and I were near the front, next to the aisle, with Aki between us. We were both wearing Hanae Mori gowns that we'd splurged on at the underground arcade.

The lights dimmed. The twang of a *shamisen* rent the air; then a spotlight illumined an ancient man in black who narrated, chanted and uttered all the characters' lines in a wheezing singsong. We were in for cultural syncretism indeed; the set – Herod's palace in Judaea – had been transformed into a seventeenth-century Japanese castle, King Herod and his manipulative wife into a shogun and a geisha, and Salome into a princess with hair down to the floor. John the Baptist, for whom, in Oscar Wilde's revisionist text, Salome was to conceive an illicit and finally necrophiliac passion, was a Jesuit missionary. The centrepiece of the stage was the massive cistern in which John lay imprisoned. It was such a fascinating interpretation that it was hard to remember that I was sitting next to a man whom I suspected of murder.

In *bunraku*, the puppeteers are dressed in black and make no attempt to conceal themselves as they operate their characters. There were three operators to each of the principals. It took only minutes for the puppeteers to fade into the background ... it made you think there was something to this ninja art of invisibility. The characters flitted about the stage, their eyelids fluttering, craning their necks and arching the palms of their hands, shrieking in paroxysms of emotion.

An American audience wouldn't be this silent, I thought.

The eerie rhythms entranced me. The rasp of the *shamisen*, the shrill, sustained wailing of the flute, the hollow tock-tock-tock of the woodblock did not meld into a soothing, homophonous texture as in Western music. Each sound was an individual strand, stubbornly dissonant. The narrator sang, or sometimes spoke in a lisping falsetto. In one scene, as Salome, his voice crescendoed to a passionate shriek that seemed the very essence of a woman's desire, a woman's frustration. He knows me, I thought ... he has seen me running from my father, bursting with terror and love. I could hardly believe that a man could portray such feelings. At the back of the auditorium, afficionados burst into uproarious cheering. From the context I guessed it was the moment when Salome demands to kiss John's mouth and he rebuffs her, and the idea of demanding his severed head first germinates in her mind ... for the Salome puppet threw herself across the floor of the stage, the three operators manipulating wildly as she flailed about in savage mimickry of a woman's despair.

Jesus, I thought. I've been there.

I looked at Aki and found that he was looking behind us, up at Mayuzumi's box. As applause continued, Mayuzumi made a little gesture with his right index finger. Aki whispered in Esmeralda's ear. She said, 'Gotta go, darlin' – be right back.' The two of them slipped into the aisle.

Was there some kinky triangle ménage between them? I could see Aki and Esmeralda in leather and Mayuzumi all tied up – the slave master playing at being the slave ... Esmeralda wasn't inhibited like me. Maybe they had become so aroused they'd slipped away to one of those notorious coffee shops, the ones with the private booths ...

I didn't want to think about it too much, and after a while I became thoroughly engrossed in the play. I couldn't follow the Japanese – it was all archaic – but I knew the original play, and the whole thing was in such a slow-motion style that you had plenty of time to figure things out.

There was the dance of the seven veils – not the Moroccan restaurant variety, but a sinuous ballet accompanied by drum and flute, and a faster section with jerky movements of the head and eyebrows and the arms obscenely caressing the air ... the seven veils were seven bridal kimonos of embroidered brocade ... the demand for the saint's severed head with which to satiate Sarome-sama's lust ... the executioner, his katana glittering in the arclight, descending into the cistern ... I gulped ... how could they be wood and cloth when I could feel their naked emotions tearing loose from them? A drum began to pound, step by pounding step as the headsman disappeared into the oubliette ...

The drums crescendoed ... the flute shrilled ... the shamisen snarled ... I heard screaming. It was my own.

A head was sailing out of the cistern, shooting up towards the stage flies! . . . a human head . . . Esmeralda's head.

For a split second I saw her torso pop from the cistern. Blood came spurting up. The puppets' kimonos were soaking. The torso thrashed and sprayed the front seats with blood. The claque began to applaud.

O Jesus Jesus it's real—

The head thudded on to the stage. Its lifeless eyes stared up into mine. I was the only one screaming. Wildly I looked about me. People turned away from me. It was as if I were somehow to blame because I had screamed. An announcement started coming over a loudspeaker. There was no panic. The audience was filing slowly out by row number, moving with purposeful precision, like ants. No panic, no shrieks, no nervous laughter. It was numbing. Jesus, I thought, they're aliens, they're incapable of feeling anything. Only the foreign guests seemed distraught. They stood in little huddles, blocking the traffic as the rest of them politely oozed around them. The stage hands were scurrying across the stage, moving props about. The Salome puppet flopped against the castle walls with its doll-neck wrung into an impossible angle.

I stared up at Mayuzumi's box. Mayuzumi was gone.

Esmeralda's head was gone. They were mopping up the blood. I could hear a police siren in the distance.

Then, up the centre aisle, framed in the doorway between two columns of departing theatregoers, I saw Aki Ishii appear as if in a puff of smoke.

Sketching.

Sketching *me*.

Jesus Christ – maybe he'd lured her away to kill her! I couldn't control my rage. I started elbowing my way towards him. The audience backed away. Oh yes. We *gaijin* all have AIDS. Aki backed slowly towards the theatre entrance. There was a shopping bag on his arm. The doors were flung wide and the snow was streaming down behind him and I was shivering in my Hanae Mori designer dress that wasn't designed for snow or serial killers.

He backed into the street. The crowd parted. Men with stretchers trotted into the theatre and a police siren screeched. I started to pummel him with my fists.

'Am I next?' I screamed. 'Is that it? Are you sucking out our souls one by one to feed your art that's going to turn to mush by Friday?'

He held his hands up. 'It's not like that at all,' he said.

The wind howled. I was hysterical by now. Fuck these people and their propriety. I shouted at a passing policeman, 'Here's your goddamn sex murderer!' He ignored me. 'That shopping bag! The head's in the shopping bag!' I tried to wrest it from him. I could feel something squishy inside it. There was blood on everything.

'How could you be so wrong?' Aki said. 'How could you fail to understand me? I told you the truth. It's not me – it's – it's—' His eyes glowed. That odour of honey and tobacco again ... startled, I remembered where I'd smelled it before ... on my grandfather's breath. I kept on hitting him with my fists but my blows were weak, dampened by snow and by my own bewilderment. You've got no right, I was thinking, no right to bring me those bad dreams ... no right to remind me ...

He grabbed my wrists. I struggled. His sketchpad flew into the snow. The wind flipped the pages and I saw face after face ... beautiful women, ... beautiful and desolate ... my own face. 'My art,' Aki said. There was despair in his voice. 'You knocked my art out of my—' He let go abruptly. Scurried after the sketchpad, his black duster flailing in the wind like a Dracula cape. He found it at last. He cried to me across the shrieking wind: 'We're both bear people. You should have understood.' And he ran off into the darkness. He vanished almost instantly, like one of those puppeteers with their ninja arts.

It was only then that I realized that my dress was dripping with blood. It was caking against my arms, my neck. The wind and the sirens were screaming all at once.

No one's going to ignore *this* killing, I thought. A consular

officer . . . a public place . . . a well-known artist hanging around
near the scene of both crimes . . .

But as I watched the audience leaving in orderly rows, as I
watched the policemen solemnly discoursing in hushed tones,
I realized that they might well ignore what had happened.

I was going to have to go to someone important. Someone
powerful. Power was all these people understood.

3

Das Unbeschreibliche,
Hier ist's getan . . .
Faust

Midnight and the snow went on piling. I walked. Snow smeared
against the blood on my clothes. I walked. I had some notion of
finding my way back to the *ryokan*, making a phone call to the
Tokyo office, maybe even to Oakland. I could barely see where
I was going.

Bear people . . .

No one in the streets. The wind whistled. Sushi pennants
flapped against restaurant entrances. I breathed bitter liquid
cold. At last I saw headlights . . . a taxi.

By two in the morning I was outside the Mayuzumi estate.
There were wrought-iron gates. The gates had been left open
and the driveway had been recently shovelled. He let me off in
front of the mansion.

A servant woman let me in, rubbing her eyes, showed me
where to leave my shoes and fetched clean slippers. She
swabbed at my bloodstains with a hot towel. Then she handed
me a clean *yukata* and watched while I tried to slip it on over
my ruined gown.

It was clear that I – or someone – was expected. Perhaps
there was a local geisha club that made house calls.

'*Mayuzumi-san wa doko—?*' I began.

'*Ano . . . o-furo ni desu.*'

She led me up the steps to the tatami-covered foyer. She slid aside a *shoji* screen, then another and another. We walked down a succession of corridors – I walked, rather, and the maid shuffled, with tiny muffled steps, pausing here to fuss with a flower arrangement, there to incline her head towards a statue of the Amida Buddha. Beyond the Buddha image was a screen of lacquered wood on which were painted erotic designs. She yanked the screen aside and then I was face to face with Dr Mayuzumi . . . naked, sitting in a giant bath, being methodically massaged by a young girl who sang as she kneaded.

He was a huge man. He was, I could see now, remarkably hirsute, like Aki Ishii; his eyes were beady and set closely together; he squinted when he looked at me, like a bear eyeing a beehive.

Behind Dr Mayuzumi, the shoji screens had been drawn aside. The bathroom overlooked the rock garden where Molly's body had been. Snow gusted behind him and clouds of steam tendrilled between us.

'Ah,' he said, 'Marie Wounded Bird, is it not? The reporter. I had thought we might meet in less . . . informal surroundings, but I am glad you are here . . . 'Tomichan! Food for our guest! You will join me for a light supper,' he said to me. It was an order.

'You have to help me, Dr Mayuzumi,' I said. 'I know who the killer is.'

He raised an eyebrow. With a gesture, he indicated that I should join him in the bath. I knew that the Japanese do not find mixed bathing lewd, but I had never done it before; I balked. Two maids came and began to disrobe me. They were politely insistent, and the hot water seemed more and more enticing, and I found myself being scrubbed with pumice stone and led down the tiled steps . . . the water was so hot it hurt to move. I let it soak into my pores. I watched the snowflakes dance around the stone lantern in the cloister at the edge of the rock garden.

'No one will do anything,' I said. 'But there's a pattern. The victims are white and black . . . people who don't belong to the Yamato race . . . maybe that's why none of you people think it's important ... the victims are all subhuman ... like me ... and I think I'm next, don't you see? The three goddesses ... the Judgment of Paris ... and the killer is subhuman too ... an Ainu.'

'What are you trying to say?' Mayuzumi said. 'You would not be attempting to pin the blame on Aki Ishii, the Grandmaster of snow sculpting?'

I gasped. 'You knew all along. And you knew that I would come here.'

Just as the heat was becoming unbearable, one of the serving maids fetched a basket of snow from outside. She knelt down at the edge of the bath and began to sprinkle it over my face, my neck. I shuddered with agony and delight. Another maid held out a lacquerware tray in front of me and began to feed me with chopsticks.

It was a lobster salad – that is, the lobster was still alive, its spine broken, the meat scooped out of its tail, diced with cucumbers and a delicate *shoyu* and vinegar dressing, and replaced in the splayed tail-shell with such artistry that the lobster continued to wriggle, its claws clattering feebly against the porcelain, its antennae writhing, its stalk-eyes glaring. I had already started to chew the first mouthful before I saw that my food was not quite dead. But it was too delicious to stop. And knowing I was draining the creature's life force only heightened the *frisson*. 'I'm sorry,' I whispered.

'Ah,' Dr Mayuzumi said, 'you're apologizing to the lobster for—'

'Taking its life,' I said. Wasn't that what Aki had said about the shrimp?

'How well you understand us.' I was conscious of a terrible sadness in him. There was more to him than just being a millionaire with a finger in every pie. 'I, too, am sorry, Marie Wounded Bird.' He ordered the maid to remove the lacquer trays. 'Yet you did not come to dine, but to accuse.'

'Yes.'

'You have proof, I hope; a man of Mr Ishii's standing is not indicted lightly. His reputation ... indeed, the reputation of the

Snow Festival itself ... would be at stake. You can understand
why I sought to discourage the press from ... ah ... untimely
revelations.'

'But he's *killing* people!' I said.

'Mr Ishii is a great artist. He is very precious to us. His
foibles—'

I recoiled. 'How can you—'

'In the grand scheme, in the great circle of birth and rebirth,
what can a few lives matter?' he said. 'But Mr Ishii's art ...
does matter. But now you are here, blowing across our fragile
world like *kamikaze*, the wind of the gods, irresistible and
unstoppable. You would melt us down, just as the spring sun
will soon melt the exquisite snow sculptures which 1.6 million
tourists are about to see ...'

I couldn't believe this. It was the most familiar line of bullshit
in the world. I was soaking in 110°, in the nude, eating live
animals and listening to the Mayor of Amity shtick right out of
Jaws. My own life was on the line, for God's sake! I remembered
Aki's eyes ... the way he had run his fingers along the nape of
my neck ... his long dark hair flecked with snow ... the quiet
intensity with which he spoke of beauty and transience and
voiced his resentment of the conquering Japanese ... could he
really be one of those Henry Lee Lucas types? I knew he had
had sex with Molly and Esmeralda. I knew he had been tracking
me. Sketching. Sketching. Smelling of tobacco and honey, like
my grandfather.

God, I wanted him and I hated myself for wanting him. For
a moment, standing in the snow amid his creation, listening to
him – Jesus, I think I *loved* him.

'Goddamn it, I can prove it,' I said. 'I'll show you fucking
body parts. I'll show you eyeballs buried in snow and skeletons
under the ice.'

I was doomed to betray him.

'All right,' said Dr Mayuzumi. 'I feared it would come to
this.'

★

The limousine moved rapidly towards downtown Sapporo. We sat in the back seat, each hunched into an opposite corner. It was still snowing. We didn't speak until we were within a few blocks of Odori Park.

At last, Dr Mayuzumi said, 'Why?'

I said, 'I don't know, really, Dr Mayuzumi. Maybe he's sending a message to the Japanese people ... about discrimination, about the way you treat minorities.' I didn't want to think of Aki just as an ordinary mad slasher. We had too much in common for that. But there was too much evidence linking him to Molly and Esmeralda ... and me. Four minorities. Lepers in a land that prized homogeneity above all things. I had a desperate need to see the killings as some political act ... it might not justify them, but I could understand such killings. Like the Battle of Little Big Horn ... like the second siege at Wounded Knee. 'Politics,' I said bitterly.

'Perhaps.' He did not look into my eyes.

The chauffeur parked at the edge of the park.

We began walking towards the Judgment of Paris tableau. Dr Mayuzumi strode swiftly through the slush, his breath clouding about his face. I struggled to keep up. I became angrier as we walked. I had come to see him with information and now it seemed he had known all along, that his coming with me now was merely the working out of some preordained drama.

The full moon lengthened our shadows. Even the snow-shovelling workmen were gone; the empty trucks were parked in neat rows along the Odori.

Dr Mayuzumi strode past the snow Sphinx and the Pyramids of Gizeh; I trudged after him, awkward in the short coat that one of the servants had lent me. I was determined not to let him take the lead. I brushed by him. I was furious now. It seemed that this whole town had been built on lies. Snow gusted and flurried. Ice-shards lanced my face. I walked. Snow metropolises rose and fell around me. I didn't look at them. I tried to quell the cold with sheer anger.

We passed the columns of the Temple of Poseidon at Sounion, the icy steps of a Babylonian ziggurat, a Mexican pyramid atop which sat a gargoyle god ripping the heart out of a hapless child. Moonlight fringed the ice with spectral colours. Had the buildings grown taller somehow? Were the sculptures pressing in, narrowing the pathway, threatening to crash down over me? A skull-shaped mountain grinned down. Trick of the light, I told myself. I stared ahead. My shoes were waterlogged.

At length we came to Mt Ida. I marched uphill. They could fix the footprints later. Dr Mayuzumi followed. We crossed the terrace with its classical friezes, its nymphs and shepherds gesturing with Poussin-like languor.

In a moment we stood inside Ishii's secret kingdom, the cave that the audience could not see. The mirror of mirrored mirrors.

There had been more tunnelling. The walls were lit by reflected moonlight and the cave seemed to stretch forever into blackness, though I knew it was an illusion. Like Wile E. Coyote, we are easily fooled by misdirecting signposts ... a highway median that leads to the edge of a cliff ... a tunnel painted on to the side of a sandstone mountain. It seemed we stood at the entry to an infinite labyrinth.

Dr Mayuzumi took out a flashlight and shone it on the interior of the cave.

There were the three statues. Molly Danzig stood with her arms outstretched. It was her – but dead, she was more beautiful somehow, more perfect ... the statue of Athena had the face of Esmeralda O'Neil. She glowered; she was anger personified. It was just as I had imagined. The third goddess had no face yet ... and neither did the boy Paris who was to choose between them.

I could be beautiful too, I thought. Cold and beautiful. I was tempted. I told myself: I hate the cold. I hate my childhood. That's why I went away to California.

Dr Mayuzumi said, 'Look at their eyes ... as though they were still alive ... look at them.'

Molly's eyes: a glint of blue in the gloom. They stared straight into mine. Esmeralda's looked out beyond the entrance. The Athena statue held a spear and a gorgon-faced shield. God, they were beautiful. But I knew the deadly secret of their verisimilitude.

'How long can the cold preserve a human organ, an eye, for example?' I said. 'Doesn't this snowclad beauty hide death? Tell me there are no human bones beneath . . .'

'You would destroy this masterwork?'

It was too late. Before he could stop me I had plunged my fingers into Molly's face. I wanted to pull the jellied eyeballs out of the skull, to thrust them in Dr Mayuzumi's face.

The face caved in. There was nothing in my fists but snow, flaking, crumbling, melting against the warmth of my hands. And then, when the snow had melted, two globes of glass and plastic. Two marbles.

I looked at Dr Mayuzumi. His look of indignation turned to mocking laughter. All my resentment exploded inside me. I smashed my fists against the statues of my two friends. Snow drenched me. The statues shattered. There were no bones beneath, no squishy organs. Only snow. Tears came to my eyes and melted the snow that had clung to my cheeks.

'A *gaijin* philistine with a stupid theory,' said Mayuzumi.

I beat my arms against the empty snow, I buried myself elbow deep. I wept. I had understood nothing at all. The marbles slipped from my fingers and skated over a stretch of ice.

I felt Dr Mayuzumi's hand on my shoulder. He pulled me from the slush. There was so much sadness in him. 'And I thought you understood us . . .'

He gripped me and would not let go. His hands held no comfort. His fingernails dug into my flesh . . . like claws.

'I thought you understood us!' he rasped. His teeth glinted in reflected moonlight . . . glistened with drool . . . his eyes narrowed . . . his mouth smelled of honey and tobacco.

I thought you understood us . . . what did that mean?

And all at once I knew. When he had greeted me in the bath, when I mumbled *I'm sorry* at the writhing lobster, had he not said *How well you understand us*? I had completely missed it before . . . 'You're an Ainu too, one who's been able to pass for a Yamato,' I said. 'You've blended with the Japanese . . . you've climbed up to a position of power by hiding from yourself . . . and it's driven you mad!'

'I'm sorry, . . . oh, I'm sorry,' he said. His voice was barely human. Still he would not let go. In the dark I could not see his face.

'Why are you apologizing?' I said softly.

'I need your soul.'

Then I realized that he was going to kill me.

The flashlight illuminated him for a moment. His face was caving in on itself. Dark hair was sprouting up through the skin. I felt bristles push up from his palms and prick my shoulders. I was bleeding. I struggled. His nose was collapsing into a snout.

'Bear people!' I whispered.

He could not speak. Only an animal growl escaped his throat. He had become my father. I was caught inside the nightmare that had haunted me since I was *winchinchala*. I kicked and screamed. He roared. As his body wrenched into a new shape, I slipped from his grasp. The cavern shook and rumbled. Snow crashed over the entrance. I could hear more snow piling up. The cave was contracting like a womb. We were sealed in. The whine of the wind subsided.

The flashlight slid across the snow. I dived after it. I waved it in the air like a lightsabre. Its beam was the only illumination. It moved across the eyes . . . the teeth . . . I could smell the foetid breath of a carnivore. I was choking on it. 'What are you?' I screamed.

He roared and the walls shook and I knew he no longer had the power of human speech. He began to lumber towards me. There was no way to escape. Except by stepping backwards . . . backwards into the optical illusion that suggested caves within caves, worlds within worlds.

I backed into the wall. The wall pulsated. It seemed alive. The very snow was living, breathing. The wall turned into a fine mist like Alice's mirror . . . I could hear the tempest raging, but it was infinitely far away.

I was at the edge of an icy incline that extended downwards to darkness.

The bear-creature that had been Dr Mayuzumi fell down on all fours. He pounced. I tripped over something ... a plastic bag ... its contents spilled on to my face. In the torchlight I saw that it was Esmeralda's head. The severed trachea snaked into the snow. There were no eyes. I bit down on human hair. I retched. There was blood in my throat. The bear-creature reared up. I screamed, and then I was rolling down the slope, downwards, downwards—

And then I was in a huge cavern running away from the were-bear my father with his rancid breath and the wind whistling through the broken window-pane and—

Darkness. I paused. Strained to listen. The bear paused too. I could hear him breathing, a savage purr deep as the threshold of human hearing, making the very air vibrate.

I swung the flashlight in an arc and saw—

The fangs, the knife-sharp claws poised to strike and—

There was music. The dull thud of a drum. The shriek of the bamboo flute and the twang of the *shamisen*, and—

The bear sprang! The claws ripped my cheeks. I was choking on my own blood. I fell and fell and fell and my mouth was stopped with snow and I was numb all over from the cold and I was sliding down an embankment with the bear toying with me like a cat with a mouse and I screamed over and over, screamed and tasted blood and snow and—

I heard a voice: *Be still, my son.* The voice of my grandfather.

I was slipping away from the bear's grasp.

Into a circle of cold blue light.

In the circle stood Aki Ishii. He was naked. His body was completely covered in tattoos: strange concentric designs like Neolithic pottery. His long black hair streamed in a wind that seemed to emanate from his lips and circle around him; I felt no wind. Smoke rose from a brazier, fragrant with tobacco and honey.

'*Tunkashila* ...' I murmured. I crawled towards him. Clutched at his feet in supplication.

The bear reared up at the edge of the circle. In the pale light I saw him whole for the first time. His face still betrayed something of Mayuzumi; his body still contained the portly outline of the magnate; but his eyes burned with that pure unconscionable anger that comes only in dreams.

'Be still,' said Aki Ishii. 'You may not enter the circle. It is I who am the shaman of the bear people. You cannot gain true power by taking men's souls; you must give in equal measure of your own.

And then I saw, reflected in the wall of ice behind us, mirage-like images of Molly Danzig and Esmeralda O'Neil. They were half human, half cave painting. They too were naked and covered with tattoos. They had become Ainu, but I saw that they were also *my* people ... they were also the Greek goddesses ... Molly, who had fled from her home and herself and sought solace in the arms of strangers, had been incarnated as domesticity itself; Esmeralda, whose diplomatic career belied her bellicose nature, had become the goddess of war. What was I then? There was only one goddess left: the goddess of love.

But I was incapable of love, because of what my father had done. I hated him, but he was the only man I had ever loved.

Three musical instruments materialized in the smoke of the incense burner. Molly plucked the *shamisen* of domestic tranquillity out of the air; Esmeralda seized the war-drum. One instrument remained: the phallic bamboo flute of desire. I took it and held it to my lips. Of its own accord it began to play, a melody of haunting and erotic sweetness. And the drum pounded and the *shamisen* sounded ... three private musics that could not blend ... until we faced the bear together.

'My son,' said Aki Ishii softly, 'you must now reap the fruits of your own rage.'

The bear exploded. His head split down the middle and the mingled brains and blood gushed up like lava from a volcano. His belly burst open and his entrails writhed like snakes. The drumbeats were syncopated with the cracking of the bear's spine. Shards of tibia shredded the flesh of his legs. Blood splattered the ceiling. The walls ran red. Blood rained down on us. Each piece of the bear ate away at itself, as though dissolving in acid. The smoke from the brazier turned into a blood-tinged mist. And all the while Aki Ishii stood, immobile, his face a mask of tragedy and regret.

I didn't stop playing until the last rag of blood-drenched fur had been consumed. Small puddles of blood were siphoning into the snow. The images of my dead friends were swirling into the mist that was the honey-tinged breath of Aki Ishii, shaman of the bear people. Only the eyes remained, resting side by side on an altar of snow. Aki nodded. I put down the flute and watched it disappear into the air. I knelt down and picked up the eyes. They were hard as crystal. The cold had marbled them.

'I'm sorry,' Aki said. The light was dimming.

'Are you going to kill me?' I whispered, knowing that was what an apology presaged.

'I'm not going to take anything from you that you will not give willingly,' said the snow sculptor. He took me by the hand. 'The war between the dark and the light is an eternal conflict. Dr Mayuzumi wanted what I wanted . . . but his magic is a magic of deceit. He was content with the illusion of power. But for that illusion, he had to feed on real human lives. This is not really the way of bear people.'

'The dead women—'

'Yes. I planted a piece of those women into the snow sculptures. We made love. I captured a fragment of their joy and breathed it into the snow. Dr Mayuzumi devoured them. They were women from three races the Japanese find inferior, but each race has done what the Ainu have not done – they have fought back – the blacks and the reds against the white men, the whites against the Japanese themselves. That was what made him angry. Our people have had their souls stolen from them. By stealing a piece of each of the three women's souls, tearing them violently from their bodies in the moment of death, he sought to give himself a soul. But a soul cannot be wrested from another person; it is a gift.'

He took my other hand. And now I saw what it was that I

had feared so much. I thought I had locked it up and thrown away the key, but it was still there . . . my need to be loved, my need to become myself.

'Now,' said Aki Ishii to me, 'you must free yourself, and me.'

I held out the bear's two marble eyes. He took one from me. We each swallowed an eye in a single gulp. It had no taste. It was like communion. And then he kissed me.

We made love as the light faded from the cavern, and when we emerged from the wall of ice, the statues were whole again, and the goddess of love had my face; but the face of Paris was still blank.

4

Das Ewig-weibliche
Zieht uns hinan!
Faust

It was a beautiful Festival. By night, thousands upon thousands of paper lanterns lit the way for the million and a half tourists who poured into the city for the first week of February. The deaths of two foreign women were soon forgotten. Dr Mayuzumi's bizarre suicide aroused much sympathy when his Ainu origins were revealed; it was only natural that a man in his position would be unable to cope with his own roots.

The death of Grandmaster Ishii was mourned by some; but others agreed that it was only fitting for an artist to die after creating his masterpiece. He was found in the cavern, nude, gazing at the statues of the three goddesses; he had replaced the image of Paris with himself. It was agreed that he had sacrificed his life to achieve some fleeting epiphany comprehensible only to other artists, or, perhaps, other Ainu.

I can't say I understood it at all. I had stood at the brink of some great and timeless truth, but in the end it eluded me.

It was a beautiful Festival, but to me it no longer seemed to have meaning. I was there in a plastic city of right-angled boulevards, a city that had robbed the land of its soul; a city that stood over the bones of the Ainu, that mocked the dead with its games of beauty and impermanence. Like Rapid City with its concrete dinosaurs ... like Deadwood with its mechanical cowboys and Indians battling for 25¢ and all eternity ... like Mount Rushmore, for ever mocking the beauty of our Black Hills by its beatification of our conquerors.

You can't understand about being oppressed unless you're born with it. It is something you have to carry around all the time, like soiled underwear that's been soldered to your skin.

I know now that I'm not one of you. You own my body, but my soul belongs to the mountains, to the air, to the streams, the trees, the snow.

I think I will go back to Pine Ridge one day. Perhaps my grandfather will teach me, before he dies, the language of the bears.

I think I will even see my father. Perhaps I can be the angel of his redemption, as I think I was for Aki Ishii.

Perhaps I will even forgive him.

———

The Pavilion of Frozen Women, the novella that opens this collection, was something of a breakthrough for me. I wrote the story for Tim Sullivan's anthology *Cold Shocks*, and the fact that it was a nominee for the World Fantasy Award is due in no little measure to his persistent and perspicacious editing ability.

Fish are Jumping,
and the Cotton is High

Every summer until the day he died, my dad used to take me on a fishing trip. He'd take a whole month off from work – when he had work, that is – and he'd throw the big trunk full of tackle into the back of his station wagon and he'd scoop me up and dump me in the front seat next to him and we'd just go, up or down I-95, until we reached a turn-off we'd never used before, then inland, down country roads, past towns with names a body couldn't pronounce, deep into cotton country, where they grew the best fish in America.

We always took Grandma with us on them trips. Not that she had much to contribute, but it felt good to have the whole family together. My favourite part of our times together was in the early evening, with the stars just fixing to come out, with the *dzzt-dzzt* of the chigger-buster and its weird blue glow, putting the tent up next to some winding creek, frying up a big old batch of bacon and flapjacks, hauling Grandma out of the suitcase and setting her up so the sunset'd shine right through her and stain them bleached old bones of hern the colour of fresh-gushing blood.

Oh, Grandma was high after so many years on the road, but after we dusted her off and hung a brand-new air freshener around her neck she was good as new, and it was better for her to be amongst her own flesh and blood than rotting away in some old hole in the churchyard back home.

I sure did love her. She was my favourite out of all my kinfolk, the only one that didn't mind my sassing.

When the fishing actually started, we'd pack her back up into the suitcase and stow her in the back of the station wagon. She was a sensitive soul.

I still remember that last summer we were all together like it was yesterday. The open road swimming in the heat, and us sitting in the cool air-conditioning listening to Dad's favourite music, which was George Gershwin in any shape or form, specially the show tunes from *Porgy and Bess*; Dad telling me stories about what it was like in the Depression; Dad telling about all the fish he used to catch down Hannibal way, especially the wrigglingest ones, the ones that got away . . .

'This time of year is best, Jody,' he told me. 'This time of year's when the fish are jumping.'

★

The name of the town was I think Sweetwater. I don't recollect the county. We cruised in about sunset, and the fish were already gathering. Along the main street was the best place to start looking. Maybe outside a beauty salon or a bar. Likely as not a town like this would only have one.

I spotted one first: she had them droopy earrings and her skirt hitched up almost all the way to her panties, and her lips were painted blood-red and her eyes were lined in heavy black. 'Slow down, Dad,' I said. 'Look, there, against that lamppost.'

'Bullcrap, sonny-boy,' he said. 'Ain't no more'n a minnow.'

'With all that make-up plastered on her face?'

'Too much make-up. You gotta look beneath the make-up. She can't be no more than twelve years old. Beneath the make-up, sonny. See that one now – there's quality.'

I knew what he meant. Her bust was about bursting out of her blouse, and her face was painted, every inch of it, in eye-popping red, black and blue. She had a beehive hairdo. Her ass was all crammed into her jeans and she was smoking a cigarette as she leaned against a mailbox outside the town drugstore.

'Now that,' said my dad, 'is a fish.'

'How we gonna catch her, Dad?'

'The usual, I think. The worm on the end of the hook on the end of the line.'

'You want me to play the worm, Dad?'

'Sure thing, son.'

He laughed. I sure was glad he was in a good mood, 'cause that meant he'd let me help with the whole job from start to finish. If he was in a bad mood, he'd lock me out of the good parts, and if he was in a really foul mood, he was liable to make me spend the night with Grandma.

We shadowed her for a couple of blocks, which was all there was to that town anyways. She never did notice. They never do. She was looking at her watch and cussing to herself. That was good. They're more vulnerable when they think they've just been stood up. After a bit she started taking bigger steps, like she was fed up and decided to walk home even though it was probably a fair piece from the town itself. She had good legs for walking, though, firm and muscular.

The town warn't hard to figure out. It didn't have but one stop sign and then it run up against open fields. Dad stopped shadowing her, took off, and let me off at the side of the road about a mile on down, just the other side of a slope, so she wouldn't know I was there till she practically tripped over me. He cuffed me a couple times in the mouth, to make it look convincing. I always hated that part.

I laid myself down and, soon as I saw her coming, I started moaning, and it warn't all play-acting neither. My dad was a mean slapper and I had a tooth loose.

'Lordy,' she said, 'what happened to *you*?'

'Oh, ma'am, please help me,' I said, 'my daddy done wore me out with his belt and tossed me out of his car and I don't know where the hell he is.'

'Why, that son-of-a-bitch!' she said, and knelt down beside me. 'Report him to the CPS, you ought to. You know what that is? Child Protective Services. They can fix you up, honey. My sister's a social worker.'

'Damn straight I know about them CPS folks, ma'am, they's what got me into this ... they took me from my parents ...

that man which beat me, he's my *foster* father.' Bleeding hearts were the easiest to confuse.

'Lordy,' she whispered, and I could see she was mighty perturbed.

'Don't tell the social workers, ma'am, they'll only find out about the time I shoplifted a box of candy from Woolworths, but ma'am, I couldn't help myself, I hadn't et in four days . . .'

'Honey, are you *hungry*?' She rooted around in her purse and produced half a Twix bar. I usually prefer the peanut butter flavour but I had to pretend I was desperate for food, so I gobbled down the whole thing and then threw in some good retching sounds for good measure.

'What's your name?' she said.

'Um . . . Jody,' I said. I always used my real name – what the hell, they weren't about to kiss and tell.

She kind of leaned down and I gripped her wrist in both hands, hard as I could. I was pretty strong even though I was only in the seventh grade. She didn't think nothing of it, just figured I was clinging on to her because I wanted attention. But it was because I heard Dad's station wagon lumbering on up the hill.

Before she knew what was happening, Dad lassoed her out of the open window, slammed on his brakes, and started reeling her in. I hung on as she got herself whip-dunked down against the car door.

'Shit, Jody, you run and call 911 right now, you hear?' the fish screamed, but that was before I got the duct tape out of my jeans pocket and shoved a snotty old handkerchief in her mouth and wound the tape around and around her face. She kicked some, but the lasso pinned her arms to her sides, and pretty soon we had her trussed up real good, like a pig.

'We oughta use her for a hood ornament,' I said, laughing.

'Nah, sonny-boy, they only do that with deer.'

We hauled her inside and stacked her up next to Grandma's suitcase. She made whinnying noises, and she thrashed around a mite, but she warn't near as much trouble as some.

There was an empty barn on some abandoned farm which

me and Dad'd staked out, about sixty miles down the road, which looked like about the perfect spot for our headquarters this summer. I couldn't wait to get there so we could start gutting the first fish of the season. We'd spent the whole night preparing for it, cleaning out the special room we were gone use, sharpening our tools.

It was about sunset when we pulled right into the barn. The air was hot and dank, but it didn't smell of cowshit or nothing; there'd been no folks on this farm for a long, long time. Dad said it was because of the recession; it'd made his job a whole lot easier. There warn't no electricity there but we had hung up some lamps in the loft, and we had most of the equipment laid out.

'Go put your Grandma somewhere decent,' my dad said. 'You know she's a sensitive soul and she don't even like to buy meat at the supermarket.'

I drug Grandma's suitcase over to a far corner so we could gut and clean without upsetting her. Then me and Dad carried our prize up the steps into the loft. She was trussed too tight to squirm much, but her eyes wiggled back and forth like lime Jell-O. We tossed a rope through a metal ring hanging from the rafter and hoisted her so she was about an inch or two off of the floor, and then I started cutting the clothes off of her.

Meanwhile, Dad was getting the instruments ready, polishing them until they shone.

'Measure her,' he said, 'and then we'll take off the gag so we can tell what she's thinking.'

I got out the tape measure. She was 37–25–39; not a bad specimen. It was a pity we couldn't stuff her and mount her. The people back home just wouldn't understand. I wrote the numbers down in the ledger so we'd always have a record. Then I put the book away in the tackle trunk, and I got out the big old Bible we always carried with us on our fishing trips.

'Ready?' I said.

'Ready.'

I ripped off the duct tape from her mouth.

'Fuck you!' the fish screamed. 'What are you, some kind of sex killer?'

Dad slapped her across the face. 'Don't you ever say that!' he shouted. 'I ain't one of them sick perverts which interferes with women and then kills them. I never do no interfering. Ain't that right, son?'

'Yeah, Dad.'

'I am an angel of the Lord, and you ain't nothing but a painted whore of Babylon. Thou shalt not suffer a witch to live. We're doing the Lord's work here, and don't you forget it. We're gone pray with you, and watch with you, and show you the error of your ways, and when we's through with you you will beg us and plead with us to send your soul flying right into the arms of the Lord's compassion. And now, Jody, let's have the harmonica.'

I fished it out of the trunk and handed it to him. He played and I sang:

> I will make you fishers of men,
> Fishers of men,
> Fishers of men,
> I will make you fishers of men,
> If you fol–low me!

It was hard to sing on key because of the way she was hollering. Finally my dad had to whup her across the face a couple of times. 'You're supposed to sing, not scream,' he said. 'Sing, bitch.' I knew how he hated getting the paint of Babylon- ish whoredom on his hands. She never did seem to appreciate what we were doing for her immortal soul. Well, he just went on slapping her until she started to croak out the words of the hymn.

After a while my dad told me to open up the Good Book and read aloud some of the parts that had to do with lusting and whoring. The important texts were highlighted in neon yellow. I read about adultery and the sins of the flesh. Didn't rightly know what some of them things were, but I knew they had to be mighty bad to deserve the kind of punishment the Lord had called us to inflict. While I read, my dad unleashed his staff of chastisement from his pants – I did the same – and the power of the Lord went into it and made it hard and strong. It was a high honour to be allowed to help with this part of the ceremony. I could feel the rapture seizing hold of my whole body.

'Why don't you just rape me now and get it over with?' she said, spitting in my face.

'You still don't get it, do you?' Dad said. 'Keep reading, sonny-boy.'

He shucked her nipples with a paring knife and dropped them in the mason jar with the others. He made a series of crisscross cuts on her belly. She screamed. He swung his staff of chastisement against her flesh and I did the same with mine, even though it only reached up to her thigh. I felt bigger than myself, like the wind of the Lord was blowing through my soul.

I held the Bible with one hand and went on reading.

'Oh Jesus it hurts it hurts,' she shrieked, 'I'll do anything I'll let you fuck me if you want just make it stop make it stop—'

Dad sighed. 'She thinks this is all about . . . lust. I've told her I ain't gone interfere with her in any way, but she still don't understand. She's too far gone to understand.'

'For them that's too far gone,' I said, 'ain't but one answer.' I ripped off one of her fingernails. Her squalling never stopped.

'Shut the fuck up!' he shouted. 'There's a lady present here! You want to wake my mother?' He hit her over the head with piece of pipe, and that seemed to calm her down a tad. It was enough for us to finish the business of anointing her with the milk of the Lord's mercy, which come spurting out of our staffs of chastisement just at that moment.

We revived her by sloshing a Diet Coke over her face, and our ministry to her went on into the night. We sliced, we diced, we chainsawed and we roto-rootered. But just like Dad promised, we didn't send her into the world hereafter until the moment she pled for it, because we warn't no killers.

When we were done, we were filled with joy, and though we

were tired we knew it was an honest day's work and that we
were storing up wages in heaven.

'Praise be to God,' Dad whispered as the fish breathed her
last, 'for we have saved you from the everlasting fire.'

The Lord rewarded us with provender. The butt meat was
always the best. We had us a small fire, fetched Grandma out
of her suitcase so she could enjoy a nice family meal; and, in
the wee hours before the sunrise, my dad and I laid down on
our pallets and talked about life, and birth, and death, and
about the Lord; about all the things that mattered in our lives.

It being high summer, it turned rainy all of a sudden. The
moisture seeped into the barn and we like to drowned from
breathing it in. I loved the sound of that rain.

Dad told me the story of how the Good Lord had called him
to this ministry. He had told the story so often I almost had it
by heart, but I didn't mind hearing it again because it was a
bond between us and every time he told the story it made me
admire him more. 'Were you real little?' I asked him.

'Littler'n you,' he said dreamily.

Mosquitoes danced in the light of the lantern. 'We lived in a
two-room shack up in the hills in them days. Every day I
studied the Bible with Brother Michael down at the Church of
Light. Sometimes he'd use his rod on me, and anoint me with
the milk of mercy, but I paid the pain no mind because it was
bringing me closer and closer to God. And every evening I
swept the house clean and said my prayers and fell asleep in
your grandma's bed. She worked late and I'd never see her
until morning, when I woke up to the smell of frying bacon.'

'Sounds like a piece of heaven,' I said softly, because all I'd
ever known was the wrong side of town, where the bigger boys
lay in wait for you after school and beat you till the crap ran
down your pants.

'Oh, sonny-boy, that it was. Until the night I slept fitfully,
and the Lord woke me from a dream. The dream was of hills
and a river. The river was beating against the wall of a dam
and the hills were pulsing with electricity. The river was full of
power. It was full of fish. That dream disturbed me and I woke

up. It was a thundering night. And I saw the most hellish sight that I ever did see. My mother was awake, and she was nekkid, and her face was painted. Her lips and her cheeks was rouged and her eyelashes blackened. There was a man on top of her, and he was bare-ass nekkid hisself, and he was interfering with her. He was sticking his rod where it shouldn't be stuck. And I was full of the wrath of the Lord, because Brother Michael done read the Bible with me that day, and we talked about sins of the flesh.

' "Stop interferin' with my mother, you hear?" I shouted.

'But your grandma, she was too far gone. Instead of realizing the error of her ways, she done pushed me off the bed and said, "Interferin'! Where d'you think *you* come from, you little bastard, if it warn't for interferin'?" I landed on the hard wooden floor and banged my ass up bad. Then I crept away to the kitchen to look for a knife.'

I could feel the horror of it as clear as if I'd been there myself. Each time Dad relived it, it became more real to me.

'What did you do next, Daddy?'

'I saved her, sonny-boy. I saved your Grandma, praise be to God, I saved her from the everlasting fire. And now—'

'Now we're a family again.' I could feel the warmth of our love deep in my heart and in my bones. We were a special family. Fishers of men. Dad kissed me and I wrapped my down bag tight around myself and listened to the pelting rain until I fell asleep.

★

That was how our summer began and it was like every summer as far back as I could remember. After we buried the fish in a ditch about twenty miles from the barn, we went on from Sweetwater to Wild Horse and from Wild Horse to Ocrapocah and Dumb Holler. We found a fish in every town and brung her back to the old barn to minister unto her. We never had to pay for our supper but once, when we stopped at a McDonald's to remind us of the lean times. My dad never once spoke a harsh word to me, and he only hit me when he had to.

The trouble started I reckon the day we reached a town called Spring Oaks. It warn't that small of a town – it actually had more'n one traffic light. Dad decided to get a copy of the local paper. It had a photograph of fish number one of the season right there on the front page. At first Dad was pleased. He pulled off the road next to a cotton field to read it.

CRISS-CROSS KILLER STRIKES AGAIN, the headline read. They'd found our first fish in that ditch. Kids'd been playing there. Somehow they'd figured out it was the same person who'd done a bunch of slayings down in Florida three years back; that was what they'd named him that time, because of the pattern of the knife cuts on her torso.

'So, what does the press have to say about me this time?' Dad said, pouring hisself a cup of coffee out of the Thermos. I skootched up closer to him and read it over his shoulder. He was a slow reader and I would sometimes help him with some of the words, whenever I seen his lips stop moving.

I read: 'Severe lacerations ... limbs missing ... genital area mutilated ... some semen stains found on buttocks suggest sporadic attempts at penetration . . .' It was the usual bullcrap. Then there was this part that said, 'Turn to page four for a specialist's profile of the suspect,' and Dad turned to that page in a hurry.

In the article, some fancy psychiatrist from Massachusetts had studied all the victims of the Criss-cross Killer and compared them all. This is what he said: 'The evidence would indicate a white male in his mid-to-late thirties. There is nothing about his general appearance to provoke suspicion. He has probably had an extremely traumatic childhood experience which resulted in the transformation of normal sexual impulses into an arcane and private ritual involving death and mutilation. Doubtless he has been imprinted with the wrong set of symbols. The danger is to over-simplify, to invest the killer's personality with a Psycho-like Pavlovian response to the trigger stimulus . . .'

'What in God's holy name does this mean?'

'Don't understand a word of it, Dad,' I said, 'honest I don't.'

'Well, I do. This high-and-mighty Yankee witch-doctor's saying I'm a pervert, that's what. He's saying I'm a sick, demented, sex-crazed, psycho killer instead of a ministering angel of the Lord.'

'Is that what he means, Dad?'

'Are you mocking me, sonny-boy? I ought to tan your hide right here and now and—'

'Dad, I didn't mean no—'

'Shut your damn mouth, Jody.'

Right then and there I knew that good times was over for the summer. The bad mood had come over him at last. Sometimes it came after only one or two fishes; this time we'd managed to stretch our precious time together through five of them – what a summer! the best I'd ever known – but the better it'd been, the worse the mood he went through when it was near over. Best to try to ride it out somehow. He just couldn't help hisself.

What I said next I reckon I shouldn't have: 'Dad, but that psychiatrist fellow was right guessing your age, warn't he?'

'Be *quiet*!'

'And it's true, ain't it, that your sex feelings ain't the same as ordinary folks'?' I thought this must be true because I always listened to the way the boys in school talked about fucking, and I never could get it to jibe with Dad's way of reckoning the facts of life. I knew Dad was right, of course, but it was a curious thing, how so many kids my age could be so ignorant, and not know the danger they stood in of eternal damnation, which meant their parents must not know nothing neither, and so on, back through the generations, all the way through to the original sin of Adam.

'I don't know what you're talking about,' he said.

'Oh, Dad, you know ... you never stick your dick into them. I never seen you stick your dick into *nobody*. Shit, Dad, I never even seen you beat off.'

I saw him go beet-red. He ripped the paper up and he threw it out of the car window and he slammed me against the dashboard and put his arms around my neck and like to strangle me. 'Don't hurt me, Daddy,' I whimpered, but he only said, 'Into the back. In there with your grandma. I don't want to see hide nor hair of you until we get home.'

'But Dad—'

'Get in there before I whup your ass with a bundle of thorns.'

I crawled into the back and opened my Grandma's suitcase and got in alongside her. Sometimes Dad would relent but this time I heard him stick the key in the padlock and I heard Dad shriek out at the top of his lungs, 'My God, my God, why hast thou forsaken me?'

It was dark. It smelled bad. Grandma's bones rattled around and the air freshener had stopped working. I held my breath a long time. The key in the padlock never turned. I could get out if I wanted to, but I knew I'd get a sound whupping if I tried. All's I could hear was the muffled sound of my dad cussing, cussing, and cussing.

After a while I could feel the car moving again. The whole suitcase shuddered and the bones kept slipping and sliding. Maybe there was another fish to fry. When the bad mood took my dad, the most we could squeeze out of a trip was maybe one more. I put my ear up to the lid and tried to listen. The station wagon was slowing down. Dad was using the charm approach. I could hear him speaking softly. He was probably driving alongside somebody, wooing her as he steered her towards a deserted street. It seemed to be going smoothly even without using me as bait. Pretty soon I heard the car door open. This was going great. She won't even putting up a struggle, just coming along voluntary. That only proved she was one of them whores of Babylon – only a whore'd get into a stranger's car without no coercion.

I heard her laughing. Well, it was more of a nervous giggle. 'You have a coffin in the back of the car!' she was saying.

'Ain't no coffin,' said my dad. 'It's a suitcase.'

She had just gone and pushed one of my dad's buttons. Dad's mood always darkens anytime a body calls Grandma's suitcase a coffin. I was curious about what was gone happen so I cautiously lifted the lid about a half inch. I saw the back of

the new fish's head and it was enough to realize she was the
best and biggest of the summer. Her hair was red as the
autumn hills and I could smell that perfume – I was right
grateful that she'd used so much because I'd about had a
noseful of the stench inside the suitcase – and it didn't take
much imagination to realize she probably had tits like balloons.
My dad can really pick them every time.

Dad turned on to the road towards our barn.

The fish said, 'You won't hurt me, will you?'

There was a pause. 'I don't hold with interferin' with
women,' he said.

She'd just done pushed another button. I could feel Dad's
rage uncoiling. I could imagine his hands just shaking and
shaking on that steering wheel and his mind racing on ahead,
thinking about the ministry, about the terrible cup the Lord
had given him to drink from.

'So you're a fag?' said the fish. Teasing. Taunting.

That was the third button.

'Bitch! don't say them things! Brother Michael was a good
man . . . a good man, do you hear? and he showed me the way
of the Lord.' He let go of the steering wheel and grabbed the
fish by the neck, both hands, and started to choke her. The car
was zigzagging all over the place but won't nobody else on the
road.

I was thinking: Dad, if she dies now before we've had a
chance to save her, she's gone straight to hell and we'll be
guilty of murder. But I daresn't say nothing because I'm afraid
of my dad's temper.

Then, all of a sudden, everything changes.

She ain't just a-kicking and a-scratching like other fish.
There's a purpose to what she's doing. She's getting the better
of him, and all of a sudden she whips out a pair of handcuffs
and next thing you know, he's cuffed to the steering wheel as
the station wagon veers off the road and into a tree.

Then she pulls out a gun.

'I'm Lt Flora Harberd,' she said. 'FBI. You have the right to
remain silent . . .'

'What the hell are you doing, ma'am?' said Dad, and he suddenly sounded ineffective and vulnerable. Almost as though Grandma were telling him what to do. Almost like a little boy. 'I was happy to pick you up. Warn't no call to start calling me names, and then picking a fight with me. You ain't no detective. You were dolled up like a who'.'

'David Lee,' she said. 'Or should I say, Billy Joe Blackburn? Johnny Raitt? How many aliases have you used, Mr Criss-cross Killer? Or are you the Swamp Thing? The Macon County Terror? Oh, yes, we've been watching you for a long, long time. I was chosen to bait you, Mr Killer, because I was the closest match to your preferred victim type. Ninety-eight per cent! They made us take a test. Computer-matched our photographs with pictures of your mother when she was a young woman working the streets. Well, mister, you're hooked now, and we're going to reel you in.'

It stung me that she was talking about fishing. It was like she didn't have no understanding of the world at all. It warn't her place to talk about the Lord's work. She was a fish, not a man.

My dad, he was just shivering and sweating all over, and I think his faith was wavering. Especially when she shoved that pistol of hers right between his lips.

'Ever suck a cock, mister?' she said. 'We have Brother Michael in custody, you know. He talked. Boy, mister, he squealed like a pig, he sang.'

My dad wailed. Like a little baby. What was wrong with him? Why warn't no thunder and lightning coming down from the sky?

'I could shoot you dead right here and now, mister,' said the fish-turned-fisherman. 'I know you're just gonna cop an insanity plea and spend the rest of your life in some asylum. It ain't right. You're scum. You should be dead.'

'Damn Yankees,' my dad said.

'Shut the fuck up and let me finish reading your Miranda rights.'

I could only see a slit of what was happening. But I could tell

that my dad won't doing nothing to defend hisself, it was like
all the fight'd gone right out of him. There was only me left to
do something about it.

She didn't know there was anybody else in the car. I didn't
have no weapon. I just grabbed a hold of the first thing I could.
I took a deep breath. She was talking about how they could use
anything he said against him in a court of law. I bust out of that
suitcase and smashed it down hard on the fish woman's head.
She looked at me with wide surprised eyes and just slumped
over in the seat.

'That was close, Dad,' I said. 'Another minute and she
could've blowed your brains to kingdom come.'

'You . . . you . . . look what you done to your grandma, Jody
. . . oh, how can you look your daddy in the eye?'

And I saw what I was holding in my hand. Grandma's skull.
I was right horrified at what I done. Carefully I put it back in
the suitcase and shut the lid back down. 'Sorry, Grandma,' I
whispered.

'Didn't tell you you could come out of there,' Dad said
angrily. He aimed to slap me across the face, but he was still
wearing his cuffs.

'Come on, Dad . . . you have to be strong.' I leaned over and
started looking for her keys. 'I know she almost had you but
we can deal with her now.' I fished out the keys, drug out a
coil of rope from the back of the wagon, and started to truss her
up the way Dad'd taught me, good and tight. Then I unlocked
the cuffs. Dad just sat there, looking at his hands. Seemed like
he didn't believe it could've happened, what with the Lord
protecting him and all. 'For God's sake, Dad, help me.'

'You tore your grandma apart!'

'Grandma's dead.'

'You *killed* her!'

'No, Dad. You did. A long time ago. You done told me so
yourself. You saved her from the everlasting fire. Praise be to
God.'

He looked all confused. 'You reckon?' he said.

'Come on, Dad. Let's get her on down to the barn.'
'Oh. Yeah.'

★

We carried her up to the loft just like we done all the others.
We moved Grandma's suitcase back inside. We slung the fish
from the rafter through the iron hook. She was unconscious, so
we didn't even bother to gag her. Everything was as it always
was, but I could see that my dad's heart warn't in his work no
more. I wished he would just slap me a time or two; even his
bad moods were better than this. His eyes had gone lifeless;
warn't no fire in them; they stared ahead like the eyes of a fish.

We cuffed her ankles with her own cuffs and we laid her
piece alongside the sacramental tools of deliverance.

All the time Dad was sharpening them tools and opening the
Bible to the right page for the start of the ritual, he was
mumbling to himself, 'I ain't pure enough, I ain't . . . I ain't the
perfect servant of the Lord . . . I have strayed . . . oh, God, I
have strayed, and now you're showing me the error of my
ways . . .'

'Dad, what do you mean, you've strayed?' I couldn't believe
what I was hearing. I loved my daddy with all my heart. He
wasn't the straying kind. He was a pillar of strength to me. He
didn't waver. The man I was seeing now, he warn't like my
dad. He was more like me.

'Once, sonny-boy, once and once only . . . I interfered with a
woman.'

The fish-detective hung from the rafter and swayed back and
forth. She was still out cold. I couldn't believe my ears. I
thought I had heard every story my dad had to tell about his
past. This was a new one. I had the feeling everything was
about to change for ever. He was unlocking the secretest
chamber of his heart to me.

'I was new to fishing,' he said. 'My understanding was still
poor. I didn't even know then that fishing was what it was. I
loved the Lord, and I wanted to bring these sinners to his
bosom, but there was things I was too simple to grasp. In them

days I was still fishing far from home, up north. I caught me a
fine one, tied her to a bedpost, and began my ministry unto
her.

'I didn't rightly know what I was doing. And she taunted
me. She teased me with honeyed words. She mocked me. "That
rod of chastisement of yours don't hurt me one bit," she said.
"It don't hurt unless to poke it right inside of me, unless you
stoke the fires of hell inside my belly." I believed her. So
trusting I was, and so ignorant of the desires of the flesh! Before
I knew it I'd pierced her in that place. And no sooner'd I spent
my milk of mercy than she screeched, "You've given me a
baby, by the grace of God; now you can't torment me, because
you can't take away the life from the innocent child."'

As he told me this, his hands were trembling. He paced back
and forth. He stumbled. The other stories he told me, they were
like pebbles, rubbed smooth in the river of his mind. This
warn't that kind of story. This was raw and jagged and full of
pain.

'What did you do next, Dad?' I said. I was afraid we'd never
get to the main business of the evening.

'It was true! The Lord revealed to me in a vision that a baby
was growing inside her – to remind me of my sin – flesh of my
flesh! What could I do? I kept her chained up, of course, cleaned
the filth off of her twice a day, fed her on scraps from your
grandma's table.'

'Did you let her go, Daddy? Did she give birth to me? Is she
my mother?'

'Don't talk about such sins, sonny-boy. It's enough that the
Lord pitied my transgression and gave you to me as a token of
his mercy.' He went on polishing his knives, but half-heartedly.

'But Dad—'

I couldn't get no more information from him, because the
policewoman started to stir. She didn't kick and she didn't
scream, she only glared at me and my dad with spiteful eyes.
Oh, she was painted all right, painted in lurid colours, and her
clothing was the fishiest I'd ever seen. Even if she was a

policewoman like she said, there was a bit of whore deep inside her, and we could still ferret it out and save her soul.

'Let's get to work, son,' he sighed.

I took out the measuring tape. She was the finest yet. I slit the clothes off of her with an X-acto knife. I found her police badge in a pocket. She hadn't been lying about that. I took out my Bible and began the reading.

'Shame on you,' said the fish, 'Mr Lee, or Blackburn, or Raitt. It wasn't enough that you should go around killing defenceless women; you had to corrupt the mind of an innocent child too. After you're in custody, CPS will take care of him, but it's going to take years of therapy before he can live a normal life . . . fucking up your own kid like that, mister . . . you asshole.'

My dad didn't even have the sense to slap her into silence.

'Pay her no mind, Dad!' I said, and started to read the story of Jezebel out of the big old Bible.

'You're not going to get away with this,' said the fish. 'I have a homing device planted on me. The police in four counties have been tracking me. Even if you kill me, they're all going to be converging on this place in just about two minutes.'

Dad's face paled. 'Don't listen to her, Dad!' I shrieked. 'She ain't got no device. Look at her, bare-ass nekkid and hanging from the rafters. There ain't no device. She's just resisting the word of the Lord is all.'

'Where's the device?' said my dad. The old spirit was starting to come back into his face. 'Where is it?'

She spit in his face.

'Where's the fucking device?'

He was yelling at the top of his lungs now. I felt a burst of pride. He was gone make it through. His faith was gone come back to him. He grabbed one of her tits and pinched it until it started to turn purple. But she didn't seem to break.

'Ma'am,' I said, 'you'd best tell him what he wants. You ain't endured the kind of pain my dad can give. He gives it with love, for the sake of your soul. Go on, tell him.'

I've never seen so much hate in a woman's eyes. She didn't have no fear, though. It was like she didn't mind nothing – not even dying – as long as she could carry my dad with her. She had the sureness of an avenging angel. The Lord giveth, the Lord taketh away. Maybe she had been sent to us. In any case, the look she gave him was enough to make him stop pinching her.

'Where's the fucking device?' he said, but it came out more like a croak.

'In my cunt,' said Lt Flora Harberd. 'You're going to have to fuck me to dislodge it, you shit-eating white trash scumbag.'

I heard the sirens wailing in the distance. A dozen sirens coming from all directions. I was afraid.

'Never,' said my father.

He picked up her piece and shot her through the heart.

Then he just stared at the smoking gun, peered so hard it looked like he was cross-eyed. I thought he was gone point it at hisself.

I said, 'Dad, Dad ... we never watched with her and prayed with her ... she never did plead for us to send her into the hereafter ... Dad, you done *murdered* her!'

The sirens were nearer now. And it started to rain.

'Why did you *murder* her, Daddy?'

'It was the onliest thing left for me to do, sonny-boy. She wanted me to interfere with her to save my own life. What is my life compared to the work we've been doing? Listen, sonny-boy, listen! I've been strong! I done resisted the last temptation!'

It thundered above the wailing of the sirens. But all I could think of was the way she jerked, and the way the blood come squirting out in all directions, like a soda fountain gone wild. This was scary. Her death was permanent. She won't never gone enter into the glory and the rapture. Oh, I was heartsick for her, and I knew that my dad had stepped over the fine line that divides saintliness from madness.

Then there come a great big echoing voice: 'Come out of the barn with your hands in the air or we're gone start shooting!'

My daddy laughed. 'My trust is in the Lord. Death ain't but the beginning.'

'Dad, ain't no use,' I said softly. 'Go on out there.'

'Not in front of your grandma! I don't want her to see me be a yellow coward! Not after all we been through together!'

'Daddy, she's dead.' I could feel tears running down my cheeks.

'Now don't you cry, sonny-boy,' he said with a tenderness I'd rarely seen in him. 'We all gone meet again on t'other side. Go on now. Go and be with Grandma. Get in that suitcase and stay there till they come for you.'

He kissed me on the cheek and walked me downstairs and made sure I had the lid down, though he didn't use the padlock. He trusted me after all we'd been through.

The thunder came again and again and again, and the sirens shrilled, and presently come the big electric voice again, telling my dad to come out of the barn. And I heard my daddy laughing, and laughing, and laughing, and finally I heard shots ring out . . . repeating shots . . . ten, twenty, a hundred of them.

I couldn't take it any more. I shoved aside the coffin lid and I saw my dad, wounded, crawling towards me.

'Daddy!' I screamed.

He hadn't been wounded in but one or two places, for all their gunfire. But I knew he warn't gone last but a minute or two. I ran to him and I cradled his head in my arms.

The voice called to us again. It was closer now.

'I got one last thing . . . to tell you,' Dad said to me. 'One last thing.'

'Save it, Dad . . . hold your talking . . . you gone be fine.'

'No. No. It's important, . . . it's about you . . . about the secret of your birth . . . about how special you are, sonny-boy. You done asked me if that whore of Babylon was your mother, and I didn't answer you. Well, she warn't your mother. Even though she bore you inside of her whorish belly for nine long months while I tried to bend her to the worship of the Lord. She warn't your mother! The Book of Job says, "Man that is born of a woman is of few days, and full of trouble . . ."

" . . . he cometh forth like a flower, and is cut down; he fleeth also as a shadow, and continueth not . . ." I said, because like him, I knew the Good Book well, almost by heart.

'You warn't born of a woman, Jody. I ripped you from that belly soon as you were big enough to breathe without that woman's help. I am your mother and your father, sonny-boy. That's how much I love you.'

'And in ripping me from her . . .'

'I found my calling. Because only when she knew she was gone die did she call on the Lord . . . only when she was in her final torment did she plead for the mercy of the Lord . . . and the milk of His mercy gushed forth on to her belly as I carved it open. It smells like a fish, sonny-boy . . . the opening of a woman that tempts man to sin . . . it smells like a fish. That's how I knew I was gone become a fisher of men. You were that angel, sonny-boy, who come to me from the belly of the woman. You were the life that come leaping out of the dust of death. You're special, son. I only come to prepare the way. You won't born of no woman, and your life gone be free of trouble. You're blessed, sonny-boy.'

'Oh, Daddy, Daddy,' I said, 'oh, save your breath, don't leave me, oh, Daddy, I love you more than anything in the whole wide world.'

'Then fetch me my harmonica.'

I found it and brought it to him. I held it to his lips. He played but a few notes, and, as the rain streamed down and the thunder burst and the police came breaking down the barn door, I sang the words of his favourite spiritual:

> 'My Lord, he calls me,
> He calls me by the thunder . . .
> The trumpet sounds within-a-my soul,
> I ain't got long to stay here.'

And then I closed his eyes for him, because he warn't breathing no more.

★

The CPS, they done took good care of me. After my grandma's funeral, they sent me to social workers and psychiatrists, and finally they sent me to a big old ranch in Northern California with horses and cows. I liked the ranch and I liked my social workers and I liked the other kids that'd been sent there, most of them from troubled homes, abused children who hadn't known the kind of love me and my daddy shared.

It's good to know that I ain't sick in the head or nothing, just that I been through some hard times, and I can be healed of the nightmares. My supervisors say I'm coming along just fine, and that maybe I'll be able to go to a foster home soon. The best thing is, a couple of the doctors here, they got excited when they heard me sing, and they think maybe when I'm older I could try out for the Grand Ole Opry. They've promised to send me to a voice coach over in Sacramento, and I sing in the church choir every Sunday.

Last week a girl named Nikki took me to the hayloft behind the stables and wanted to look at my thing. She showed me hers, too.

'You can play with it if you like,' she told me 'Go on. Touch it.'

It felt good. I felt the stirrings of the old rapture. My loins were about bursting with it. I kissed her, too. I'd never tasted living human flesh before. But when I lifted my finger to my nose I could smell the taint of stale fish, and it brought back all the memories.

I killed her.

———
———

Fish are Jumping, and the Cotton is High was originally written for an anthology called *Monsters in Our Midst*, edited by Robert Bloch. I owe 'Uncle Bob' many debts; not the least of them is that, as a result of being asked to write for this anthology about psychopaths, I found myself for the first time able to write a story without any fantasy element whatsoever. This was a liberating experience. I soon began to discover so much horror, fantasy and magic in the real world that the entire focus of my work began to shift away from the genres I loved so much as a young man.

Fire from the Wine-dark Sea

Once upon a time there was a man who had two sons, twins. They had wild wheatfield hair that rustled in rough winds and was bleached still whiter in summer, and pale freckles, and smiles that burst out (teeth crooked and all) like sunlight after a stormfall, and great dark darting daunting eyes.

People would stare at them, searching for a difference, and they usually couldn't find one. They also stared because they were shockingly beautiful kids. Of course the man could tell the difference; he was their father.

For the man, what was difficult was another thing – having two such beautiful children, and knowing that he loved one of them better . . .

I've started this all wrong, haven't I? When you've got the Poetry Chair at some obscure New England university, you feel an obligation to talk this way, to write this way; it's the literary syndrome. Because words are in themselves beautiful things. Like gems. Like clothes. Like coffins. Hiding the hurt.

Well. Shit.

You see, this man I'm writing about. It's no fairytale. It's not an archetypal hypothetical mythopoeic paradigm out there in a house by the sea, scribbling ironic Byronic laconic verses into a tattered notebook. Maybe this man exists, but the man in this story isn't him.

He's me.

So I think I'll desist from this 'universalizing' crap now. I only began that way because it's so scary, trying to write about something real, something that happened. You want to escape into 'he did this', 'he did that.' And yet . . .

It's because of this very story that I don't ever want to run away from anything again.

First Person.

Summers we lived by the sea, on our estate two miles down from the village of St Joan – it's pronounced *Sinjun* by the natives – in an old house ghosted with grandfathers, on Delenda Circle that curved off Moore Avenue that ran from the village and route 311, past Charley's Cliffs and along the Cape for many miles. From my window and from the boys' window you saw the sea mostly, a ribbon of beach at high tide, and a fuzzy Tuckatinck Island, white and grey-green.

Mornings Sandy and Claude would go running before I woke, up the avenue a bit and then into DuPertuis Lane, twistier than a cat-pawed yarnball and smelling of old earth and moss and tall woods peering over the mist . . .

One morning I was meditating on the sunny side of an egg when Sandy burst through the kitchen door. Everything always exploded from silent black-and-white to technicolor Sensurround whenever he came into a room . . .

'Harry!' he yelled. 'Harry! We've found a friend!'

'Who—'

'Coming up behind us! Running behind, up DuPertuis Lane, rounding the corner – c'mon, Harold, Mr Vance, come see!'

He stopped for a breath. Christ, what a kid! With a grandly unselfconscious movement he swept back his hair. It remained a mess, moss-sprinkled and mussed up by the morning wind. Then he chucked his sneakers over the table. They arced up over the eggs and crashed on the stoneware tiles, and he smiled a little.

'Sandy, who is he?' I said.

'We don't know, Harry.'

Then Claude stood quietly in the doorway, his face gridded by the screen, and the sunrise shooting sparkdarts through his hair.

The room temperature seemed to drop a notch.

'Hi, Dad.'

It's funny, how Sandy never called me that. Always – with a

wryness concealing awkward tenderness – 'Harold', or 'Harry', or 'Mr Vance'. Kids that age hate to give anything away . . . yet it was Sandy I loved the most, wild Sandy.

'Sandy—' I touched him but he slipped through my fingers like sea spray.

Claude said, 'Dad, he's very strange, the man. I don't know if I like him. He keeps babbling on about . . . oh, weird stuff.'

'He's terrific!' said Sandy.

'Yah,' said Claude, coming in and pressing against the doorhinges to make them squeak. He sat down at the kitchen table. He moved unsteadily, like a typical thirteen-year-old; in this he was different from Sandy, who moved with his whole being, elementally, like a wild animal. He took off his sneakers very carefully and put them down on either side of a tile-crack, to make a completely symmetrical pattern.

I watched them both for a while. What kind of weirdo had they picked up at the beach or in the woods? I looked from one to the other; Sandy's eyes seemed to trust you so blindly, while Claude's were never innocent; they had a way of shaming you, of putting you in the wrong.

Then I heard a voice from outside. 'Phew! Bare feet are no good for running along your roads.' It was a rich voice, like someone playing the cello in a marble bathroom.

'Jesus Christ,' I said, 'do you guys have to bring home everyone you meet? Can't a fellow eat his breakfast?'

'But Dad—' said Claude.

'Harry, you'll like him,' Sandy said, and I swallowed my exasperation for a second, and then the room went dark because the stranger filled the doorway completely.

He was tall, fair, with a torn white tunic on, and a trim beard. He was sunburnt. He didn't smile. I looked at him rather belligerently . . .

And he transfixed me with his eyes, dark and formidable, as my sons' eyes could be sometimes, and cold as a winter wind. And then I noticed that his hair was streaming behind him like fire. But there was no wind in the room.

I started to say something angry, but my lips were chilled shut . . .

Then the coldness melted away and he seemed all friendliness. 'These . . . *sneakers*, you called them,' he said, half-laughing, 'a fabulous, exotic treasure indeed! Hermes could not be swifter than a stripling shod with these . . .' He knelt down to look at Sandy's Adidases, carelessly thrown there on the brown tiles. He picked one of them up and began to poke it, as though he'd never seen such a thing before.

I got my voice back then. 'Of all the nerve! Marching into a stranger's house like this, peering at his things—'

He rose up then, and stared at me very seriously until I felt guilty – the way Claude could always do – and said, 'I've come an awful long way.' His hair never stopped billowing. 'Thousands of miles. Would you turn me out, Mr Vance? Your boys have been most kind to me . . .'

'Who are you?' I said, more quietly.

'I am,' he said, 'Odysseus, King of Ithaca.'

'See, Dad?' Claude said. 'I told you he was weird.'

'Now look here . . .' I was desperately scanning the newspaper in my mind. There had to be some kind of headline like PSYCHOPATH FLEES EMERGENCY WARD, something like that. I floundered for something to say and came out with, 'Okay, so you're Napoleon. Or Odysseus. Whatever. How come you're not speaking ancient Greek then?'

'I am.'

And then I saw it.

When he spoke, it wasn't in lip-synch. I mean what I was hearing didn't synchronize with what his mouth was doing. I mean, my God, it was like watching a Godzilla movie. And then there was the hair. And the tunic, too . . . lashed by a still tempest.

Now I was really frightened.

Claude said, 'It's being translated straight into our minds. Like you know, telepathy, some kind of radar, something . . .'

But Sandy didn't say anything at all. He seemed just to accept the stranger, to know he was all right, without looking for an explanation.

'I've left Ithaca for good,' the stranger said. 'After ten years of war, ten years of high adventure, who can stay home? And that Penelope ... so perfect, so patient and everything. Every time I so much as looked at her she would accuse me with her eyes, never meaning to of course, but you just knew she was swallowing her suffering and trying to look beautiful for you. She has her loom now, and I – I wander over the sea, landing in new countries and new epochs, exchanging gifts with the strange new people I encounter ...'

'Either that, or you're a hell of an actor,' I said. The eggs had grown cold now.

'Harry, can he stay here?' Sandy pleaded. 'He has to get supplies, and—'

'Well ...' I saw that Claude had turned away and was staring at the wall. There was so much eagerness in Sandy's eyes ...

'It would please me much, sir, if I could call you my guest-friend,' Odysseus said.

I didn't know what to think.

Claude got up suddenly and said, 'Dad, I'm going up to the den to use your typewriter.' He had this craze for doing concrete poetry, picked up from a wacky creative writing teacher in his school.

I watched my son cross the living room and run up the stairs, his fingers skimming the banister. Not looking at the man, I said, 'If only I could believe your story ... but it can't be happening, can it? You can't be real.'

But Odysseus said: 'Mr Vance, you are a poet. You of all people should know how tenuous the line between reality and fantasy is. If the line *itself* is a fantasy, then fantasy must of necessity be real ...'

'You talk like Odysseus *should* talk,' I said, 'wily, word-twisting, devious. You ought to do well in our century.' It was easy to play along with him; he made it all sound so plausible.

'So can he stay, huh, Harry?'

I saw them exchanging a look. He had my son quite hypnotized. Well, that wasn't surprising. I scrutinized his face, still avoiding his eyes, searching for a trace of deceit, and I couldn't find anything at all ... and the wind on his face never stopped blowing.

I knew he was looking at me, and without meaning to I was raising my eyes to meet his ... they were so dark ... even in the morning light, they were crystallized night.

'Wait till you see his ship!' cried Sandy.

Odysseus laughed. 'It isn't much of one, judging by the monstrosities I have seen breasting the tides in the midst of nowhere ...'

'He has a *ship*?'

'You can see it from the window!' and Sandy had run to the stairs and was springing up them like a cat.

Odysseus said to me, 'Beautiful child. Beautiful ... "sneakers".' He was holding up one of Sandy's, hefting it from hand to hand. And then he smiled a broad sunny smile and gathered up his tunic more tightly around him, bracing himself against the wind I couldn't feel, and we went up to the boys' room on the second floor.

I could hear Claude tapping laboriously on the typewriter in my den.

Sandy was gazing out of the window. Without turning around, he beckoned for me to come and stand by him. I stood over him and he didn't push me away; and I saw a little boat moored on the beach, on our private dock, next to our own boat; nothing strange about it.

'That's it?'

'No, Dad,' he said – he never called me that! – and pointed. Out over the dark water, sparkle-kissed, to where Tuckatinck Island blocked the horizon. 'Don't you see it? *That* boat's only his little shuttlecraft.'

I couldn't see anything at first. 'What do you mean, Sandy?'

And then I saw a vague white outline, as though a cloud had settled on the distant shoreline. Perhaps a mast. Perhaps a sail. Perhaps a prow chiselled into a nude woman with wide-open arms. I couldn't tell ...

'See, Harry?' He was yelling excitedly. 'There are people walking the decks, the sails are flapping—'

'Damn it, I can't see a thing! I guess you just have better eyesight than me.'

'You suck shit, Mr Vance!' he said, childish suddenly.

I turned around and tried to resolve the cloud that hugged the island into a firm-outlined ship with planks, masts, rivets, but the haze remained a haze.

I shrugged. 'I guess your peculiar friend will be with us for a few days, huh?' I looked at the man expectantly.

'Just long enough to look around,' said Odysseus. 'Already I long for the sea, for tastier adventures. But I'd like to take something with me, a souvenir perhaps . . . at every port, you see, I must receive some gift from the local inhabitants, because I am a King.'

He and Sandy exchanged a look.

In that moment I knew I was jealous.

'Sure,' I said, as Claude's typing pelted the silence.

*

Claude woke me up by putting on one of Laura's records. The one of Beethoven's last piano sonata, the opus 111, with the long impossible trills that seem to stretch from your guts to the end of the sky. Laura had played it at her last concert.

(Laughing Laura! The arms like wild cranes in flight. Sweeping up from the keyboard like Sandy springing from the diving board by Charley's Cliffs. Laughing alone in the Albert Hall before the audience came on, confounding the ushers. Darting from the Underground at Piccadilly Circus. Stepping in front of a double-decker bus.)

'Dad? . . .'

(Coming back to the States. Clearing the coffin through customs.)

Claude: a slim shadow crossing the bed, bisecting the triangle of dawn light from the half-closed shutters.

(Four years ago? Really?)

'Dad . . .'

I felt a pang of guilt suddenly. I couldn't think why, except that I'd neglected the kid, as always. 'Hey, Claudius, why aren't you out there running with Sandy?'

'He took Odysseus with him.' Then – the anguish in his voice all out of proportion with what he was saying – 'Dad, he lent him *your* sneakers!'

I suppressed the unreasonable, unadult annoyance I felt.

'Besides,' he said, 'I hate to run. I only do it to be with him.'

'And now?'

'He's with the immortal stranger.'

– the piano had reached the first of the long trills –

'Daddy, I think he's surrounded by some kind of time-shield, you know, like a force field. It keeps him locked away from your universe, you know. And we don't know what he's really saying either. It's all dubbed, but the translation could be wrong, you know like in those Swedish movies when they're really saying "oh fuck" or something and it comes out "jeepers". Or he's come bursting through from an alternate universe—'

'Yeah.'

I didn't really understand what he was saying. You know faculty kids. Smart as hell, old before their time; smart-assed, too. He was hiding something though, under the froth of words. I said, as gently as I could, 'What's up, kid?'

He sat down on the bed then. I could feel him against my knee, and I could feel the tension between us like a jack-in-the-box ready to pop. 'You love him a lot, don't you, Dad?' he said. 'More than me.'

I was silent.

'That's all right, Dad. I want you to know that. I do too.' He was talking to the shutters, trying not to see me. 'But sometimes I don't think he's really there at all. He's like a wind or a fire, not a person. Like Odysseus.'

– the long trill went on and on, the piano strained, high, high, touching the sky –

'Jesus Christ!' he said. 'Why do you have to be deaf before you can write such great music?' And I saw he'd been crying.

It wasn't like him. He was always the one with no emotions.

'All right, Claudius. Get your clothes on. You and I are going to drive to Hyannis. Right now.'

'How come?' But his face lit up. I sat on the bed and threw open the shutters. Light spilled out over the waxed oak floor. 'Do we have to wait for the others?'

'No.' He was really smiling now, though he looked like he hadn't had any sleep. 'Look, Odysseus wanted a souvenir, didn't he? Maybe we can get him something really nice, and then maybe he'll go away.'

Downstairs, Laura's record clicked.

*

Then, in the afternoon, Sandy made me drive him and Odysseus to Laura's grave, which was five miles past the last of Charley's Cliffs. Claude had already hidden the parcel we had bought in the den, in the desk drawer under the typewriter.

We were in our ancient Austin, with Claude nestled against me as if terrified, and Odysseus in the front seat too, watching the view, and Sandy in the dog seat. Odysseus seemed preoccupied; his eyes flitted from cliff to pebble-strewn roadside to forest wall. We took a left into the cemetery and I saw the grave.

I walked ahead, not wanting to be too close to the stranger, and Claude was huddled against me the whole time. The cement path was broken by veins of moss and tufts of grass, and the sun shone so fiercely that the newer gravestones, the ones that had been washed recently, blazed.

Claude whispered, 'Do you think it'll work? The present, I mean.' We walked on quickly so as to be out of earshot.

'For $39.95,' I said, 'it better.' Then I said, 'Christ, I'm scared.' We came up to the grave and stopped suddenly. I knelt down and saw that there was a clumsy wreath of wildflowers on the ground. 'Did you do this?' I asked Claude.

'No.'

I turned and saw Sandy. He looked away. And then Odysseus was behind us, his shadow eclipsing the gravestone.

Claude said, under his breath, 'You shouldn't have brought him here. This is *our* place.'

In the heat-haze, in the oppressive bright stillness, still the stranger's hair caught fire and flamed, still his tunic rustled; and still his lips moved differently from the sounds we heard. 'Wives,' he said, sighing. 'I too have a wife.'

'Then why don't you go back to her?' I said, angry. Already he'd lured Sandy into his power and he'd driven Claude to near hysteria. 'What's your game, stranger? All right, so you're *not* an escapee from a mental home, but what do you want from *us*?'

'Nothing that you would not give freely.'

Sandy said, 'I told him about Mom, Harry. We ran down to the very end of DuPertuis Lane this morning, maybe three miles. He loves your sneakers . . . I played him Mom's records.' His light blue T-shirt was plastered to his skin, his hair damp-glistening. 'He wanted to pour a libation here's all.' He looked at me. His eyes seemed to conceal nothing.

I picked up the crude wreath and put it on top of the gravestone. The marble had already worn away some; you couldn't read her name unless you got the exact angle of sunlight.

'I too have a wife,' Odysseus said. 'She sits at home and weaves enormous tapestries. And sometimes she rips them up and begins again, and rips them up and begins again . . .'

'Don't you feel sorry for her?' I said.

'No,' he said. But not too convincingly. 'I like the sea and the changings and the constant new strangenesses of new shores. To be at home is to be rooted, like rocks, like trees; I can't feel *real* that way. Sometimes I am a wind. I am what slips through people's fingers.'

'Oh?'

He went on, 'You should all be thankful to my wife Penelope though. If she were to stop weaving, you'd all come to an end, most likely. You see, a millennium ago she became sick of all those scenes of heroes and Titans and beasts. She became a little more speculative, a little – how do you people say it these days – science-fictional? And what she weaves, of course, is the truth.'

'Bullshit,' I said, 'the world has existed far longer than your Greek mythology ever did.'

'When a good writer writes, doesn't the story seem to stretch far beyond the writing itself? Don't the characters seem to have histories from long before the first page? But they don't, you know.'

Claude said, 'So you're saying that you sprang into being because Homer sang of you, Odysseus?'

Odysseus' face clouded for a moment. Then he said, 'Homer? Now who is that?'

'You can't see where you came from either!' Claude said. 'No one can, unless they stand outside where they came from.'

'Let's talk of other things,' Odysseus said, in a hurry. 'It hurts me to think of my wife alone at her loom. I've never stopped feeling guilty.' Then, 'You know, one of you boys might want to come with me when I leave.'

He said it so casually. Too too impromptu. That's how I knew that this was why Odysseus had come. I stared at my two sons. Both were terrified.

'But think of it!' Odysseus cried out. 'Think of the open sea, the wind on the wine-dark waves, the giants, the cyclops, the golden princesses, the enchantresses ... and of being immortal. For we are not real as you are real; we are far more than real. We are the old things that do not change.'

'I won't leave my father,' Claude said hesitantly.

'I'll say you won't!' I said.

We all looked at Sandy. He was so small ... then suddenly Claude said, 'Maybe one of us is *meant* to go. If so, I'll go, Dad. If one of us has to. I know you'll never want to lose Sandy, and it's the only way—'

'Hold it, kid,' I said. 'Nothing's going to change. Nobody's going anywhere. Except Odysseus. He's going straight back to the nuthouse.'

Sandy was shaking with anger, struggling to get something out, and then—

'Fuck you, Odysseus!' he screamed. 'Leave us alone, just get out of our lives, just fuck off!'

In the appalling silence I saw:

(Laura's arms, anger, hammering the dead piano, Laura tearing the music, Laura's eyes from the coffin depths)

—Sandy backing away into the dead stone.

'It's all right,' Odysseus said gently. 'I don't insist.'

And then there was more silence. From behind the silence, from behind the cliffs across Moore Avenue, came the whisper of the unseen sea.

★

And so in the evening we went to the beach and sat on the sand and ate broiled hamburgers and watched the sun setting behind us, partly over the cliffs, partly over Tuckatinck Island, a little over the open sea.

He was going to leave in the morning.

After the afternoon's explosions, I just wanted to relax. I knew that he was leaving and that there was nothing to worry about any more. Odysseus sat with his feet just touching the water, telling tall tales. He looked out to sea the whole time; and though I knew his ship was meant to be docked by the island, I still could see nothing. Only a haze that enveloped the rocks and rose and shifted in colour from white to blue-grey, like the fur of a Siamese cat.

We were waiting for Claude. Sandy was away in the water, jumping up and down.

Claude came clutching the parcel, running out of the house. He made a breeze with his running. He made the sand fly. For a moment I thought he was Sandy.

'So you still don't see my ship?' Odysseus was saying. 'Your son there now, he does.'

Claude crashed down beside us. The sand poured into my cutoffs. He thrust the parcel at me. I caught his eye for a moment; his look said, *This won't work*.

'Come back, Sandy!' I hollered. 'We've got something to do!'

He ran over the waves, a dark streak over the pink and grey . . . and tumbled in front of us. Sand and water on my face.

I said, 'We're sorry to see you go.'

'I know you are not,' said Odysseus, not playing along.

I handed him the parcel.

He opened it and took out the sneakers . . . soft suede Adidas, fawn with pale blue stripes, size twelve, nesting on layers of tissue. He seemed very thoughtful.

'Thank you,' he said, and there was much sadness in his voice. 'I will wear them often when I tread strange shores, and I will think of your beautiful children, the ones who would not come with me, the ones who loved their father better than the wild wide ocean.'

'Tell us another story,' said Sandy. 'Tell us about Troy.'

'You don't want to hear about it.' A wind had sprung up; for once the billowing of his hair seemed to match reality. He stroked the sneakers. Behind the habitual coldness of his eyes I thought I saw some indescribable yearning. It was truly terrible, and I was afraid.

'I can show you,' he said, 'the fires of Troy. I can show you if you can see them. Look there at the island, over by the ship . . .'

But all I could see was the shifting haze, pinker now in the twilight.

'Don't you see the fire across the wine-dark sea?' said Odysseus. 'Don't you see the slaughter, don't you see the screaming women being dragged to the ships?'

The haze twisted; I saw nothing.

Then Sandy burst out: 'I see it all, Harry! I see everything! I see the walls crumbling and the horse standing behind the walls and the fire burning the horse and the children screaming in the streets . . .'

'Cut the crap, Sandy!' Claude said tightly. He was trembling all over.

'Your son has vision, then,' Odysseus said. 'He is like one of us.'

Sandy said, 'It's terrible, Harry! Now they've dragged a child from its mother, they're going to throw it down from the walls, and the walls are falling, falling—'

The sky was fire-blood-red. But I saw nothing.

Claude was shaking Sandy now. 'It's all lies, Dad! He's just making it up! He doesn't see those things!' he screamed. And Sandy's eyes were frozen (like Laura's eyes, crystallized and cold watching me from the coffin)—

I put out my arms and covered the boy's eyes. He pushed me away. 'I've got to see, Harry. I've got to,' he whispered. And I saw that Odysseus no longer seemed interested in us. He had stood up and had put on his new sneakers and was springing lightly up and down on them, laughing for joy.

Red rays like fire fingers grasping the water—

'That's enough,' I said. I lifted Sandy up in my arms. He held me so tightly that I couldn't breathe.

'Harry,' he said, 'you gotta come running with me.'

I saw that Claude had gone back inside, and so I walked Sandy to the front of the house, where our sneakers were, and then we set off down Delenda Circle, into the red-streaked darkness.

It was hard at first. Mostly I watched the pavement. When I looked up, Sandy was running free, pounding the ground and leaping in smooth curves, gazing straight ahead. The woods were so much taller than him ... we crossed Moore Avenue and turned into DuPertuis Lane.

'Don't tail-gate!' Sandy shouted.

We ran on. The rhythm of foot-thuds became a heartbeat. I was lost in a leaf-moist stillness. We ran flat out and the lane corkscrewed, it was alive, it was a snake's gullet, we were flowing into its gut, like blood, like bile.

'Damn it, wait for me!' I cried.

He was deep into the wood now. Darting from shadow to shadow. I was so tired I could hardly think. My sneakers crunched on twigs and winced away from pebbles.

And then we stopped.

Why had he made me do this? Later I would realize: he was

showing me he possessed me. I belonged to him no matter what.

We sank down on the wet ground, against a tree.

Sandy said, 'Dad.'

He said it shyly. He wasn't used to calling me Dad. But defiantly too. Because I *was* his father. He shook a dead leaf from his hair and smoothed out a crease in his T-shirt and a moonbeam fell across his face . . .

Even in this darkness his eyes could still flash like sunlight from a gap in a thundercloud. I waited. This was his show. I didn't know what was coming. It could have been a storm. Or nothing at all.

(Laura's eyes breaking out from behind the crook of the piano)

'Dad, will you love me for ever?'

'Of course, Sandy,' I said, tense.

'And Claude? You're going to stop pushing him away from you?'

'I don't know what you mean.'

'Don't lie, Dad.'

A leaf fell.

'Christ, Dad . . . can't you think of her as a human being? Can't you remember the *human* things about her? I make you think of her, don't I, Dad? But she isn't real any more. And I don't think I am, either. You never did see the ship, did you, Dad, or the fire from the sea?'

'Let's talk about something else.'

The forest pressed in on us. We really *were* in the serpent's gut. And Sandy seemed so far away from me, even though he stood so close I could smell the fabric softener through the sweet odour a young boy's sweat.

'I have to go with Odysseus, Dad.'

'No, Sandy, please,' I said, 'don't play games with me, you'll kill me.'

'I saw the ship. I saw the walls crumbling. I saw the fire.' He spoke without emotion. 'I'm part of his world, Harry. But that's not why I have to go.'

I waited.

'If I stay here I'm going to go on breaking your heart, for ever,' he said, talking into the ground.

'How can you say that?' I said.

'You're so ashamed about feeling one way about me and one way about Claude. Your guilt's a scary thing. And it's only that you're afraid of him ... because he's so like you. People think they love the things they can't be. That's all you see in me, Dad.'

He had drained me. I couldn't talk. All I could think of was him: leaping from diving rocks, running in the darkness, sliding down the banisters.

'Daddy, before I go, I have a gift for you, too.'

This was his gift. He laughed me Laura's laugh until the trees laughed in the close darkness, until his laughing dried up, and then I caught the laugh from him and laughed too, laughed hysterically until I couldn't stop crying.

Then he said, 'Let's go, Dad.'

In the moonlight I saw that his lips no longer matched his words.

*

There's a little bit of the stereotype that's true. I do possess a tattered notebook and I do go around writing in it: lines that become poems, sometimes, but usually are just lines that go nowhere, smoke-trails of a skywriter that disperse in the wind.

I carried the notebook out to the beach.

I saw two sets of sneakerprints: size twelve and size six.

They led to a point in the sand and stopped.

'I think the stranger was Death,' I whispered to myself.

Claude said, startling me – I didn't know he was there – 'No, Daddy, no. Sandy went away because he loved us. To kill your mourning. To give me a chance.' He looked so serious. He hadn't slept. I wondered if they had stayed up talking all night. I wanted to know every word that had passed between them. But I was not a breeze that could squeeze through a half-closed shutter, nor a mist that could cling to a bedpost; I was only a father.

We looked out to sea. A high wind sprang up and blew the fog away from Tuckatinck Island, and the fog drifted, skimming the water, towards the sunrise, blushing against the grey of sea and sky.

'It's the ship!' Claude yelled. And he jumped up and down frantically and waved. 'Goodbye, goodbye, Sandy!' and rushed out into the low tide . . .

'Do you see the ship?' I called out to him.

'No.'

We turned and went into the house. Claude had left the record on. The one of Laura playing the opus 111.

Jesus Christ! Why do you have to be deaf before you can write such great music?

And then I saw that we are all deaf, and blind too. If we were not, if we could see, we would be like Sandy. We wouldn't need visions, or art. We would run after the truth until we melted into a breeze, into sea water, into sunlight.

That's why art is all lies.

I saw my son in the doorway. I thought he was Sandy for a moment. Then I crushed him hard against me in my arms as though I would never see him again.

And Claude said, 'I'm not Sandy, Daddy. But some day . . .' and behind the grief, his eyes sparkled for a moment . . . 'some day, could we go running in the woods?'

I wrote another line in the book:

art is the dark glasses a blind man wears . . .

—————

Fire from the Wine-dark Sea was written in 1978, and was my first attempt to write a story in a voice that was not science fiction. Like 'Fish are Jumping', it's a story that deals with fathers and sons and about the relationship between the concrete world and the inner world. According to my wonderful agent, Eleanor Wood, my entire career would have been different had she been my agent at the time I wrote this story. 'I would have sent it to some literary magazine,' she told me, 'and you would have long vanished from the ghetto of genre.' I'm not sure that's true, but I'm including the story in this collection at her behest. Completists should note that I've rewritten it somewhat.

By the way, this is – almost – a true story, as you will know if you ask my old friend Deborah, to whom it is dedicated.

Chui Chai

The living dead are not as you imagine them. There are no dangling innards, no dripping slime. They carry their guts and gore inside them, as do you and I. In the right light they can be beautiful, as when they stand in a doorway caught between cross-shafts of contrasting neon. Fuelled by the right fantasy, they become indistinguishable from us. Listen. I know. I've touched them.

In the '80s I used to go to Bangkok a lot. The brokerage I worked for had a lot of business there, some of it shady, some not. The flight of money from Hong Kong had begun and our company, vulture that it was, was staking out its share of the loot. Bangkok was booming like there was no tomorrow. It made Los Angeles seem like Peoria. It was wild and fast and frantic and frustrating. It had temples and buildings shaped like giant robots. Its skyline was a cross between Shangri-La and Manhattan. For a dapper yuppie executive like me there were always meetings to be taken, faxes to fax, traffic to be sat in, credit cards to burn. There was also sex.

There was Patpong.

I was addicted. Nights, after hours of high-level talks and poring over papers and banquets that lasted from the close of business until midnight, I stalked the crammed alleys of Patpong. The night smelled of sewage and jasmine. The heat seeped into everything. Each step I took was coloured by a different neon sign. From half-open nightclub doorways buttocks bounced to jaunty soulless synthrock. Everything was for sale; the women, the boys, the pirated software, the fake Rolexes. Everything sweated. I stalked the streets and sometimes at random took an entrance, took in a live show, women propelling ping-pong balls from their pussies, boys buttfucking on motorbikes. I was addicted. There were other entrances where I sat in waiting rooms, watched women with numbers around their necks through the one-way glass, soft, slender brown women. Picked a number. Fingered the American-made condoms in my pocket. Never buy the local ones, brother, they leak like a sieve.

I was addicted. I didn't know what I was looking for. But I knew it wasn't something you could find in Encino. I was a knight on a quest, but I didn't know that to find the holy grail is the worst thing that can possibly happen.

I first got a glimpse of the grail at Club Pagoda, which was near my hotel and which is where we often liked to take our clients. The club was on the very edge of Patpong, but it was respectable – the kind of place that serves up a plastic imitation of *The King and I*; which is, of course, a plastic imitation of life in ancient Siam ... artifice imitating artifice, you see. Waiters crawled around in mediaeval uniforms, the guests sat on the floor, except there was a well under the table to accommodate the dangling legs of lumbering white people. The floor show was eminently sober ... it was all classical Thai dances, women wearing those pagoda-shaped hats moving with painstaking grace and slowness to a tinkling, alien music. A good place to interview prospective grant recipients, because it tended to make them very nervous.

Dr Frances Stone wasn't at all nervous though. She was already there when I arrived. She was preoccupied with picking the peanuts out of her *gaeng massaman* and arranging them over her rice plate in such a way that they looked like little eyes, a nose, and a mouth.

'You like to play with your food?' I said, taking my shoes off at the edge of our private booth and sliding my legs under the table across from her.

'No,' she said, 'I just prefer them crushed rather than whole. The peanuts, I mean. You must be Mr Leibowitz.'

'Russell.'

'The man I'm supposed to charm out of a few million dollars.'
She was doing a sort of coquettish pout, not really the sort of
thing I expected from someone in medical research. Her face
was ravaged, but the way she smiled kindled the memory of
youthful beauty. I wondered what had happened to change her
so much; according to her dossier, she was only in her mid-
forties.

'Mostly we're in town to take,' I said, 'not to give. R&D is
not one of our strengths. You might want to go to Hoechst or
Berli Jucker, Frances.'

'But Russell . . .' She had not touched her curry, but the
peanuts on the rice were now formed into a perfect human face,
with a few strands of sauce for hair. 'This is not exactly R&D.
This is a discovery that's been around for almost a century and
a half. My great-grandfather's paper—'

'For which he was booted out of the Austrian Academy? Yes,
my dossier is pretty thorough, Dr Stone; I know all about how
he fled to America and changed his name.'

She smiled. 'And my dossier on you, Mr Leibowitz, is pretty
thorough too,' she said, as she began removing a number of
compromising photographs from her purse.

A gong sounded to announce the next dance. It was a solo.
Fog roiled across the stage, and from it a woman emerged. Her
clothes glittered with crystal beadwork, but her eyes outshone
the yards of cubic zirconia. She looked at me and I felt the
pangs of the addiction. She smiled and her lips seemed to
glisten with lubricious moisture.

'You like what you see,' Frances said softly.

'I—'

'The dance is called *Chui Chai*, the dance of transformation.
In every Thai classical drama, there are transformations – a
woman transforming herself into a rose, a spirit transforming
itself into a human. After the character's metamorphosis, he
performs a *Chui Chai* dance, exulting in the completeness and
beauty of his transformed self.'

I wasn't interested, but for some reason she insisted on giving
me the entire story behind the dance. 'This particular *Chui Chai*

is called *Chui Chai Benjakai* ... the demoness Benjakai has been
dispatched by the demon king, Thotsakanth, to seduce the hero
Rama ... disguised as the beautiful Sita, she will float down
the river towards Rama's camp, trying to convince him that his
beloved has died ... only when she is placed on a funeral pyre,
woken from her deathtrance by the flames, will she take on her
demonic shape once more and fly away towards the dark
kingdom of Lanka. But you're not listening.'

How could I listen? She was the kind of woman that existed
only in dreams, in poems. Slowly she moved against the tawdry
backdrop, a faded painting of a palace with pointed eaves. Her
feet barely touched the floor. Her arms undulated. And always
her eyes held me. As though she were looking at me alone.
Thai women can do things with their eyes that no other women
can do. Their eyes have a secret language.

'Why are you looking at her so much?' said Frances. 'She's
just a Patpong bar girl ... she moonlights here ... classics in
the evening, pussy after midnight.'

'You know her?' I said.

'I have had some ... dealings with her.'

'Just what is it that you're doing research into, Dr Stone?'

'The boundary between life and death,' she said. She pointed
to the photographs. Next to them was a contract, an R&D grant
agreement of some kind. The print was blurry. 'Oh, don't
worry, it's only a couple of million dollars ... your company
won't even miss it ... and you'll own the greatest secret of all
... the tree of life and death ... the apples of Eve. Besides, I
know your price and I can meet it.' And she looked at the
dancing girl. 'Her name is Keo. I don't mind procuring if it's in
the name of science.'

Suddenly I realized that Dr Stone and I were the only
customers in the Club Pagoda. Somehow I had been set up.

The woman continued to dance, faster now, her hands
sweeping through the air in mysterious gestures. She never
stopped looking at me. She *was* the character she was playing,
seductive and diabolical. There was darkness in every look,
every hand-movement. I downed the rest of my Kloster lager

and beckoned for another. An erection strained against my pants.

The dance ended and she prostrated herself before the audience of two, pressing her palms together in a graceful *wai*. Her eyes downcast, she left the stage. I had signed the grant papers without even knowing it.

Dr Stone said, 'On your way to the upstairs toilet . . . take the second door on the left. She'll be waiting for you.'

I drank another beer, and when I looked up she was gone. She hadn't eaten one bite. But the food on her plate had been sculpted into the face of a beautiful woman. It was so lifelike that . . . but no. It wasn't alive. It wasn't breathing.

★

She was still in her dancing clothes when I went in. A little girl was carefully taking out the stitches with a seamripper. There was a pile of garments on the floor. In the glare of a naked bulb, the vestments of the goddess had little glamour. 'They no have buttons on classical dance clothes,' she said. 'They just sew us into them. Cannot go pipi!' She giggled.

The little girl scooped up the pile and slipped away.

'You're . . . very beautiful,' I said. 'I don't understand why . . . I mean, why you *need* to . . .'

'I have problem,' she said. 'Expensive problem. Dr Stone no tell you?'

'No.' Her hands were coyly clasped across her bosom. Gently I pried them away.

'You want I dance for you?'

'Dance,' I said. She was naked. The way she smelled was different from other women. It was like crushed flowers. Maybe a hint of decay in them. She shook her hair and it coiled across her breasts like a nest of black serpents. When I'd seen her on stage I'd been entertaining some kind of rape fantasy about her, but now I wanted to string it out for as long as I could. God, she was driving me mad.

'I see big emptiness inside you. Come to me. I fill you. We both empty people. Need filling up.'

I started to protest. But I knew she had seen me for what I was. I had money coming out my ass, but I was one fucked-up yuppie. That was the root of my addiction.

Again she danced the dance of transforming, this time for me alone. Really for me alone. I mean, all the girls in Patpong have this way of making you think they love you. It's what gets you addicted. It's the only street in the world where you *can* buy love. But that's not how she was. When she touched me it was as though she reached out to me across an invisible barrier, an unbreachable gulf. Even when I entered her she was untouchable. We were from different worlds and neither of us ever left our private hells.

Not that there wasn't passion. She knew every position in the book. She knew them backwards and forwards. She kept me there all night and each act seemed as though it had been freshly invented for the two of us. It was the last time I came that I felt I had glimpsed the grail. Her eyes, staring up into the naked bulb, brimmed with some remembered sadness. I loved her with all my might. Then I was seized with terror. She was a demon. Yellow-eyed, dragon-clawed. She was me, she was my insatiable hunger. I was fucking my own addiction. I think I sobbed. I accused her of lacing my drink with hallucinogens. I cried myself to sleep and then she left me.

I didn't notice the lumpy mattress or the peeling walls or the way the light bulb jiggled to the music from downstairs. I didn't notice the cockroaches.

I didn't notice until morning that I had forgotten to use my condoms.

★

It was a productive trip but I didn't go back to Thailand for another two years. I was promoted off the travelling circuit, moved from Encino to Beverly Hills, got myself a newer, late-model wife, packed my kids off to a Swiss boarding school. I also found a new therapist and a new support group. I smothered the addiction in new addictions. My old therapist had been a strict Freudian. He'd tried to root out the cause from some childhood trauma – molestation, potty training, Oedipal game – he'd never been able to find anything. I'm good at blocking out memories. To the best of my knowledge, I popped into being around age eight or nine. My parents were dead but I had a trust fund.

My best friends in the support group were Janine, who'd had eight husbands, and Mike, a transvestite with a spectacular afro. The clinic was in Malibu so we could do the beach in between bouts of tearing ourselves apart. One day Thailand came up.

Mike said, 'I knew this woman in Thailand. I had fun in Thailand, you know? R&R. Lot of transvestites there, hon. I'm not a fag, I just like lingerie. I met this girl.' He rarely stuck to the point because he was always stoned. Our therapist, Glenda, had passed out in the redwood tub. The beach was deserted. 'I knew this girl in Thailand, a dancer. She would change when she danced. I mean *change*. You shoulda seen her skin. Translucent. And she smelled different. Smelled of strange drugs.'

You know I started shaking when he said that because I'd tried not to think of her all this time even though she came to me in dreams. Even before I'd start to dream, when I'd just closed my eyes, I'd hear the hollow tinkle of marimbas and see her eyes floating in the darkness.

'Sounds familiar,' I said.

'Nah. There was nobody like this girl, hon, nobody. She danced in a classical dance show *and* she worked the whore-houses ... had a day job too, working for a nutty professor woman ... honky woman, withered face, glasses. Some kind of doctor, I think. Sleazy office in Patpong, gave the girls free VD drugs.'

'Dr Frances Stone.' Was the company paying for a free VD clinic? What about the research into the secrets of the universe?

'Hey, how'd you know her name?'

'Did you have sex with her?' Suddenly I was trembling with rage. I don't know why. I mean, I knew what she did for a living.

'Did you?' Mike said. He was all nervous. He inched away from me, rolling a joint with one hand and scooting along the redwood deck with the other.

'I asked first,' I shouted, thinking, Jesus, I sound like a ten-year-old kid.

'Of *course* not! She had problems, all right? Expensive problems. But she was beautiful, mm-mm, good enough to eat.'

I looked wildly around. Ms Therapist was still dozing – fabulous way to earn a thousand bucks an hour – and the others had broken up into little groups. Janine was sort of listening, but she was more interested in getting her suntan lotion on evenly.

'I want to go back,' I said. 'I want to see Keo again.'

'Totally, like, bullshit,' she said, sidling up to me. 'You're just, like, externalizing the interior hurt on to a fantasy-object. Like, you need to be in touch with your child, know what I mean?'

'You're getting your support groups muddled up, hon,' Mike said edgily.

'Hey, Russ, instead of, like, projecting on some past-forgettable female two years back and ten thousand miles away, why don't you, like, fixate on someone a little closer to home? I mean, I've been *looking* at you. I only joined this support group 'cause like, support groups are the only place you can find like *sensitive* guys.'

'Janine, I'm married.'

'So let's have an affair.'

I liked the idea. My marriage to Trisha had mostly been a joke; I'd needed a fresh ornament for cocktail parties and openings; she needed security. We hadn't had much sex; how could we? I was hooked on memory. Perhaps this woman would cure me. And I wanted to be cured so badly because Mike's story had jolted me out of the fantasy that Keo had existed only for me.

By now it was the '90s so Janine insisted on a blood test before we did anything. I tested positive. I was scared shitless.

Because the only time I'd ever been so careless as to forget to use a condom was ... that night. And we'd done everything. Plumbed every orifice. Shared every fluid.

It had been a dance of transformation all right.

*

I had nothing to lose. I divorced my wife and sent my kids to an even more expensive school in Connecticut. I was feeling fine. Maybe I'd never come down with anything. I read all the books and articles about it. I didn't tell anyone. I packed a couple of suits and some casual clothes and a supply of bootleg AZT. I was feeling fine. Fine, I told myself. Fine.

I took the next flight to Bangkok.

The company was surprised to see me, but I was such a big executive by now they assumed I was doing some kind of internal troubleshooting. They put me up at the Oriental. They gave me a 10,000 baht per diem. In Bangkok you can buy a lot for four hundred bucks. I told them to leave me alone. The investigation didn't concern them. They didn't know what I was investigating, so they feared the worst.

I went to Silom Road, where Club Pagoda had stood. It was gone. In its stead stood a brand-new McDonald's and an airline ticket office. Perhaps Keo was already dead. Wasn't that what I had smelled on her? The odour of crushed flowers, wilting ... the smell of coming death? And the passion with which she had made love. I understood it now. It was the passion of the damned. She had reached out to me from a place between life and death. She had sucked the life from me and given me the virus as a gift of love.

I strolled through Patpong. Hustlers tugged at my elbows. Fake Rolexes were flashed in my face. It was useless to ask for Keo. There are a million women named Keo. Keo means jewel. It also means glass. In Thai there are many words that are used indiscriminately for reality and artifice. I didn't have a photograph and Keo's beauty was hard to describe. And every girl in Patpong is beautiful. Every night, parading before me in the neon labyrinth, a thousand pairs of lips and eyes, sensuous and infinitely giving. The wrong lips, the wrong eyes.

There are only a few city blocks in Patpong, but to trudge up and down them in the searing heat, questioning, observing every face for a trace of the remembered grail ... it can age you. I stopped shaving and took recreational drugs. What did it matter anyway?

But I was still fine, I wasn't coming down with anything.

I was fine. Fine!

And then, one day, while paying for a Big Mac, I saw her hands. I was looking down at the counter counting out the money. I heard the computer beep of the cash register and then I saw them: proffering the hamburger in both hands, palms up, like an offering to the gods. The fingers arched upwards, just so, with delicacy and hidden strength. God, I knew those hands. Their daintiness as they skimmed my shoulder blades, as they glided across my testicles just a hair's breadth away from touching. Their strength when she balled up her fist and shoved it into my rectum. Jesus, we'd done everything that night. I dropped my wallet on the counter, I seized those hands and gripped them, burger and all, and I felt the familiar response. Oh, God, I ached.

'Mister, you want a blowjob?'

It wasn't her voice. I looked up. It wasn't even a woman.

I looked back down at the hands. I looked up at the face. They didn't even belong together. It was a pockmarked boy and when he talked to me he stared off into space. There was no relation between the vacuity of his expression and the passion with which those hands caressed my hands.

'I don't like to do such thing,' he said, 'but I'm a poor college student and I needing money. So you can come back after 5 p.m. You not be disappointed.'

The fingers kneaded my wrists with the familiarity of one who has touched every part of your body, who has memorized the varicose veins in your left leg and the mole on your right testicle.

It was obscene. I wrenched my own hands free. I barely

remembered to retrieve my wallet before I ran out into the street.

★

I had been trying to find Dr Frances Stone since I arrived, looking through the files at the corporate headquarters, screaming at secretaries. Although the corporation had funded Dr Stone's project, the records seemed to have been spirited away.

At last I realized that that was the wrong way to go about it. I remembered what Mike had told me, so the day after the encounter with Keo's hands, I was back in Patpong, asking around for a good VD clinic. The most highly regarded one of all turned out to be at the corner of Patpong and Soi Cowboy, above a store that sold pirated software and videotapes.

I walked up a steep staircase into a tiny room without windows, with a ceiling fan moving the same sweaty air around and around. A receptionist smiled at me. Her eyes had the same vacuity that the boy at McDonald's had possessed. I sat in an unravelling rattan chair and waited, and Dr Stone summoned me into her office.

'You've done something with her,' I said.

'Yes.' She was shuffling a stack of papers. She had a window; she had an air-conditioner blasting away in the direction of all the computers. I was still drenched with sweat.

The phone rang and she had a brief conversation in Thai that I couldn't catch. 'You're angry, of course,' she said, putting down the phone. 'But it was better than nothing. Better than the cold emptiness of the earth. And she had nothing to lose.'

'She was dying of AIDS! And now *I* have it!' It was the first time I'd allowed the word to cross my lips. 'You *killed* me!'

Frances laughed. 'My,' she said, 'aren't we being a little melodramatic? You have the virus, but you haven't actually come down with anything.'

'I'm fine. Fine.'

'Well, why don't you sit down. I'll order up some food. We'll talk.'

She had really gone native. In Thailand it's rude to talk

business without ordering up food. Sullenly I sat down while
she opened a window and yelled out an order to one of the
street vendors.

'To be honest, Mr Leibowitz,' she said, 'we really could use
another grant. We had to spend *so* much of the last one on
cloak-and-dagger nonsense, security, bribes, and so on; so little
could be spared for research itself ... I mean, look around you
... I'm not exactly wasting money on luxurious office space,
am I?'

'I saw her hands.'

'Very effective, wasn't it?' The food arrived. It was some kind
of noodle thing wrapped in banana leaves and groaning from
the weight of chili peppers. She did not eat; instead, she amused
herself by rearranging the peppers in the shape of ... 'The
hands, I mean. Beautiful as ever. Vibrant. Sensual. My first
breakthrough.'

I started shaking again. I'd read about Dr Stone's great-
grandfather and his grave-robbing experiments. Jigsaw corpses
brought to life with bolts of lightning. Not life. A simulacrum
of life. Could this have happened to Keo? But she was dying.
Perhaps it was better than nothing. Perhaps ...

'Anyhow. I was hoping you'd arrive soon, Mr Leibowitz.
Because we've made up another grant proposal. I have the
papers here. I know that you've become so important now that
your signature alone will suffice to bring us ten times the
amount you authorized two years ago.'

'I want to see her.'

'Would you like to dance with her? Would you like to see
her in the *Chui Chai* one more time?'

*

She led me down a different stairwell. Many flights. I was sure
we were below ground level. I knew we were getting nearer to
Keo because there was a hint of that rotting flower fragrance in
the air. We descended. There was an unnatural chill.

And then, at last, we reached the laboratory. No shambling
Igors or bubbling retorts. Just a clean, well-lit basement room.

Cold, like the vault of a morgue. Walls of white tile; ceiling of stucco; fluorescent lamps; the pervasive smell of the not-quite-dead.

Perspex tanks lined the walls. They were full of fluid and body parts. Arms and legs floating past me. Torsos twirled. A woman's breast peered from between a child's thighs. In another tank, human hearts swirled, each neatly severed at the aorta. There was a tank of eyes. Another of genitalia. A necklace of tongues hung suspended in a third. A mass of intestines writhed in a fourth. Computers drew intricate charts on a bank of monitors. Oscilloscopes beeped. A pet gibbon was chained to a post topped by a human skull. There was something so outlandishly antiseptic about this spectacle that I couldn't feel the horror.

'I'm sorry about the décor, Russell, but you see, we've had to forgo the usual decoration allowance.' The one attempt at dressing up the place was a frayed poster of *Young Frankenstein* tacked to the far wall. 'Please don't be upset at all the body parts,' she added. 'It's all very macabre, but one gets inured to it in med school; if you feel like losing your lunch, there's a small restroom on your left ... yes, between the eyes and the tongues.' I did not feel sick. I was feeling ... excited. It was the odour. I knew I was getting closer to Keo.

She unlocked another door. We stepped into an inner room.

Keo was there. A cloth was draped over her, but seeing her face after all these years made my heart almost stop beating. The eyes. The parted lips. The hair, streaming upwards towards a source of blue light ... although I felt no wind in the room. 'It is an electron wind,' said Dr Stone. 'No more waiting for the monsoon lightning. We can get more power from a wall socket than great-grandfather Victor could ever dream of stealing from the sky.'

And she laughed the laughter of mad scientists.

I saw the boy from McDonald's sitting in a chair. The hands reached out towards me. There were electrodes fastened to his temples. He was naked now, and I saw the scars where the hands had been joined at the wrists to someone else's arms. I saw a woman with Keo's breasts, wired to a pillar of glass, straining, heaving while jags of blue lightning danced about her bonds. I saw her vagina stitched on to the pubis of a dwarf, who lay twitching at the foot of the pillar. Her feet were fastened to the body of a five-year-old boy, transforming their grace to ungainliness as he stomped in circles around the pillar.

'Jigsaw people!' I said

'Of course!' said Dr Stone. 'Do you think I would be so foolish as to bring back people whole? Do you not realize what the consequences would be? The legal redefinition of life and death ... wills declared void, humans made subservient to walking corpses ... I'm a scientist, not a philosopher.'

'But who are they now?'

'They were nobody before. Street kids. Prostitutes. They were dying, Mr Leibowitz, dying! They were glad to will their bodies to me. And now they're more than human. They're many persons in many bodies. A Gestalt. I can shuffle them and put them back together, oh, so many different ways ... and the beautiful Keo. Oh, she wept when she came to me. When she found out she had given you the virus. She loved you. You were the last person she ever loved. I saved her for you. She's been sleeping here, waiting to dance for you, since the day she died. Oh, let us not say *died*. The day she ... she ... I am no poet, Mr Leibowitz. Just a scientist.'

I didn't want to listen to her. All I could see was Keo's face. It all came back to me. Everything we had done. I wanted to relive it. I didn't care if she was dead or undead. I wanted to seize the grail and clutch it in my hands and own it.

Frances threw a switch. The music started. The shrilling of the *pinai*, the pounding of the *taphon*, the tinkling of marimbas and xylophones rang in the *Chui Chai* music. Then she slipped away unobtrusively. I heard a key turn in a lock. She had left the grant contract lying on the floor. I was alone with all the parts of the woman I'd loved. Slowly I walked towards the draped head. The electron wind surged; the cold blue light intensified. Her eyes opened. Her lips moved as though discovering speech for the first time ...

'Rus . . . sell.'

On the pizza-faced boy, the hands stirred of their own accord. He turned his head from side to side and the hands groped the air, straining to touch my face. Keo's lips were dry. I put my arms around the drape-shrouded body and kissed the dead mouth. I could feel my hair stand on end.

'I see big emptiness inside you. Come to me. I fill you. We both empty people. Need filling up.'

'Yes. Jesus, yes.'

I hugged her to me. What I embraced was cold and prickly. I whisked away the drape. There was no body. Only a framework of wires and transistors and circuit boards and tubes that fed flasks of flaming reagents.

'I dance for you now.'

I turned. The hands of the McDonald's boy twisted into graceful patterns. The feet of the child moved in syncopation to the music, dragging the rest of the body with them. The breasts of the chained woman stood firm, waiting for my touch. The music welled up. A contralto voice spun plaintive melismas over the interlocking rhythms of wood and metal. I kissed her. I kissed that severed head and lent my warmth to the cold tongue, awakened passion in her. I kissed her. I could hear chains breaking and wires slithering along the floor tiles. There were hands pressed into my spine, rubbing my neck, unfastening my belt. A breast touched my left buttock and a foot trod lightly on my right. I didn't care that these parts were attached to other bodies. They were hers. She was loving me all over. The dwarf that wore her pudenda was climbing up my leg. Every part of her was in love with me. Oh, she danced. We danced together. I was the epicentre of their passion. We were empty people but now we drank our fill. Oh, God, we danced. Oh, it was a grave music, but it contented us.

And I signed everything, even the codicil.

*

Today I am in the AIDS ward of a Beverly Hills hospital. I don't have long to wait. Soon the codicil will come into effect, and my body will be preserved in liquid nitrogen and shipped to Patpong.

The nurses hate to look at me. They come at me with rubber gloves on so I won't contaminate them, even though they should know better. My insurance policy has disowned me. My children no longer write me letters, though I've paid for them to go to Ivy League colleges. Trisha comes by sometimes. She is happy that we rarely made love.

One day I will close my eyes and wake up in a dozen other bodies. I will be closer to her than I could ever be in life. In life we are all islands. Only in Dr Stone's laboratory can we know true intimacy, the mind of one commanding the muscles of another and causing the nerves of a third to tingle with unnameable desires. I hope I shall die soon.

The living dead are not as you imagine them. There are no dangling innards, no dripping slime. They carry their guts and gore inside them, as do you and I. In the right light they can be beautiful, as when they stand in the cold luminescence of a basement laboratory, waiting for an electron stream to lend them the illusion of life. Fuelled by the right fantasy, they become indistinguishable from us.

Listen. I know. I've loved them.

Chui Chai is a modern-day Frankenstein story mostly set in Bangkok's infamous Patpong district. It was originally written for an anthology called *The Ultimate Frankenstein*, edited by Byron Preiss and John Betancourt. To my surprise, it's turned out to be one of my most frequently reprinted stories.

By the way, I changed the geography of Bangkok slightly in the story, so that no one would go looking for the nonexistent places described in it . . .

Though I Walk through the Valley

Uncle Will never meant no harm. Dude, he was *down*. Last Christmas he gave me a Super Nintendo and a dirt bike. Once a month or so we'd like get drunk and stoned and shit. When my brother was gunned down in a drive-by, he took me down to Hollywood after the funeral and bought me a big old chocolate sundae, and he told me I could come and live with him if I wanted to. And I'm all, 'Thanks, but like I don't want to hurt Mom's feelings even if she don't got no feelings since she became a junkie.'

He's all, 'I hear you, but don't be such a stranger any more. I only live two floors down. I like you, Oz. You really have your head screwed on straight for a kid who's had so much shit happen to him in his life. So maybe you can do me a favour, talk some sense into Little Ferdie; he's so fucking stubborn.'

That's how I come to see a lot more of my cousin Ferdie, and how I found out that Uncle Will was a child abuser.

Cousin Ferdie was twelve like me but he was totally skinny with big bulging eyes like a hunger poster. When I started hanging out at Uncle Will's apartment after school, or when I would ditch, I didn't see much of him. His door'd be closed and there wasn't no reason for me to go in and see him and maybe he wasn't even home, maybe he was like out cruising with his own friends somewheres. I didn't like Ferdie. He was so quiet he made you nervous, and when he would say something it would be like sudden, out of nowhere, something that had nothing to do with anything . . . like when my grandmother would do her speaking-in-tongues thing in church.

I didn't go to Uncle Will's to see Ferdie anyways. I was there to see Will. He was always there because he'd been laid off for three months. His girlfriend, a directory assistance lady, was paying all the bills, except his liquor bill which he would get the money for by standing at the entrance to the Sacramento Free-way with a big old sign that said he was homeless. By lunch-time he would always have enough for a couple of forty-ouncers.

He often had his homies over. There was Bill and Ted, forty-year-old surfers, from the apartment next door, and Armando, who was dying of AIDS, and Lupe the hooker, and Jungle George the loan shark, but most of all there was Mr Death, an old black dude with long white hair. His real name was Daniel Moreau. Mr Death was his professional name. He was a *houngan* – a voodoo witch-doctor. Retired that is. Used to hang out with Baby Doc in Haiti. Told wild stories: political prisoners getting burning tyres hung around their necks, magic potions, and zombies, naturally, except the way he told it, there wasn't nothing supernatural about them. He was my favourite of Uncle Will's friends, but his stories about Haiti made the East Valley sound like buttfuck Egypt, I mean *nothing* happens here except like, drive-bys and drug busts and shit.

My cousin Ferdie was usually nowhere to be found. That was fine with me. Then, one too-hot day in April, I totally saved his life.

It was kind of an accident. I was at the 7-Eleven trying to buy a pack of cigarettes. Usually the dude just sells them to me but this time I think it was a different person even though it's like hard to tell them apart. He stood there, six feet six in his turban, and he's all, 'You cannot be purchasing cigarettes here, young man.'

I'm all, 'Why not?' and he's all, 'Because you are being too young,' so I'm all, 'You motherfucking camel jockey,' and slamming the hardpack on the counter and jamming out of the store. But because I'm in such a hurry, everything I've jacked starts tumbling out of my pocket: two Twix bars, a packet of condoms, a bag of peanuts and a Bic lighter.

'Shoplifter!' he screamed, and started loping out from behind the counter.

But I'm all, 'So what are you gonna do about it, fag?' because I knew I could outrun anybody, and I started running, but he pushed some kind of alarm button and I didn't make it out of the parking lot before a cop car pulled in and two big dudes jumped out with big old PR-24s. They started chasing me but they didn't know the alleys like I did. I lost them but then I heard the sirens and I knew they were going to try and head me off somewhere. I hopped a chainlink fence and dove through a hole in a churchyard shrubbery and I came out behind our apartment building. I was in an alley that was too narrow for the squad car to squeeze through but I seen it through the gap and the lights flashing and I knew that they'd be running after me again and I didn't feel like getting beat up. Them plastic ties they put around your wrists can really cut you.

I shimmied up the wall where a orange tree grew, swung over the branch, and found myself on the balcony outside my cousin's room. I could tell they hadn't seen me because I heard them running all the way past the complex shouting, 'Stop you little *cholo* shit stop or I'll shoot your fucking face off,' and I knew I'd gotten clean away. They'd never even gotten a good look at me since they thought I was a *cholo*; I may dress like one but I don't look like one.

So I slide open the door into Ferdie's room and there he is, standing on a chair with a belt around his neck, tightening the buckle and getting ready to kick. His eyes were all empty and he had wet his boxers.

I didn't waste no time, I just grabbed a hold of him and yanked the belt out of the buckle. There was like a red bruise all around his neck where the leather had cut it. I lifted him up real easy (he was a head shorter than me) and carried him to the lower bunk and I'm all, 'What do you think you're doing, dude?' and pulling off his boxers and drying him off with a Ren and Stimpy towel.

'Jesus, Ferdie,' I said, 'you could at least have pissed in the bathroom.'

'Not allowed in the bathroom.'

'What do you mean?'

'Not allowed to leave my room for two weeks on account of I'm stubborn.'

'Not even to go to the bathroom?'

'Sometimes there ain't no one out there to let me out in time.'

I tried Ferdie's door. It was locked from the outside. Then I heard my Uncle Will's voice: 'Don't you try the door, it's no use, I'll double your time if I even hear you breathe.'

I held my breath. This was another Uncle Will than the down dude I could get stoned with. I'd never heard Uncle Will scream like that before. Never even heard him raise his voice.

Ferdie was all shivering even though it was probably 106 outside and the swamp cooler wasn't working too well because of the humidity. I looked around the room for some clean underwear, but when I found it he wouldn't let me take away his towel. I had to trick him and whisk it away and that's when I saw all the bruises because he stepped out from the shadow of the bunk, into the harsh summer light. There were some thin red stripes, like maybe an electric cord, and some wide purple ones with punctures, like the buckle end of a belt, and a couple of cigarette burns. I was too shocked to say anything at first, and then all I could say was 'Why?' because something this bad had to have a reason, it couldn't just happen.

And he's all, 'I dunno.' And he shrugged. 'I guess it's because I'm stubborn, that's all, stubborn.'

'How stubborn?'

'I forget. I think I wouldn't eat my cereal.' He gave a sharp giggle, like a girl. 'I don't like Captain Crunch.'

There had to be more to it than that. I figured maybe he wasn't thinking straight seeing how he'd just been this close to history. Uncle Will wasn't like one of them dudes on *Geraldo*, you know, one show they had with like kids who had been locked up in cages, used in satanic sacrifices, shit like that. Was he? I've known Uncle Will since the fourth grade, when we moved down to the Valley from the trailer park in Lancaster. Maybe Uncle Will had gotten weird from being laid off so long.

'You still shouldn't of tried to kill yourself,' I said. 'It's a sin.'

'I know, Oz,' Ferdie said, 'but hell can't be no worse than this.'

Then he looks at me with big sad sunken eyes and picks at a scab on the back of his hand. The way he looks at me is all, *I'm in hell now, Oz, and you gotta help me, cuz I'm sinking fast.* But I still couldn't believe that Uncle Will would have done that to him. I didn't like Ferdie, you understand, on account of he could stare anyone down and he made you nervous just being around him. And he read books, too, and he could toss off a string of facts that would make you feel totally stupid and want to punch his head in. But he was my cousin and you know, family is all you have, and less and less of it because they keep getting gunned down in your back yard.

'You don't got to help me any,' Ferdie said, 'next week they're gonna put me on Ritalin and maybe I won't be so stubborn no more.'

I'm all, 'Shit, Ferdie, of course I'll help you.' I gave him a piece of bubblegum that I'd jacked along with the other stuff, that hadn't fallen out of my pocket. He swallowed the whole thing. 'Me and Uncle Will are homies. Maybe I can find out what's making him act this way.' Because I still thought that it was just some kind of temporary craziness and I could get Will to come to his senses, and I knew we couldn't turn him in, because that would tear the family apart forever.

*

So I waited for a couple of hours and I snuck back over the balcony and around to the front of the apartment building. Mr Death and Uncle Will were sitting in the living room chugging their forty-ouncers. They were talking in whispers and they didn't see me come in. So I sat down on the bean bag behind Will's armchair and pretended like I wasn't there.

Uncle Will's all, 'I don't know what to do, I try so hard, he's so stubborn.'

'I would say you was probably stubborn too,' Mr Death said. 'Stubborn runs in families.' His voice was deep and it rolled like a tubular wave. The way he talked wasn't like the black people in my school exactly, I mean it had like a foreign lilt to it, French or something.

'Yeah,' Uncle Will said, 'I reckon I was. Stubborn I mean. My dad used to whip the shit out of me. But Ferdinand's a different kind of stubborn. He's stubborn like a block of granite that you want to carve into a statue and it won't give. Drugs don't help him, whipping don't make it any better.'

It's weird. *Stubborn* ain't a word you hear people use much about kids, well, just old people, and they're more'n likely talking about a mule or a dog when they say it. When I heard Uncle Will talking this way it was, you know, like when I heard his voice booming through Ferdie's locked door – it didn't sound like the Will I knew, my bud. Suddenly I realized that it sounded like Grandpa.

And like I'm all cold suddenly, cold and clammy, even though the air from the electric fan is as burning hot as the smoggy air outside. Because I seen my grandfather dead, at the wake. They made me kiss the corpse on the cheek. The make-up rubbed off on my lips and I sucked in a cold and bitter-tasting wind. Even though that had been a totally hot day too, a heat wave, and me six years old and standing on a crate and sweating like a motherfucker.

Uncle Will said, 'I wish there was another way.' And popped the cap off the second forty-ouncer. 'Jesus, I try so hard but him and me, it's like I'm butting my head against the biggest-ass wall in the world.'

And Mr Death said, 'Well, Will, there *be* other ways. There is things in the world you can only see if you choose to open your eyes. There is doors you can unlock but only if you know they there.'

I could tell that like, Mr Death was about to totally launch into one of them stories of his. Maybe if Uncle Will got all involved in the story I could slip out from behind the armchair and act like I just arrived. But Will cut him off and he just said, 'Daniel, I got no patience for your bullshit today. I'm scared, man, scared for me and my son. What if I accidentally kill him one of these days? I ain't a bad man, I ain't a murderer, but the kid just plain makes me go berserk.'

'Well, back at home there is a little trick I do,' Mr Death said.

'And after I do this little trick, my patients they all calm, they do what they told, they never ever complain no more.'

'What is it, some kind of voodoo therapy?'

'Maybe you call it that.'

'Is it expensive?'

'Not for you. You can't afford not to have it done. You drinking yourself into the grave because how much it trouble you. You want to feel that love God say you got to feel for the child of your own loins.'

'I'd give anything.'

'And you will. Not just anything. Everything.'

'But what will you give Ferdie in return?'

'I will give him a new life,' Mr Death said. 'A kind of being born again, starting with a clean slate.'

That's when I really got scared, because before you can kind of be born again you have to kind of die. And I knew Mr Death was talking about turning Ferdie into a zombie.

*

I didn't come out from behind that armchair until long after Daniel Moreau had gone home and Uncle Will dozed off after his second forty-ouncer. I crept up the stairs to my mom's apartment. She was lying on the living room floor, past noticing anything.

I dreamed about my brother. I never saw him dead because they couldn't fix his face and so they had a closed coffin funeral. Then I dreamed Ferdie was dangling from the end of a noose, swinging like a busted naked light bulb. Then I dreamed about Grandpa. Bending down to kiss the body. His eyes popping open. Staring straight at me. Fixed. Like the lens of a camcorder. Staring. Videotaping me, my lips still freeze-dried from brushing his cheek, too scared to scream.

Then I dreamed it was me in that coffin, and I'm all rigid but not from death, only from terror because the three of them are standing around me and all of them are dead and all of them with their fixed-focus eyes . . .

I woke up and I thought: Uncle Will didn't come to the

funeral. I didn't meet him for another three years. I wondered why he didn't come. I'm all, I think I'll ask him tomorrow. I looked over at the VCR and the timer said 3:30 in the morning. I tried to go back to sleep.

But like, every time I closed my eyes I would see all three of them again. *Night of the Living Dead* style, with their arms hanging limp and shambling around my grave. And their heads swivelling like the security cameras at the K-Mart. And that's how it goes on, all night long, so I can't get to sleep, so when I finally do it's almost dawn and I know I'm going to have to sleep through first period or totally ditch.

★

I got up around twelve. I couldn't leave the house because there's always a cop prowling around somewheres and they can't wait to truss your wrists with them plastic ties and haul you off to school. So I decided to go down to Uncle Will's apartment.

Actually I went down the fire escape first, slipped Ferdie a couple of cookies and a wine cooler – he just sat staring into a broken television set – then worked my way back around to the front, let myself in.

Uncle Will gave me a big old hug and I told him I had nightmares all night long and he's all, 'It's okay, son, I'm here for you, calm down now.'

And I'm all, 'Dude, I dreamed everyone was dead.'

'You've had it rough, kid.' He steered me towards the sofa and gave me a couple of Valium. 'You want to hang out here for a while? Your mom don't give a shit.'

I sat on the sofa juggling the Valium from hand to hand. 'Uncle Will? Why didn't you go to Grandpa's funeral? Like, he was your dad, wasn't he?'

'Don't got no father,' said Uncle Will.

'Well but . . . Uncle Will? Why do you beat up on Ferdie so much?'

'Because he's a stubborn little motherfucker.'

'Yeah, but . . . over not eating his cereal? I mean like, cigarette burns and shit?'

'How d'you find out?'

'I saw him yesterday.'

'Saw him? I told him to stay in his room!'

'I know, I went in through the balcony.'

'I told him not to—' I could see that Uncle Will was getting real pissed. Frothing at the mouth almost. He strode down the corridor to Ferdie's room and started trying to kick it in.

I'm all, 'Don't you have a key?' and he like calms down, but only a little bit, and fumbles in his jeans and pulls them out and unlocks the door. There's Ferdie, sitting on the bunk in just a pair of *Terminator 2* boxer shorts and criss-crossed with cuts, and I see what Uncle Will means when he says *stubborn* because there ain't one shred of fear or self-pity in Ferdie's eyes, he just glares at Will and there's more anger coiled up in them eyes than you can imagine. Will just throws himself on Ferdie and he's all punching him and Ferdie just sits there, taking it, but no matter how hard he's hit he never gives up one little bit of that fury that's in his eyes. After a while I couldn't stand it no more and I'm all trying to pull Will off of him and I'm all, 'You're crazy, dude, you're not yourself, you're fucking possessed or something.'

And then it all suddenly snaps to. Ferdie, rigid, Uncle Will stepping back, looking away from those blazing eyes. 'It's them eyes,' he said, 'it's all because of them eyes. Devil eyes. They just keep daring me and daring me. They taunt me and they haunt me.'

He grabbed my shoulders and pushed me out of Ferdie's room and then he slammed the door shut behind us and locked it again. 'I got to do something,' he said. 'Or else I'm going to murder him, I really am.'

Once Ferdie was out of sight he started changing back into the Will I knew. 'Let's go cruising,' he said. 'I can't stay cooped up here. I'll keep thinking about *him*.'

So we took off down the San Fernando Road towards Sun Valley, past Foothill Division, with speed metal all blaring on the stereo. I had to shout and he did too. And he's got his arm around me the whole time, and he's all, 'Ozzie, I wish you were my kid. We have such good times together.'

'Don't you love Ferdinand, Uncle Will?'

'I love him with all my heart.' But there's no tenderness in his voice when he says it, only fear. 'I don't know why I want to kill him so bad. He's got some devil in him.'

'Maybe it's in *you*, Uncle Will. You know' – we turned a sharp corner, bounced across the railroad tracks somewhere around Tuxford, nothing but big old grey warehouses covered with taggers' writings, and the smog totally hiding the San Gabriel Mountains from sight – 'when you were all screaming and shit, you sounded like another person. You sounded almost like Grandpa.'

'Your grandfather was a good man. He never laid a hand on me. Do you hear that? Don't you ever forget that.'

The tape was getting chewed up, so I had to stop the stereo and pull out the cassette and wind the little ribbon back with the end of a Pilot marker. So we caught the end of some news thing and it was that the cops were all found not guilty up there in Simi Valley, and then Uncle Will switched the radio off. 'Motherfuckers,' he said softly.

'Uncle Will, where are we?'

We were threading down a narrow winding road, half paved, half dirt, and weeds waist-high on either side of us, and like, it was suddenly getting dark. Then, poking out of them weeds, there's a big old sign that reads *Daniel Moreau, Doctor of Divinity*. I get that chilly feeling inside me again because of what I heard them talking about last night, which I've been trying to forget all day.

'I'll be damned,' Uncle Will said. 'It's Mr Death's place.'

After we parked we had to walk through a path winding through trees and weeds and here and there little piles of rocks, pyramids kind of, decorated with bunches of wildflowers. Like the place was a kind of homemade graveyard. The house wasn't much more than a shack, and it was set way in back of the lot. It looked abandoned, but when we got closer we could see the TV flickering behind closed blinds, and Uncle Will knocked on the door. There wasn't no answer but we went in anyways.

Mr Death was in a Lazyboy rocking back and forth and

looking at the television. 'Gone be riots,' he said softly. 'I just know it.'

Uncle Will's all, 'Gosh, Daniel, I don't know what happened. We were just cruising is all, and the road twisted and turned and we somehow ended up here.'

'I been expecting you.' Mr Death's voice was all booming and hollow. On TV, the sun was setting and the streets were totally filling with angry black dudes and they were shouting and breaking store windows and beating up Koreans and shit. 'You come for that service we done talked about.'

'No, Mr Death,' Uncle Will said, 'I swear, we were just passing by.'

'You at your wits' end, Will. And Mr Death he at the end of every road.'

Now I was getting totally scared because the way Mr Death was talking, it was like this house, this whole encounter, was supernatural somehow. And I was staring at the TV, it was Fox 11, and I could see fire running down the streets of South Central, and once in a while they cut to the videotape of the Rodney King thing, I remembered us driving past Foothill Division, I thought of my dream and my grandfather's shambling towards me with camcorder eyes.

'Don't be ashamed you come to me,' said Daniel Moreau. 'You done tried everything you can. You a good man, Will, but you have one streak of darkness in you, and maybe this gone lighten your darkness, maybe not.'

'I just ... want to be able to love my son ... you know. The way I love Ozzie, my nephew.'

And the way he said it, it made me feel like me and Ferdie were more alike than I'd of ever thought; like Ferdie was my own self's shadow, locked up in a dark room, sucking the hatred out of Uncle Will so that all that was left for me was his love. We were different like night and day, but the sickness in Uncle Will's mind had made us Siamese twins, joined at the heart.

'Give me a few minutes,' said Mr Death, 'and I'll get all my tools.'

'How much is this going to cost me?'

'It against the law for me to charge for this kind of thing. But you make a voluntary donation, that's fine.'

'How much?' said Uncle Will, who always counted every dime, even when he was panhandling for change next to the freeway.

'You will know what the price will be,' Mr Death says, 'and it will be the right price.'

We followed him into the kitchen which was totally filthy. On the counter there was a bell jar with a big old frog inside, and hanging from the ceiling where a light bulb should be there was a bunch of dried puffer fishes. At first I thought the frog was dead but he was only sleeping, and Mr Death lifted the jar and made me hold him in both my hands, and then he jabbed it in the head with a needle, so it was dead and undead at the same time, and then he cut down one of the puffer fishes and got a whole mess of other shit off the shelves and then he throws everything, including the dead twitching frog, into like this big old blender, and he like turns it on.

While it's whirring all I can think of are frog-in-a-blender jokes.

Okay so then he pours this gooey mass out of the blender and then he does something with it in the microwave and finally he's all pounding it in a mortar and he's all mumbling in some kind of foreign language. After a while the chemicals and the dead animals were reduced to about a handful of dark powder and Mr Death used a flour scoop to fill a Ziploc bag with it. A black and white TV on top of the microwave was on the whole time and the riots were getting uglier every minute, but so far they hadn't mentioned San Fernando, it was all like mostly downtown.

'You know,' Mr Death said, 'if we cruise up to Mulholland Drive, we'd see, the whole city she a sea of fire.'

He closed his eyes like he was remembering that sea of fire. But I knew that Mr Death had been here the whole time. Maybe he had an inner eye for seeing things like that. Or he could send his spirit out hovering over the city. Maybe that was how we been led to his house ... shit all I know is he scared me, and I couldn't take my eyes off the things he was doing, and maybe it was the words he mumbled and maybe it was the two Valium, but my mind was all fuzzed up and I couldn't see straight.

Mr Death put the powder in a black tote bag and took a human skull out of the refrigerator and he stuck that in the bag too. Then we drove back to the apartment and what was weird was it only took a minute or two to get back and I never seen the road we took before. In front of the complex there wasn't nobody cruising, only a patrol car with its lights flashing at the corner of Aztec and Hubbard. We went indoors and the TV was on and it showed a helicopter view of the city and like Mr Death said, it was a ocean of flames and the people were streaming down the streets like termites.

We went to Ferdie's room and we found him exactly where he was sitting before, on the bunk bed facing the television.

Mr Death is all, 'We must introduce the *coup poudre* through a cut in the skin; it has to get into the bloodstream before it start to work.'

'Come here, Ferdinand,' said Uncle Will.

Ferdie comes towards us. He's thin as a shadow and there's his eyes, clear blue and deep sunken and full of rage, and some of his welts are bleeding a little bit where he's been picking scabs.

'And now,' says Mr Death, 'please remember, my homies, there is no magic, no superstition. This a ancient and venerable science that come all the way from BaKongo times. The *coup poudre* gone send the boy into the sleep of no dreaming, and then, when he come back, he don't be stubborn no more.'

I'm all, 'You're gonna kill him, dude!'

Mr Death said, 'Death is transformation.'

Ferdie comes up to Uncle Will. He only comes up to his chest. His sandy hair is all matted. I'm all, 'What the fuck do you think you're doing, Uncle Will?' but he pushes me away real rough like, I never seen him be this rough to me before, he sends me reeling across the carpet and I hit my head against the bunk post. I'm all, 'Why are you hurting me, Uncle Will,' but then I look across the room and I see a strange thing in the cold light of the street lamp through the orange tree that leans against the balcony: I see Uncle Will take Ferdie into his arms with all the tenderness that he shows me, sometimes, when he knows I'm going through a lot of pain, and he hugs him, and he's all, 'Ferdie, I'm only doing this because I want us to be a real family, I'm doing this for you as much as for me,' and while he's hugging him his fingernail is searching out a long thick scab that goes diagonally all the way across Ferdie's back like a burned-on shoulder strap, and he's all digging his fingernail into it, flicking off the dry blood and exposing the quick, slick flesh. And the weird thing is there is a kind of love between them, or anyways a kind of dependency, because they are like each other's liquid sky, they are each other's addiction. Uncle Will still has Ferdie in his arms and he turns his back to me so I can see right into Ferdie's eyes and them eyes are all shiny, like the contact lenses a monster wears in a cheesy horror movie. But Ferdie's smiling too, like he's telling me, *This is what I've been waiting for. Yeah, maybe you like saved my life yesterday but you couldn't snatch me away from Mr Death for ever.* And I'm all like standing with pain pounding in my skull from hitting the post and breaking out in a cold sweat because now Mr Death has crept up behind Ferdie, with his cupped hands full of the powder, and even bending down he's a head taller than them and standing against the balcony door he's all black and shadowy and big and terrifying, and then I guess when there's enough raw flesh showing he like blows the powder all over Ferdie's back and he begins to chant and the powder goes everywhere, it wraps itself around the three of them like a cloud for a moment and then it all gets totally swallowed up in the dust and darkness of the room.

That's when Ferdie starts to scream.

Uncle Will's all, 'God damn it, bitch, stop whining or I'll whip your motherfucking ass to kingdom come,' but Mr Death puts his hand on Will's shoulder and says, 'It too late, my friend, you already have.'

*

We left him screaming and went into the living room and Uncle
Will broke out a brand-new bottle of Jack Daniels. We drank
the whole thing in less than fifteen minutes and then we got
totally fucked up on weed and downers. We had to. Because
that screaming went on and on and it made me feel cold all the
way into my guts. I don't know how long it went on but when
I finally woke up it was because Uncle Will was prodding me
with an empty bottle, and he's all, 'Help me load him into the
car, dude.'

'Where's Mr Death?'

'Gone already. But he's left us a note.'

The note read:

> Bring him to my house
> Bury him in my yard
> Wait

And that's what we did. We found an open wooden box
lying out under the trees, all ready to receive the body, and we
dug a hole and buried Ferdie and we set up a pile of stones like
we seen other places in Mr Death's yard. We hung around all
day. It got to late afternoon and Uncle Will kept going up to
the house and knocking but the whole place was locked up.
When the sun got near to setting Will was all pacing up and
down and he's all, 'We can't stay after sunset, there's a fucking
curfew on and we'll have to spend the fucking night if we don't
leave now.'

'But we can't just leave Ferdie behind.'

Just when Will was about ready to explode, this beat-up old
Packard comes screaming into the driveway and there's Mr
Death. He's all dressed in black and he has a bottle of pills in
his hand and he throws it to me and the bottle says on it,
Datura. 'Sorry I'm so late,' he said, 'I had to see my pharma-
ceutical contacts. It difficult to track anybody down with all
them riots going on.'

'What's that stuff for?' said Uncle Will.

'Insurance,' said Mr Death. 'Now let's dig up your new son.'

Digging him up took a lot longer than burying him because

every now and then Mr Death stopped to chant and then, when
the moon came out, he went into like a trance and his eyes
totally rolled up into their sockets, he danced around us,
hollering and shrieking.

But we finally pulled the coffin back out of the ground and
we opened the lid and there was Ferdie, his eyes wide open,
trying to breathe and his knuckles and knees were all bloody
from clawing and kicking at the coffin lid. Mr Death forced a
pill down his throat and he calmed down, and Mr Death's all,
'Ferdinand, you a zombie now. You one of the living dead. You
understand what that mean?'

Ferdie nods, slowly, and yeah, I can tell that he's changed. It
ain't that he looks much different. There ain't no smell of dead
things on him, just the usual toilet smell because he didn't have
nowhere he could go in that box we buried him in. His eyes
have that look though. The look I remember from my grandpa.
The camcorder look. The eyes suck in, but they give nothing out.

'Now,' Mr Death says, 'embrace your father, and don't you
be stubborn again, cuz next time you dead for good.'

'I won't be stubborn,' Ferdie says, and he sounds more like a
toddler than a twelve-year-old, 'I love my father.'

We went back to the house and camped out on the living-
room floor because of the curfew. Ferdie lay on the floor and
slept with his eyes open and didn't move a muscle. Maybe Mr
Death was right when he said this was all science, not magic,
and maybe it was true that Ferdie wasn't really dead but had
only been called back from a coma caused by the nerve poison
in the puffer fish, but I knew that Ferdie didn't think so. Ferdie
had watched zombie movies before. He knew that he didn't
have his soul no more. He knew he was just a animated corpse.

★

I didn't ditch too much that week because of the riots and there
was so much to talk about with my homies. A lot of them had
taken the bus down to South Central and did their own looting
and they were all telling me about their new watches, Sega
Genesises, boomboxes, shoes they jacked. I couldn't tell them I

had spent the last two days raising the dead so I pretended I didn't care. In fact, whenever they tell me about all the shit they stoled, I'm all, 'Who cares? It ain't no challenge looting a big old Circuit City with five hundred other people and the cops too scared to come in. Me, I can jack a CD player right from under the security guard's eyes. I'm down and you ain't.'

So anyways I didn't see too much of Uncle Will that week. But whenever I would go there, the apartment was totally different. It was all clean and vacuumed and all the forty-ouncer bottles were all neatly lined up against the wall ready to be recycled. The blinds were all up and the living room was flooded in sunlight. At first I thought Uncle Will must have a new girlfriend but actually she had dumped him and it was just him and Ferdie living there now. And it was Ferdie cleaning the house. One time I caught him at it. He was all dusting the blinds and he was dressed different, too, in freshly laundered Bugle Boys and a white T-shirt.

'Yo, Ferdie,' I said.

And he's all, 'Hello, Ozzie, can I get you something to drink?' like he's a fucking waitress at Denny's or something. I was amazed and I just let him fetch me a wine cooler from the refrigerator. Then he went back into the kitchen and I followed him. He didn't walk like a zombie. He wasn't all shambling. He held his shoulders back and stood straight and didn't slouch around like a wuss. And he was all smiling. I mean, all the time. Only his eyes didn't smile. His eyes took everything in, gave out nothing.

I'm all, 'What the fuck's happened to you?'

'I think I'm enjoying being dead.'

'Ferdie, you ain't dead. Mr Death explained the whole process to us. The datura makes your mind all fuzzy but you ain't *dead*.'

He's all, 'Of course I am. It's what I been praying for all my life. I'm happy now and so is my dad. You should try it, Oz. I look at you and I see, you're so unhappy.'

'I seen dead people before,' I said. I thought of Grandpa. I thought of my brother, which I never saw dead but they all told me about his brains being splattered on the pavement and his eyeball impaled by the hood ornament of a parked Impala. 'You ain't one of them.' But his eyes, his eyes ... 'And I don't want to be one neither.'

'Suit yourself,' he said, and scrubbed the counter with a sponge, scrubbed it to death even though it was already shiny except the spots where his scrubbing had wore off the laminate.

Uncle Will came home.

Ferdie's all 'Daddy!' and he runs over to embrace him. Uncle Will kisses him on the cheek. He takes a pill out of his pocket and feeds it to Ferdie. They hug each other again. It's kind of sickening actually, like *The Waltons*.

'Shit,' he says, 'last one. I'll have to ask Mr Death for more.' Then he sees me and he's all, 'Oh, it's you.'

I'm all, 'I stopped by to see what's up.'

Uncle Will looks me over and then he's all, 'Look at you, Ozzie, jeeze you're a disgrace. Look at them jeans. What are you doing wearing them jeans, they look like they're about ten sizes too big.'

'It's the style, Uncle Will.'

'Fucking *cholo* style. You want people to think we're nothing but white trash?'

I backed away in a real hurry. I looked at Ferdie but he didn't seem to think anything was wrong, he was hanging on every word Uncle Will spoke, like a ten-year-old girl at a NKOTB concert.

'And what are you doing drinking that wine cooler anyways?'

'You always let me drink wine coolers, Uncle Will.'

He knocked the bottle out of my hand and Ferdie dove after it, caught it one-handed, got on his hands and knees to sponge the mess off of the carpet. While I was all standing there stunned, Uncle Will slaps me hard right across the mouth a couple of times. I can't believe this is happening to me even when I start to taste blood.

And Ferdie's all smiling.

'Uncle Will,' I said softly, 'you never done this to me before.'

'I'm seeing you with new eyes, you good-for-nothing juvenile delinquent scumbag.'

'Come on, Uncle Will, you said yourself every kid has to steal a few cars and jack a few stereos once in a while, and get drunk. You said it was just a phase, that I'd get over it, that it was like harmless.'

'Don't sass me.'

But it's hard to get out of the habit of answering back because it's always been this close between me and Uncle Will and I can't understand why he's turned against me until I realize that it's the Siamese twin thing, that Will can't love his zombie son without hating me. So I'm all backing out of there real fast because I think any minute now he's going to start laying into me with his belt or his fists or a cigarette, I get out of there as fast as I can and I go sprinting up the stairs three steps at a time to my mom's apartment, the place where I most hate to be.

★

Mom was sitting at the counter and what was weird was she was actually making dinner when I arrived and the whole living room smelled of enchiladas. She was all dressed up, too. I realized she had been out looking for a job, and she didn't look wasted. She was all shredding lettuce and watching television, which was showing the riots, naturally.

'How's the job market, Mom?'

She's all, 'I actually *got* a job today, Oz, they're going to train me to be a checkout lady at Alpha Beta.'

'Coolness.'

'I get a discount on food, too. We're not gonna be hungry no more.'

'We wouldn't be hungry, Mom, if you would have spent them disability checks on food instead of—'

'I know, I know. Let's not argue about it no more. I want to start again. I done a lot of things I regretted in my life. And Jesus, I don't know how to tell you this, but ... there was this lady from the rehab program, she got my name off some

mailing list, she was over here to talk about shared needles and
. . . Jesus, Oz, do you think I have it?'

'Don't say that, Mom.'

'I'm scared to take the test, son. I'm scared to stick another
needle in me and I'm scared not to because if I don't then I
know I'm going to be scared by everything around me, the
whole world.'

She's all crying and the oven timer goes *dingdingding* so I
took the enchiladas out and then I put my arm around Mom's
waist and let her cry for the longest time, and dinner was
totally cold when we finally got around to it, but it's the
thought that counts and it was like the first dinner she'd made
in six months.

After we ate I asked her what Grandpa was like. 'Was he
ever mean to you?' I said. 'Did he like hit you and stuff?'

'No. I got everything I ever asked for. It was Will he hated.
He always said Will was stubborn. He'd lock him up in the tool
shed for days at a time. Me, though, he loved me. He loved me
to death. His love was a scary thing. It engulfed me. It ate me
up. I guess that's why I became a junkie.'

And then I understood everything. Uncle Will's sickness
didn't just come from nowhere. It had been handed down
through the generations and maybe, one day, it would even
come down to me. Grown-ups are always all, what a big deal it
is to grow up, to become mature, to set aside childish things as
my grandma says, quoting the Bible . . . I ain't grown up yet
but I already know that growing up is a big old joke . . . you
don't grow up. You just live through your childhood again and
again and again until the day you die. Your childhood is who
you are.

'I'm going back down to Uncle Will's place,' I said. 'There's
something I just got to tell him.'

'All right,' she said. 'But don't go outside. The curfew hasn't
been lifted yet and you don't know what the cops will do,
they're in such a state over these damn riots.'

Yeah. We could hear sirens in the distance. Mom switched
channels and an anchorman was talking about the fires again

... behind him, the city was burning ... in a little window on the screen, they were replaying the video of the Rodney King beating for the millionth time. They had pre-empted the fucking *Simpsons*. They showed a clip of Pat Buchanan visiting South Central. He might just as well have been an alien from *Close Encounters*.

I went down to Uncle Will's to tell him my big new insight. I figure if he would have known that he was just slow-motion-replaying a scene from his childhood over and over, he could maybe step back from it, get it in perspective, and then maybe we could pull Ferdie back from his so-called death and Will out of his madness. But when I got to Will's I could tell that things had gone wrong, more wrong than they ever were before.

Will and Ferdie were standing on opposite sides of the living room. Between them, on the big TV, was the bird's-eye-view of the ocean of fire. Will was shouting into his portable phone. 'God damn it,' he was saying, 'I need the fucking pills *now*, he's getting stubborn again, I'm gonna fucking lose control!'

He had run out of datura. But what difference did it make? Ferdie was standing there and he was all submissive, all smiling, didn't seem like he was doing nothing wrong.

I heard Mr Death's voice, 'You know I can't come out there now. The curfew. And my supplier he way out in South Pas.'

And Uncle Will's all, 'Fuck, fuck, fuck, I'm fucking desperate!'

He slammed the portable phone against the wall. Then he turned and saw me. 'Kid's being stubborn again,' he shouted. 'He won't mind, he just stands there, won't do what he's told.' Then he turned to Ferdie and screamed, 'I want you to whine, you hear! I want you to wipe that grin off your face! I'm sick of watching that smile day in day out!'

Ferdie tried to frown but the smile was soldered on his face. He said, 'But I can't be unhappy, Dad. I have the kindest father in the world. I have a great life.'

'You don't even *have* a life, you're just an animated corpse, and I want you to obey me!'

Ferdie's all, 'Okay, Dad. I'm as sad as you want me to be.'

And he goes on smiling. And Uncle Will's going berserk, I mean like, more berserk than he's ever been before, he's like frothing at the mouth and shit. And Ferdie just goes on smiling. And Will's all, 'I'm gonna hurt you, Ferdie,' but Ferdie's all, 'I don't hurt any more, Dad. There ain't no hurting where I am, the dead country.' And he goes on smiling.

Uncle Will picks up the first thing he sees which is one of the empty bottles lined up against the wall and he strides over to Ferdie and he starts swinging it and it cracks against the wall and he cuts Ferdie's face a couple of times and Ferdie goes on smiling. Will socks him in the jaw and a bloody tooth flies on to the carpet and Ferdie smiles a gap-toothed smile, wider than ever. Will's weeping with rage and he just goes on punching and punching and for a long while I'm all standing there and staring because I can't believe it's happening, it's worse than I've ever seen before. I forget all about the big old revelation I was going to make. I think maybe even though it's true, that we're all together in this generational cycle of violence, that just saying it isn't going to make it stop because we're stuck in it, we're part of it, we're the spokes of the wheel and when the wheel turns we can't just turn the other way. I'm so full of despair I want to go hang myself like Ferdie was trying to. I want to be dead.

While I'm all standing there with these terrible emotions raging through me, Uncle Will's never stopped trying to whip that smile off Ferdie's face. And now he's all, 'You ain't dead, you ain't dead, it's just your stubbornness speaking, and I'm going to *shock* you back to the way you are, you can't escape from me by playing possum cuz I know you're inside there and you're laughing at me, laughing at me ...' and he sounds just like Grandpa used to sound sometimes. I stand there and watch while he ties Ferdie to a chair with an extension cord and now he's all getting more cords out of a drawer and I realize that when Uncle Will says *shock* that's exactly what he means, he's going to fry Ferdie's brains and this time he'll *really* be dead. And finally this shocks *me* out of my despair and I do what I should have done the first day I saw my cousin cut and bruised and caged ... I crawl over to where the phone's lying on the carpet and I pull up the antenna and I dial 911.

It takes for ever to get through because of the riots I guess. And the whole time Uncle Will's all storming through the house and throwing things around and there's blood all over Ferdie's white shirt but Ferdie's all smiling, smiling, smiling, and even I can feel a piece of Uncle Will's madness in me, the smile that goes on and on and driving you all crazy and shit. Then there's a lull in the shouting, Uncle Will's out of breath or something maybe, and that's when I get through to the police and I give them our address and tell them there's a child beating going on right now and please come, please Jesus come fast or I think my cousin's going to get fucking killed.

I put down the phone and I see the two of them, face to face, frozen in a moment of concentrated rage. Uncle Will turns to me and says, real soft like, 'Traitor.'

I'm all, 'I'm sorry, Uncle Will.' And I'm thinking of the times Uncle Will's been good to me, put his arm around me, wiped my tears with his sleeve, and all the time there's been a mirror image of this love between us, locked up like a dirty secret. And I'm all crying. We can hear sirens in the distance. They're already coming.

'I've gotta get out of here,' says Will. 'Can't let them catch me. There's a warrant on me, parking tickets and shit, car registration, I don't know.'

'You got nowheres to go, Uncle Will. There's a curfew.'

Someone is knocking on the door.

Uncle Will bolts past both of us towards Ferdie's room. I let the officer in and she takes one look at Ferdie, tied to the chair and covered in blood, and she's all pulling out her gun and running towards the back of the house.

I untie Ferdie and then me and him follow. We hear the rustle of the orange tree and we know he's going down into the alley. The sirens are wailing from every side now. The police officer's all, 'Stay right here, kids. I'm going down to radio for help.'

So there's me and there's Ferdie standing on the balcony

looking down through the branches of the orange tree into the alley below. And there's Uncle Will. Staggering. Confused. Two police officers come in from Aztec and two from Astoria and they have their PR-24s out. They don't read him no rights, they don't call out to him to surrender. They just surround him and they start beating the shit out of him with their power blows. The whistling of the nightsticks and the crunching of bones blend in with the other sounds of the night, the swaying of the orange branches, the rattling of garbage cans, the thrum of helicopters, the wail of sirens and stray cats. The night air totally smells of citrus and smog and garbage and gunsmoke. Though this is all happening for real and not on television there's something about it that's less real than television: it's because we're standing in the warm wind of night and seeing the San Gabriel Mountains through the veil of smog and we feel small and we feel powerless, not like TV where you're bigger than the people on the screen and you can turn them on and off with a flick of a remote. I look down and I don't see a man I used to love, I only see flesh and bone and blood, and I try to feel but I don't feel nothing, *nothing*.

And like, now I understand why Ferdie prefers being dead.

The beating goes on and on and afterwards Uncle Will isn't moving no more and I'm sure that he's not gonna see the morning.

And I'm all, 'Ferdie, come back from the dead now. You don't have to be dead no more. We've killed him.'

But Ferdie doesn't come back from the dead. I look into his eyes and they have the lifeless look of a camcorder lens. There won't be no videotape of Uncle Will to play on national television. No, there'll just be the videotape that's burned into me and Ferdie's brains, with the erase tab popped forever.

Ferdie smiles. And smiles.

And smiles.

*

Me and my mom and Ferdie are in family counselling now. We were on a waiting list for a foster home for a while, but nobody wanted us. Mr Death has disappeared, and we've never been able to find his house again.

Our counsellor says it's true what Mr Death said: that there's no magic to what happened, that Ferdie never was dead or came back from the dead. He says that Uncle Will wove a tapestry of illusion around us, that we were trapped inside his warped reality. He says that coming to terms with this will help us to change, to heal.

Well like, *I've* changed. I hardly drink no more and I never shoplift. I try to read books sometimes, like Ferdie used to. Ferdie don't read books. I don't think he's even growing any. He's all frozen in time.

But Ferdie hasn't stopped smiling. He smiles through everything: happy times, sad times. A defence mechanism, the counsellor calls it. My mom says, 'Give him time and one day he'll feel again.'

Sometimes I ask him if he's ever going to come back. And always he's all, 'Nu-*uh*.'

'Why not, Ferdie?' I'll ask him. Because like, there's no reason for him to play dead no more. Mom's in rehab and we're getting taken care of, and he don't have to feel pain all the time like he used to.

But he'll just look at me with them dead eyes, and he'll say, 'I like it better here.'

Though I Walk Through the Valley is a story I wrote shortly after the infamous Los Angeles 'riots', or 'uprising', of 1992. But it's not really about the riots as such. It was inspired by the real lives of three kids from a depressed neighbourhood who showed up at my house one weekend, who taught me what it's *really* like to live in LA.

It's the first of three stories in this collection that are about both theology and zombies.

Hunting the Lion

I have never liked eunuchs. I must confess a certain queasiness in their presence; in this I fear I am behind the times, and possessed of a kind of naïveté most unsuitable for one who practises the craft of the private detective in this modern world, this Ninth Century since the founding of the greatest nation on earth.

It was nevertheless a eunuch who was ushered into my triclinium at the hour of cena. I was drinking a goblet of undiluted Falernian and attempting to disentangle a dish of calves' brains sautéed in egg and honey, all the while dictating a letter to the steward of my Sicilian estates. I did not take kindly to being interrupted, but the creature whose presence now graced my dining room was not the kind of person one could ignore if one had any regard for one's political prospects.

He had the singularly inappropriate name of Eros. He wore a gold-fringed tunic dipped in purple (making up in ostentation for what he lacked in virility) and, when I showed him the couch, waddled towards it like an animated blood pudding.

'Rejoice,' he said in his clipped demotic Greek, 'O Publius Viridianus! I trust I find you in good health? Ah, but I see you are at dinner; perhaps I should come back at a more convenient hour.'

'No hour could be more convenient,' I said with practised insincerity. I made to proffer the Falernian, then changed my mind and called for an amphora of Lesbian wine. Eros hemmed and hawed until I dismissed the scribe and whisked aside the arras to show that there were no spies. Even then he stared about like a caged beast. At last I said, 'Come, come; I know you didn't come here to admire the murals. You just had your own house in Baiae done by the same artist, though I understand the mythological scenes you selected weren't quite as tame as the ones here – the rape of Ganymede, was it not?'

'How did you know? – but of course, such is your business – I imagine you've a thick dossier on me by now.'

'You flatter me,' I said. Not to mention yourself, I thought. 'I am not nearly as omniscient as is rumoured. Nevertheless, it delights me that I am deemed capable of providing service to no less a figure than the – third? – undersecretary of the – privy purse, is it? – division of Caesar's household.'

'You will be well paid,' Eros said. Wine dribbled from his lips. He took another swallow. There is nothing more unnerving than a fidgety eunuch. 'That is, if you – ah – accept the commission.' He emptied a purse full of gold aurei on to the dining-table. One of them skittered into the brain omelette. 'An advance, perhaps.' I did not look at the money, though I wondered where such a supply of gold could have come from, what with the recent debasement of the coinage. I did not imagine that many of the coins would bear the image of Nero Claudius Drusus Germanicus, our current God of State.

'You haven't told me what the commission is.'

'Haven't I?' He looked around again.

'My good man,' I said, 'I think you can see from my surroundings that I do not lack money; why, the very idea of your offering me so much seems not a little vulgar – I no longer make my living by spying on the mistresses of the nobility, tracking down changeling heiresses switched at birth by inattentive nursemaids, children running away to join the foreign legionaries, and the like. Now and then, as a favour, I might essay a little investigation, but . . .'

'Name your price, Viridian! I've no time to haggle . . .'

I smiled. 'There will be a price. I take it we are not speaking of some petty patrician whom it would be politically expedient to embarrass. You want me to hunt . . . nobler game. The lion rather than the jackal.'

'Q. Drusianus Otho, to be precise,' said the eunuch, his voice dropping to a whisper. 'Now that I've revealed this, I may as well tell you that, should you refuse the assignment, I have been given authorization to order you to commit suicide.'

Probably a bluff, I thought, shrugging. And even were it not, it would not do to appear overly concerned. After all, I am a real Roman and not some freedman's son ... at least, not since I bribed a palace scribe 2,000 denarii to 'purify' my birth papers. Pity I had to kill him afterwards, but one can't be too careful nowadays.

He immediately began to imbibe the Lesbian and, though I had not asked him to share my cena, to attack my homely brain-and-honey omelette with gusto. I let him eat while I pondered my prospective target.

This Drusianus was an influential man. He was related by adoption to the Imperial family and also, by the marriage of his cousin to the Lady Octavia, to the Emperor's discarded ex-wife and through her to the Julian Divinity himself – thus he could claim, with more justification than many would require, to be descended from the goddess Venus on both sides. He was extremely rich – had served as editor of the games on a number of occasions, and owned both a gladiatorial school and a menagerie most noted for its abundance of lions – but had kept his nose remarkably clear of politics, apart from serving as consul once or twice. He didn't indulge in loose women or little boys – at least no more than was politically correct under our artsy-fartsy régime – and his home life was a model of uxoriousness and probity. A lion indeed, I thought. No wonder they want to bring him down.

'Why?' I asked at last, after giving Eros a chance to sit around quivering for a few moments. 'He seems harmless enough. Why, he wasn't even part of the Pisonian conspiracy.'

The eunuch pulled a little scroll from his tunic and handed it to me. It contained a poem that purported to be by Petronius, although I could tell by its stylistic infelicities that it was some second-rate imitator. The poem extolled the virtues of this Drusianus while castigating the Emperor's excesses; clever little thing actually, in a mindless sort of way – the sort of ditty one might compose while squatting in the communal shit-house at the public baths.

'If you don't mind my saying so,' I said, 'this hardly seems something to get all flustered about. The man obviously had nothing to do with this poem; what's more, it's abysmal. I can dig up dirt for you – you know my reputation for finding *merda* in unlikely places – and undoubtedly I will be able to discover something, however picayune, to bring about the downfall of this member of the Noble Order of Equites. But why bother? You know how expensive my services are; it is well known that I have many scruples, and that I charge by the scruple. How many scruples will I have to overcome to finger the most honourable man in Rome? More than this,' I said, clapping my hands for someone to come and gather up the gold pieces scattered all over my triclinium table.

'But Caesar is annoyed,' said Eros. 'And you know what he's like when he's annoyed.'

And that, of course, was that.

★

I spent the evening scouring through my files on Drusianus. I knew him only by reputation – we did not go to the same sort of parties – and his reputation was amply backed up by my researches. His wife Volumnia had been one of the Christianoi for a while, but, after being interrogated by the secret police, had done the sensible thing and turned in all her contacts; I doubted it was anything more than an indulgence in the cult-of-the-month fever that infects our city in the summer heat.

I had a lot more information about Eros. Castrated though he was, he had slept with everybody who was anybody in Rome. He was a Syrian of some sort, born a slave into the household of one Polycrates, owner of a chain of brothels that promised uniform prices and service from Gaul to Gaza; as a boy had first attracted the attention of the Lady Claudia Procula, wife of Pontius Pilate, procurator of Judaea, by his acrobatic skill with his tongue; brought back to Rome; several bills of sale later, earned his freedom and ended up buying out his former master

Polycrates, whereupon he lost his entire fortune in a venereal disease scandal, and ended up working for the imperial house under an assumed name . . .

Exciting reading, almost as good as an evening at Petronius's house.

Drusianus was editor of the current spectacle season. Opening day was tomorrow, the Kalends of August . . . auguries pointed to a steamy, hellish day. With the Great Fire and its subsequent Grand Spectacle only two years past, the games were bound to be lavish, but I did not doubt that Drusianus had paid for them out of his pocket, without a qualm; he was not the sort of person who ever needed to ask the price of anything.

Perhaps the Lady Volumnia would be a likelier target; she had fallen prey to the treacherous Christianoi once; perhaps she was still tainted by the bloody Oriental rites they were known to practise.

It was time to don the first disguise of the evening.

*

I spent a few minutes propitiating the household gods by the hall entrance, lighting incense and wringing the neck of a small dove in expiation for the impieties I was about to commit. I took a last look in a bronze hand-mirror and had to admit that my handiwork was impeccable. I had built up my nose with a liberal application of clay, applied a false beard, put on a white robe and wrapped around my head a prayer-shawl such as the Judaeans use.

Of course, it would not do to be seen after dark in this costume, here in the old-money south side of the Palatine, so I called for my litter, drew the curtains tight shut as though I was a cloistered Greek matron slipping off to a night-time tryst, and proceeded downhill towards the seamy side of town. The bearers moved at a brisk trot and I was pleased not to have to quirt them. I avoided the great squares and took only back streets.

It was a quiet night – many had gone to bed early, doubtless anticipating the early morning commencement of the games –

but now and then a link-boy ran down a passageway waving his torch to light the way for some drunken reveller, and once I spied, through the peephole I had made in the curtain, a group of centurions gang-raping a slave-woman against a bakery storefront. A lone graffiti artist scrawled 'Arrius is a nefarious retiarius' along a wall while his friend pissed noisily alongside.

At length we reached a taberna by the Judaean quarter on the other side of the Tiber, and I abandoned my litterbearers there with a bag of copper and the admonishment that they were not to get too drunk or they would feel the lash on my return. The litter was parked in one alley, and from another alley I emerged in my Judaean garb, shawl about my head, mumbling to myself in what I hoped was a passable imitation of the Aramaic tongue.

The night life was in full swing. The tabernae were open; whores in whiteface walked the streets, as did young children with their tunicae hitched up above their buttocks; the smell of bread being baked for the morning rush mingled with the odour of animal blood running into the street from a slaughter-house that practised ritual killing in the Judaean fashion. There was an all-night bank across the street – for the Judaeans engaged in moneylending at all hours of the day or night – and I went there to deposit my bag of aurei, for the Judaeans are the only people in Rome with whom I would trust my money, and I have accounts under different names in Jewish banks from Rome to Alexandria, all earning a hefty rate of interest.

'Rejoice, Ioannes!' The voice was a resonant bass. Quickly, I allowed myself to flow into my persona: Ioannes of Damascus, physician, philanthropist, thrower of good parties – thoroughly Hellenized on the surface, thoroughly subversive at heart.

I was not surprised to find the banker, an Alexandrian by the name of Chrysolithos (he found his true name, David ben David, too ethnic for his social aspirations) still up, doing his accounts by lamplight; he was only too happy to take my money, and smiled as he counted it out.

'It must be a good life,' he said, 'this specializing in the diseases of the rich.'

'The rich have many slaves,' I said, affecting an expression of wounded piety, 'and those who have nothing are most likely to need riches in heaven.'

Chrysolithos cackled. 'Converting the heathen is all very well,' he said, 'but I'm glad you're lining your pockets too ... it's the Roman way, after all ...'

'Rome terra opportunitatis,' I said.

I pocketed the receipt and, looking furtively from left to right, made the sign of the fish in the air.

Chrysolithos immediately became defensive. 'Look, you're not going to go on and on about *that* business again, are you? Ever since the secret police cleaned up the catacombs for spectacle-fodder two months ago, you won't find much—'

'I'm looking for the Lady Volumnia Drusiana,' I whispered. 'She's in terrible danger! Her husband has angered Caesar – *anything* could bring about his political downfall – especially her involvement with *us*—'

'Don't say "us", Ioannes, please! Oh, I know my wife talked me into this New Age nonsense for a while, but—'

'By Jupit – I mean, by the blessed Paraclete!' I said. 'Do you mean to deny your saviour, as did Simon Cephas the fisherman? Reprobate! Do you still cling to earthly things when you should be thinking of the life to come?' I rather enjoyed giving that speech; I must admit that I was really getting into the role.

It was at that moment that the Lady Volumnia walked into the room.

I gasped, for she was every bit as sensuous as I last remembered her – her features delicate, her nose aquiline, her dark hair luxuriously bunned, her gazelle-eyes imbued with fragility and a certain coldness. Though she was past forty, her breasts had not succumbed to time, and the robe she wore was designed to reveal more than it concealed.

She looked at me guiltily – it was, of course, because she thought I was this Ioannes fellow, an elder of the banned cult to which she had once subscribed.

'Daughter Volumnia! – but what are you doing here? – at this hour, unchaperoned, in a dangerous sector of town?'

'I am not entirely unattended,' she said. Behind her stood a black man of impressive height, clad only in a leopard-skin. I had not realized that Lady Volumnia's taste ran to Numidian gladiators; perhaps this was going to be an easier job than I thought. After the austerity of the Christianoi, she could not be blamed for wanting to have a little fun.

'This is Babalavus,' she said, 'a mage of the Iorubae, a tribe that dwell in the yet-unconquered regions where lies the source of the Nile.'

I smiled. There's a charlatan on every block in Rome, waiting to hoodwink a credulous rich woman out of a few million. Such a charlatan, in fact, was *my* role that night. 'Have you abandoned then, Volumnia, the faith of the Christianoi? Have you ceased to attend the love-feasts?' I had to know.

'Oh, Ioannes,' she whimpered, falling to her knees before me, 'forgive me for being such a weak woman! Would that I were a slave, and had no position in society to lose for belonging to a subversive religion! Then I would gladly go to a thousand love-feasts every night. Really, I didn't mean to denounce anyone in the faith, it's just that – well – most of them weren't really our kind of people anyway, so I suppose they were more or less expendable . . .'

I made the sign of the cross over her and mumbled a few nonsense words, hoping that she and Chrysolithos would take them for the Christianoi ritual of 'speaking in tongues'. It must have worked, for the two of them immediately placed their palms together in an attitude of reverence, their glazed eyes fixed on me like a pair of village idiots. By the Pudenda of Venus! How I hate these weird Oriental cults!

We stood for a moment in a sort of tableau of religious ecstasy, and then Lady Volumnia, all business, got up and said to the banker, 'Listen, the reason I came is – I have to make a rather large withdrawal.'

'Precisely how large, O Clarissima?'

'Well, you know I've no head for figures, but – well, two million denarii?'

'Such a sum might be rather difficult to come by in cash—'

I was all attention now, even as I stood there mimicking the servile unctuousness of a preacher of the Christianoi.

'Perhaps one and a half million—' said the Lady Volumnia.

'My Lady, you will bankrupt me! Of course, bearing in mind the substantial penalty for early withdrawal from your interest-bearing equity account—'

How well I knew this ploy of Chrysolithos's! By the time Volumnia received her money, she would end up owing him more than she'd ever paid in; such were the perils of high finance in a world in which our Emperor has melted down the very vestments of the statues of the gods to help eke out a currency that is, at best, half silver and half lead.

'I'll have to give it to you in gold, Clarissima,' Chrysolithos said, 'and of course, there'll be an exchange rate deduction . . .' He called for a slave to bring out some bags from his vaults.

Meanwhile, my attention was drawn to the mage Babalavus. He stood with his arms crossed, every bit the bodyguard. I would wager that he was not a Christianos, for the followers of that sect have a look about them, a strange cross between the hangdog and the insolent. They have a complete disregard for human life, even their own, for they believe that they will shortly be resurrected and the world will end in an apocalyptic conflagration. There was something distinctly unnerving about him, for he stared back at me and would not be stared down, even though it is customary for the lower classes to be a tad more circumspect in the presence of patricians. I could well believe that Lady Volumnia had taken him for her lover, though a million and a half seemed a steep price to pay for the services even of so stallion-like a physical specimen.

Unless it was hush-money . . . a cover-up . . . unless this were only the epigraph to a veritable epic of scandal in high places . . .

Then again, Volumnia and the Numidian were not exactly lovey-dovey; a practised eye like mine can almost immediately tell if two people are involved in a clandestine intimate relationship, but with these two I had the distinct impression that something else was going on . . . some darker secret.

'Please, Ioannes, holy man,' Volumnia said, 'do not be too harsh with me for my lack of faith! I have a plan that will redeem me in your eyes ... that's why I need the money, you see ...'

What a stroke of luck! She was going to incriminate herself. I would have no trouble at all arranging for her husband's political demise if I could uncover some kind of bribery scandal ...

At that moment I felt a sneeze coming on. I knew that my clay nose would be turned into a projectile if I stayed for another minute. It was time to retreat. 'May the Sacred Paraclete guide you and comfort you,' I said in sacerdotal tones. 'I must go now and tend to my lost sheep. Rejoice, O Volumnia Drusiana, Chrysolithos and Babalavus!'

'Such a model of Christian piety!' I heard Lady Volumnia remark as I passed from the hall into the street. It was getting towards the ninth hour. Keeping to the shadows, I made my way back to my litter, rousted the bearers, and returned to an alley next to the bank to await the emergence of my prey.

*

An hour later – it was not yet dawn, but the sky was already tinted red, for in the summer the night hours are shorter – Lady Volumnia and her companion emerged from a side door, the latter slinging a jingling sack over his shoulders. Babalavus whistled and two litters appeared: a plain one and one bearing the minotaur-crest of the Drusiani. Side by side, they made off down the alley, curtains open wide so I could see they were deep in conversation as they rode.

'Follow them!' I whispered to the head bearer. 'And be as inconspicuous as you can!' We started to move. I peered through my peephole while wrestling with the elaborate garments and make-up for my next charade. It was good to be able to sneeze at last.

The litters moved slowly. It was easy to follow at first. Whenever they stopped, we ducked behind a convenient pillar or fountain. I did not think they were lovers now; else why

would the Lady Volumnia be so brazen about being seen in
public with this so-called mage, not even bothering to keep the
curtains of her litter drawn?

Another alley now – a street of smithies – I could hear the
clank of chains and the clink of hammer on anvil – and
somewhere in the distance, a slave being noisily chastised. The
mage looked at the moon, which, though full, was paling fast
in the impending sunrise; a look of concern crossed the Lady's
face ... the litterbearers went into a trot, and a lead-tipped
quirt materialized in her delicate little hand.

'Faster!' I said. 'But stay out of sight!' My litter swerved to
avoid a chamberpot that was being emptied from an upper
window.

My quarry took a left turn and suddenly we were in a fish
market. Though it was the dead of night, the square was
bustling. Dozens of carts were lined up, with slaves and
peasants hastening to unload their wares before the dawn
deadline – for horse traffic is not permitted in the city from
dawn to sunset – and the smell of fish and horsedung was
overpowering. Already the cooks from the great houses on the
Palatine were out in force, snapping up the best fish for the
evening's orgies. I followed the two litters closely as they wove
in and out of the stands. The litterbearers were moving briskly,
purposefully. Suddenly they stopped in front of a stall and
purchased a few fish. Lady Volumnia did not even bother to
have them wrapped. She said something and the bearers began
sprinting back downtown, towards the Old Forum.

It was harder to follow them now. The avenues were broader
and there were fewer monuments to duck behind. We collided
with a bevy of partygoers, garlanded, drunk, and singing lewd
songs, and wove in and out of a procession of Cybele-worship-
pers on their way to the Temple of Magna Mater. A beggar
tried to climb into my litter and had to be shaken off. At last
the two of them turned sharply into a narrow passageway. It
was difficult not to be seen, and my front bearers were literally
pronging the buttocks of the aftmost litter-slaves of the Lady
Volumnia when our way was blocked by a old plebeian,

wheezing as he tried to push a cartful of chickens out of a rut. I braced myself for a collision. It came.

I barely had time to take in the spectacle of the three-litter pile-up. Chickens ran amok. A fishy projectile had landed in my lap. It was, I noted ruefully, the common pufferfish, hardly a delicacy, and poisonous besides. Lady Volumnia screamed as she attempted to disentangle herself from the Numidian, the chicken vendor and the chickens, and litter-slaves were rolling about in the excrementa, their livery ruined.

Fortunately, I had already finished donning my next disguise, and when I emerged, veiled and forbidding, from the litter, the Lady and her Negro witch-doctor were both aghast to discover that they had collided with the litter of the Clarissima Julilla Juliana, the aged, prim, severe and intractable second high priestess of the College of Vestal Virgins.

It is one of my most convincing disguises.

'Dear me, my children,' I said, brushing the pufferfish off my stola, 'you really ought to watch where you're going.'

Even my own slaves were impressed, and many of them quickly kneeled and began muttering every formula of aversion they could think of.

'O sacred one! Forgive me for profaning – I had no idea—' the Lady Volumnia began, and then suddenly, inexplicably, winked at me with a kind of nudge-nudge informality that suggested some kind of womanly conspiracy of concealment. Meanwhile, the black mage seemed to have gone into a trance, for his eyes had rolled up all the way into their sockets and he was looking from side to side in the manner of a hungry lion, occasionally muttering the phrase 'Oba kosó, oba kosó.'

In the distance, a cock crew.

Lady Volumnia roused herself in alarm. A shaft of predawn half-light made the dust dance in the noxious air. 'Hurry, Babalavus!' she said, trying to shake him out of his ecstasy. 'We're losing the moon!' Turning to me, she said, 'By your leave, Clarissima,' and, bowing, added, 'I will see you at the games, perhaps.' Then she clambered back aboard with her pufferfish under her arm and, tossing a purse to the disgruntled chicken vendor, quirted her bearers uptown. Babalavus set off with equal dispatch towards the gates of the city. I could not follow both; besides, it would be undignified for a Vestal Virgin to go charging through the streets at night.

What was I to do? I bade my bearers run alongside Babalavus for a few minutes, doffed my robes and, making sure that I could be seen turning in the direction of the Capitoline, slipped out of the far side of the litter, now garbed in the loincloth of a common slave.

I ran behind Babalavus's litter. It was hard to keep up as we raced downhill. Past the rickety insulae of the impoverished, the many-storied slum buildings whose roofs leaned across the alleys and blocked out the twilight, where dirty immigrant children played amid piles of refuse . . . past dingy temples of unfashionable cults, where priests with scruffy tonsures prayed in empty vestibules in unfamiliar tongues . . . past whorehouses frequented by washed-up gladiators and slumming patricians . . . I could see where we were heading . . . a catacomb whose entrance lay just beyond the walls behind the intersection of the Appia and Nomentana.

I tapped the hindmost bearer on the shoulder. Ran up alongside him and showed him an aureus that I had had concealed in my mouth, and explained to him what I wanted. The other bearers, panting as the leader called out the rhythm, were concentrating so hard that they did not notice when, without skipping a beat, I changed places with the slave and – thanking the gods that it was still pretty dark – changed loincloths with him also, for the bearers were a matched set. I was counting on the mage having hired the litter rather than owning one, so that he would not notice me, for one hired litterbearer is much like another.

The litter stopped at the entrance and Babalavus stepped out. He was carrying an amphora under his arm which appeared to be in the shape of a human skull. He seemed already to be drifting into one of his trances. He called for a torchbearer. As luck would have it, that torchbearer was me.

We descended. The steps were steep. The stench of rotting

plebeians filled our nostrils. I held the torch high for him but he seemed to need no light, for he moved about as one possessed, rocking his head from side to side and now and then springing like a panther. We went deeper. There were white flowers and mushrooms and strange herbs growing from cracks in the floor. Once he paused to pluck some leaves from the eye-sockets of a human skull. Always he sang to himself. Sometimes his voice was high-pitched, like a child's; other times he appeared to be answering himself in a mellifluous bass. Now and then he paused to gather his roots and flowers and to throw them into the skull-amphora.

I was beginning to suspect that this was no Christianos.

Dead bodies lined the walls. Some niches were occupied by two or three corpses. Some had been incompetently mummified; others were just skeletons; many were fresh, and bore on their limbs and torsos evidence of the torture that must, by law, be inflicted on all slaves who give evidence in a court of law. The odour was nauseating, but I had a rôle to play.

Babalavus danced and chanted a while longer, then stalked up and down a passageway looking for something. At length he selected the skull of a child and slipped it into his amphora. He motioned to me to go on up.

I was not displeased when we once more achieved the upper air. The sun was just rising now, and I could see, along the Appian way, the long line of horsecarts hastening to leave the city before their owners were arrested for disobeying the ban on daylight equestrian traffic.

*

It was a simple matter to change places with the slave once more – he had been waiting in the portico of a nearby temple of Mithras – and to slip back to my own litter, wherein, once safely ensconced, I could once more assume the apparel of the Lady Julilla. I had lost a few hours. Nevertheless I made it to the Temple of Vesta just in time for the ceremonial blessing of the hearth and was able to go through the motions of the rite without any of the other Vestals noticing either my excessive perspiration or my inappropriate gender.

As soon as it was over I retired to the chamber of the Lady Julilla – fortunately, I had a duplicate key – just in time to see a shadowy figure slipping out of her window.

'By the Sacred Mysteries!' cried the Lady Julilla, springing from her bed with astonishing alacrity for one of her years, and sprinting behind the nearest arras. 'I have been profaned – my honour violated—'

'Relax, O Clarissima!' I said, as I sat down on a tripod next to the window. 'It is only me.' I squinted as I looked out, but all I could see was a rather corpulent figure waddling at top speed through the garden, now and then bumping into a stone Silenus or satyr. Once more, I hadn't arrived quite in time to discover the identity of the Lady's paramour.

The Vestal – who, upon realizing it was only me, had come out of hiding and was now seated upon a couch, powdering her face and looking at me with hauteur – said, 'Ah, Viridianus. I trust the morning service went smoothly?'

'Most smoothly, Clarissima. No one suspects that you are in your bedroom trysting with—'

'Be nice, O Publius Viridianus!' she said, peeling an apple. 'You know very well that if I am ever discovered, my life is forfeit; the virginity of the Vestals is inviolable. But I've been stuck in this dump since the age of sixteen, and a girl gets to wondering what it's all about, if you know what I mean ... you won't gain a thing by turning me in, you know that. I'm a Roman of the Julian gens, and descended from the goddess Venus; I know how to die properly.'

'True, Clarissima, but a certain curiosity—' I glanced once more at the garden, but the priestess's fat lover had managed to escape.

'Curiosity was not part of our deal, Publius Viridianus,' she said, relapsing into that sternness of demeanour for which she was well known. She pulled a bag of silver from under the couch and threw it to me. 'Our arrangement still stands, I trust. I need you to impersonate me at the games as well today; I have . . . ah . . . a business meeting to attend to . . . a little matter of the Temple archives.'

'As you wish, Clarissima,' I said, noting with satisfaction that her plans jibed perfectly with my own.

★

I was, I confess, rather tired when I finally reached the Circus of Nero and staggered up to the Vestals' balcony. A venation was in progress, but the heat and the humidity had rendered the mob restless, and only the distribution of the lunchtime lottery tickets had been able to prevent them from getting ugly. There are only so many gazelles, wolves, jackasses, ostriches and hippopotamoi one can watch being slain on a sweltering day in August without being driven insane with boredom. The Vestals' balcony was only half full; after showing me the deference due my putative rank, my fellow virgins mostly gossiped or licked their snow cones or nibbled at a tray of succulent kebabs assembled from thrushes' tongues, finches' gizzards, and the like.

I was able to observe the editor's box at my leisure, since it was next to the Vestals' and separated from me only by a marble frieze.

There was my quarry at last, in full view, every inch the lion. Q. Drusianus Otho was reclining on a gilded couch, with slaves and dancing girls at his feet. Suckling pigs stuffed with figs and apples sat ignored on silver platters; oiled Nubians wielded impressive peacock-feather fans; a couple of centurions squatted, rolling the bones, under a makeshift canopy put together from three javelins and a cloak.

Sitting next to him was Volumnia, heaving prettily. Behind them stood the Ioruba mage. They weren't sweating one bit after the adventures of the previous night. I was not surprised to see that Eros was there too, looking shiftily about. He was the only one to show any interest in the suckling pigs.

There was another woman there too, with gold dust in her hair, her face powdered to the colour of packed snow, wearing

a king's ransom in purple silk, plucking idly on a kithara. She
was singing, and everyone stopped now and then to applaud.

I was somewhat bemused when I realized that this Lady was
none other than Himself the God of State, His August Divinity,
L. Domitius Ahenobarbus to his friends, Nero-666-The Beast to
his treasonous and godless detractors, many of whom were
fated to perish before our eyes that very day. The aria he was
singing was none other than the fiendishly virtuosic *Hecabe's
Lament* from Euripides' *The Trojan Women*. I'm no critic, but
there seemed to be a number of wrong notes in his rendition.

As the carcases were dragged off, the Emperor launched into
a rousing rendition of something of his own. I was thankful
that I knew nothing about modern music; I could not tell the
wrong notes from the right. I was, however, saved from having
to comment by the miraculous emergence of the face of Petronius Arbiter from the thighs of a voluptuous Celtic woman; he
made some pronouncement, the Emperor nodded daintily, and
everyone clapped.

I took out a wax tablet and began making notes as the
Amphitheatron was being filled with water for a simulated sea-
battle. I kept an ear cocked, for one of the occupants of the
editor's box might well reveal something I could use.

What had I found out?

Imprimis: the tableau of glorious dissipation that was visible
in the editor's box was a mere simulacrum; in fact, I was
witnessing a vipers' nest of seething intrigue. Someone had
written a poem in a blatantly inferior pastiche of Petronius's
style in order to discredit Drusianus; Lady Volumnia, guilt-
ridden over turning in so many Christianoi, had dug deep into
her pockets to form an alliance with a bizarre African magician;
Eros was watching everybody, hoping someone would fall
from grace so that he could move up the ladder of power;
Petronius was not long for this world, for I had been invited to
his suicide party later in the week; the Lady Julilla – that is to
say, myself – was fooling around and decidedly non intacta;
none of the pieces were falling into place for me.

Had the Emperor really sent Eros to destroy Drusianus, or

did the eunuch have his own agenda? Should I deliver the innocent patrician up on a platter, or was I risking my own downfall by essaying something that the Emperor had *not*, in fact, commanded?

Was it not entirely possible that the entire thing was a ruse, and that it was I – the knower of secrets – who was the quarry? Had one of my thousand disguises finally been seen through?

These are the kind of questions a detective must wrestle with daily, and I fell into a kind of reverie.

A theological argument was now going on in the editor's box, and now and then a phrase penetrated my miasma of self-examination . . .

'Resurrection of the body!' the Emperor was saying. 'What a curious concept. These Christianoi must be quite, quite mad.'

'It is not as uncommon as all that, Divinitas,' – I recognized the resonant bass of Babalavus – 'for amongst the Iorubae, and also the Kikongii, our neighbours, malefactors are often sentenced to become *nzambi*, the Living Dead . . . they are first poisoned with a powder whose active ingredient is the ground-up liver of the homely pufferfish . . .'

Pufferfish!

I came to all at once. Resurrection! and pufferfish! Were the Christianoi poisoning themselves in the hope of coming back to life? Was not their sign of recognition a fish? And had I not last seen the Lady Volumnia climbing on to her litter with a brace of pufferfish tucked under her arm?

In the arena below, two ships were having at each other with catapults. In a humorous touch, the projectiles were neither rocks nor flaming brimstone, but political prisoners – Christianoi of dwarfish stature, each one bundled and trussed into a compact sort of a ball. Since catapultae are not really designed for hurling humans about, it was impossible to aim them. The crowd screeched and hooted as Christianoi crashed into the sea or brained themselves against the embankments. Now this was not only purest entertainment – full of human interest as the prisoners bobbed up and down, trying to extricate themselves from their bonds only to find themselves being devoured by crocodiles which were now being released into the waters – but a practical thing too, since the flooding of the arena also functioned as a rudimentary air-conditioning system, and the water was constantly being cooled with cartloads of Alpine snow.

I was really beginning to enjoy the show when a man was catapulted right into the Vestals' pavilion. His head struck the marble floor and his brains spritzed my robes, my wax tablet, and my eyelashes. Fortunately I had the presence of mind to scream in falsetto.

I had seen and heard enough for the day. 'I have been profaned!' I cried. 'I must return at once to the Temple of Vesta to be purified!'

I turned and made for the secret passageway by which the Vestals may come and go as they please without being subjected to the indignity of plebeian frottage. I was more upset than I wanted to admit to myself. I had seen the dead man's face, in the split second before the big splat. To my astonishment, it was the face of someone I knew – someone who ought have been able to afford to buy his way out of this unholy mess.

I was going to have to get myself a new bank account.

*

I was finally getting a moment to myself, taking a postprandial soak in my private tepidarium, when the nomenclator announced the arrival of Lady Volumnia Drusiana. She stalked into the bathroom and flung a purseful of gold at my head. The two Spanish masseuses fled in panic.

'Take this!' she screamed. 'You vulture! You parasite! You open-sphinctered catamite!'

'The first two I allow, Clarissima, but really you do go too far in accusing me of—'

'Oh!' she turned away from me and began weeping copiously, and I availed myself of the opportunity to slip into something decent.

'There, there,' I said, 'let's hear all about it now.' I escorted her to the library, where three of my scribes were in the process of reproducing Petronius's *Satyricon* in triplicate – for the novel makes a nice gift for someone on whom one has amatory designs. I shooed the scribes away and offered Volumnia a drink from the jug of best-vintage Lesbian I kept on my desk.

'You've got to help me!' she said, flinging herself on to the nearest couch. 'My life is in ruins – my husband's political future has been horribly compromised—' She pulled a little scroll from her bosom. I was not surprised to see that it was a copy of the insulting poem that had been attributed to the Arbiter of Elegance himself.

'Oh, I've already read that,' I said. 'And a million and a half denarii won't be enough to overcome my scruples—'

'One and a half—! How could you possibly—' She stared at me, for in my demeanour and accent there was absolutely no trace of Ioannes of Damascus, the fanatical prophet of the Christianoi.

'Yes,' I went on, 'you were consorting with an elder of the banned sect last night, weren't you? One' – I pretended to consult my notes – 'Ioannes of Damascus. And you were visiting the offices of another Christianos, a certain Chrysolithos, were you not? Who is now—'

'Dead,' she whispered. 'I'm going to have to open another bank account.'

There was a pause while I took out a tablet and prepared to take some more notes.

'Anyway,' she said, 'I don't have all the money any more. He took a twenty percent commission, the poor dead soul! And there were other – expenses. I can only offer you what I threw at your feet – if you'll only call off the hunt. Don't say you're not after him – I was told this by no less a figure than the third undersecretary of the Emperor's privy purse!' So Eros was playing both sides against the middle! So much for him! 'My husband, as you well know, is innocent of all wrongdoing. Never has a man been more loyal to his Emperor. It is I who have been weak, I who have gone from faith to faith, never finding certitude in this complex modern world!'

As she shrugged out of her clothes, I realized that there was also to be compensation of another kind. The Lady Volumnia, though not young, possessed a statuesque voluptuousness which certainly lived up to her name. She palpitated curvaceously against the harsh right angles of my shelves of papyri.

'My dear Clarissima!' I said, tossing down the last of the Lesbian. 'This display of your not unappetizing charms renders me quite inarticulate,' I added, stooping to litotes in my confusion.

She smiled. There was nothing for it but to bed her, on the instant, in the half hour or so before my next appointment. She clawed, whinnied and bounced about with such enthusiasm and vigour that I was glad I had recently had all the lecti cubicularii in the house reupholstered.

Afterwards, I assuaged my guilt by leaving a nice juicy leg of lamb as an offering to the house gods.

It was time for me to return to the games, this time as myself.

*

Caesar too was Himself by the time I arrived. Garbed once more as a man, wearing a towering diadem of solid gold and a floor-length purple robe embroidered in gold thread with suns and moons, Himself was enthroned on a chair of state, with the outrageously beautiful Statilla Messalina at his side. I was glad to see that he was getting over the apotheosis of the Empress Poppaea, whom he had accidentally kicked to death one drunken evening.

It was almost the hour of cena, and the day was cooling off; a Greek tragedy, put on at the Divinity's behest, had just been booed off the stage, and the stage manager had been forced to bring on some Christianoi as an entr'acte. They were being eaten by lions, but as no one ever pays much attention to last year's hits, they were being watched only by the most devoted fans of Christianoi-bashing.

I hastily paid my respects to the God of State. 'Aye, Divinitas,' I said, and quickly switched to Greek, for the Emperor hated the uncouth jangle of the vulgar tongue. 'Rejoice, Auto-krator,' I said. 'I didn't have the chance to pay my respects earlier . . .'

'Pity; you missed my new poem. I'd sing it again, but I'm not dressed for it anymore.'

'I am crushed,' I said. 'But maybe I'll have a chance to borrow it from the Library; I know it's not the same as hearing it from your Divine Lips, but—'

'Poor little Viridian,' said Nero. 'As tone deaf as can be, yet he still attempts, in his small way, to sit at the feet of the Muse.'

The reason I had come back to the games was because I was sure I was missing some vital piece of information. I noted that Drusianus and Eros were deep in conversation, and that Lady Volumnia and her curious magician were absent; Petronius, on the other hand, was leaning on the balcony, watching the Christianoi being eaten with profound fascination. I supposed that, since he was about to die himself, he was finding something in common even with this most tedious of spectacles. I was really looking forward to his suicide party; it's not every day that a patrician decides to go out in style.

Since Petronius was as good as dead, I decided I might as well whip out the scurrilous poem and show it to the Emperor.

'What do you think of this, Divinitas?' I said. 'It – ah – came to my attention last week.'

He took it from me, looked at the first few lines, and began to chuckle. I became uneasy. I looked at Drusianus, but he was still deep in conversation with Eros.

'What a terrible thing!' said Nero, looking deep into my eyes. 'Who do you think could have perpetrated such blasphemy?'

'Well, it *looks* like Petronius, and yet there's something – ah – something – ah—' I wanted to protect Petronius from the imputation that he might have written this inferior piece of doggerel, and yet . . .

'Something – ah – something—' There was a feverish glint in his eye, and suddenly I knew what I was going to have to say.

'It looks like Petronius, only far, far *better*, of course!'

I knew at once that I had said the right thing, for the Emperor

beamed and threw me a bag of money. The old fox had written
the thing himself – was doubtless disseminating it as a test of
loyalty! Well, that certainly put paid to Eros' contention that he
had hired me at Caesar's behest.

'Far from being displeased at him,' said Nero with his mouth
full of peacocks' brains, 'I am thinking of giving Drusianus
some kind of political appointment . . . a consulship perhaps, or
even a procuratorial position . . . I've even assigned a high-level
member of my staff to . . . ah . . . act as his financial adviser . . .'
He indicated the eunuch.

It dawned on me that Eros's financial advice was probably
the last thing Q. Drusianus Otho needed. It was the eunuch's
greed that had led him to try to pay me into effecting the man's
downfall, that much was certain. I had taken Eros's money and
owed him some kind of investigation; I had also taken the
money – not to mention the lubricious fluids – of the Lady
Volumnia, and I owed her something too. And who had turned
Chrysolithos in? Surely not the very Lady who relied on him
for all her banking needs at odd hours of the night.

The God of State lost interest in me, since I wasn't talking
about the arts. He called Petronius over for a chat about Homer.
I had to admire the poet's sang-froid; he gave absolutely no
indication that he was planning to commit suicide, and I was
sure that it would come as a complete shock to Nero, who
hated surprises.

Idly I watched the next number, a small group of Andabatae.
These are the lowliest criminals, who are given helmets without
eyeholes and unwieldy weapons, and swing blindly at each
other until all are slain – an incorrigibly tasteless entertainment,
and fit only for the vulgar element.

The fight was drawing to a close, and slaves were removing
the helmets of the slain and fastening hooks to their feet so that
they could be dragged out through the Gates of Death. Now
the sun was low on the horizon, and the few remaining
wretches, staggering about, cast huge shadows against the sea
of togas in the patricians' balconies. One could not see too
clearly what was going on, but it chanced that a ray of

flickering, sooty light, cast upon the arena by a Christianos who was being burned alive on a lofty display cross, fell upon the face of one of the dead Andabatae just as he was being hauled away.

It was the face of Chrysolithos the banker.

Surely I am imagining this! I thought to myself. I squinted; the red sunlight made my eyes water; yet still I could have sworn, by Jupiter and all the Immortals, that that face was none other's. There was even a great red smudge on his temple whence, earlier that afternoon, his brains had been spurting forth upon my virginal garments.

Chrysolithos had died twice in the same day.

Somehow – my detective's intuition assured me – the resurrection of the old Judaean banker was the key to the whole affair.

For was not resurrection also the crux (no pun intended) of the Christianoi religion? Did these people not believe so strongly in a physical afterlife that they had not hesitated to set fire to Rome itself, the quicker to bring about their prophesied apocalypse? Were they not so confident of this resurrection that they did not even mind being killed in the circus? Why, instead of showing the proper terror when being eaten by lions, they would stand around singing their catchy hymn tunes, completely undermining the public service aspect of their deaths. These people really believed in resurrection all right.

Well, what if they'd actually found a way to do it?

There was only one way to find out, and to do that I would have to slip around to the Gates of Death as soon as the games were done for the day.

*

Sunset over the Amphitheatron: I was just in time to catch the imposing figure of Babalavus climbing out of a litter and speaking to the guards at one of the back entrances. I was in costume once more, impersonating Ioannes of Damascus. As soon as Babalavus was admitted, I crept up behind the two guards and, placing my hands about their necks, put them both to sleep with a certain nerve pinch that induces a temporary state of narcosis. I followed Babalavus down the dank staircase. He was too intent on his business to notice me.

There is no sight more depressing than the bowels of a circus. The stench of animal dung was everywhere; in the half dark one could make out the cages of exotic beasts. Cramped though the bestiaries were, the human prisoners fared even worse, for they were a far less valuable commodity. One could hear, from behind dungeon doors, the screams of the panic-stricken and the frenzied copulations of those who knew this lovemaking would be their last. From some torture-chamber lower down came the crack of the flagellum, the squeak of the rack, the hiss of the red-hot iron on human flesh, and, of course, the ever noisome screaming.

Babalavus strode through labyrinthine corridors, turning this way and that with the confidence of one who had come here often. I followed. After a while he ascended some steps, and we were in a chamber with an egress into a back alley.

We had arrived at the hall of the butchers, where the criminals killed that day were being methodically quartered and shoved into large baskets by slaves. Arms, legs, heads and buttocks protruded from enormous containers which were even now being loaded on to carts; the meat would be sold to various menageries around the city, for the wild animals at the circus itself had to be kept hungry.

The butchers worked quickly, but there was still a heap of some two or three hundred corpses, their feet still pierced from the hooks that had been used to haul them off the sand. Little boys were engaged in divesting these corpses of clothing, jewellery, hairpins, anything that could be recycled. Indeed, I thought, the entertainment industry has been hard hit by the Emperor's financial cutbacks!

Concealing myself behind the pile of dead bodies, I watched Babalavus bargaining with one of the overseers. There were a few relatives hanging around, hoping to bribe one of the slaves into releasing their lamented for a decent burial; a sobbing couple rooted through the piles of body parts, looking for their son.

Babalavus took out a bag of gold and presented it to the overseer. Greed gleamed in the man's eyes; he turned, barked out an order, and presently a wagon pulled up to the entrance, and – as Babalavus pointed to one corpse after another – they were loaded on to the cart. I recognized Chrysolithos amongst the fallen. I thought I saw a few other Christianoi too.

This was no time for reflection. I had to find out what was going on.

Quickly, under cover of the wall of dead bodies, I disrobed, smeared myself with dead men's blood, plunged my arms into an open abdomen and pulled out a piece of intestine with which to drape myself ... then, when no one was looking, I sneaked behind the busy butchers and managed to clamber on to the cart while Babalavus's back was turned.

As chance would have it, I had landed right on top of Chrysolithos. He was dead all right. They were all dead. It was a necrophiliac's dream come true; alas, this has never been one of my favourite perversions. More bodies were being shovelled on top of me. A woman's half-amputated breast rammed into my mouth, almost suffocating me; blood oozed into my nostrils and slicked my limbs so that I slid back and forth like a fish at the market. The stench was almost unendurable.

When the cart began to move, things got even worse. Even now it irks me to recall the discomfort of our journey. Every rut, every cobble made the bodies slip and slither and marinated me in their bodily effluvia. I could see nothing, for there were at least three layers of dead people crammed on top of me. I could hear the voice of Babalavus urging the horses on and singing snatches of barbarian music.

*

At length we stopped. The bodies – myself among them – were unloaded one at a time. I concentrated on acting out my most demanding role, that of a corpse. I felt myself being lifted by the arms and legs. I made myself limp. They laid me down on a rocky surface. When I finally permitted myself to peek, I saw that I was lying in an immense morgue. The bodies of Christianoi lay in neat rows on the stone floor of what seemed to be a vast cave; it was one of the natural chambers into which the catacombs led, though I could not remember which one. To my surprise, Chrysolithos the banker lay not two paces from me, to my left; eviscerated as he was, he was not a pretty sight.

Suddenly, I heard a familiar voice shriek out: 'By the Sacred Paraclete! It's Ioannes of Damascus! Oh, how could they have killed such a holy man?' The Lady Volumnia ran out from the shadows and knelt by my side, covering my face and chest with so many kisses that I feared that, in my nakedness, I would accidentally reveal my lust.

'Do not worry, my Lady.' It was Babalavus, standing beside her. He was clad only in a loincloth. His face was hideously painted in whiteface with streaks of black and red. 'If Shangó wills it, he will not be dead for long.'

There were others like Babalavus in the background, some with drums and marimbas. Other Negroes clutched chickens and turtles in their arms.

From somewhere far away, I heard Christianoi psalms being sung. One of their love-feasts was taking place. It was cold, and it was hard to keep my teeth from chattering.

At last, the love-feast seemed to end, and Christianoi crowded into the chamber. Volumnia and Babalavus were handing out phials of some potion. At length, Babalavus addressed the throng: 'O Christianoi,' he said, 'it has become necessary, for political reasons, for the Lady Volumnia to denounce some of you to the secret police in order to save her husband's career. You will probably be arrested before dawn, so that you can be ready in time for the morning tableaux.'

His announcement caused a sensation as some wailed, others complained, and others still cried out their jubilation at the propinquity of their redemption.

'Doubtless a number of you are afraid that the resurrection of the body will not occur as promised. That is why I have been invited to join you, and why I have prepared this potion. Do not forget, in your hour of martyrdom, to swallow the pufferfish elixir before going onstage! Otherwise the magic will not work . . .'

Several of the crowd began to voice their objections. Some complained that the blessed apostle Simon Cephas had made no mention of any pufferfish elixir. Others shouted that Babalavus was no Christianos and had no right to order them around. Like every other Judaean sect, the Christianoi love to quarrel over the minutiae of dogma, and do so even when death is imminent. At length, the Lady Volumnia appealed for silence.

'Please, my brothers and sisters—' she said. 'Just do what he says. The police are even now making their way towards this catacomb. You're all going to die anyway, so you might as well be decent about it.'

A chorus of *amens* and *hallelujahs* echoed around the cave. Then, at a signal from Lady Volumnia, there began an ominous music, all drums and high-pitched keening and grunts and babblings. Above it all I could hear the phrase 'Oba kosó!' repeated over and over. I knew it must be a ritual formula of these Iorubae.

At that moment, Babalavus went into a trance.

He fell to his knees and began to heave and buck like an angry minotaur. His pupils vanished into their sockets, and animal cries emanated from his throat. Sweat poured down his face and torso.

'Behold! He is speaking in tongues!' Lady Volumnia shouted, though I knew very well that this was nothing of the kind.

Babalavus began to do a jerky sort of dance. He leapt over corpses. He made clawing gestures in the air, as though he were possessed by some jungle creature. The pounding went on. It was hypnotic. Suddenly he was holding the skull-amphora in his hands, and asperging us corpses with its contents – a foul-smelling concoction of herbs and blood.

Then he was joined by his tribesmen, whooping wildly as they sliced the heads off turtles and chickens and began to slop their blood liberally over us. It was becoming harder and harder to play dead. Soon I was going to have to sneeze, or cough, or—

Chrysolithos began to twitch! As the chanting rose to a deafening pitch, as the black mages pranced about and sprinkled us with foul fluids, all the corpses fibrillated wildly. I soon realized that I had better start wiggling myself, or I would look out of place. I started to jerk about with a vengeance, and when the corpses began to stand up, each with a glazed look in its eye, I too scrambled to my feet and attempted to mimic their rhythmic swaying. Soon the corpses were all lumbering this way and that, each one with a look of profound bewilderment, as though awakening from a drunken stupor. Chrysolithos was going round and round in circles, as one who has been struck in the head with a poker.

I heard Lady Volumnia cry out above the uproar: 'Behold the resurrection promised to you by the Christianoi prophets! Death is an illusion! You will not die in the arena tomorrow; as long as your body can be recovered in one piece, you will be brought back to life as good as new! Zombificati sunt!'

What kind of a word was *zombificatus*? It must been that we had been made into *nzambi*, the Living Dead of which Babalavus had spoken to the Emperor. But as I looked around me I could see that this resurrection was a far cry from that promised in the utterances of the Christianoi. These *nzambi* were hardly human. They gibbered. Intestines dangled from their ripped abdomens. Arms and legs were missing. Heads lolled. Sputum and vomitus dribbled from their lips, and brain tissue trickled from their cracked skulls. It was hard for me to appear as disgusting as they, for I had no wounds; but I shambled and gibbered and swung my arms aimlessly along with them, while trying to work my way up to where Lady Volumnia and Babalavus were standing so as to be able to hear what they were saying.

'You have done well, O Babalavus!' she was telling him. 'I shall not forget how you allowed me to betray the Christianoi, thus salving my husband's reputation, while at the same time providing this supernatural means of assuaging my betrayal of the religion I hold so dear . . .'

A piercing shriek issued from Babalavus's throat. All at once the music stopped. We *nzambi* stood, waiting, a little threatening. The unzombified Christianoi backed away, terrified – who would not be? – and I do not doubt that many were reconsidering the most cherished tenets of their faith.

At that moment, bucinae blared. We heard the tramp-tramp-tramp of Roman soldiers. It was the Praetorians. They burst into the chamber so quickly that there was no time for a stampede. The crowd were too stunned to scream. With professional speed and detachment, the secret police clapped everyone in chains – living and dead – and marched us all back to the Amphitheatron, flogging us for good measure as we staggered along the dim streets.

*

I was thrown into a cramped prison cell along with my *nzambi* companions. There were also Christianoi who were not yet zombificati. Most sat around praying to their God, but one or two were heard bitterly complaining that this death and rebirth was somehow not quite as advertised. One was even suggesting that, if they should survive their martyrdom, they should bring suit in the tribunes' court against the cult for making these false claims. I had no time for specious arguments or theological speculation. I had to get out of there before the morning spectacle, for I did not possess a phial of the pufferfish elixir which had, it seemed, to be imbibed shortly before death for the Ioruban ritual to work.

In the flickering torchlight, I could see that some of the *nzambi* were gnawing on each other's innards. It was entirely possible that one would not even survive until the show started. I stumbled forward to the portal, which had a tiny grille through which I could see one of the guards. I banged to get his attention.

'My good man! I,' I said importantly, 'am Publius Viridianus, private investigator. I was spying on the Christianoi on the

Emperor's behalf; I have been apprehended in error. Release me at once!'

The guard peered at me. 'Publius Viridianus, the most famous detective in Rome?' he said. 'Try another one! You don't look a bit like him with your big nose and your straggly beard!'

I plucked off my false nose and thrust it in his face. He raised an eyebrow. 'False nose, eh?'

I started pulling my beard off. 'This is false, too. Look, hurry up, I don't want my cover blown; luckily the Christianoi are too busy arguing about dogma to notice our conversation.'

'By the pudenda of Venus!' said the decurion. He called for the keymaster and in a few moments I was free, and had a good woollen cloak to cover my nakedness. It turned out that the guard was quite an intellectual, for he would not let me depart until I had autographed a scroll of my memoirs which I had been vain enough to have published the previous year, and which he just happened to be reading.

'On no account,' I said, 'must you reveal that I have been here tonight. I will ensure that you are amply rewarded – but if this gets out—' I made a throat-slitting gesture.

'High political intrigue, is it, sir?' said the decurion. 'I loves a good intrigue, by the Gods! Don't you worry about the reward, just you mention me in the next volume . . . it's Olus Dolabella, and you must remember to spell my praenomen the plebeian way, O-l-u-s, not A-u-l-u-s; it's a point of pride in my family you see, we've been spelling it that way since my great-uncle done divorced my patrician great-aunt, she was one of the Scipiones, you know—'

'Yes, yes,' I mumbled, hoping that my litterbearers would still be waiting at the other entrance of the Amphitheatron.

'Treacherous lot, them Christianoi,' he continued. 'What a stroke of luck we had this tip-off from the Lady Volumnia. I wonder what's in it for her! I understand these people' – his voice dropped to a whisper – 'eats human flesh, they does.'

'They do indeed,' I said, shuddering as I remembered the sight of one *nzambi* nibbling at another's loose body parts.

He wanted to know everything about their foul practices and orgies. I persuaded him to shut up only by letting him keep my nose as a souvenir, and giving him the slip while he gazed at it in adoration.

It surprised me a little to see Eros wandering through the corridors, scribbling feverishly on a wax tablet. He did not notice me, for I hid myself in the shadow of an archway. He met Babalavus; they had a brief conversation; he handed the magician a bag of money and they parted company. Why was he up so early, and what was he doing here, so far from the offices of the Imperial privy purse? Ah, but of course – the Emperor had appointed him Q. Drusianus Otho's financial adviser. Naturally he would be at the games, checking the figures – how many Christianoi at so much overhead per victim, how many tons of hay for the elephants, that sort of thing. But why was Babalavus in his pay?

Interesting, I thought; very interesting.

★

The mosaic stones were finally beginning to fall into place. But I still had to figure out who was behind it all – who stood to benefit – who was manipulating whom, and why. I would have to go through another day of spectacle, disguised as the Lady Julilla once more, for only from the Vestals' box could I eavesdrop on everything that was going on in the Editor's Pavilion. Unfortunately, I wasn't slated to be her double that day; nevertheless, I figured that she would not mind, since there was nothing she despised more than carrying out the endless round of litanies and sacrifices that were her lot.

It was the tenth hour; in two short hours (and the night hours are shortest in summer) would come dawn. I urged my bearers to make haste.

It was simple enough to enter the Temple of Vesta and to take the secret passageway that led from the main courtyard to the private vestiarium next to Lady Julilla's bedroom. A dozen sets of ceremonial robes hung from hooks. The Lady, with her back to me, was already up and seated on a sella, pinning her shawl in place with a silver fibula. She did not hear me enter, for I am nothing if not stealthy. I crept up behind her and tapped her on the shoulder.

She turned around and, seeing me, screamed.

I managed to cover her mouth just in time. Her scream became a gurgle.

'Just what in the name of all the Gods are you doing here?' I said.

'I might ask the same thing of you,' said the Lady Volumnia, for that was who it was. 'To tell you the truth, the Lady Julilla asked me to – ah – impersonate her at a morning sacrifice, because she had another – ah – appointment.'

So that was why Lady Volumnia had winked so knowingly at me the night our litters had collided! Thinking that I was that wayward old Vestal Virgin, she had assumed I was returning from some tryst! I could not help laughing. 'I was about to impersonate her myself!' I said. 'I never realized that she had more than one – ah – accomplice.'

As I said this, I was taking a robe off the wall and getting into it. I put on one of Lady Julilla's wigs and, sitting down in front of the mirror, started applying the whiteface and dabbing kohl on my eyelashes.

'You really seem quite professional at it,' said the Lady Volumnia. 'Well, I'm pleased to learn that I'm off the hook today; I'm really too tired to pull off the charade.'

'Up all night?' I said.

She clammed up.

'I know all about the zombifications,' I said. She gasped. 'Don't worry – I really see no harm in it – the Christianoi are criminals, and I really don't care whether they die once or a thousand times. And you know, it isn't really resurrection at all – the elixir seems to put them into a kind of catatonic state, and when they are awakened in the zombification rite they are not quite themselves anymore. But I'm not going to berate you for playing on the credulity of a bunch of losers.'

'Thank you,' she said. 'I love my husband so much, O Viridianus! Even when I allowed you to possess this admittedly shopworn body of mine, it was because I love my husband and will stop at nothing to prevent him from coming to harm . . . you do understand, don't you?'

I murmured something appropriate about the power of conjugal love.

'I mean,' she said, 'I had a lot of fun at the Christianoi meetings, singing those tuneful hymns and chumming with slaves and riff-raff; there's something so *elemental* about the lower classes, you know. Of course, I had to betray them for the sake of my husband's reputation, but I was so plagued by guilt about it—'

'You're a very sensitive soul, Clarissima,' I said.

'That's why, when Eros introduced me to Babalavus—'

So the plot was thickening even in the moment of its unravelling! Somehow Eros had engineered the whole thing . . . but why?

I explained to Volumnia why I needed to go to the circus in the guise of the Vestal Virgin. 'Why don't you stay here,' I said, 'while I go into Julilla's bedroom and tell her I'll take her place today? I'll only be a moment.'

She nodded, then kissed me for luck. I placed the last layer of veils over my head and crept into Lady Julilla's cubiculum.

'Lady Julilla, it's me,' I said. There was no answer, but I fancied I heard a faint scuffling noise somewhere in the chamber. Perhaps it was merely a mouse. A single lamp burned by the Vestal's bedside. She was not in bed. Nor did I see any telltale bulges behind the drapes. It was a sparsely furnished room, as befitted its occupant's otherworldly vocation; a few busts of Emperors stared at one from marble pediments of various heights; there was a couch and an altar for private devotions. Several fumigators spewed clouds of incense into the air, which added to the gloom. Near the window was Lady Julilla's capacious bed, wide enough for the entire Praetorian guard, it seemed, canopied with veils of damascene.

I had no time to wonder about the Lady's whereabouts, for I heard someone scrambling at the open window and I dived into the bed.

To my horror, a blubbery mound of flesh, perfumed to the gills and attired in the height of *nouveau-riche* tastelessness, came tumbling through the window, rubbed its backside, stood up, began to shamble towards me, panting like a hippopotamus with sunstroke.

'My beloved,' it squawked. 'I simply had to come. I could stay away no longer!' It was all too apparent that the Lady Julilla's secret lover was none other than the emasculated Eros, and that if I did nothing I would soon become the receptacle of his sacrilegious lust!

It was too late. Eros bounced on to the bed, arms outstretched, and I had to duck to avoid his proffered lips. 'I've pulled it off,' he gloated, 'the impudent get-rich-quick scheme I told you of . . . soon it will all pay off . . . and then I'll be able to take you away, far from here . . . far from the long arm of Caesar . . . beyond the reach of Rome itself! Yes, my darling; you have but to say the word and I am yours for ever!'

I am no fool. I realized that all I had to do was lie there, avoiding the eunuch's advances, and he would eventually cough up the solution to the entire puzzle. Once more I wriggled free of his grasp, making little whimpering noises such as I imagined the randy old hussy might make were she there to reciprocate the creature's passions.

'Oh, Julilla, you're such a tease,' Eros said. He managed to get me in a kind of amorous wrestling lock, and his mouth descended on mine.

'You're so masterly,' I said, 'but I've got a headache.'

'Headache – splendid!' he said. 'I know how you love it with a dollop of pain.'

Pain! Clearly the Lady Julilla's appetites had been rendered decidedly deviant by her years of abstinence.

'I have my flagellum right under my tunic, my dear,' said Eros.

'Er . . . it's that time of the month,' I temporized in my best falsetto.

'You adorable old minx,' he said, 'you know it hasn't been that time of the month in fifteen years . . .'

So much for that. I prepared to either give myself away or yield to his caresses. I allowed him to chase me around the bed for a while, and then said at last, in sudden inspiration, 'Before we consummate our love, O Eros, tell me more of your brilliant machinations! You know how ... aroused I get with talk of political intrigue ...'

Eros let go of me. I clasped my hands, fluttered my eyelids, and looked as adoring as I could. I had guessed, correctly, that political gossip was, for the ageing Vestal, the most stimulating kind of foreplay.

'It's chicanery at its most devious!' he said. 'Syrian political savvy, Judaean financial wizardry – combined with the secret black arts of unconquered lands! I've hired a Negro mage to reanimate the corpses of hundreds of Christianoi, so they can be killed over and over again in the arena. And the Christianoi love it! They think it's their day of resurrection or something.'

'But – what advantage can this bring you?'

'Women and mathematics simply don't mix, do they?' he said, and I did not remind him that his equipment was little different from a woman's. 'Look, the Christianoi are reckoned into the expenses of the games at so much per head, based on the overhead amortization of previous games ... do you follow?' I did not, but continued to listen raptly. 'A certain sum is charged against the privy purse per Christianos for his execution; in other words, the execution, which would normally be carried out by the state, is franchised out to the editor of the games. Another sum is also charged against the editor's accounts to cover the actual cost of execution; this is a pro rata share of the total costs of the executions, as calculated from previous spectacles, with allowance for the debasement of the currency and so on and so forth. The upshot of all this is, a properly placed person – such as – ahem – the Imperially-appointed financial adviser to Q. Drusianus Otho – can, by recycling the Christianoi over and over, funnel money from both the privy purse *and* the editorial budget into his own – ah – slush fund, from which—'

'Surely you did not concoct so labyrinthine a scheme entirely by yourself, O Eros!' I said.

'Well, I did have help from a certain Judaean banker, one Chrysolithos – but luckily I was able to have him silenced – and to seize his estate besides,' he said, grinning.

'Chrysolithos! Good heavens, my family banks with him.'

'Oh, the bank will go on as usual,' Eros said. 'It will merely be serving other interests.' He began stroking my neck. 'But enough of this nonsense! Let us get down to the real business of the morning—'

'But wait! I am so worried for you ... won't you get in trouble? What of Drusianus and the Lady Volumnia?'

'Oh, I've already taken care of *them*. Babalavus the mage has convinced that airhead that she's saving her Christianoi friends from death while simultaneously protecting her husband from scandal ... I have that detective to thank for that, whatsis-name—'

'Publius Viridianus.'

'Yes – I have hired him to look for hanky-panky, and he will soon find that – because of the recycling of the Christianoi – that goody-goody prig's books will not be in order – he will have been found to have cheated the Imperial privy purse – at which point – zombificatus! And his vigilant denouncer will be in a fine position to – ah – take over the Villa Drusiana, which has the most splendid view of Vesuvius.'

The gig was up. But just as I was about to whip off my disguise, the eunuch seized me in his surprisingly powerful embrace and planted his tongue firmly against my gritted teeth. If I attempted to speak, that tongue would surely gain admittance into that cavity whither no man – let alone a gelding – had ever gone before.

At that moment, however, Lady Volumnia rushed into the room and began pummelling the eunuch with her fists. I was so startled I almost bit off his tongue.

'Monster!' she screamed. 'You told me that Viridian had been sent to discredit my husband – but you never told me *you* had hired him to do it!'

'Juli – J–J–Julilla!' he said, looking from me to Volumnia. 'Volumnia!'

'You, my dear Eros, are ruined,' I said, ripping off my veils and dropping my voice back to its commanding baritone. 'You may as well commit suicide now, for the Praetorians will be knocking on your door by sunset.'

'P. Viridianus!' he shrieked.

'Indeed,' I said, as I wiped the kohl from my eyes.

The eunuch looked at his two accusers in some bewilderment for a moment. Then he said, 'You'll never get away with this. I have the ear of Caesar! He'll never take the word of a known Christianos and a two-sestertius detective over that of a trusted civil servant. I'll hire the best lawyers in Rome! By the time I'm through with you—'

At that moment there came a sound like the rumbling of an earthquake. We all stared at the bed. It was quaking. The bedposts were clattering against the marble floor. I heard the jangling of an untuned lyre.

At length, an imposing figure emerged from under the bed, clutching his instrument, garbed in a cloak of Imperial purple spangled with stars and moons.

We all prostrated ourselves.

'Divinitas!' we said.

'The ear of Caesar, eh?' said the God of State, glaring at the gelatinous Eros. 'Guards! Arrest this thing!'

★

And so, at the last minute, an extra number was inserted in that afternoon's games, between the Rape of the Sabine Women by trained jackasses and the battle between Pygmies and Amazons. The punishment would fit the crime – Eros was to suffer an undignified end, the application of a molten gold enema – but would be one that would only be appreciated by true afficionados, since it was hard to see and lacked spectacle.

Lady Julilla had been invited to share the editor's pavilion, as had the Divinity himself, who sat upon a gilded cathedra shaped like a rearing lion. I asked her if she regretted seeing her erstwhile lover's demise.

'Not at all,' she said, biting delicately into a snow cone flavoured with crushed berries. 'He was a brute.'

'But how did the Emperor come to be hiding under your bed?'

'Oh, he always does that. You see, the idea of a Vestal Virgin coupling with a eunuch excites him greatly; it is the closest he can come to being reunited with his mother, whom, as you know, he was forced to have murdered. So we came to a little – agreement. Were the God to couple with me himself, it would be a dreadful impiety and bring about the downfall of the Empire; but since Eros was a eunuch, strict propriety was observed.'

Wonders would never cease. Despite her licentious lifestyle, the old bag had managed to remain entirely intacta and true to her vocation! She was, I had to admit, a Roman through and through, able to answer the most bewildering moral dilemmas with pragmatic solutions.

They were hauling away the last of the violated women and Eros was now being wheeled in on an ingenious contraption that would allow him to spin slowly while he agonized, thus providing even the plebeians with a decent view of his suffering face. There was desultory applause from the audience; most were bored, waiting for the Pygmies and Amazons.

Eros was brought over to our box so that he could pay the customary respects to the Emperor before being killed. He appeared to have gone quite bonkers. 'Rejoice, Autokrator!' he cried, and waved merrily at us. 'Don't you worry – I'll be back!'

Perhaps a last-minute conversion to Christianity?

'I'm thinking of giving Babalavus your old job,' said the Emperor. Then he took out his lyre. 'You have been a very fine civil servant, O Eros, and afforded me much amusement besides.' He winked at the Lady Julilla. 'I shall therefore pay you the supreme compliment – I shall accompany your death with a song of my own composition.'

He began to sing. It was very modern.

Lady Volumnia came sidling up to me. 'Oh, Viridian,' she said, 'we're having a big party at our house tonight to celebrate my induction into the mysteries of Astarte – do come; my husband owes you a debt of gratitude and I have pledged to – pay it myself.' She smiled seductively.

'The cult of Astarte – that's the one where the women give themselves randomly to passers-by, isn't it?' I said. It was really difficult to keep these Oriental cults straight, though it did not surprise me that Lady Volumnia had already found a new one to amuse herself with.

Eros screamed. Politely, I looked away.

'I really can't go,' I said. 'I've a dinner party at Petronius's. In fact' – I looked at the sun – 'it's almost the eighth hour now, and cena is at nine.'

So saying, I turned my back on the entrancing if not unblemished Volumnia, on honest Drusianus and careful Julilla, and on our magnificent and fun-loving Divinity, and furthermore on the entirely satisfying excruciation of the eunuch Eros and the marmoreal splendour of the Neronian Amphitheatron. I left the spectacle behind in order to spend a last evening with C. Petronius Arbiter, a dinner of classical simplicity and artful conversation.

What happened at that dinner is, of course, known to all men; after reading us his letter to Nero in which he catalogued the Divinity's many infamies, he caused his physician to open his veins and died as elegantly as he had lived. So famous is that dinner party that it eclipsed all memory of my exploits; and while the name of Petronius will live on, the scandal of Eros the eunuch, the titillating amours of the Lady Julilla, and the multiple resurrections of Christianoi by the art of zombification are all things that, I am sure, history will mercifully forget.

Hunting the Lion is the second of the tales about theology and zombies in this collection. It's also a hardboiled detective story, a

Roman spectacle, a *Night of the Living Dead*-style horror story, and a story about corruption in the entertainment industry. I just wanted to see how many genres I could squeeze into a single story.

This was originally written for *Weird Tales*. I have to admit that it's weird.

Mr Death's Blue-eyed Boy

Darrell Sachsenhauser loved money and hated children. Children had always frightened him, even when he was a child himself.

He did not know why, although by middle age he had paid a great deal of money to therapists, analysts and occultists to find out. There were those who wanted to probe his dreams; they elicited little but recurring images of wild, fanged creatures with slitty eyes. They tried to regress him to that singular trauma of childhood that always seemed to motivate their clientele; but this client did not seem to have had much of a childhood at all; he had sprung into being some time around puberty; they could find no mismanaged potty training, no virulent rape, no devastating primal scene. It seemed to the Freudians that the trauma must be so deeply lodged that only a larger infusion of cash could draw it out; and so Darrell Sachsenhauser, who loved money more than he loved himself, went to the Jungians instead.

The Jungians tried to get him to confront his Shadow and communicate with his Anima, only to discover that he seemed to have neither. A variety of New Age therapists had a go, but they ended up telling him that he simply didn't want to change. And then there was a shamaness who told him that some enemy had worked a spell on him, and that he should bury a thousand dollars in a certain graveyard by the light of the full moon; Darrell Sachsenhauser balked at that and so received no succour from the spirit world. The last straw had been Marilyn Firth, whom he'd run into at the Long Beach coin fair: beautiful in a shopworn kind of way, a former Jungian, now some kind of vaguely Joseph Campbellian counsellor; she had tried to help him communicate with his inner child, only to discover that there was no inner child within him – a shell without an oyster, she'd called him in a fit of pique.

At least she had been good in bed. Surfers always were. They bucked and heaved in time to an imagined tide.

After he weathered his mid-life crisis, it occurred to him that the attempt to fathom his phobia had become increasingly subject to the law of diminishing returns; he gave up trying to find out why. He merely avoided them whenever possible; and when, as often in the course of his daily business, he could not do so, he kept his distance as best he could.

It was not necessarily as discomfiting a phobia as it might appear. Darrell Sachsenhauser lived in an all-adult condominium and he took a circuitous route to the coin store in order to avoid passing the playground and the elementary school. However, there were times when they did cross his path. After all, the coin store was a public place. There *was* a sign in the window that read NO CHILDREN ALLOWED, but it was not, of course, enforceable.

One particular Sunday he had planned to close the shop early. The last customer was a snotty-looking child who was clearly not about to buy anything; and Darrell wanted to count his money without having to experience the unreasoning terror he suffered in their proximity. He retreated to the furthest corner of the store, switched off a few lights, and began emptying the display cabinets so he could put the coins back in the safe. But the child seemed to sense where he was. When Darrell looked up, he was right there, sniffing the dusty air like a rat.

'Scram,' Darrell Sachsenhauser said. 'Show's over.'

The child had a skateboard under one arm and a T-shirt with neon pink skeletons dancing against black. 'Wow!' he said. 'Is that, like, really a *billion* on that banknote? How much is it worth?'

In his thirty years as proprietor of a second-rate coin store in the northeast side of the San Fernando Valley, Darrell had got pretty fucking tired of that question. Nevertheless, having to concentrate on the stock answer distracted him from the terror. He rattled off: 'It's *Notgeld*, emergency scrip put out by local governments during the great inflation that hit Germany after World War I . . . a billion marks could buy you maybe a dozen eggs . . . that's how Hitler came to power, by taking advantage of the economic—' He paused. The unease was creeping back up on him.

The kid just stood there. Feral. Ready to pounce. Beady-eyed, slavering. No teary-eyed moppet, but a monster, a vampire. Darrell mopped the sweat from his forehead. Damn you, disappear! he thought. *Retro me, Satanas!*

'You okay, dude?'

. . . and something clammy slithering down his spine. 'Take it,' he said. 'You can take the goddamn thing for a buck if you'll get out of the fucking store so I can close up!'

'Fresh,' said the child, 'gimme two of 'em, dude.'

Darrell selected a worn City of Bamberg 'eine Milliarde Mark' note and a crisp Heidelberg 'zwei Millionen', hurriedly inserted them into mylar envelopes and handed them to the boy. He tried to make himself relax with the thought that, even at the discount, he was still clearing a 400 per cent profit. You could buy German *Notgeld* by the carton. It was worthless. A novelty item at best. His pulse raced. Any minute now he'd be gasping for oxygen—

The door clanged shut. Darrell was safe.

He put away more coins. He turned off the neon sign. Smog-filtered sunset streamed in through the window bars. He coughed. It had been a narrow escape. Another minute or two and he might have fainted dead away, like the time his neighbour's nieces came over to use the swimming pool.

Darrell packed up the last of the gold, a handful of 2x2s containing liberty half-eagles in shitty condition, slammed the safe shut and lugged it into the toilet, where he had a secret panel behind the medicine cabinet. That's where he kept the real treasures: an Athenian dekadrachm of the archaic period, a roll of CC Morgans, a mint state Caligula denarius with an

unrecorded reverse ... coins that could one day put him in a
mansion on Mulholland. Coins he had killed for.

He held up the dekadrachm, feeling its weight and the
weight of its past. The face of Athena was in profile, but the
eye was askew; it glared straight up at him. Time hadn't
touched the coin since some Ionian merchant hoarded it away
in a wine jug and buried it against catastrophe. Darrell had
snatched it right under the nose of that Turkish dealer in a Paris
hotel. Then the dealer had died, somehow. Heart attack. Poison.
Darrell couldn't recall.

Darrell held the Turk's death between his fingers, a chunk of
metal with the face of a goddess.

There was a tap at the window.

Quickly Darrell put away his guilty pleasures. He locked the
medicine chest and came out of the bathroom. There was a
shadow in the doorway. He mouthed 'We're closed. Go away.'

The shadow didn't leave. It was a slender figure in a leather
coat, silhouetted in sunset and the flicker of sushi bar neon
signs. It was banging hard now. Any minute it would set off
the alarm. Insufferable. But it least it wasn't another kid.

It was a sharp-featured young woman with a page-boy
haircut. She pummelled the door with operatic desperation.

'Closed! Come back tomorrow.'

A high-heeled patent leather boot jammed the doorway.
*'Bitte. Entschuldigung, Herr Sachsenhauser. Sie müssen mir ja
helfen.'*

'I don't do any of this old country talk, lady. Just English.'
Darrell could understand German perfectly, but he had no
memory of ever having learned it.

'Mr Sachsenhauser?' A limousine was waiting by the kerb.

Darrell looked her in the eye. Could she possibly know about
the trail of blood that led to the medicine cabinet in the lavatory
of his coin store? Was she Interpol, maybe? But why so
distraught? Why the heaving sex appeal? Surely anyone with a
dossier would have known that his interest in women was
confined to his regular Saturday night outing to Mrs Cherni-
kov's – quick, impersonal, and modestly priced.

'I have been searching for you for months, Herr Sachsen-hauser.' She handed him her business card.

It read:

> *Eva Rotwang*
> *Office of the Municipality of Hameln*
> *Westfalen, Germany*

'You've come a long way, lady,' he said.

'It was necessary.' Maybe she *was* with Interpol after all. But Darrell had never killed anyone in Germany. Or robbed a collection. No. He'd always kept his hands off Germany. The Fatherland, he supposed, although he had no memories of it. He started to fidget. 'There isn't much time, Mr Sachsenhauser. Your passport is in order, I hope? But of course it is; you travel a great deal.'

'Am I going somewhere?' he said. Sensing his unease, she tugged at his sleeve and pulled him out of his store so that they stood, face to face, on the sidewalk. She no longer seemed distraught. She gripped his wrists. Her mid-calf overcoat and leather gloves were overpoweringly Aryan. She seemed strong . . . so different from the wishy-washy Marilyn. She allowed him a moment to lock up and set the alarm system. Then the chauffeur ushered him into the back seat.

He protested that he had his own car, but no one listened. The Rotwang woman followed. 'Are you kidnapping me?' he said.

'No, of course not,' said Eva Rotwang. In a few moments they were on the Ventura Freeway. She picked up the car phone and dialled, said, '*Ja, ja,*' a few times, hung up.

'*Nach dem Flughafen,*' she said to the driver.

'Bullshit,' Darrell said. 'I'm not going to the airport. Do you have a warrant?'

Eva Rotwang pulled something out of her purse. 'Do you recognize this man?' she said.

It was a Polaroid shot: a pretty nondescript man, actually, long, scraggly blond hair, not too thoroughly shaven – the caveman type. His cheeks were hollow and his face gaunt . . . it was an Auschwitz sort of a face . . . a skull.

Mr Death, Darrell thought. But he had no idea who he was, and said so. 'Whatever you're looking for,' he said, 'you obviously have the wrong man.'

'I don't think so.'

Darrell peered at the photograph again as the freeway crossed the Santa Monica Mountains. They were speeding; these people were used to the Autobahn.

The man in the picture was wearing some kind of mediaeval costume, he realized, one side red and the other side yellow; maybe he was an actor. But still, it wasn't someone he had robbed or cheated. No, Darrell told himself firmly, I don't know him. And yet . . .

Eyes on a cavern wall, dancing in candlelight . . .

'The man insists on seeing you, asking for you by name. And he's very persuasive.'

'How so?'

'Enough to cause the city of Hameln to send me here to get you . . . by hook or by crook.'

'I don't even know where the fuck Hameln is.'

'In Westphalia. Germany. But you know of it, *natürlich* . . . the rats . . . the Pied Piper . . . the thirty Guilders . . .'

'Oh, you mean Hame-*lin*.'

'Ja, ja, Hameln. Hamelin is the anglicized version.'

'Well, listen, Eva, or whatever your name is, this doesn't seem to have much to do with me, so if you're not arresting me, you might as well let me off at the next exit. I'll take a cab home.'

'You don't understand . . . we'll pay you.'

'Usually, in a kidnapping, it's the kidnappee who pays.' They were really flying down the San Diego Freeway now. He reckoned they'd reach the airport in about ten minutes. Perhaps he'd be able to lose her there.

The Rotwang woman said, 'If not for the sake of a reward, then at least do it for the children!'

'Now you've really said the wrong thing.' She scrambled in her purse and produced several more Polaroids. They were all kids. Cute little blond things. Children in sailor suits. Children waving Nintendo Gameboys and Barbie dolls. Each image filled him with revulsion. They're only pictures, he told himself, but he found himself sliding towards the window. 'Children make me nervous. It's a phobia of mine.' He gazed at the billboards as they reeled by, strident in the purple-streaked smog of sunset. The Polaroids were all over the seat and he caught the reflection of one of them in the window ... eyes superimposed over the cityscape ... floating in the void. Animal eyes. Hungry. Glowing in the dark. Devil eyes.

'I *hate* children,' he said softly.

'In that case,' said Eva Rotwang, 'you won't mind coming to Hameln. There are no children there at all, you see. They've all vanished. And you're the only one *he'll* talk to.'

★

It was an old familiar dream ... the cave ... the cold. And the hunger. Seeping into his bones. And the darkness. The only sound a steady drip ... drip ... drip ... echoing. Echoing. Drip. Echoing. Then slowly, out of the cold and dark, a faint light. Flickering. Ebbing now, sucked back into the limestone void. Ice-floes that hugged the interior of the mountain. Dark. Dark.

Candlelight ...

Flash! The glint of a razor-sharp incisor. A hint of drool. A deathsmile forming out of the dimness ... eyes that burn crimson ... eyes. Eyes. And then the laughter: squeaky, metallic, punctuated by the drip–drip–drip ... and the cold. The cold. Eyes. More eyes. Eyes. Screeching.

The laughter of feral children.

Darrell screamed.

★

He felt a cold compress against his brow. 'There, there.' A familiar voice . . . one he had never thought to hear again. 'My, my, our inner child's sure going through a shitload of anxiety today.'

'Marilyn Firth?' said Darrell. 'Get out of here, go back to Santa Monica, find some new yuppies to torment.'

She stood there, resplendent in sari and – this was new – dreadlocks. The Indo-Jamaican look. Underneath it, still the middle-aged surfer woman from Santa Monica. 'Now you listen to me, Darrell. You're not paying for my services, so don't have a cow. Me all taken care of, mon.'

'Talk about an identity crisis,' Darrell said. 'You with your bleached hair and your Santa Monica sun-weathered face and your' – he noted that she had now become a dothead – 'third eye.'

'Hey, I found myself, okay? In Jamaica, on the rebound from you, I might add. More than can be said of you, you old miser.'

Eva Rotwang was coming through the partition into the first-class section now. 'What a commotion,' she said. 'Do you want me to ask for you some sleeping pills? We have a doctor on board, at your disposal.' Darrell seemed to be the only passenger in first. 'I see the doctor has found you.'

'Yes. Give me a Valium or something. And get this witch-doctor off the plane.'

'Got a parachute?' said Marilyn, shrugging. 'Relax! Money's no object to these people; they *desperate*.'

He looked at Eva. 'What possessed you people to bring *her* along? Don't you know she's a total charlatan? Her psychic powers come and go, just like her quaint and colourful West Indian accent.'

'Oh, you've no imagination, Darrie . . . we're all spokes in the great cosmic wheel. Karma, mon. Hey, we could have sex. Old times' sake.'

'I'm sorry,' Eva said. 'Our records indicated that . . . you're not the most stable of individuals . . . and this woman was listed as your most recent therapist.'

'And you didn't want me to flake out on you while I negotiate
with the Pied Piper.'

There was a long silence as the women looked at each other,
each waiting for the other to do something. At last Darrell said,
'Okay, give me the damn tranquillizer.'

But the nightmare came back as soon as he closed his eyes. It
was more vivid than ever. And this time he could not wake
himself up, because he had taken one Valium too many. The
children laughed all the way from Los Angeles to Hamburg . . .
all the way through customs . . . all the way along the Autobahn
. . . all the way to the office of the mayor of Hamelin.

★

Sculpted wood panelling; frayed carpeting; on the ceiling, a
baroque fresco of cupids, nymphs, shepherds and the like.

They were sitting at a round table. Each wore a business suit
of the identical shade of grey, and each wore a dark blue tie.
They were the city council: all male, all old, all tired. Darrell
had not had time for even a coffee break; the two women
ushered him in, standing on either side of him, as though he
were their prisoner.

'*Herr Sachsenhauser,*' one of them, bearded, perhaps a nona-
genarian, began. '*Wie glücklich, daß Sie schon angekommen sind.*'

'He won't speak German, Dr Krumm,' said Eva Rotwang.
'Darrell Sachsenhauser: the distinguished members of our city
council. Unfortunately, the mayor will be unable to attend this
meeting.'

'He is in hiding,' said the old codger, and introduced the
others quickly by name; Darrell soon forgot who they were.
Confusion was kicking in. They weren't Interpol. They had
dragged him halfway across the world because they thought he
could save their children. He, the one person in the world who
could not be in the same room as a child without experiencing
a mindless, uncontrollable panic.

A man in a butler's uniform came into the room. He was
carrying a television set. He set it down in the middle of the
round table and Dr Krumm finally remembered to invite

Darrell to sit down. The seats were dark green leather, the central heating oppressive. The butler turned on the television, and one of the councillors activated a speakerphone.

'There he is,' said Dr Krumm.

It was the straggly-haired blond in the mediaeval costume. '*Er ist im Gefängnis,*' said one of the other councillors.

'You jailed him?' said Darrell.

'Of course we did!' said Krumm. 'He could be a serial killer or something like that. A madman preying on ancient legend.'

The man on the screen looked up at them; a prison guard handed him a telephone. He seemed unsure of its purpose, but after a brief explanation from the guard he lifted the receiver.

'I want to speak to Sachsenhauser,' he said in a strangely accented German. Even through the speakerphone's distortion, there was something compelling about his voice. His eyes, too, were hypnotic, so sunken that they were encircled with shadow.

'Herr Sachsenhauser is here now,' said Dr Krumm. 'Enunciate clearly, though; he hasn't spoken the *Muttersprache* for a long time.'

Darrell said, 'Good morning, Mr Death,' in German, surprising himself by how easily it leapt to his tongue.

'Why do you call me that?'

'I . . . I don't know.'

'It is not I who kill the children.'

'What are you accusing me of?'

The stranger said, 'Five hundred years ago, your many-times-great-grandfather made a pact with me. I have come to collect the money. With, of course, the accumulated interest.'

Dr Krumm said, 'Which comes to, Herr Sachsenhauser, four quadrillion, seven hundred and twenty-two trillion, sixteen billion, four hundred and twelve million, six hundred thousand and seventeen Marks and thirteen Pfennigs!' And he handed Darrell a piece of computer printout on which were row upon row of figures . . . and that ominous final figure, 4,722,016,412,600,017.13, underlined and circled.

'These folks mad as hatters,' said Marilyn Firth. 'Just my kind of people.'

Dr Krumm went on, 'We have a document that has been in the city archives for some centuries. It is an ... ah ... a sort of trust deed. It certifies that ...' He put on a pair of horn-rimmed spectacles and rummaged in a drawer. Then he looked up in frustration. The butler came in, sideways, bearing a silver casket; Dr Krumm took out a xerox of a handwritten document. 'I'll translate it for you: "in consideration of services rendered to the municipality of Hameln, the sum of thirty Guilders, plus interest, to be awarded, to be collected no sooner than one hundred years from this date, with the children of the town, their bodies and souls, to be pledged as mortgage collateral ... that this agreement be binding upon myself and my heirs until such time as the obligations therein be fully discharged, as witness of which I herewith commit my living soul and the souls of my heirs living or as yet unborn ... signed this day by me, having been granted such authority by the citizens of the municipality of Hameln, Antonius Sachsenhauser, mayor."' Krumm removed his glasses and looked expectantly at Darrell.

'What the hell is this supposed to mean?' Darrell said. 'Anyway, everyone knows what *really* happened ... oh, I don't mean *really*, I mean in the fucking fairy tale ... the Piper *did* get paid ... with those children ... good fucking riddance ... and ...'

'Apparently not,' said Dr Krumm. 'Apparently there was some kind of compromise ... the Piper agreed to ... ah, carry paper, as you might say in the mortgage business ... and the balloon payment has come due.'

An even more geriatric fellow, jabbing his finger in the direction of Darrell's face, said, 'You are the only traceable living descendant of Antonius Sachsenhauser, author of this document.'

'Awesome,' said Marilyn. 'I mean, it's like, a visitation from the collective unconscious. I think I'm in love!'

'Bullshit,' said Darrell Sachsenhauser.

'Oh, but it's beautiful, mon,' Marilyn said. 'It's not just that

Berlin Wall she come a-tumbling down; it's the wall between reality and illusion ... the wall between mythic time and modern time. This is so cool I could piss myself.'

'I'm not descended from any mayor of Hamelin,' Darrell said. How could they possibly know such a thing when even he himself had no memories of childhood, of being *anybody's* heir? And how could a fairy tale come true? Was it all something to do with the childhood Darrell could not remember, the childhood that seemed to have been walled up within the same mountain walls that had hidden the children of Hamelin? It was too ridiculous for words. Yet here were all these decrepit old Krauts, sitting around a table in a plush old office building, waiting for him to be their Messiah. 'It's beyond belief.'

'And yet ...' said Marilyn, causing all eyes to turn to her, even the eyes of the madman in the prison cell ... 'and yet he does have this irrational fear of children.'

... the cave ... the cold ... the laughter ...

The old men all looked at each other, nodded, muttered, murmured, as if Marilyn's revelation proved everything.

'You will negotiate with the Piper,' said Dr Krumm. 'You'll be well paid.'

'Your city doesn't have a good track record in paying for pest control,' Darrell said. It was easy to fall into the reality of the fairy tale because all of *them* believed it.

'You'll like what we have to offer.' The butler, suaver than ever, came in with another casket, this time gold. Inside, on a blue velvet lining, lay a coin. A dekadrachm. It was a twin of the one in Darrell's bathroom safe. Except that *this* one was perfect. The last such dekadrachm to be auctioned had sold for $600,000, but it had only been in EF.

Darrell reached out to grab the box, but the butler snatched it away. 'You certainly know what I like,' Darrell said, 'but somehow—'

'There is, of course, also the leaden casket,' said Eva Rotwang. The butler whipped it out, opened it, and Darrell saw what was inside: a photograph of a dead Turkish coin dealer in a Paris hotel. There was another photograph of a glass case full of ancient coins, with one conspicuously missing. There was a third photograph – a close-up of the glass case – a fingerprint.

'I'll be damned,' said Darrell. 'You *are* from Interpol.' Eva smiled a little, then clammed up.

'This is *so* fucking mythic!' squealed Marilyn.

'You have twenty-four hours, give or take a few,' said Dr Krumm. 'That's the deadline *he* gave us.'

'What if he has nothing to do with the disappearance of your children? What if he's just some lunatic taking the credit and trying to blackmail the city?'

'That is possible. But walk our streets . . . look out over the town square from your hotel window . . . go to the playgrounds . . . you will see that there are no children in Hameln. *None!*'

And all the old men began to weep.

★

Darrell did walk the streets. There were indeed no children in Hameln. If, as their records seemed to indicate, Darrell Sachsenhauser had actually been born in Hameln, and had emigrated to America with his parents and aging grandfather some time after the war, it was strange that he felt no twinges of recognition.

Darrell walked down cobble-stoned alleys, past rococo churches, past squat apartment complexes and mediaeval storefronts. Toyshops were boarded up. In a pastry shop, old women in black dresses sipped hot chocolate and glared at each other. In Los Angeles, there would be times when Darrell was just walking down the boulevard to buy a magazine . . . feeling quite safe, quite at peace with himself . . . and then there'd be a shrill cry in the air . . . a child whizzing by on a skateboard, brushing against him, and his nostrils would get a sudden blast of that smell they had, an odd amalgam of ketchup and chocolate and sweat and *Teenage Mutant Ninja Turtles* bubble bath. The contact would last for a split second and yet by the time he'd reached the newsstand he'd have become a nervous wreck, unable to remember what he had come for. Or sometimes, just the dread that such an encounter might occur would be enough to reduce him to a gibbering idiot.

After an hour of walking, he had yet to feel that dread. There was no turning a corner and suddenly running into one of the creatures, sprinting towards school. There was no metal-tinged laughter.

There really were no children here. Darrell could breathe deeply without fear of sucking in their breath, their odour. After another hour or so, strolling along the left bank of the Weser, it occurred to him that this was the first time he had ever felt free from oppression. He walked with his head held high, unafraid. All cities should be like this city. He waved at passers-by, but no one waved back. It was autumn and moist rotting leaves fluttered along the narrow streets, and people walked with their eyes downcast. One storefront was plastered with dozens of Polaroids of children, with a banner that read, 'Wo sind die Kinder?' and Darrell was tempted to shout back, 'Who cares where they are?'

At length he found himself beside a souvenir stand that sold plastic Hong Kong rats and wooden flutes. There was no vendor. It stood beside a stone gate, an obvious tourist spot, though there were no tourists; a Latin inscription noted that this gate was dedicated, two hundred and seventy-two years later, to the hundred and thirty children abducted from the town and immured within Mt Poppen. Sitting down on a bench, feeding the pigeons with a bag of bird seed pilfered from another abandoned souvenir stand, Darrell could see the celebrated mountain itself, rearing up behind the town's sky-line, an unharmonious blend of the sixteenth and twentieth centuries. He helped himself to a Pilsner. It occurred to him that they must be following him, and sure enough he could see the leathery outline of Eva Rotwang in the shadow of the gate; but he didn't care. It was wonderful to know such freedom from anxiety. The therapists hadn't been able to do it. Maybe there never had been anything wrong with him ... just with the rest of the world.

'Pretty grim, huh?' It was Marilyn, sitting down on the bench beside him, opening an apple juice.

'On the contrary,' said Darrell, 'I've never felt better in my life.'

'Oh, you old solipsist! I didn't mean you, I meant this town.'

'I don't miss them.'

'Oh, don't be silly. How would the human race replicate itself without children? Your ancestor did the right thing, in a way ... life expectancy was much shorter in the Middle Ages ... you eliminate one generation, you kill the whole town.' She wasn't putting on some accent now, which meant she was dead serious.

'You're buying this malarkey?'

'You take their money, you take their shit,' she said. 'Besides ... when old Krumm there was telling you how the children were all gone ... and you were just staring into the Piper's eyes, on the monitor ... there was something in your expression ... it didn't look like doubt to me. It looked like *recognition*.'

'Maybe,' Darrell said. Two women, dressed in black, walked past, not looking at them. A man walked towards them wheeling a baby carriage, but Darrell felt no *frisson* at all ... as the man went past them, Darrell realized that the carriage contained only a Cabbage Patch Kid ... and the man was weeping.

'I can totally tell what you're thinking, mon,' Marilyn said. 'You've been inside that cave with the laughing children and you're all shuddering inside – and now for the first time you feel the walls crumbling.'

'Maybe,' Darrell said again. But as he breathed the clean pure childless air, he thought: I don't need healing.

'Me think maybe time for you to try to touch your inner child one more time.'

'I thought it had been scientifically determined that I *have* no inner child.'

'Ain't no living being don't not have no inner child,' she said.

'Speak English!' said Darrell, cringing at the quintuple negative.

'Tubular!' she said, and rubbed the red dot on her forehead. 'But Darrell Sachsenhauser, I am a shapeshifter in my own way, you see; I dart from mythos to mythos; yet the heart is always the same. But, it seems, not your heart; perhaps you aren't human after all. What were those photographs they were blackmailing you with?'

'Nothing. I killed someone once. I think.'

'Eww! Let us explore.'

And then, right there in the empty plaza, Marilyn Firth began to dance. At first it was only with her eyes; they darted back and forth to a music Darrell could not hear; yet after a while, as by hypnotic suggestion, he thought he could hear a kind of rhythm in the cooing of pigeons, in the flapping of old news-papers in the wind, in the footsteps of the passers-by, heads bowed, who were too absorbed in the community's grief to be interested in the strange woman dancing. Marilyn danced and Darrell watched her eyes . . . fluttering . . . glittering . . . strobing . . . suddenly she began to whirl. Her sari began to unravel . . . and unravel . . . and unravel . . . veils of sheer silk jetted out in all directions . . . she unwound and unwound and unwound herself and still the silk seemed infinite . . . like a magician's string of handkerchiefs . . . billowing upwards, twisting, weaving into mandala-like patterns against the grey sky.

I must be dreaming, Darrell thought. But the colours were more garish than any dream . . . crimsons and ceruleans and vermilions and apple greens and cadmium yellows . . . dancing . . . dancing.

'You never used to do this sort of thing,' he said.

She didn't answer him but he could hear her voice pounding in his head like the wind in a tubular wave . . . *I've learned a lot of new tricks, Darrie. And you've helped me. You've heard the cracking of the cavern walls, not me . . . you told me you were ready . . . now take me. Take me into your dream. We will go together so you need not be afraid. We will go together and this time you will be awake, conscious, understanding.*

Darrell still could not believe that this phantasmagoric display could lead to a therapeutic epiphany, but he could not help be mesmerized by the streams of colour as their patterns shifted and undulated. After a time it seemed that the silk was darkening, taking on the shades of the overcast sky. He could smell the wet limestone and the dust that had hung for centuries in the sunless air. And the cooing of the pigeons ... wasn't it transforming itself into the mocking laughter of children ... children with predatory eyes?

And Marilyn danced, and the cave walls coalesced out of the lowering sky. The veils rained down around him and hardened and turned to stone. And it became dark. And he could hear the drip–drip–drip of water. And he felt the fear for the first time that day. Until Marilyn's voice echoed in the chamber: *Speak to me from your dream. Tell me what you see.*

'There's a cave.'

Yes.

'There're voices. Laughing. Cruel voices. The children.'

This is a dream, Darrell, but it's a waking dream. And it's a journey. There are caves within caves, and the darkest cave is the one inside your own soul. Tell me what you see.

'I see eyes.'

But wait a minute! There were more than eyes. There were names attached to those eyes. There was a *real* cave. Wasn't there? Darrell stood up, grew accustomed to the darkness that was shot through with streaks of phosphorescence. He turned a corner and saw—

The dead Turkish coin dealer, mummified, sitting up in his coffin, holding out the glistening silver dekadrachm and—

Deeper. Deeper into the labyrinth. He steadied himself against clammy walls. There were cave paintings here. He could hear the pattering of rodent feet. Movement in the shadows. A pair of eyes. Nothing now. The laughter came closer. The hairs on the nape of his neck prickled.

Go on, said the voice of Marilyn Firth.

He didn't know at what point the cave became, not the metaphorical caverns of his recurring nightmares, but a real cave. He had stepped through the wall behind which he had sealed his childhood. Images of it were hurtling through his mind in a surreal montage—

The belt buckle lacerating his buttocks, the rhythmic refrain of *Pay the Piper! Pay the Piper!* and—

Mr Poppen . . . the town square with the mediaeval gate, the tourists, the plastic rats, balloons, the mousetraps in the attic, weathered faces of dead parents, sneaking over the bridge and pissing into the Weser . . .

Grampa showing him his most treasured possession. It's a hammered silver coin, thirteenth century, some German principality . . . 'I was disappointed because it was all tarnished. I wanted precious coins to be shiny.' He laughed ruefully.

Saxenpooper! Saxenpooper! Childish voices ringing out in the clear summer air.

. . . another country. A cave. Children. He hadn't always been afraid of children, he realized . . . and this discovery filled him with awe. 'There's a cave,' he told Marilyn. 'A real cave this time. It's in America. It's summer, a hot wild place, Montana maybe. In the summer I stay with Grampa. Or maybe my parents are already dead. Yes. I just remembered the funeral. A car crash.'

Tell me what's happening.

. . . 'I'm a child. It's an unfamiliar feeling because I've never been able to remember it before . . . how big things seem . . . how slender my hands and feet . . . I'm with my friends, Stevie Dunn and Mikey Austin and Johnny I can't remember his last name. We're dissecting a rat. It's neat. It was stuck on a glueboard in Mikey's mom's sewing room. It's still alive but barely. I just stuck a pin through its head, one of those shiny pins that come stuck in brand-new shirts, the kind you wear to church. Okay, the rat's sort of twitching now. Its guts are neat. I didn't know there was so many of them. It's fun. Johnny says, "Pretend like we're Mr Death." That's the name of a child-murderer in this part of the state . . . there's been a manhunt for some months now.

'Mikey says, "Mr Death slices off their heads. He eats their brains." Johnny says, "Bull. It's their livers." Mikey says, "Nu-

uh." And I just watch the rat twitching, twitching, twitching, but finally I put it out of its misery by squishing its head with a rock. The odd thing is that I'm not scared of these children at all. I'm more scared of the rat, even though it's a helpless thing, and now it's not even moving any more.'

Go on.

Images came flooding now. 'Stevie comes running. "C'mon, Saxenpooper! There's something you gotta see." It's deeper in the cave. Deeper. We follow him. We're in a tunnel. We have to go in single file. There's a little bit of light because the walls are glowing. Mikey remembers his flashlight and he turns it on and then it gets weird because of the beam of light that darts back and forth. There's graffiti scrawled on the walls. Skeletal figures. A mediaeval dance of death.

'The cave widens. There's candlelight or something. Flickering. First thing we see, crouching behind a low ridge of limestone, is a face. Larger than life. Painted on the wall. Its eyes are a clear deep blue and it's holding a flute to its lips. It's a face that shows no emotion at all but to me it's scary. It's a thin, pinched face, like a skull. I look a little lower and see that he's wearing a mediaeval costume, one side red and the other side yellow. And I can almost hear the music.

'"Jeepers," Mikey whispers. "What is it?"

'"It's a shrine or something. Or a human sacrifice place. Yeah."

'Around the image of the Piper are children. They're not realistically painted, but drawn the way a kid might draw them . . . a circle for a face, a wavy line for the lips, a sketched-in skirt or overalls . . . only the eyes seem real. You can't help looking into those eyes. They're the eyes of creatures who were human once, but now they've gone dead. But the candlelight lends them a kind of life.

'"Jeepers Creepers," Mikey whispers urgently. "There's a bum in here."

'We look at where he's pointing. There is an old man huddled against the far wall, and there's a candle on either side of him and that's where the flickering light is coming from. And he's wearing a tattered piper's costume . . . and he has a flute in his hand ... and he's trying to blow a tune. So I haven't imagined the music after all. "It's Mr Death!" Stevie says suddenly. "This must be his secret hide-out or something."

'The old man is my grandfather. But I don't dare say anything. I'm starting to feel the fear now, for the first time.

"'Let's *get* him," says Mikey. "C'mon, there's four of us and only one of him."

"'I bet this is where they're all buried," says Johnny, the littlest.

'Mikey takes a rock and heaves it at my grandpa. It hits him in the forehead and he gets up and I can see a spot of blood between the eyebrows ... it doesn't seem to hurt him.'

Oh! Cosmic! Mythic! The wounding of the Fisher King! The opening up of the third eye!

But Darrell had no time for the intrusive voice of Marilyn Firth. In all the time he had lived without a memory, without a past, the world had been populated with phantoms, two-dimensional figures. Oh, God, this was different. He could taste, touch, smell this memory.

Darrell? Darrell?

'My grandfather stands fully erect. He's holding up the flute like a talisman. Mikey and Johnny and Stevie are throwing stones like crazy now. They're screaming, "Take that, you baby-killer ... take that." And my grandfather just stands there, tottering a little, there's a big gouge in his left cheek and his arms are pitted and bloody. And Mikey says, "He ain't much. Let's kill the fucker. Let's carve him to bits." He takes a Swiss army knife from his shorts. "Yeah," Stevie says, "let's do him." And I'm watching all this, not participating, and I see the three kids converge on my grandfather and surround him, and they're pummelling him with their fists and bashing him with rocks and biting and scratching, and he's just standing there. Finally I can't take it any more and I scream, "Grandpa," and he looks up at me. The boys are surprised for only a minute and then they go on beating up on him, I guess they're too much into it now to stop ... there's all this rage in them ... their eyes are glowing. They're laughing as they kick him and punch him in the stomach. Finally I run down there and I'm trying to pull them off him . . . and he just stands there, taking it . . . his eyes darting back and forth . . . as though there were hundreds of kids, all over the cave, kids with glistening fangs and slitty eyes . . . and I wrest the flute out of Grandpa's hand and then I bring it smashing down on Mikey's head and I hear bone cracking . . . I see blood trickling down his face . . . I see a whitish goo squishing out of the fractured cranium and . . . Stevie and Johnny step back. And I say, "Grandpa, Grandpa," and my two friends are chanting, "Mr Death, Mr Death, Mr Death." And Grandpa says to me, "Now we have to go all the way." Suddenly he's strong. He's like a demon. He grabs the two boys. He slits the throat of one of them, then the other. I help him, I hold them down. We pile the bodies up in front of the icon of the Pied Piper. We're soaked with blood. I taste the blood. The blood's all gooey and crusting on my skin and hair. And I'm crying and saying, "What's going on, what are you doing here, why did we kill them, are you Mr Death?"

'Grandpa's weak again. He looks at me and I see hopelessness in his eyes as he says, "Damn kids. They're out to destroy you, body and soul, because of who you are. They know about the past. They haunt you wherever you go. They lurk in the shadows. They leap out at you from the darkness. Their eyes glow and their teeth glisten. It's always been this way." I say, "Why, Grandpa, why?" and he says, "When the Piper comes, you pay him. You hear? *Pay him!* Then all this will end."

'The dead boys are stacked in a heap. We don't suck out their livers or anything like that. We just light candles around them and leave them as an offering to Piper. The pictures of the children on the walls seem to draw life from the dead boys because now their eyes are animated. I can hear them laughing. My grandpa puts his bloody arms around me and says, "Forget, my blue-eyed boy, forget." And I forget.

'Except for the nightmares . . .'

Darrell followed Marilyn's voice, out of the cavern within the cavern, back to the square beside the memorial gate. She sat down beside him, securely cocooned in her sari now. There was no evidence around them of any supernatural happenings. There were only autumn leaves skimming the cobbled pavement ... and pigeons ... and the sun setting ... and the lengthening shadow of Mt Poppen.

'What was that all about?' cried Darrell. 'Was that true? Did all that really happen?'

'When was the last time you wept, Darrie?' said Marilyn, her arm around his shoulder, her other hand swabbing at his cheek with a fold of her sari.

Darrell said, 'I don't know. Back then, I guess.'

Marilyn said, 'So maybe I am a kind of sorceress after all, and not the crank you think I am. Reality has warped itself around you so that you'll get to replay this ancient myth. You can be a fatalist, and you can say, myths are eternal, the outcome can't be changed ... or maybe you can face up to this Mr Death ... and find the peace that's eluded you all your life. Good?'

And Darrell Sachsenhauser returned to his hotel and slept all night without dreaming. When he awoke, he had a plan.

*

Darrell asked Dr Krumm's office to buy up all the *Notgeld* they could find. 'You can even print more, if you have to,' he said. 'Just make sure it adds up to the four quadrillion or whatever it is.'

'But it is worthless,' said Dr Krumm.

'That,' Darrell said, 'is in the eye of the beholder.'

To Eva Rotwang, he said, 'When you threw him in jail, did you confiscate any items?'

'Yes.'

'Any flutes? Pipes? Shawms? Woodwind instruments of any kind?'

'A wooden flute.'

'I'll take that with me too.'

They piled up the sacks of money in the Piper's cell. Then they left the two of them alone together. Darrell faced the nemesis he had not known he had until the previous day; he looked him square in the face; and he cheated him of his quadrillions.

Mr Death examined the sacks of useless money with interest. 'It's only paper,' he said. 'Astonishing.'

'But paper with promises written on it,' Darrell said. 'And that makes it more than paper; that lends it a kind of magic.'

'I suppose you're right,' said Mr Death. 'I'm glad you understand that a bargain is a bargain.'

The Pied Piper was a little man after all, despite the monstrous icon on the cavern wall. In real life, locked in the cell, with his two-day stubble and his unwashed joker's costume, there was nothing to him.

Darrell handed over the flute.

The Piper broke the flute across his knee. Then, with his sacks of money, he vanished.

As Darrell left the prison, his new dekadrachm in a velvet pouch in his pocket, he heard children's laughter. It didn't bother him anymore.

★

Darrell had dinner with Marilyn in one of those riverside coffee shops: schnitzel, one of those desserts drowning in whipped cream, a lot of beer to wash it down. He told her, 'You were right. I shouldn't be fatalistic about it. Guilt's not genetic. I didn't do anything wrong.'

Although he thought to himself: I *have* killed people.

But what did it matter now? The flute was broken. The phobia was no more. Soon he would be back in Los Angeles. He would think of the trip to Hameln as one of those weekend therapy retreats he'd tried so frequently in the past . . . only this time it worked.

'You really *are* a sorceress after all, Marilyn.' A wind rose from the river and blew out their candles. A girl ran past, her pigtails flying. Darrell laughed.

'I'm not a sorceress,' said Marilyn. 'Whatever it was you did, *you* did. And if there's any price to pay, *you'll* pay it.'

'What price?' He couldn't resist taking the dekadrachm out

of his pocket, sliding it out of the pouch, as the waiter relit the candles. 'What's to pay? I got away with it. The way I always do.'

Marilyn smiled and scratched the dot on her forehead. It wasn't a real dot at all; just a stick-on thing. She peeled it off and stuck it in her purse. Sensing his surprise, she said, 'Hey, all the girls do it this way now.'

That night, she showed him that the sari, which had seemed endless, could in fact be completely unwound. They made love; he remembered how well she used to thrash about; tonight though, it was he who thrashed with newly-learned abandon, and she who, eyes closed, rode him, serenely, as though he were a surfboard and their bed the infinite sea. And then, as he drifted into sleep, she left him.

*

Later that night, Mikey Austin stood by his bedside. He was still eleven years old, and his brain was still oozing from the crack in his head.

'Long time no see, Darrell Saxenpooper,' he said. And laughed that high-pitched, metallic laugh that had haunted Darrell all those years.

But Darrell wasn't afraid. 'Oh,' he said, 'a ghost.'

'Come on,' said Mikey. And his eyes glowed. And he gripped Darrell's hand in his death-cold fingers. 'Time for you to go now.'

'Where to?' said Darrell. 'Is this a fucking dream?'

'No more dreams, Darrie.' The cold of Mikey's touch was burrowing into his flesh and creeping up his bones. 'You know where we're going.'

He tugged and Darrell found himself getting out of bed. Mikey walked quickly. They penetrated the wall of the hotel room and sank through the floor ... they reached the town square. It was deserted, and there was a full moon, and the dead leaves glistened like tarnished silver.

'Come on! Quick! You don't have much time left,' Mikey said. And laughed again. And this time Darrell did feel a ghost

of the old terror. But the cold had seeped deep into him and he
was too numb to shiver.

They reached the café beside the Weser. The tables and chairs
were overrun with rats. Rats darted back and forth over the
flagstones. Rats swam to and fro in the brackish water. The
only sound, save the sighing of the wind, was the pattering of
rodent feet; for he and Mikey made no noise as they trod the
cobble-stones of the city.

They flitted through the memorial gate. They skirted the
Autobahn for a moment. There were no cars. Then they turned
uphill, towards Mt Poppen. There was a winding path that
narrowed, narrowed, narrowed, narrowed, narrowed, and the
mountain loomed higher and higher until there was no sky,
and still the pathway narrowed until it was a man-wide cleft
cut into the face of the rock . . . and finally there was no
pathway at all . . . there was only the mountain . . .

. . . and the darkness. The cold. And the hunger. Seeping into
his bones. And the darkness. The only sound a steady drip . . .
drip . . . drip . . . echoing. Echoing. Drip. Echoing. Then slowly,
out of the cold and dark, a faint light. Flickering. Ebbing now,
sucked back into the limestone void. Ice-floes that hugged the
interior of the mountain. Dark. Dark.

'Hey, there, Saxenpooper! Been a while!'

Flash! The glint of a razor-sharp incisor. A hint of drool. A
deathsmile forming out of the dimness . . . eyes that burn
crimson . . . eyes. A shock of blond hair and a slit throat. And
the blood, drip–drip–dripping.

'Stevie?' Darrell said.

'You should've paid the Piper with real money,
Saxenpooper.'

'Johnny?'

'There's a lot of us here, Saxenpooper. And there's only one
of you,' Johnny said. His voice buzzed in his severed wind
pipe.

'But I didn't put you here! *He* did. It wasn't me who made
that bargain.'

'There's only one bargain, and you all made it,' said Stevie.

'You and every Sachsenhauser and every man who can't come to terms with Mr Death.'

'You can cheat the Piper, but you can't cheat yourself,' said Mikey.

'You're our new Mr Death, now,' said Stevie. 'Neato.'

Darrell looked around. The panic gripped him. He couldn't breathe. His pulse pounded. Darkness . . . and the eyes. Glimmering, glowering, angry. Then the laughter: squeaky, metallic, punctuated by the drip–drip–drip of children's blood . . . and the cold. The cold. Eyes. More eyes. Eyes. He could smell their breath . . . and the sweat and the junk food and the baby shampoo . . . as they surrounded him, touching him, sucking the warmth from his body with their icy fingers . . . and laughing. Laughing. Laughing.

This time it would never end.

Mr Death's Blue-eyed Boy was originally written for an anthology entitled *Phobias*, edited by Richard Gilliam, Ed Kramer, Wendy Webb and Martin H. Greenberg. I am frightened of many things, so it was hard to focus on one particular phobia; eventually I settled on a fear of children. The story gave me a chance to revisit the folk tale of the Pied Piper, and eventually led to my creating an entire cycle of short fictions that were modern retellings of fairy tales, often in some disturbing psychosexual context.

The Steel American

The steel American was different from all the others. Not that there was any real doubt that he was an American. He spoke English, after all, not Russian; besides, the Russians had just come through the village the week before with their annual promises of tractors and medicine.

He was different because he came alone. Because he was completely encased in platelets of jointed steel, like a television robot. And because he came to *me*. He was *my* American.

At the crest of the hill, past the old stone temple where the man who used to be my husband had meditated, hardly moving, for the last ten years, there was a waterfall where the women used to bathe, mornings, coyly draped in their sarongs. Behind the waterfall was a cave most people were afraid to enter, for it was inhabited by a malevolent spirit, but I've always been good with spirits. The back of the cave opens into a deep, still pool at the bottom of a well of rock. Nobody knew about this pool except me. My mother showed it to me the day after I had my first period, and she told me that its waters contained the secret of our family's youthful appearance. Indeed, until the day she died, my mother had an inexplicably smooth complexion, and it seemed that she aged all at once, within minutes, just before she passed away. It could have been the water, but then again my mother was a shaman; it could have been some other magic.

I too was beautiful. No need for false modesty in a story like this. Yet, in his fortieth year, my husband had turned from me, left me sleeping, crawled out of the mosquito net, climbed the hill, entered the sacred brotherhood of *sangkha*. I was a widow and not a widow.

And every morning at sunrise I bathed in the secret pool, waiting, perhaps, though I did not know for whom I waited. Until I met the steel American.

It was the morning after the last Russian left. I had left my *panung* in the cave. That was one of the reasons I kept the pool so secret; although I was a married woman, I loved to bathe naked, like a child. In this private place, I could let the cool water invade every cranny of my body. As I stood embracing myself, it seemed sometimes that the water itself loved me. It was alive and it made me come alive. It touched places my husband had never learned to touch. It made me forget the shame of having been forsaken.

But not for long. I climbed back up into the cave. Sunrise was pouring down the limestone well. I sat in a shaft of light, drying my hair with my husband's old *phakhomah*. The void inside me ached. I wanted to pray to the guardian *vinyaan* of the hill, but I did not know what to wish for.

At that moment, I heard a crash – iron on rock – like a kettle clattering on the stove. I turned and saw the steel American. At first I didn't think he was human at all; the metal he wore glowed pink and orange in the circle of morning light. The television in the village had not worked in over a year, but I remembered the movie with the robot. No doubt robots were commonplace in America. At first I assumed he was no longer working; perhaps, like transistor radios, he ran on batteries. I did not cover myself, since he did not seem to me to be sentient, but merely a simulacrum of a man.

At that moment the visor slipped and I found myself staring into his eyes. It was too late for modesty, so I just stood there and gaped. The eyes were the colour of the secret pool itself: sometimes brown, sometimes blue, depending on the light; a wisp of golden hair straggled from the helmet. His cheeks were lined and hollow; he seemed to have endured many lifetimes' suffering; but his eyes were the eyes of a boy. I thought he was beautiful, and I was ashamed that I thought him beautiful, and it brought back the memory of my husband, sitting in the lotus position in a pavilion at the monastery and gazing for hours at some inner beauty I could never impersonate. And I began to weep.

'Demons,' said the steel American, 'when you are tired of cajoling, you try tears. But I won't be moved.'

I could understand him after a fashion because I had been learning to read the Bible with Father O'Malley.

'What are you doing here?' I said. 'You're exhausted ... wounded too. You're not a deserter, are you?'

'Of course not,' he said. 'Get thee behind me.'

'I can't ... you're leaning against the wall.'

'Temptress! Whore of Babylon!' he gasped, and then he slumped back again. Father O'Malley used those words sometimes; it was hard to tell whether they were meant for insult or for lovemaking. Why would a wounded American call me names? I recovered enough of my sense of proprieties to slip my panung back on and tuck the fabric around my silver belt, and to throw on my blouse; then I took my plastic *khan* and filled it from the secret pool; then I knelt over him – he was stretched on the cavern floor, his hands clasped together like a corpse prepared for cremation – whispered an ancient formula for making lustral water, threw in a few petals from some wildflower that bloomed from a crack in the rock – I sprinkled the magic liquid over him and waited for him to awaken.

This time, he was a lot more civil.

'Are you an angel?' he said.

'Good,' I said. 'The last time I was a demoness.' I went on sprinkling the water and whispering the meaningless syllables that came unbidden to my lips.

'What country is this?'

'That's a good question,' I said. 'The Russians have told us we're in a liberated zone; you people have told us we're part of a great free nation; all I know is that this mountain is called Doi Xang, that we're a village of Thai speakers, that below us there's a village where they speak Hmong. We're not actually *in* a country, though everyone around us thinks we're in *his*.

We grow opium and raise pigs and ducks. I know that there's a war going on a few kilometres down the mountain, to the northeast of us. Sometimes, at night, we can look down on the flaming jungle and smell the smoke; it's a choking chemical smell mixed with the odour of burning flesh. When the television worked, we sometimes used to see news about the war. But we could never figure out what it was about, so we would switch over to *Lost in Space* or *Leave it to Beaver*. But then, you see, the war doesn't touch us. Nothing does, not even the monsoon. It's because our temple is built over one of the sources of the river.'

The steel American looked at me, wide-eyed and only half-comprehending. I eased his helmet off and his hair, matted and unkempt, fell on to his shoulders. A rancid odour came from inside his iron casing. I wondered how long it had been since he'd removed his armour. I tried to tug off one of his gauntlets. He pushed me away. 'No!' he said. 'I've sworn to live inside this metal shell until the day my quest is fulfilled.'

'I see. It's a bargain you've made with your god.' That was easy to understand; I had tried to deal with the Four-faced Brahma for winning lottery numbers, but I never seemed to come up with the right offering. Or perhaps it was his way of telling me that my special powers were not meant to benefit myself, but the whole village.

'But it's not good for you,' I said ... 'what you're wearing wasn't designed for the tropics. Your god would surely understand.'

'I'm afraid not,' said the steel American. 'He's a hard god. Harder than the steel I gird myself with.'

'I know,' I said, thinking of Father O'Malley, tormenting himself whenever a woman crossed his mind.

'They said I would travel far and wide. And it's true. I've traversed the burning desert of time itself, and I'm still no closer to my goal. They said there'd be a castle of temptation atop a mountain, and a sorceress.'

'Well, this is a castle of sorts, and I did tempt you. Though I didn't mean to. And I *am* a sorceress. I know how to curse, and how to heal. Though for healing I usually prefer penicillin.'

'Your words are dark,' he said. 'Tell me your name, mysterious lady.'

'My name is Mali,' I said. '*Jasmine.*' He looked at me with the kind of longing a pubescent boy has; he did not even know the nature of his longing.

'I am Sir Perceval.'

'Should I call you Sir, or Mr Perceval?'

'Tempt me no more,' he said. I clutched his metal hands in mine. 'I hurt so much I think I'm dying.'

'We can heal you,' I said. 'It's the least we can do.'

'But I have to find the grail!'

'*You* want the grail?' I said. Foreboding gnawed at me. Of all the things demanded of us through the years, by the CIA and the Russians and the Vietnamese and the missionaries and the landstealers, this was the first time someone had asked for something we actually possessed. And it was the one thing we could not give, because it would mean the death of our way of life.

'There's nothing for you here,' I said. 'When your wounds have healed, you can go on your way. Though you've wandered so far astray in space and time that I don't see how you can find your way back.'

'You're lying,' said the steel American. His jointed fingers dug into my hands and stained them with blood and rust. 'You're the sorceress they told me of. This is the castle atop the hill, and this is the stream that heals all wounds.'

I gazed into his eyes and knew that in his purity he saw past my dissembling. What could I tell him? 'Yes,' I said, staring past him at the sweating limestone, 'yes, I was lying. I am that sorceress.'

*

I had to move him out of the cave myself; I didn't want anyone to find out about the secret pool. He was delirious by then; our conversation had taken place in a moment of relative lucidity.

After I had dragged him out to the other side of the waterfall, I saw my daughter Pailin pounding the washing by the side of the stream while her half-brother, Smaan, sat watching from the back of a water-buffalo. I called out to them.

'We've got a new visitor,' I said.

My daughter gathered her washing; Smaan went running back to get help; they managed to heft him on to the village chief's Landrover, and we drove him down to the temple hospice.

I left him lying on a straw mat, in between a pregnant woman and a man with a gangrenous leg, who had crawled all the way to our village from a prison camp in the hope of being healed.

I didn't want him up and about and frightening the villagers, so I placed a sleeping spell over his eyes, and I told Smaan and his friends that if they said anything to anyone I would make sure they were reincarnated as cockroaches; they nodded and ran off to play among the ruined pagodas that jutted from the wild grass like the mountain's teeth. He would sleep at least until evening; by then, perhaps, I would have a plan.

My daughter sat cross-legged, mixing a love potion on the veranda of our house, her baby slung across her back. Smaan was still trying to fix the television.

The baby squalled. 'Oh, mother, hold her for me,' Pailin said.

I took the child in my arms. 'You're using my mortar and pestle,' I said. 'I wish you'd use your own things when you do experiments.'

She was pounding furiously: locusts, hemp, toadstools, a little horse fat. 'Your things have more magic than mine do,' she said, 'and I need the strongest I can get.'

She seemed barely older than my grandchild. I wondered whether she, too, would age all at once, in the minutes before her death. Although the baby was half-Russian – we hadn't been able to save the father – no one dared ridicule my daughter, because they were afraid I would send a spirit in the night.

'You don't need to attract a husband yet; you're only thirteen.'

She smiled and looked away. There was no need to remind me that she had been offered five thousand baht for a two-year contract at a brothel in Chiang Rai.

'The new American,' she said, 'is the most beautiful man I have ever seen.' Suddenly I noticed a strand of blond hair in the mixture and I realized that my daughter was in love. With a man who was forbidden to make love! I knew what it was like to love such a man, and my heart ached for her.

'Don't think about him. He's made a bargain with Phra Yesu, the Christian god; he is not allowed to remove his iron skin.'

'That's ridiculous, Younger Mother,' said Smaan. 'How can he shit?'

'Who knows?' I said. 'A sliding panel, perhaps.'

'Well,' said my daughter, 'if he can have a sliding panel for that, he might just as easily have a sliding panel for the other.'

'That's absurd,' I said, but then I thought, why not? The Americans are not entirely human. The Vietnamese, the montagnards, even the Russians are easier to fathom.

*

I went to see Father O'Malley first, because of all our visitors he was the craziest. Madmen are best at penetrating to the core of things.

The father's church, like all the other buildings in the village, was on stilts, and thatched. It was the time of the year that we hang phallic fetishes from the eaves of our houses to make sure that the earth renews itself. The sandalwood phallus brushed my face as I walked on to the veranda. I knew Father O'Malley would remove it as soon as he found it, but someone would soon sneak another one back up; there are some things that you just don't trifle with.

I washed my feet from the rainwater jar and left my sandals in front of the threshold; then I took some holy water, crossed myself and genuflected as I went inside. O'Malley sat on the altar, scratching his head: a fat, balding, sweaty man. An electric fan, powered by the battery of a van that idled outside,

blew right in his face; the rest of the church was stifling hot.
The air was thick with opium smoke.

'Oh, Mali,' he said. 'Come for your reading lessons? Or
perhaps you're in need of religious succour? It's Sunday, isn't
it? So hard to keep track.'

'You haven't kept track for five years, Father.' It had been
that long since O'Malley staggered into our village, gibbering
about women being raped to death and babies sliced in two.
There were no wounds in his flesh, but his soul seemed ravaged
beyond repair; even now he had barely begun to heal. We
couldn't in all compassion send him back out, so he was
allowed to build his church, though of course no one wor-
shipped there.

'We were studying the Apocalypse, weren't we?' he said,
reaching behind the altar for a weatherbeaten Bible.

'Yes. But I don't want to read about religion today. Can we
go back to what we were looking at last week ... the Arthurian
romances?'

He laughed. There was a whole pile of books – mostly
reclaimed from corpses found rotting in the jungle – and among
them was *A Child's Treasury of Arthurian Tales*. That was where
I'd first read about the grail, and that was how I had been
certain that it was in our village.

He opened that book and I got into position, that is to say I
lay, face up, on the altar and unclasped my silver belt, and
undid the buttons on my blouse. Father O'Malley discreetly
turned his back and faced the bamboo crucifix. One hand held
the book open; the other reached behind, grasped at the air for
a few moments before landing, by accident it seemed, on my
exposed breast. Lightly the fingers drummed as Father O'Malley read to me and I listened, filling in the words I couldn't
understand with my own vision of how things must have been
in the olden times ...

*Phra Yesu, the Christian god, who was an incarnation of the god
Vishnu, made his disciples drink his blood from a silver cup called the
Holy Grail. It was a magic blood which could heal the universe. But
Phra Yesu was attached to material things and could not free himself*

from the sexual desire for Mary Magdalene, who was an incarnation
of Maya, the deceiving one, who tempted Buddha under the Bo tree.
So Phra Yesu was made to suffer crucifixion instead of being granted
enlightenment. And the silver cup was lost.

This was the gist of what I gleaned from the priest's dis-
course. I could not make out all the words, but oh, the severe
beauty of their sounds! I loved the clash and grinding of those
English consonants, the elusive imprecision of those vowels.
Father O'Malley's left hand had worked its way to my pubes
now, and his index finger was warily circling my clitoris. I tried
to concentrate on puzzling out the story, but his touch had
already begun to tease the waters within me.

The Fisher King lay wounded in his castle ...

'Yes, yes,' I said, 'but who is Sir Perceval?'

'Let me find where it talks about him.'

Softly his left hand skimmed the hair of my pubis. I trembled.
I was thinking of the first time my husband touched me. He'd
started to waken my body and then without warning he
shuddered and fell still ... the mosquito netting hung heavy,
drenched with the moisture of night. Lizards barked as they
darted from cupboard to cupboard. I lay awake while my new
husband slept; sometimes, through the wire-mesh window, the
sky lit up with the soundless fire of the distant war; I was
sixteen; my husband was thirty-five; I cried as I fingered the
amulet I wore to ward off the spirits that cluster around at
night, when we are most vulnerable. In those days, the war was
still far away. These days we could hear it as well as see the
flashes in the jungle.

The pure fool came to Klingsor's stronghold ... the maidens danced
around him, displaying their wanton charms and daring him to fall
into temptation ...

Father O'Malley dropped his book. He sighed. Perhaps he
had ejaculated beneath that sweat-soaked cassock of his.
Abruptly he knelt at the altar, retrieved a bundle of *mayom*
branches that he kept tied up next to his bag of frankincense;
he unbuttoned his cassock, stripped down to his waist, and,
gazing intently at the face of Phra Yesu on the cross, began

whipping himself furiously. He showed more passion than when he had furtively caressed me. I lay on the altar, unfulfilled, just as I had with my husband. This was how our reading lessons generally ended up.

When Father O'Malley finished flagellating himself, he eased his cassock back over his bruised flesh, went to the back and got a bottle of Coke and two glasses. I buttoned myself up quickly and joined him in one of the pews, sipping my soda and watching him try to ignore his pain.

'I don't know why you beat yourself afterwards,' I said. 'Surely you know that the sex drive can't simply be flogged away.'

'Then how does your husband manage?'

'He's a holy man,' I said, and looked at the floor.

'So am I,' said Father O'Malley. He too looked at the floor. A gecko ran past with a struggling dragonfly in its mouth.

'Perhaps you were a holy man once,' I said, 'but you have fallen from grace. Or so you claim.'

'We are all fallen,' he said.

'Don't you want to make love to me just once? Don't you feel hypocritical, clutching the book of learning with your right hand and groping me with your left, and feeling so filthy afterwards that you have to flagellate yourself?'

'Of course I want to make love to you,' he said, his voice trembling, 'but that is between you and your husband. It's what God has ordained.'

'I'm afraid my husband is journeying towards the extinguishment of desire. And I'm left out.'

To distract him, and to prevent him from falling prey to his temptation and having to hurt himself again, I told him about the steel American and his quest for the grail. I told him that the man lay up at the hospice, lost in an enchanted sleep.

'He was wearing armour?' Father O'Malley paged through the *King Arthur* book until he found what purported to be a picture of Sir Perceval.

'That's him!' I said. 'But more emaciated. And then the artist doesn't do justice to his eyes. His eyes stare right past things as though they're not there. I wasn't even sure he felt anything when he saw me naked.' A thought occurred to me. 'He hasn't come to take you back, has he? I mean, you *are* a deserter after all. Or a spy.'

'It's nothing like that. It's just that ... well, he's not real anyway. He's like everything else in this damned village ... an illusion. You know as well as I do that I can't go back ... that you're all part of some *Twilight Zone*-like hallucination that I'm having ... that I'm really out in that jungle with my left arm shattered, drowning in a swamp of leeches ... my death is still going on, a split second stretched out to for ever.'

'There, there,' I said, stroking his hand. 'Of course we're an illusion. Life itself is an illusion, according to the Lord Buddha. My husband could tell you more.' A feature of Father O'Malley's madness was that he believed he was dead, and that this place was some kind of psychedelic purgatory. 'But you'll want to be on hand when he wakes up. He might need another American to talk to.'

'He'd be English, not American.'

'Makes no difference ... American, Russian, Martian, suit yourself.'

'Maybe he'll need spiritual counselling,' Father O'Malley said.

'You really miss being a priest, don't you? I mean, you haven't made any converts here ... except for Nit, the village idiot, and she thinks that drinking the sacramental wine is just another word for giving you a blowjob.'

'I've failed her. But I can't go back. I don't have the guts to face ... what's out there. Beyond the—'

A sacred *saisin* ran the perimeter of the village. Every evening I would walk all the way around, making sure the cord was taut, looping it through banana trees and bamboo thickets, whispering the words that keep away evil. O'Malley was convinced that beyond the *saisin* was another universe, a world more real than ours.

Leaving the church, I saw that Smaan and his friends were

kicking something around. It was a human head. Russian, from the headgear. I yelled at them to stop.

'The head is the seat of the soul,' I said. 'Show some respect. The pigs will eat it if you don't give it a decent cremation.'

'But we found it outside the *saisin*,' said Smaan. 'And it's only a *farang*'s head anyways.'

I glared at him, and at length he lifted the head up high, like a flag, and the boys marched off towards the jungle, whistling *She's Got a Ticket to Ride*.

I had an exorcism and a childbirth that afternoon, so it was almost evening by the time I went in to look at the Holy Grail.

★

I don't know how long the Holy Grail had been in our village. Before the grail, there had been other relics. There used to be a herb called *moly* that could cure even death; a bearded adventurer named Gilgamesh had come for it. That was in my mother's time. Or maybe my grandmother's. We had a golden fleece once, but all that remained of it was a shiny hank of wool.

The Holy Grail took many forms. It was never that shimmering golden chalice hovering in the air, haloed with rainbow light, like in Father O'Malley's book. There were times when its power had resided in a broken Coke bottle. But for a few years now it had been that lowliest of household objects, the *khan* we use for drawing from the stoneware jars, tall as a ten-year-old boy, that we set out for catching the waters of the monsoon. Sir Perceval had already seen the grail; he had come within a finger's breadth of touching it.

There was a locked room in the temple that held these treasures. The women of my family had held the key to the room since the beginning, before there was even a temple, before the Indians came to our country and converted the people to the teachings of Buddha: in the days when everyone listened to the spirits of tree and rock. In those days they didn't need people like me to interpret the language of spirits. Then we learned from the Buddhist missionaries that the spirits were illusions; that we ourselves are but shadows.

Nothing exists.

In the main hall of the temple I knelt with three joss sticks before the ten-metre-long reclining image of Lord Buddha. I said my *namo dasa* three times, stuck the joss sticks in the burner, drank in the sweet smell of incense. Then, making sure no one could see me, I crawled on my hands and knees under the tiers of altars stacked high with fruit and flowers and fresh eggs, and I crept underneath the statue, past the stucco hem of Lord Buddha's robe, until I faced the wall with the faded fresco of a gateway guarded by angels.

The key was a mantra that I repeated three times; then I was inside the room.

The room that was also the well of rock above the pool of still cool water.

The plastic *khan* I had bought at the Sunday market in the next village for twenty-five satang ... which I'd filled with healing water and sprinkled over the steel American ... it lay on a slab of rock beside the pool, where I'd last left it. I felt an overwhelming relief. The relic had a mind of its own; there were times when it refused to be found.

I held the *khan* in my cupped hands. The room spun around me. I muttered the mantra three times in reverse and presently I found myself outside, treading across the stepping-stones to the pavilion beside the stream.

My husband sat there in his saffron robes, in the lotus position, on a reed mat; my stepson, his *phakhomah* hitched up, stood thigh-deep in the water casting a fishing-net.

I prostrated myself before him, keep my distance so that he would not be polluted by the touch of a woman.

'Holiness,' I said, 'there's a new American. He's asking for the grail.'

'Then you must give it to him,' he said.

There were those in the village who believed that my husband neither ate nor slept, and that he had sustained the lotus position for over ten years. I knew better, but you can't argue with superstition.

'How can I?' I said. 'We gave away the golden fleece. We gave away the golden apples of the sun. The magical herb. The mistletoe. The urn of the demon's heart.'

'We are a very giving people.'

My stepson held a wriggling fish in both hands. He held it up, laughing. 'Breakfast, honoured father!' he said.

'Don't wave it at me now,' said my husband. 'Temptation, you know.' For monks may not eat after midday.

'But,' I said, 'everyone for miles around knows that this is the village that heals. The war rages around us and we're untouched. Wounded men come crawling past the *saisin* and we cure them. Without the grail—'

'Oh, nonsense. It's just an old plastic bowl that you bought for twenty-five satang.'

My husband placed his prayer fan in front of his face and chanted for about half an hour. The words of the mantra spoke of transience and the insubstantiality of fleshly desires. Smaan gutted fish and tossed them into a bucket. The pavilion smelled of sandalwood and night-blooming jasmine; moisture was condensing out of the evening air.

At length my husband stopped his chanting. He continued the conversation as though no time had elapsed at all. 'You see,' he said, 'we are in the business of fulfilling secret desires ... that's why the travellers come here ... and that's why they often find it so hard to leave. That is how the ones who come here are healed. That is why some cannot be healed ... they just don't have the yearning to be healed.'

'I can't believe that Father O'Malley's secret desire is to fumble around inside a woman's *panung* ... and to whip himself afterwards.'

'Yet he won't get up and walk away.'

'If that *is* what he really wants, though, doesn't it mean his mind is sick and that we haven't succeeded in healing him at all?'

'It's not our place to say who is sick and who is whole.'

As always, my husband spoke in riddles; as always, I knew that the answer to my dilemma lay somewhere in his words. He launched into another bout of chanting. I wanted to fling myself at him and shout, 'What about *my* secret desire, what about my need for you to come back down from the mountain and put your arms around me and make me fully a woman?' But I knew he would only answer with an enigmatic smile.

'I'm taking the fish home for Pailin to cook,' Smaan said, and he started to lope downhill, swinging the bucket and whistling.

'The boys were kicking around a human head this afternoon,' I said. 'Any moment, the barrier's going to break and the horrors beyond the *saisin* are going to leak into our world ... don't you care about that?'

A bomber passed overhead. Behind the next ridge of mountains, the evening sky was bright with the aurora of warfare.

My husband said, 'Remember the story of King Vessandar, who gave away his very children – those most precious to him – to a beggar, because he had managed to free himself even from love itself, that most persistent of desires. It was only when he had relinquished even love that he was free to be reborn as the Lord Buddha.'

*

I went down to the hospice. I cured a lame child, and I let a man die in peace who had been consumed by tuberculosis, whose every breath was agony. Then I went to the room where Sir Perceval lay. Father O'Malley was already there; he sat beside the knight with open Bible, peering at the words in the light of a kerosene lamp.

On the walls, the frescoes of heaven and hell seemed to dance.

'Back off,' I said. 'I'm going to wake him now.'

I waved my hands over the steel American's eyes.

'Don't listen to the woman,' Father O'Malley said to him as he stirred. 'She is a seductress; she'll lead you away from your quest.' Always woman the evil one, woman the temptress, sex as the ultimate darkness; I marvelled at the alienness of Christian thinking.

The eyes opened. They fixed on me. I knew that I was beautiful, like my mother, and that no man save my husband could resist me. I wondered whether he could still be moved by carnal passion or whether, inside that cage of steel, he had succumbed to atrophy. I had to know, because it was the only way to keep my village safe from him.

'You're the angel who tempted me by the pool,' he said.

'Is the grail the thing that you truly desire?'

'Yes.' But the eyes told me a different story, and I dared hope that I could win my people a reprieve from the entropy that afflicts all transient things.

'Then I'll have to give it to you,' I said. 'This village is the place that rewards all seekers with the object of their quest. If the grail is what you truly desire, meet me at midnight at the secret pool, the one only you and I know about.'

I left so Father O'Malley could hear the knight's confession.

★

I found my daughter still concocting her potion, and I told her I was going to have to borrow it.

'Oh, mother,' she said. 'At your age.' I was twenty-nine years old. 'You know it will only work if there's something there to work with.'

'I believe there is.'

'Oh, mother! *I* wanted that man to make love to me! All day I've been dreaming about the milk-white skin beneath the steel, unburned by the sun and moon. It's cruel of you to take him from me.'

'Trust me, Pailin.' I embraced her. I was glad now that she had used my implements to make the potion. 'There will be others. Your time will come.'

I sat in meditation until I felt the spirit of my mother, and her mother before her, and so on, back to the beginning of time, take possession of me, one at a time. At midnight I walked back uphill to the temple, crawled behind the giant statue of Lord

Buddha, and murmured the mantra that opened the wall to the secret pool beyond the cave.

The steel American was already there, kneeling by the side of the water, his hands clasping his sword. He had doffed his helmet as was proper in the presence of the divine. When I appeared, on the rock in the centre of the pool, with my *panung* bound tightly about my breasts, he looked up.

'I have brought you your heart's desire,' I said. The same words that my ancestresses spoke to the world's great wanderers. I held out to him the plastic *khan* filled with my daughter's potion.

'I knew you were an angel,' said Sir Perceval. 'I've kept myself pure. I've done everything I knew how to try to be worthy of this moment. Deo gracias.' Humbly he stretched his hands out to receive the relic.

I held the plastic bowl in my hand and I knew what he saw: a jewelled chalice, cunningly wrought, floating on a cloud of light. I stood above him as he knelt.

'Look into my eyes,' I said, and as he gazed up at me and the moon behind me I poured the sacred water and the love potion over him so that the liquid grazed his lips and scalded the scales of reality from his eyes . . . and I said, 'Perceval, Perceval, I am here to give you the thing you most desire. You have fulfilled your vow and you no longer need that armour. Free yourself, Sir Perceval.' I did not add, *Free me,* but I felt myself strain against the cage of my ensorcellment, the cage I had crafted around myself, the cage of my self-inflicted shame . . . and the pure fool, whose eyes betrayed his true desires because he did not have the art of dissembling, he cried out, 'Yes, I have fulfilled my vow!' and all at once the armour seemed to melt from him and scatter across the cool still water like a million beads of quicksilver.

Oh, he was beautiful. His skin was so pale it seemed to be wrought from the very moonlight. His penis was like a fetish carved from teakwood. His hair streamed up towards the stars as though drawing upon their brilliance. And his eyes – in the moments before they lost their innocence – were the eyes of a child. I knew then that I loved him, had always loved him even before I knew he existed for me to love.

I unloosed the knot that held my *panung* over my breasts and it too swirled away; and he seized the bowl and drained the potion and then he kissed me; and I was awakened; and we made love, in the circle of moonlight, in the water that churned and lashed and trickled in time to our passion as though it were one with the waters inside us, our blood, our sweat, our sexual fluids. I was beautiful and I knew that he found me beautiful; I knew that my breasts were ripe and fragrant as young mangoes, and my breath as intoxicating as the jasmine of the evening. I gave him all I had withheld from other men. The void that no one had filled, I let him fill; took him into myself, like a mother receiving her child back into the womb and saying to it, *Do not be born, for the world is full of suffering.* It was my last and finest magicking.

And afterwards, when I held him in my arms, feeling the water's turbulence die down, I watched the steel American grow old and withered and disintegrate into the pool ... his eyes last of all, still fixed on mine even as his flesh lost all its substance ... I watched him fade into the past whence he had come ... and I still held the plastic *khan* in my hand, and knew that the village would endure.

*

Our television sputtered to life soon after that. But my eyes became too dim to watch it, and now I sit on the steps where visitors leave their shoes, chewing betelnut and letting my grandchildren describe the images they see. On this television, they tell me, brutal images of war alternate with reruns of *I Love Lucy*.

Today Father O'Malley came to visit me. He walks with a cane now. We read together from the book of the Apocalypse, and for old times' sake he touched me; we made love as old people do, getting more comfort from our closeness than excitement.

'Will the steel American ever be back?' I mused, as we lay together beneath the mosquito netting.

'How should I know? I'm only a deserting army chaplain, not a shamaness.'

The *saisin* had been brought in closer to the village, and now, when we walked over to the stream, it was rare to find that it was not red with human blood, or there were no bloated corpses floating slowly towards the main river. 'Do you still believe that our village isn't real?'

'Yes,' he said. 'If I leave, I will find that a thousand years have passed, or that I am dead and buried.'

Afterwards, he did not whip himself. He is coming to terms with his secret nature.

Tomorrow is my husband's funeral. Everybody is happy, as he led an exemplary life and we are glad to hasten him towards nirvana.

I no longer bathe in the sacred pool. For me there is no cave behind the waterfall. The mantra in the temple no longer works; it ceased to work shortly after I told my daughter the secret.

But I still try to go back. For, though I loved him and killed him, though I fulfilled his desire by relinquishing my own, though I lied to him by telling him the truth, and betrayed all that he believed in . . . I cannot exorcise him from my mind. All my life I waited for the void to be filled, only to find that no void can be filled, no hunger satiated, until the day the soul steps away from the ceaseless cycle of *sansara* and dissolves in the cool still pool at the heart of the world.

Sometimes I toy with the idea of leaving the village. Beyond the *saisin* there are many roads. Perhaps, circling back on myself, I will find the steel American again, and my own young self, unchanged, still charged with magic.

The Steel American is my Vietnam War Holy Grail story, and was originally written for an anthology called *Grails*.

Gingerbread

When we went to live in Hollywood, we saw many wonderful things. We saw many cruel things. Some people touched our hearts and some people touched our bodies. We grew up much too fast, and when we were all grown we found we'd been trapped in our childhood for ever.

This is me, Greta Blackburn, writing all this down so my brother Johnny will one day remember if he chooses to. I can write real good now because there are a lot of books here and they let me take as many as I want into my room and I can keep them there without signing for them or anything.

On Sundays, a screenwriter comes to the institution and tells us stories. His name is Bob, and he is unemployed. But I've never seen him panhandling for money, and he wears expensive clothes. He is nice, kind of, and he never lays a hand on us. He is a volunteer. The Writers Guild has this program where they send writers to talk to people like us. It's supposed to keep us anchored to the real world.

Bob encourages me to write and he makes me keep a diary. Every week he reads what I've written and corrects most of the grammar. He doesn't correct all of it because sometimes he thinks it's charming the way it is.

I know I am too old to listen to stories but I go because of my brother. He doesn't talk much anymore, but I think he is taking it all in. The time Bob told us the story of Hansel and Gretel, I could see that Johnny was paying attention, because he fixed on Bob with those clear blue eyes. That made me listen too. That's how I finally figured out what Titania Midnight was. I hadn't been able to put my finger on it, not until I heard Bob read us that fairy tale, but the moment I realized it, it was obvious.

Titania Midnight was a witch.

★

We didn't meet her until the second time. The first time our parents tried to dump us, they didn't succeed. That's because Johnny had snuck down to the kitchen for a Snickers bar, and he overheard them in their prayer meeting. He woke me up by banging on the ladder that goes up to the top bunk. 'Greta,' he said, 'they're gonna take us away and . . . and they're gonna *ditch* us.'

I was groggy and I thought he'd wet the bed again, but he just kept shaking me, and finally I crept out of bed, just so he'd calm down, and I went downstairs with him.

They were in the living room. There was a drape we used to hide behind whenever we listened to them arguing. It was a nice living room with big vinyl sofas, a mahogany piano and a painting of Jesus over the fireplace, with big kind eyes. I couldn't see Daddy but I knew he was standing right in front of that painting and drawing his authority from the Lord. 'It's all settled, Martha,' he was saying, 'no ifs, ands or buts about it. I've prayed on it, and I've begged the Lord to take this cup from us, but he said, "I've made up my mind, Jed, and there ain't nothing more to say about it." And you'd best obey me, because you're my wife, and the apostle Paul says—'

'Maybe it wasn't the Lord talking to you. I mean, to abandon your own kids . . . maybe it was . . . someone else . . . you know . . . *mimicking* the Lord.'

'You calling me a Satanist, Martha?'

'Told you,' Johnny whispered, and he gulped down his second candy bar.

'But how can we know they'll be all right?' Mom said.

'We have to trust in the Lord. They'll be provided for, long as they don't stray from the paths of righteousness.'

I hugged my brother and said, 'We have to make a plan.'

Later, when we were settled in again, Daddy came into our

bedroom. He checked to make sure Johnny was snoring. Then he sat down on the bottom bunk next to me and slowly peeled down the sheet. I half opened my eyes. In the blue glow of the Smurfs nightlight my father's face looked like the face of a demon. As usual, I pretended to be fast asleep, and I waited for it to end. But this time he didn't start right away. Instead, he began to talk, in a sweet voice full of hurting, a voice I'd never heard him use before.

Daddy said, 'Forgive me, I'm not a bad man, there's just something that comes over me and I can't help myself...' and then, 'if only you knew how much I love you baby but I can't talk about those things I'm just a sinner and your mother don't understand...' and then he called me tender nicknames he would never use when I was awake. But after a while his voice grew harsh, and he said, 'God damn them to hell, them Ayrabs and them Chinks that take away a decent Christian's job, and them usury-practising Kikes that caused this damn recession and take bread out of our mouths ... the Krauts should've never let them crawl out of them ovens, damn them, damn damn damn,' and he called me *bitch* and *whore* and I just squeezed my eyes tight shut and made myself very small and very far away until he was all done with me.

The next morning, after breakfast, they made sure we brushed our teeth, then we got into the station wagon and set off. Daddy had to go to a job interview first, and we waited in the car. He came out looking dour.

'God damn all them Goldbergs and Goldsteins and Goldfarbs and Gold-shitass-Satan-worshipping baby-sacrificing Jewboys,' he said. 'A decent Christian can't get enough to feed his family, and they own half the damn country.'

'Jed, please don't curse,' said our mother, 'not in front of the children.'

They left us at some shopping mall, told us they'd pick us up in an hour, and went away. But we were prepared for that, and we had memorized every turn and every street name, and by sunset we managed to walk all the way home.

Daddy prayed on it all night. He didn't even come into our

bedroom. Johnny peed the bed, but I overslept and didn't strip the sheets. They didn't notice, just fed us breakfast and told us to wait in the garage.

The second time, they locked us in the trunk and they drove and drove, and Johnny was carsick and we could hardly breathe. Johnny cried all the way. Partly it was the sugar that made him hard to deal with. I guess that's why they wanted to ditch us. Still, I was the one who took care of him most of the time. I'm a good girl.

★

When we woke up, we were in a blind alley, and it was night. There was a dumpster leaning against the wall, so I knew that we wouldn't go hungry. But it was cold and I didn't know how late it was or how long we had been there. Johnny was whimpering because he hadn't had a candy bar in a long time. From beyond the wall we could hear a buzzy kind of music and there were neon lights flashing in rhythm to it. There were people chattering, too, and the sound of spiked heels on concrete, and, now and then, a police siren. But inside the alley it was all quiet and dark.

'It hurts all over,' Johnny said.

'Maybe we should go back to sleep for a while,' I said, because I knew that when you're asleep there is no pain. We curled up together but the pavement was damp and cold, and finally we climbed up on the dumpster and found comfy places among the trash, which was not bad; back home, Daddy sometimes made us sleep in the garbage to teach us a lesson. He'd say, 'You're poor, and you're white, so you might as well be trash too.' I got a better deal because Johnny had a lot of fat on him and his butt made a pretty good cushion after I wedged it tight against the metal casing with a beer bottle.

The next time I woke up, it was still night, and I was looking into Titania Midnight's eyes. She was shining a flashlight in my face, and she was all in shadow, except for her eyes. They were sunken into a mess of wrinkles, but they were young eyes, and kind, like the painting of Jesus in our living room. 'By Isis and Hecate,' she said, 'I've struck gold tonight.'

That was when Johnny woke up and he started carrying on like he always does. 'Double gold,' said Titania Midnight, 'even though the second nugget is a little . . . dare I say it . . . *larded*.'

'That ain't nice,' I said. 'Johnny can't help being, um, *ample*. It's his glands.'

'Oh, I daresay, I daresay. But within the chrysalis, something beautiful, no? You'll come with me, of course; you'll want food.'

'I had pizza earlier. It was still warm even, two slices, pepperoni. But Johnny has to have his sugar fix or he'll get crazy.'

'I've just the thing.' She rummaged in a tote bag and gave something to Johnny. 'Baked it myself. Gingerbread is best. I think it blends a lot better than brownie mix.'

'Blends with what?' I said.

'Oh, oh, you innocent, wide-eyed creature. Fundamentalist parents, I'll bet. Raped you too, I wouldn't wonder. Maybe not the boy, he's so *gelatinous*. No wonder you bolted.'

I didn't understand what she was talking about, but she seemed kind, like in the parable of the good Samaritan. Johnny gobbled the gingerbread cookie greedily and asked for another one.

'Oh, nonsense,' she said, 'you'll be stoned out of your ever-loving mind.'

She asked us our names and she told us hers. I thought it was a fishy-sounding name, but I didn't want to be impolite. I'm a good girl.

'Well,' she said. 'Come along now. You'll be wanting to freshen up. Get a decent night's sleep and all that. No time to stand around chit-chatting. Hollywood's like the Forest of Arden. Anything can happen. Sorcery. Gender confusion. Love potions that make you see a donkey as a sex object. Whew! But it's a magic place. You'll see. Wonder piled on wonder.'

I helped Johnny out of the trash and dusted him off a little bit. We followed Titania out of the alley and that's when the lights and the music hit us full blast. God, it was wild. Posters tall as buildings with painted ladies on them and musclemen in just their underwear, and a big Chinese dragon that lit up and wall-to-wall cars and hip-hop make the pavement quake and skateboarders with long hair on one side and bald on the other and people snapping pictures everywhere and stars on the sidewalks and a dinosaur climbing up the side of one building ... oh, it was Disneyland. I held Johnny's hand tight because he gets frightened easily. But actually he didn't seem to mind even though he had never been among so many people in his life. His eyes just seemed to go all glassy. The gingerbread must have been real good.

Everyone seemed to know who Titania was. People would come up to her and she would smile at them or wave. The colours of the lights kept changing and sometimes she seemed young and sometimes she seemed old. She had a nose like a parrot's beak and her lips were red as cherries and her eyelids were all covered with gold paint. A man in a white suit came up to her and pointed at us, but she said, 'Don't you touch any of my babies, you hear? They're too good for the likes of you.'

And I whispered in Johnny's ear, 'She's nice. She'll protect us. Maybe she's our guardian angel.'

'Yeah,' Johnny said, and then he giggled for no reason at all.

We turned down a side street and then another one. This was a narrow street and all dark, except for one neon sign, blinking, and it read

PSYCHIC READER AND ADVISOR
DONUTS

and I knew that there had never been any place like *that* where we came from. From the street it seemed like just a regular doughnut place and there were a couple of customers inside including a policeman. Next to the entrance was a real narrow unpaved alley with high walls and there was a side door. Titania used three keys to let us in, and then she punched in a code on the security pad inside the doorway.

Inside there was a dingy living room. A black girl was lying

on the rug watching *Murphy Brown*. The clock on the wall said
3 a.m., so it must have been a videotape. She looked up at us.
'Hey,' she said, 'I thought you said no more kids.'

'No jealous fits, now, Laverne,' said Titania, 'you really must
learn to share.'

'Where they gone sleep?' Laverne said. 'And what about
lardass there? You could strip him and sell him for parts, maybe,
but in one piece, he wouldn't even make it round the block.'
She frowned and flicked the remote to MTV. I knew it was
MTV, even though we didn't have cable back home, because it
showed Satanic stuff.

'Oh, you cruel heartless beast,' Titania said, but there was no
malice in the way she said it. 'Put on the light; let's have a look
at this one. Ai, ai, ai . . . what are we to do with him?'

Laverne got up and switched on a naked light bulb that
swung from the ceiling. All of a sudden the room was harshly
lit. I could see more of the room. One side of it was all drapes;
they were a tad open and I could see through to a big kitchen,
maybe where they made the doughnuts. The walls were
covered with signed photographs of famous actors. The shag
carpeting was spotty . . . one or two places looked like puke
stains. Titania and the black girl were leading Johnny by the
hand until he was right under the light, and they were studying
him, like dissecting a frog in school.

'You know,' Titania said, 'Laverne, you are too ready to flush
people down the toilet bowl of existence. This one has possi-
bilities. Notice the eyes, how big they are. They are the eyes of
an angel. And the flesh, well, the flesh . . . even though we are
not Michelangelo, can we not see David in this block of marble?
Can we not whittle? Hone? Hollow the pudginess so the
cheekbones stand proud, even arrogant? And look at his
sullenness. The lips can be worked into a wilful pout. Strip
him for parts indeed!' They were all poking him and looking at
his teeth and looking down his shorts and Johnny started to
cry. And Titania let go of him and made Laverne step back,
and she said, 'That's it. The finishing touch. Listen to that

weeping. It's like the cry of the seagulls over some solitary isle in the bitter cold North Sea.'

'I think I know what you're getting at,' Laverne said slowly.

'What *is* she getting at?' I said, and I could feel my stomach curl up.

'He will be our fortune!' Titania cried, and kissed Johnny wetly on the lips, which caused him to make one of his goofy faces. They laughed. 'He'll have the beautification room,' Titania said. 'As for . . . Greta, was it? . . .'

'I ain't sharing my room with no honky greenhorn,' Laverne said.

'Oh, you were always selfish.'

'You can tell she's not right for us!' Laverne said. 'She gots a strong firm body like a who', but she don't have a who's eyes. She be needing one of your magic potions every time she goes to work.'

Suddenly, for the first time, I panicked. 'You can't split us up!' I said. 'We've never been apart, not for one minute! And I'm the only one who can tell when his sugar's off.'

That set both of them to laughing, and Johnny to carrying on still more, and I could feel a few tears brimming up in my eyes too, until it dawned on me that there would be no visit from Daddy tonight. I realized I had died and gone to heaven.

★

The beautification room was about the size of a large closet but it had a TV and a VCR. It could only be locked from the outside. The door had a little glass pane where you could look in. There was no toilet but Titania gave him a potty that she made me empty once a day. She fed him on nothing but water and little blue pills. I told her he needed sugar but she said, 'It's okay, hon, this is just for a little while, the dexies will get him thinned down, bring out those dimpled cheekbones.'

Titania was the only one who had the key, but you could talk to Johnny by putting your ear right on the pane to listen, and putting your lips up to the glass and talking soft enough so the sound wouldn't carry beyond the corridor. But I couldn't touch

Johnny and I knew that upset him. Still, I didn't want to complain too much to my host. I was a good girl, and I had been through a lot worse times than this.

It wasn't much fun sleeping with Laverne at first though. She used to hog the thing you folded out to sleep on (she called it a futon) and she would talk about me as though I wasn't there, and even when she talked directly *to* me she made it sound like I was stupid. But a lot of the time she was gone all night, and I could sleep by myself, which was great because it was a tiny room, the size of a large bathroom maybe, with no windows.

When Laverne got home – it didn't matter how late it was – she kicked me out of the futon so I was at least halfway on the floor. She would turn on the television and smoke cigarettes.

She was addicted to the Jeffrey Dahmer case, which was on the late, late news every day. 'I *love* Jeff,' she would say. 'I think he's beautiful. He eats people alive. He's the Grim Reaper.'

I didn't know if that was a satanic thing to say or not. I shut up about it mostly. But no matter how late she came in, she would always go flick, flick, flick with the cable controller until she found some piece of news about him. It was scary how obsessed she was. The third night, even though I was afraid she'd bully me and tell me to shut up, I just came out and asked her why she didn't watch something more pleasant. She only said, 'Sometimes I wish he'd carve *me* up.'

'But why would you say that?' I said. 'Aren't you happy here?'

'Sure,' she said, 'sure, Laverne happy.'

In the dark room all I could see were her eyes, large and round and full of disappointment. I thought she was just contrary. Things were good for us girls. We had a lot to eat. And even though Titania didn't let Johnny eat anything at all, it was true that Johnny was shedding his rolls of fat. By the third day, looking at him through the pane in the door, I could see what Titania meant. Johnny was beautiful, and I cussed myself out because I, his own sister, hadn't seen fit to notice a plain fact like that, right under my very own nose. His eyes were getting more and more like the eyes of the Jesus that hung in our living room over the fireplace.

'Titania,' I said over dinner, 'you must know magic or something.'

'I do,' she said. 'Finish your corn muffins and take Johnny his pills. And empty his chamberpot and weigh him and get dolled up, because we're going into Beverly Hills.'

I used to watch *Beverly Hills 90210* every week, of course, so naturally this was the most exciting moment for me since we arrived in Hollywood. Titania made me borrow some of Laverne's clothes. They were tight and skimpy but Titania kept telling me I looked beautiful. Then she made me put on make-up so I looked like a painted whore of Babylon. I guess I did anyway, because though I had never been to Babylon I'd heard Daddy talking about them often enough, and I knew they weren't good girls like me. But I was afraid not to do what Titania said because she had been so good to me. And then again I thought of Johnny, locked up in the beautification room, with the ugliness melting away from him with the pills and the starvation, and I knew that what Titania was doing was a dark mystery ... like the changing of water into wine. If Titania could really work miracles, she had to be connected to the Holy Spirit somehow, because Daddy told me that Satan can't *really* do miracles, he can only deal in illusion.

And when I looked in the little hand mirror Titania gave me, I really was beautiful. It wasn't an illusion. I looked like, I don't know, Julia Roberts. It sure made me happy to know I could be beautiful even though I had never been in a movie.

Titania came out of her room and she was wearing a long black gown, studded with rhinestones. She wore so much make-up she seemed to have no wrinkles at all. In the harsh light of the living room her face seemed to be made of porcelain. Laverne came in for a moment and when she saw me dressed that way she turned her nose up at me.

'Bitch,' she said.

'Now don't you carry on,' Titania said. 'You can be *so* immature sometimes, Laverne.'

But I was sorry because I figured Laverne was a little envious because she wasn't coming with us, and I said, 'Why can't we bring her along?'

Laverne said, 'She taking you cause you white.'

'Now you know very well that that simply isn't true,' said Titania. 'Each of us has his appointed place in the cosmos. You have yours, and Greta will have hers ... and a splendid place it will be,' she added, handing me a gingerbread cookie out of her clutch. I nibbled it as she went on, 'Come on, now, Greta. It's time you learned the ropes. And really, dear, we must do a little better than *Greta*. So *plain*, so, I don't know, *Teutonic*! What about Anastasia? Or Renée? Carina? Perhaps some advice, Laverne? You people always have such unusual names.'

'I hate you,' Laverne said. 'Gimme one of them cookies.'

'In time,' said Titania, and it seemed that her porcelain face grew taut and brittle, 'but now, get your black ass back out on the street and don't come back until you've made your quota for the night.' She didn't sound like the same woman at all; she had a scary voice, like those women who sometimes get possessed and have to have the devil cast out of them in church. Then Titania turned on the charm again and said to me, 'Honey, we're off.'

★

A limo picked us up and we went on to the freeway. Actually we went way past Beverly Hills – I got a chance to look at all the posh houses – and then down a winding road that hugged the ocean. I watched television and Titania fussed with my hair. I flick-flick-flicked until I saw the image of Jeffrey Dahmer on the television screen. He was being tried and his face filled the whole TV screen. I didn't think he was beautiful at all, and I sure didn't want to get cut into pieces and eaten. I wondered what it could be that made Laverne think that way. After all, life is a precious gift.

The limo drove past solitary beach houses. There was a house shaped like Darth Vader's face, peering from the side of a cliff. There was a house that seemed to be made of vines, and another all glass, and another all chrome. It was gloomy and you could hear the ocean sighing even through the closed windows of the limo. Titania was putting on more make-up. For the first time since I'd known her, she seemed nervous, tapping the armrest with her tapered fingernails, smudging and redoing her lipstick over and over. When she thought she was all done, she said to me, 'Now, Anastasia, I'm going to introduce you to a *very important* person. He can really change your life if you're good to him. I want you to do what he says, even if it seems a tad peculiar to you . . . do you understand?'

I nodded as I watched on television that they weren't going to send Dahmer to the electric chair after all, since they don't do that kind of thing in Milwaukee. That was strange to me, that you could kill all those people and not be killed yourself. It went against the Bible. But I had been thinking less and less about the Bible these days.

Where the party was there was a long wooden deck that ran on stilts beside the sea. The house was wooden and all white. There were maids in black uniforms and all the guests wore black even though it wasn't a funeral. Inside the house there were big splotchy paintings and sculptures made of wire and the guests sat in small groups, drinking and sniffing some kind of Nutrasweet into their noses. I was scared and stood in a shadowed corner, but Titania just ploughed right into the crowd, screaming out endearments like 'darling' and 'honey' to people even though I could tell she didn't care about them at all.

'Titania Midnight!' said a woman who was wearing enough jewellery to sink a ship. 'You have just *got* to do a reading for me.'

'Well,' said Titania, 'the moon is full and the night is bright.' She blinked her gold-lidded eyes and her lashes *rippled*, I don't know how to describe it except once, in school, before my parents took us out because they'd been teaching about evolution, I saw a paramecium-thingy in a microscope, and it had those little legs, *cilia* they call them, and they were just like Titania's eyelashes. 'Come, Anastasia,' she said, and it took me

a minute to remember it was me, and we went out to the deck,
to a private place that was surrounded by potted plants.

Titania sat on the redwood planks, in front of one of those
electric waterfalls where the water comes down all beads, and
she pulled a deck of cards out of her clutch, and she handed
them to me. The woman squatted across from us and I realized
I had seen her before, in *All my Children* maybe. Titania shuffled
and the movie star woman shuffled and then they handed me
the deck and whenever Titania held out her hand I was to give
her one of the cards, face down. And Titania would turn it up
and lay it down on the deck in a cross kind of pattern, which
reminded me of the Lord's crucifixion. Then she closed her eyes
and mumbled to herself . . . I guess she was praying in tongues
. . . and she said things like, 'Oh, no, oh, no. You won't want to
hear this, honey, but . . . the other one . . . he is darker, isn't he?
I think, a swarthy man, hairy also, and . . . wearing a gold
chain: thick.'

'Oh, my God,' said the movie person, 'I can't wait until I
totally tell all my friends . . . this is, oh God, *uncanny*. Well, it's
a platinum chain actually, Herbie's, you know, *allergic* to gold
and all. Can you relate?' she added, turning to me, but I don't
think I was supposed to answer.

Then I looked up and saw the blond beautiful man with long
hair. He was wearing a black suit and he had an earring in the
shape of a scythe, dangling all the way down to his shoulder.
He wore mirror shades. Maybe Laverne was in love with Jeff
Dahmer, but she'd probably think again if she saw this man.
He had a little stubble, like Jeff did in the courtroom – but
everything else about him was much more beautiful.

'You old witch,' he said to Titania. 'What have you conjured
up today?'

Titania saw that I was staring at him with my mouth wide
open. She said to me, 'Anastasia,' and she nudged the base of
my skull so I'd look more demure, with downcast eyes, 'this is
your host and mine, Dana Harrington. I think you had better
call him Mr Harrington.'

'But what about the dark hairy man with the platinum chain?'

said the movie star woman. 'Do we get to, you know, like, *do* it?'

'Hold your horses, hon,' said Titania, taking the next card and flipping it through the air, 'you have the Death card. I think you should wait until after the divorce. Or else . . .' She made a throat-slitting gesture.

'*Shit*,' said the movie person, 'the fucking trust fund. The palimony. I'd better lay in a supply of Seconals.'

'Go with Mr Harrington,' Titania said to me.

I followed Mr Harrington through the party crowd, which parted for him like the sea. We reached a bedroom that was all white and didn't even have a television in it. There were toys on the white carpet . . . boy's toys, but the kind that are a few years out of date, I mean, Transformers, TMNT action figures, and stuff. Above the bed there was a huge painting in a gold frame, and it was a picture of a boy. He was a thin boy with big eyes, but in a strange kind of way he reminded me of Johnny. I couldn't help thinking of Johnny at that moment, wondering what he was doing and whether he had wet himself yet. There was a tray of chocolates next to the bed and he offered them to me. I had one. There was a weird liquid in the middle, which tasted the way Daddy's breath used to smell some nights. It made me feel a bit woozy, but part of that was from the gingerbread I'd had earlier. I had a few more chocolates.

'How old are you, Anastasia?' said the blond beautiful man.

'Fourteen. And my name's really Greta.'

I said I was older than I really was. Later I found out you can get more money if you say you're younger. He took off his shades. He had the clearest eyes; I couldn't decide if they were more like Jeff's or more like Jesus.

'Do you like the chocolate liqueurs? Have some more.' He smiled. He was nice. I wondered if he would start calling me names, like Daddy. But he just made me sit next to him on the bed and he toyed with my hair. I was scared my hair would get messed up and Titania would be mad at me so I just sat there, all stiff, eating the chocolates.

'I want you to know that I'm not a bad man,' said Mr
Harrington. 'I do have ... *weaknesses* ... but I'm in therapy
now. You really needn't worry about me hurting you or
anything like that. I'm the last person in the world who would
do that.'

'I know you're a good man, Mr Harrington,' I said.

'I'm an important man,' said Mr Harrington. 'Maybe I could
do something for you one day.'

'I got everything I need,' I said. 'You don't have to worry
about me, Mr Harrington.' But he had already slipped a
hundred dollar bill into my hand. 'You sure got a lot of art
here.'

'I'm a collector. I only have the most beautiful things in the
world here. Like you. I have an insatiable appetite for beauty. I
eat it up. I consume it and afterwards I'm still hungry. You
know. The Chinese food syndrome.' I wasn't sure what was so
great about some of those splotchy paintings, but I was too
good a girl to point that out to him.

'Who's that?' I said. I pointed to the portrait that reminded
me so much of Johnny ... not fat little Johnny but the Johnny
that Titania was squeezing out of Johnny's flesh ... the ideal
Johnny, Johnny Angel.

'It's my son,' he said.

'He looks nice.'

'He's dead.'

'I wish I'd of known him.'

'You would have liked him. Everyone did. He was everybody's favourite Hollywood kid. He was precocious but not
obnoxious. He was bright enough to be witty but not enough
to be an egghead.' Mr Harrington looked away from me,
remembering.

'How did he ... I mean ...' I knew I shouldn't have said
that. Because Mr Harrington turned to me and he was so full of
rage I was afraid he was going to slap my face.

'Don't!' I said and I shrank back, and that left him kind of
dazed, staring at his hand.

'Violently,' he said at last. 'He died violently.' I saw a tear in the corner of one eye form slowly, like a drop of condensation on a glass of soda, and slide down his cheek. I wondered whether, right now, Daddy was crying over me. Probably not, I thought. Mr Harrington was a very special kind of man, blond, beautiful, and caring. He wiped his eye on a sleeve, and he smiled a little, and put his mirror shades back on again so I couldn't see his eyes anymore.

Then he fucked me.

★

Titania Midnight allowed me to keep ten dollars out of the hundred and things got better for me after that night. I did parties and dates every night except Sunday, when I helped out in the doughnut shop, stirring the big vat of batter and putting the croissants into the monster oven in batches, a hundred at a time. Sometimes I made as much as a hundred dollars a week. I became good at make-up. I became more beautiful. And so did Johnny. But when I went into his little room to take him his pills and empty his potty, I tried not to look at him too much. He would mumble things I didn't understand. I think it was because of all the videotapes he watched. He didn't have anything to do but look at television. It was lucky there were a lot of tapes: musical comedies, slasher movies, pornos and even some that weren't in English.

Johnny's skin had a shine to it now, like a polished vase. It glowed as though there were a candle burning inside him, and I could see what Titania meant about his cheekbones. But I'd clear out of the room as quickly as I could, every morning. I felt guilty, I suppose. I knew that somehow I had betrayed him. Once in a while I'd slip him a piece of gingerbread.

Titania had taught me how to make it, from sautéing the dried marijuana in butter beforehand to kill the taste, to rolling the dough and fashioning it into flat little men with raisin eyes, noses and mouths. 'Creating life in the laboratory,' Titania called it, sipping her coffee and wolfing down three or four powdered doughnuts, her favourite. It sure seemed to give

Johnny life because he'd just wolf that thing down. He was always sad and that was part of what made him beautiful.

Titania even showed me the larder where she kept all the fixings for her special treats. There was a jar full of white powder, and mortar and pestle, and dried toadstools, and a big brown envelope full of marijuana. There was a corrugated brown box marked *Valium*. And a whole lot of other stuff that you could use in baking to get unusual results.

The best times of all were when it was real late at night, and Titania would let me sit in on her readings. They were in a big room way in back, and it was hung with black velvet drapes and there would always be music playing there, the kind of music where you can't quite catch the melodies even though they are almost the same thing, over and over, twisting around one or two notes. I would sit in shadow and hand her the cards. Sometimes she told them I was a mute, or retarded, because they were afraid I would betray their secrets. They would look at me and say, 'Poor thing,' and stuff, and I had to pretend I couldn't understand.

After the last customer left, Titania would show me how it all worked. Every card, she said, is a window into another world. There's what you see and there's what you don't see. Look at this one: what are the wolves howling at that's just beyond the edge of the picture, the thing that we can't see? Is that a lobster or is it a scorpion in the water? When you open yourself up, she told me, you can hear what the wolves are saying. And more. You can hear the voices that speak from all over that hidden world. You can hear the weeping of the moon. Listen. Listen. Turn over another card.

Tonight the card was Death.

The first time I'd flipped up Death had been at Mr Harrington's party. Death was a bent old skeleton-man with a scythe, grinning. Mr Harrington had a scythe hanging from his left ear. The ground was strewn with severed heads. Jeffrey Dahmer had heads in his refrigerator, apartment 213, the same number as our area code in Hollywood. Looking at the card this time made me all shivery and I wanted to cover it with another card.

Laverne poked her head in the doorway. 'Eww,' she said, 'someone gone die tonight.'

Titania took both my hands in hers and said, 'Dear, dear, dear! The first lesson for the good clairvoyant is this: *Thou shalt not kill the goose that layeth the golden eggs!* Imagine, honey, the horror of telling some Hollywood fashion plate, "Eww, someone gone die!" You'd never survive a fortnight in the biz.'

'But what if I get the feeling that someone *is* going to die?' I said. 'I have to tell the truth, don't I? Ain't that what the gift of prophecy is all about?'

'Laverne, go check on the chocolate dips, there's a dear.' Laverne threw a roll of twenties on the floor, slammed the door, stalked off down the hall. The money crossed the Death card and all you could see was the tip of the scythe. Titania flicked the money out of the way and whispered, 'Now, my dear dear dear disciple, now we come to the greatest mystery of them all. Death is not death. Death is transformation.'

'Oh, I get it. Like the death and resurrection of the Lord.'

'Bingo! Aren't you the clever one.'

'So if I draw the Death card, I have to tell the questioner that . . .'

'There will be a transformation. No, no, there is no death. Chrysalis and butterfly, corpse and maggot, life rolls over into life, death is a tango through eternal night. Look at your little brother . . . how he has shed his fleshy self . . . how he is translated into the ethereal! Ai, ai, ai, Johnny Angel indeed!'

I stared and stared at that card, but I couldn't figure it out.

★

In the morning, Johnny moaned and carried on, and he was mumbling and muttering and he had a fever. His skin was all translucent and you could see the veins. I mopped up his sweat with a dish towel and he tossed and turned in my arms, but I couldn't understand anything he was saying, until, looking straight past me, he said, 'The man with the big curvy sword.'

The room became all cold. I thought I felt someone breathing on my neck. Johnny seemed to see someone, standing behind me, swallowing both of us in his shadow. Maybe it was the fever, or maybe he really could see something; he's gifted that way; in church, he always used to know when someone was possessed.

After the blast of icy breath died away, I couldn't feel anything any more. But Johnny could still see whatever it was he saw. I knew it was terrifying him because he started to piss himself, which he normally only does in his sleep.

I fed him gingerbread men until he dozed off. Then Titania came in with a Polaroid camera, and she made me lay him down, very carefully, like a dead body on a bier, and she took three or four snapshots of him all lying there, asleep with his eyes wide open.

★

I have a lot of men inside me now. I've sucked little pieces of them into myself. One day the little pieces will dissolve and I'll be able to piss them away and become all clean again inside.

They liked it when I called them Daddy. Maybe they didn't have daughters of their own. Sometimes when she sent me out to work, Titania brewed me what Laverne used to call her magic potion. The potion made me crazy. I learned how to buck and heave and make those little panting noises. But oftentimes they liked it better when I played dead, closed my eyes, pretended to be asleep. That was the easiest to do, because I learned it from home. It was different from home though. Because sometimes they told me jokes, bought me little gifts, tried to treat me like a real person. They didn't call me names. And they gave me money, so that I wasn't worthless any more.

I'll hardly ever watch television or go to the movies these days. You never know when one of them's going to appear. And then I'll feel all queasy inside and I have to excuse myself to go to the bathroom.

After a while, maybe because she wasn't Titania's favourite any more, Laverne kind of drifted away from us, and some-times she'd stay out all night. One day they were yelling at each other and Titania screamed, 'Go away, get what you want,

I dare you,' and sent Laverne sulking into the neon night, and Laverne never came back.

I saw one evening on *A Current Affair* how Jeff Dahmer had his own groupies who used to hang around the courtroom waiting for a glimpse of him. You'd think they would all be a bunch of fat wannabes but no, some of them were good-looking, not the kind of people who needed to get a life. I had this idea that Laverne had maybe taken the bus out to Milwaukee to become one of the groupies. Since the verdict, Jeff had not come on television as often anymore, so that was probably why I had not seen Laverne on TV. Maybe in a year or two, if they ever had one of those 'What ever happened to—?' type shows, I could see Laverne, hovering outside the walls of a bleak grey prison, and she'd still be calling out to him, 'Come and get me too, because I love you.'

I did see Laverne on television, but it wasn't how I imagined it. They were pulling her body out of a dumpster. I think it was the same one Johnny and I had slept in, that first night in Hollywood.

Later Titania and I went down to the morgue to identify the body, because we were all the kin Laverne had. She was in pieces, but it was her all right. Her hands had been cut off and strung around her neck with a length of her own intestine, and one of her feet was poking up out of her, you know, down there. Her skin was just like Johnny's, translucent. She had never been that black but now she was almost yellow. Her eyes stared past me the way Johnny's stared that time, seeing someone I could not see. It still seemed to me that she was sneering at me, even now that she had been shuffled and redealt.

In the pocket of her jeans, they had found a Jeffrey Dahmer trading card. I knew then that this death had been the death she'd prayed for. It was hard to believe that a man in a prison far away could have reached out, heard her wishes and granted them, maybe by sending down some divine ambassador to wield the scythe that had sliced her into thirteen pieces. After all, Daddy had always told me that only God can do things like that. But he also said God can be anyone, anywhere, anytime.

Maybe even inside a serial killer.

It made me sick, and later I asked Titania how she could still say to me, 'There is no death.'

But all she would say was, 'You have to look past those things.' And she took a sip of the hospital cafeteria coffee.

Sure, she'd said, *sure, Laverne happy.*

Now I couldn't get any of them out of my head: the bone man swinging the scythe and Dahmer and the head in the refrigerator and Mr Harrington and the dead boy who'd died violently, *violently*, and my brother transforming into an angel inside that beautification room. 'God, why'd you have to bring me here?' I screamed at her. 'Did you make this happen when you told her she would get what she'd always wanted? Is this another one of your magic spells?'

'Temper, temper,' she said. 'I have to open all the doors in the dark castle, dear; you have to gaze at the searing face of the deity; yes! Oh, Anastasia, oh, Renée, you have looked the demon in the eye and know him to be yourself!'

It was then that I knew Titania Midnight was crazy. Only Johnny could know if she was sick in the head or whether some devil had taken possession of her body. I was half crazy myself, because I loved the old woman, because she was what I had to cling to in the madness that whirled around me. The city of night had given me a thousand fathers, but only one mother. I cried then, and I hugged her and told her it would all come out all right in the end.

After all, she still had me, and I could do double the work to keep us all afloat. And I did.

*

There was another party at the Harrington place. It was another Harrington place, actually, not the one in Malibu, but the one actually *in* Beverly Hills. The house was different but the room was the same. It was uncanny. The room was a kind of shrine I guess. There was probably one like it in every house the beautiful blond man owned.

The bed, the portrait of Mr Harrington's son, even the outdated toys that were scattered on the rug in exactly the same places. Mr Harrington gave me two hundred dollars this time because by now he had found out my real age, plus now I was real good at behaving just the way he wanted. Right after it was over I fell into a deep sleep because it was the best way to stop feeling the pain.

When I woke up, Titania Midnight was in the room, and so was Mr Harrington, fully dressed now in his tuxedo, ready to go to some premiere. They were sitting on the edge of the bed.

'Can we talk? She won't wake up, will she?' said Mr Harrington.

'Not if she drained that Valium cocktail to the last drop.'

Mr Harrington said, 'You've been very good to me, Titania. In accommodating, well, my tastes. But there was something else you were going to look for ... I don't know how much progress you've made.'

'A lot. I want you to see some Polaroids,' Titania said. I kept my eyes closed because I didn't want them to know I could hear them. I could hear Titania rummaging in her purse, could hear papers rustling, and then I heard Mr Harrington sigh. 'The eyes. The sadness. The crisp hard curl of a lower lip that can't quite twist into a smile. He's so beautiful you could eat him up.'

'No poetry, Titania,' said Mr Harrington. And he sighed again.

'No poetry? But how can you say that when you see these pictures? But it gets better. No papers. No dental records. No milk cartons. No television appeals. He does not exist. Not until you spring him, fully-formed, into the world. Come for him tomorrow midnight.'

'I'll have the cash.'

They didn't talk for a long time. It took time for the weight of what they were saying to settle in. I pretended to sleep until they left the room. Then I got up and prowled around. I didn't go back down to the party because then they might know I'd overheard them. I tiptoed across the toy-strewn rug. Titania had left her purse on the dresser. I was sure she'd been showing Mr Harrington the Polaroids of Johnny and I was right. That's what they were. I held one of them up to the lava lamp and I glanced up at the portrait of Mr Harrington's son. Titania had caught the look exactly. Somehow, she had turned Johnny into this dead boy. It was like Johnny's body was an empty glass and you could pour in any soul you wanted. Maybe the pills did more than melt away his fat. And Mr Harrington was a collector, he'd told me. Was he planning to collect Johnny? I became real frightened and I guess my hand was trembling because I knocked the purse on to the floor.

A lot of stuff fell out: a key ring, a packet of Dunhills, a driver's licence. I knelt down and tried to put everything back in. I looked at the licence too. It showed Titania's picture, but the name on it was Amelia Goldberg. Hadn't Daddy said something about Goldsteins and Goldfarbs ... sacrificing babies and taking away his job? It didn't seem possible that Titania Midnight could be one of those people. She didn't even know who my father was, so how could she take his job? And it wasn't *her* who had killed Laverne.

Or was it?

I didn't want to think such terrible things about the woman who had taken me in, given me a job with decent wages, and tried to share so much of her wisdom with me. But it sure made me think. There was more to all this than I had ever dreamed. It really scared me.

Especially when I finally put my clothes back on and I went back down to the party, and I saw Dana Harrington gliding through the thick of the crowd, smiling a little, in a world of his own, and the scythe in his ear catching the light from the crystal chandelier. He moved among the chatter, and the clinking of cocktail glasses, but he himself seemed to be inside his own private silence.

★

That night I dreamed about the beautiful blond man, and the scythe swinging and people screaming and their heads flying through the air like bloody soccer balls. When I woke up I wished Laverne would be lying on the futon next to me, even if she would kick me half on to the floor. It was real late and I knew that even Titania would be asleep by now, either in her bedroom or in the reading room, slumped over a deck of tarot cards, or in the easy chair in the big kitchen among the unbaked doughnuts.

I had a feeling I had to see Johnny. It was Johnny who had spied on Daddy's prayer meeting and who had had the presence of mind to come and warn me. It was only fair I should tell him about things I overheard. So I pulled on a long *Beverly Hills 90210* T-shirt, and I crept down the corridor to the beautification room.

I looked at my brother. He was leaning against the wall, staring at the television. He didn't seem to see me. I put my lips to the pane and whispered his name a couple of times, but he didn't look up. Then I tried the door. It was unlatched. I wondered how many times it had been unlatched in the past, how many times we could have escaped. Except where would we have escaped to? Titania had fed us ... me, anyway ... loved us, for all I could tell. I slipped into the room and I was almost touching him before he seemed to notice me. 'Johnny,' I said, 'Johnny, I think they want to do something to you, I don't know what.'

Johnny said, 'I don't like the pornos that much. I seen all that stuff before, at home. Westerns are cool. The horror movies are the best. I love Freddy Krueger's fingernails.'

'Johnny, can't you hear me?'

'When I close my eyes the movie still goes on. The man with the curvy sword is dancing in the street. Under the neon lights. The flashing Mann's Chinese sign makes a dragon on his face because his face is like a mirror.'

God, I thought, thinking of Mr Harrington's shades as he moved up and down, up and down, seeing my face get big and small, big and small. 'Johnny,' I said, 'are there mirrors over his eyes? Is the curvy sword dangling from his ear? Is he a beautiful blond man dressed in black?'

Johnny giggled. But that was because of something on the television. 'You have to tell me,' I said, 'it's real important.'

But Johnny began to babble in tongues. He was always a lot closer to the Lord than I could ever be. He carried on for a while, waving his arms and making his eyes roll up in their sockets, but without the gift of interpretation I couldn't understand what he meant. But finally he switched back to English and he said, 'The skull.' And pointed straight at the television screen. But all I could see was a Madonna video.

'Come on, Johnny. Let's run away. I don't think this place is safe any more. I think they're gonna do something really bad to you. Look, I got a couple hundred bucks saved up, tips and stuff. I know we don't remember how we got here, but maybe we can find a better daddy and mommy. I met a hundred new daddies here and most of them were pretty nice to me. You could have all the candy bars you wanted. You wouldn't have to be this way.'

Johnny turned to me at last. The room was dark except for the pool of grey light in front of the television. He sat up. He was wearing only a pair of yellowing BVDs and his whole body was shiny, like the TV screen, and his eyes were haunted and deep. His hair was as pale as the hair of the blond beautiful man, and his fingers tapped at the empty air. 'We can't go,' he said softly. 'You can't run away from the man with the curvy sword.'

I hugged Johnny and said, 'I got a plan, Johnny. We'll be okay.' I didn't know what the plan would be yet, but my mind was racing. We'd use my money to buy a bus ticket to Disneyland. We'd find a mommy and a daddy and a tract house in a green green suburb. We'd overdose on gingerbread and fly into the sky.

I tugged at Johnny. He started to budge, then I heard the key turn in the latch of the prison door. I looked up sharply and saw Titania's face in the television's ghostly light. She must have just come back from a Beverly Hills reading, because her face was powdered to a chalky whiteness, and her lips painted the crimson of fresh blood, and there were charcoal circles around her eyes. She sniffed like a hungry she-wolf, and her lips twisted into a sharp-toothed smile. Then she faded into shadow.

Titania Midnight was more than mad. She was evil.

I held Johnny in my arms the whole night long, and didn't sleep until dawn.

*

The blond beautiful man with long hair was coming at midnight. I knew that from overhearing that conversation. I didn't have that long to do what I had to do. I went to Titania's secret larder and pulled out about forty Valium, and ground them up with the mortar and pestle, and I folded and sifted them with a half cup of powdered sugar. I poured the mixture into an envelope, tucked it in my jeans, and went out to work.

Work was not too bad that day. All my dates were regulars, and I already knew how they all liked it. So I didn't really have to concentrate very hard. I just let myself drift, and I swallowed just enough gingerbread to loosen up my soul, and not enough to cut the kitestring that held me to the real world. Everyone was pleased with me and I got a lot of extra money, which was good because maybe me and Johnny would need it later.

I stayed out as late as I dared. When I came home it was already an hour before midnight. I found Titania in the kitchen of the doughnut shop. She had turned off the neon and pulled down all the shades and hung up a sign on the door that read ON VACATION – CLOSED. She had a whole pot of coffee out and, even though she wasn't going out anywhere, was dressed to the teeth. She had on a long black robe embroidered with suns and moons and stars. Her eyelids were painted in rainbow glitter, and her lips were midnight blue. When she saw me she became all agitated and she started to cackle.

'Tonight's the night, my baby Anastasia,' she said. 'No more slaving over a hot kitchen for you! No more blowjobs in BMWs. You're going to be a princess now, and Titania's going to be

queen of the wood. Be a dear and do me up some powdered
doughnuts. Mama Titania'll be back in a few minutes.'

I fetched the doughnuts and dipped them in the Valium
powder. She was gone for a long time and I became more and
more nervous. I took the croissants out of the oven and stacked
them up. I wondered why she was still baking if we were
supposed to be on vacation . . . and rich besides.

When Titania came back, she had Johnny with her. He was
wearing a brand-new blue suit with crisp, sharply creased short
pants. Titania had moussed his hair and brushed it. It was hard
for Johnny to stand in the light. He kept blinking and he seemed
not to know where he was.

Titania said, 'Things will be different now, Johnny. You'll be
able to eat anything you want. Would you like some candy?
Would you care for a doughnut?' She snatched one from the
plate I had so carefully arranged and handed it to him. Then
she stuffed one into her own mouth. While she was busy
chewing I pried the doughnut loose from Johnny's fist and gave
him something else, a chocolate éclair. He sucked on it, savour-
ing the cream.

'My two little darlings,' said Titania Midnight, 'tonight Mr
Harrington is going to come for you. Well, the deal is only for
Johnny, but I think we can manage to get Anastasia thrown
into the package . . . oh, my angels, how I slaved to make you
ready for this moment! But tomorrow it's curtains for Titania
Midnight, reader, adviser, pimp, and doughnut manufacturer
extraordinaire . . . and now . . . for my next transformation . . .
enter Amelia Goldberg . . . rich bitch from Encino . . . estate
broker . . . millionairess . . . queen of the glitterati . . . oh, it'll be
splendid, splendid, splendid, my honey babies!'

I said, 'There's a picture on Mr Harrington's wall. He says
it's his son. He says his son died violently.'

'I know,' said Titania. 'So sad, isn't it? Torn to pieces by a
mad slasher. Time, indeed, for a new son.'

'You're lying!' I said. 'You made Johnny into an angel so Mr
Harrington could kill him! He's the man with the big curvy
sword, the Grim Reaper, the Jeffrey Dahmer man!' How could

I have been so stupid before? Daddy always told me that people like her liked to sacrifice babies. He said they shouldn't have let them crawl out of the ovens. Titania had sent Laverne out to die with a single sentence. She had said that death and transformation were the same thing, and now she was telling us to get ready for transformation. Right. For death.

He's so beautiful you could eat him up.

Wasn't that why the oven was still on?

'We ain't going where you tell us any more,' I said. 'We ain't going to die for you. It's too much to ask.'

Her face started to transform then. There really was a demon inside. I could tell by the way her eyes burned and her fingernails raked the air.

'Whore!' she screamed. 'I take you in ... you *nothings* ... I make something of you, I see the chance to pull all of us out of the gutter ... and you dare defy me ...' She lunged at me, but that was when the Valium kicked in and she sort of folded up and then I pushed her with all my might. Right into the oven. She slid in easy. I slammed the door but that didn't keep out the stench. And then fumes began pouring into the kitchen. There was a smell like burning plastic, maybe from her clothes, and another smell, like barbecuing lamb, that made my mouth water in spite of what I knew it was.

I started coughing. The smoke detector went off and the alarm screeched and I could hear clanging and buzzing and a siren in the distance, and I stood there for a long time, too numbed to move, until I realized that the fire was going to eat all of us up unless I took Johnny by the hand and steered him out of the doughnut shop.

There was smoke all over the street and the whole place was burning up. There was a Rolls Royce parked in the alley and the blond beautiful man was standing there, all dressed in black, with the scythe dangling from his ear.

'Get away from him,' I said to Johnny. 'He'll cut you in pieces.'

But Johnny just stared at him, and he kind of smiled. And he began walking towards him. I ran after him, trying to pull him back, crying out, 'No, Johnny, no!' but he wouldn't listen.

Mr Harrington took off his mirror shades. He was just staring at Johnny as though he was looking at a man from Mars. Then he started to weep.

'He does look just like him,' he said softly. 'Titania was right.' He started to reach forward to touch Johnny and that was when I lost control.

'I killed Titania! Now you can get out of our lives too!' I screamed. And I pummelled his black silk jacket with my fists. But he was hard and strong and hollow.

'She's dead?'

'I shoved her in the oven,' I said. 'Goddamned baby-sacrificing Kike.'

'Oh, my God,' said Mr Harrington. 'Where did you learn to say such hateful things?'

'From Daddy,' I said.

'You killed her.' He started to back away from us. 'She wasn't an evil woman. In her way she did try to help you. It's true that she trafficked in young flesh . . . but . . . no one is so evil they deserve to be . . .' The odour of burning meat wafted across the alley. 'Poor Titania.'

'Poor Titania? She was gonna give Johnny to you . . . so you'd kill him and cut him in pieces and eat him . . . like Jeffrey Dahmer.'

'She didn't tell you? I was going to adopt him. Both of you, probably. You could have lived in Beverly Hills with me and had everything you ever wanted. For years I've wanted a new son . . . and Titania knew the dark country where you live, the forgotten, the abandoned children. I promised to pay her well to find me a kid who looked so much like . . . like . . .'

'Don't give me that bullshit. You fucked me.'

He winced. 'I wish you wouldn't use that language.'

The smoke blended right into the smog of night. I just glared at Mr Harrington. I think he saw my anger for the first time. Maybe I shouldn't have lain there, leaving my body behind while my mind drifted far away. Maybe I should have looked him straight in the eye and shown him all my rage, all my frustration at being so weak and powerless. Then maybe he wouldn't have done it to me. But it was too late now. I could see now that the powerful emotion that had shaken him when he first saw us might have been the beginning of love. But it was fading now.

'I'm not a bad man,' he said. 'I'm ... a weak man. I would have been good to you.'

Johnny said softly, 'I'm gonna pee my pants.'

'But of course I can't adopt either of you now. My reputation ... the scandal ... you know how it is. I'd better go.' Now I could see that he thought of us as slimy things ... cockroaches ... vermin. 'I'll call 911 from the car.'

He kissed Johnny on the forehead and touched my hair. Then he got back in his Rolls Royce and drove away, and we stood in front of the burning doughnut shop, waiting for the fire department.

★

Sometimes I see the blond beautiful man on television. But I change the channel. In a few months the court will send us to a foster home, if they can find one. But it might be hard since I'm a murderer.

After Bob read the last entry in my diary, the one where I talked about the fire at the doughnut shop, he told me that it made him cry. I don't know why. *I* never cry. I don't have time because I have to look after Johnny.

After he read 'Hansel and Gretel' to us, I told Bob my witch theory, and he shook his head slowly and said, 'Greta, there's only one kind of magic in the world. You made magic when you wrote the words that made me cry. Words can be black magic and they can be white magic, but they are the only things that can transform us. Even a movie starts with just words on a page, a screenplay.'

That's why I go on writing it all down. If I write enough words down, maybe we can still have the things we long for

... the tract house, the mommy and daddy, the green green suburb far away. But so far nothing has come true.

I guess I'm not that good at witchcraft.

———————
———————

Gingerbread was the first of a series of stories I've been writing that retell well-known fairy tales in the dark milieu of present-day Los Angeles. 'Though I Walk through the Valley', elsewhere in this volume, is also one of these stories, based on a story in Grimms' Fairy Tales called 'The Stubborn Child', which seldom appears in children's collections because of its unmitigated violence.

Darker Angels

One day there'll be historians who can name all the battles and number the dead. They'll study the tactics of the generals and they'll see it all clear as crystal, like they was watching with the eyes of the angels.

But it warn't like that for me. I can't for the life of me put a name to one blame battle we fought. I had no time to number the dead nor could I see them clearly through the haze of red that swam before my eyes. And when the gore-drenched mist settled into dew, when the dead became visible in their stinking, wormy multitudes, I still could not tell one from another; it was a very sea of torsos, head and twisted limbs; the dead was wrapped around one another so close and intimate they was like lovers; didn't matter no more iffen they was ours or theirs.

I do not recollect what made me stay behind. Could be it was losing my last shinplaster on the cockroach races. Could have been the coffee which warn't real coffee at all but parched acorns roasted with bacon fat and ground up with a touch of chicory. Could be it was that my shoes was so wore out from marching that every step I took was like walking acrosst a field of brimstone.

More likely it was just because I was a running away kind of a boy. Running was in my blood. My pa and me, we done our share of running, and I reckon that even after I done run away from *him* and gone to war, the running fever was still inside of me and couldn't be let go.

And then, after I lagged behind, I knowed that if I went back they'd shoot me dead, and if they shot me why then I'd go straight on to the everlasting fire, because we was fighting to protect the laws of God. I just warn't ready for hell yet, not after a mere fourteen years on this mortal earth.

That's why I was tarrying amongst the dead, and that's how I come to meet that old darkie that used to work down at the Anderson place.

The sun was about setting and the place was right rank, because the carrion had had the whole day to bloat up and rot and to call out for the birds and the worms and the flies. But it felt good to walk on dead people because they was softer on my wounded feet. The bodies stretched acrosst a shallow creek and all the way up to the edge of a wood. I didn't know where I was nor where I was going. There warn't much light remaining and I wanted to get somewhere, anywhere, before nightfall. It was getting cold. I took a jacket off of one dead man and a pair of new boots from another but I couldn't get the boots on past them open sores.

You might think it a sin to steal from the dead, but the dead don't have no use for gold and silver. There was scant daylight left for me to rifle through their pockets looking for coins. Warn't much in the way of money on that battlefield. It's usually only us poor folks which gets killed in battle.

It was slippery work wading through the corpses, keeping an eye for something shiny amongst the ripped-up torsos and the sightless heads and the coiling guts. I was near choking to death from the reek of it, and the coat I stole warn't much proof against the cold. I was hungry and I had no notion of where to find provender. And the mist was coming back, and I thought to myself, I'll just take myself a few more coppers and then I'll cross over into the wood and build me a shelter and mayhap a fire. Won't nobody see me, thin as a sapling, quiet as a shadow.

So I started to wade over the creek, which warn't no trouble because there was plenty of bodies to use as stepping-stones. I was halfway acrosst when I spotted the old nigger under a cottonwood tree, in a circle which was clear of carrion. He had a little fire going and something a-roasting over it. I could hear the crackling above the buzz of the flies and I could smell the cooking fat somewhere behind the stench of putrefying men.

I moved nearer to where he sat. I was blame near fainting by then and ready to kill a body for my supper. He was squatting with his arms around his knees and he was a-rocking back and forth and I thought I could hear him crooning some song to himself, like a lullaby, in a language more kin to French than nigger talk. Odd thing was, I had heard the song before. Mayhap my momma done sung it to me onc't, for she was born out Louisiana way. The more I listened the less I was fixing to kill the old man.

He was old all right. As I crept closer I seen he warn't no threat to me. I still couldn't see his face, because he was turned away from me and looking straight into the setting sun. But I could see he was withered and white-haired and black as the coming night, and seemed like he couldn't even hear me approaching, for he never pricked up his ears though I stood nary a yard or two behind his back, in the shadow of the cottonwood.

That was when he said to me, never looking back, 'Why, *bonjour*, Marse Jimmy Lee; I never did think I'd look upon you face again.'

And then he turned, and I knew him by the black patch over his right eye.

Lord, it was strange to see him there, in the middle of the valley of the dead. It had been ten years since my pa and me gone up to the Anderson place. Warn't never any call to go back, since it burned to the ground a week after, and old man Anderson died, and his slaves was all sold.

'How did you know it was me?' I asked him. 'I was but four years old last time you laid eyes on me.'

'Your daddy still a itinerant preacher, Marse Jimmy Lee?' he says.

'I reckon,' said I, for I warn't about ready to tell him the truth yet. 'I ain't with my pa no more.'

'You was always a running away sort of a boy,' he said, and offered me a piece of what he was roasting.

'What is it?'

'I don't reckon I ought to tell you.'

'I've had possum before. I've had field rat. I'm no stranger to strange flesh.' I took a bite of the meat and it was right tasty. But I hadn't had solid food for two days and soon I was a-heaving all over the nearest corpse.

He went back to his crooning song, and I remembered then that I had heard it last from his own lips, that day Pa shot Momma in the back because she wanted to go with the Choctaw farmer. I can't say I blamed her because leastways the man was a landowner and had four slaves besides. Pa let her pack her bags and walk halfway acrosst the bridge afore he blew her to kingdom come. Then he took my hand and set me up on his horse and took me to the Anderson place, and when I started to squall he slapped me in the face until it were purple and black, saying, between his blows, 'She don't deserve your tears. She is a woman taken in adultery; such a woman should be stoned to death, according to the Scriptures; a bullet were too good for her. I have exercised my rights according to the law, and iffen I hear one more sob out of you I shall take a hickory to you, for he who spareth the rod loveth not his child.' And he drained a flask of bug juice and burped, I did not hear the name of Mary Cox from his lips again for ten long years.

Pa was not a ordained minister but plantation folks reckoned him book-learned enough to preach to their darkies, which is what he done every Sunday, a different estate each week, then luncheon with the master and mistress of the house or sometimes, if they was particular about eating with white trash, then in the kitchen amongst the house niggers. The niggers called him the Reverend Cox, but to the white folks he was just Cox, or Bug-juice Cox, or Blame-Fuckster Cox, or wretched, pitiable Cox, so low that his wife done left him for a Injun.

At the Anderson place he preached in a barn, and he took for his subject adultery; and as there was no one to notice, I stole away to a field and sat me down in a thicket of sugar cane and hollered and carried on like the end of the world was nigh, and me just four years old.

Then it was that I heard the selfsame song I was hearing now, and I looked up and saw this ancient nigger with a patch over one eye, and he says to me, 'Oh, honey, it be a terrible thing to be without a mother.' I remember the smell of him, a pungent smell like fresh crushed herbs. 'I still remembers the day my *mamman* was took from me. Oh, do not grieve alone, white child.'

'How'd you come to lose that eye?'

'It the price of knowledge, honey,' he said softly.

Choking back my sobs, a mite embarrassed because someone had seen me in my loneliness, I said to him, 'You shouldn't be here. You should be in that barn listening to my father's preaching, lessen you want to get yourself a whupping.'

He smiled sadly and said, 'They done given up on whupping old Joseph.'

I said, 'Is your momma dead too, Joseph?'

'Yes. She be dead, oh, nigh on sixty year now. She died in the revolution.'

'Oh, come,' I said, 'even I know that the revolution was almost a hundred years ago, and I know you ain't that old, because a white man's time is threescore years and ten, and a nigger's time is shorter still.' Now I wasn't comprehending anything I was saying; this was all things I heard my pa say, over and over again, in his sermons.

'Oh,' said old Joseph, 'I ain't talking about the white man's revolution, but the coloured folks' revolt which happened on a island name of Haiti. The French, they tortured my *mamman*, but she wouldn't betray her friends, so they killed her and sold me to a slaver, and the ship set sail one day before independence; so sixty years after my kinfolk was set free, I's still in bondage in a foreign country.'

I knew that niggers was always full of stories about magic and distant countries, and they couldn't always see truth from fantasy; my daddy told me that truth is a hard, solid thing to us white folks, as easy to grasp as a stone or a horseshoe, but to them it was slippery, it was like a phantom. That was why I didn't take exception to the old man's lies. I just sat there

quietly, listening to the music of his voice, and it soothed me
and seemed like it helped to salve the pain I was feeling, for
pretty soon when I thought of Momma lying on the bridge
choking on her own blood I felt I could remember the things I
loved about her too, like the way she called my name, the way
her nipples tasted on my lips, for she had lost my newborn
sister and she was bursting with milk and she would sometimes
let me suckle, for all that I was four years old.

And then I was crying again but this time they was healing
tears.

Then old Joseph, he said, 'You listen to me, Marse Jimmy
Lee. I ain't always gone be with you when you needs to open
up your heart.' Now this surprised me because I didn't recollect
telling him none of what was going through my mind. 'I's gone
give you a gift,' he said, and he pulls out a bottle from his
sleeve, a vial, only a inch high, and in that bottle was a doll
that was woven out of cornstalks. It were cunningly wrought,
for the head of the doll was bigger than the neck of the bottle,
and it must have taken somebody many hours to make, and
somebody with keen eyesight at that. 'Now this be a problem
doll. It can listen to you when no man will listen. It a powerful
magic from the island where I was born.'

He held it out to me and it made me smile, for I had
oftentimes been told that darkies are simple people and believe
in all kinds of magic. I clutched it in my hands but mayhap he
saw the disbelief in my face, for he said to me with the utmost
gravity, 'Do not mock this magic, white child. Among the
coloured people which still fears the old gods, they calls me a
houngan, a man of power.'

'The old gods?' I said.

'Shangó,' he said, and he done a curious sort of a genuflecting
hop when he said the name, 'Obatala; Ogun; Babalu Ayé . . .'

The names churned round and round in my head as I stared
into his good eye. I don't recollect what followed next or how
my pa found me. But everything else I remembered just as
though the ten years that followed, the years of wandering,

Pa's worsening cruelty and drunkenness, hadn't never even happened.

It was as though I had circled back to that same place and time. Only instead of the burning sunlight of that summer's day there was the gathering cold and the night. Instead of the tall cane sticky with syrup, we was keeping company with the slain. And I warn't a child no more, although I warn't a man yet, neither.

'The *poupée* I give you,' old Joseph said as I sat myself down beside him, 'does you still got it?'

'My pa found it the next day. He said he didn't want no hoodoo devil dolls in his house. He done smashed it and throwed it in the fire, and then he done wore me out with his hickory.'

'And you a soldier now.'

'I run away.'

'Lordy, honey, you a sight to see. Old Joseph don't got no more dolls for you now. Old Joseph got no time for he be making dolls. There be a monstrous magic abroad now in this universe. This magic it the onliest reason old Joseph still living in this world. Old Joseph hears the magic summoning him. Old Joseph he stay behind to hear what the magic it have to tell him.'

Like a fool, I thought him simple when I heard him speak of magic. It made me smile. It was the first time I had smiled in many months. I smiled to keep from crying, for weeping ill becomes a man of fourteen years who has carried his rifle into battle to defend his country.

'You poor lost child,' said Joseph, 'you should be a-waking up mornings to the song of the larks, not the whistle of miniés nor the thunder of cannon. You at the end of the road now, ain't nowhere left for you to go; that's why us has been called here to this valley of the shadow of death. It was written from the moment we met, Marse Jimmy Lee. Ten years I wandered alone in the wilderness. Now the darker angels has sent you to me.'

'I don't know what you mean.'

'Be not afraid,' he said, 'for I bring you glad tidings of great joy.' I marvelled that he knew the words of the evangelist, for this was the man who would not go hear my father's preaching.

He nibbled at the charred meat. For a moment I entertained the suspicion that it were human flesh. But it smelled good. I ate my fill and drank from the bloody stream and fell asleep beside the fire to the lilt of the old man's lullaby.

*

I had not told old Joseph all the truth. It warn't only the need to run that forced me from my father's house. Pa was a hard man and a drinking man and a man which had visions, and in those visions he saw other worlds. He was unmerciful to me, and oftentimes he would set to whipping the demons out of me, but everything he did to me was in keeping with Holy Scripture, which tells a father that love ain't always a sweet thing, but can also come with bitterness and blows.

I had visions too, but they warn't heavenly the way his was. I would not wear my shoes. I played with the nigger children of the town, shaming him. I ran wild and I never went to no school. But I could read some, for that my pa set me to studying the Scriptures whenever he could tie me down.

This is how I come to join the regiment:

We was living in a shack in back of the Jackson place, right next to the nigger burial plot. Young Master Jackson had all his darkies assembled in the graveyard to hear a special sermon from my pa, because the rumours of the 'mancipation proclamation was rife amongst the slaves. There was maybe thirty or forty of them, and a scattering of pickaninnies underfoot, sitting on the grass, leaning against the wooden markers.

I was sitting in the shack, minding a kettle of stew. Through the open window I could hear my pa preaching. 'Now don't you darkies pay this emancipation proclamation no mind,' came his voice, ringing and resonant. 'It is an evil trickery. They are trying to fool you innocent souls into running away and joining up with those butchers who come down to rape and pillage our land, and they hold out freedom as a reward for treachery. But the true reward is death, for if a nigger is captured in the uniform of a Yankee it has been decreed by our government that he shall be shot without trial. No, this is no road to freedom! There is only one way there for those born into bondage, and that is through the blood of our saviour Jesus Christ, and your freedom is not for this world, but for the next, for is it not written, "In my father's house there are many mansions."? There is a mansion for you, and you, and you, and you, iffen you will obey your master in this life and accept the yoke of lowliness and the lash of repentance; for is it not written, "By his stripes we are healed" and "Blessed are the meek"? It's not for the coloured people, freedom in this world. But the wicked, compassionless Yankees would prey on your simplicity. They would let you mistake the kingdom of heaven for a rebellious kingdom on earth. "To everything there is a season." Yes, there will be mansions for you all. Mansions with white stone columns and porticoes sheltered from the sun. The place of healing is beyond the valley of the shadow of death . . .'

My pa could talk mighty proper when he had a mind to, and he had a chapter and verse for everything. I didn't pay no heed to his words, though, because there is different chapters and verses for niggers, and when they are quoted for white folks they do not always mean the same thing. No, I was busy stirring the stew and hiding the whiskey, for Pa had always had a powerful thirst after he was done preaching, and with the quenching of thirst came violence.

After the preaching the darkies all starts singing with a passion. They done sung *All God's Chillun Got Wings* and *Swing Low, Sweet Chariot*. Pa didn't stay for the singing but come into the shack calling for his food. It warn't ready so he throwed a few pots and pans around, with me scurrying out of the way to avoid being knocked about, and then he finally found where I had hidden the bottle and he lumbered into the inner room to drink.

Presently the stew bubbled up and I ladled out some in a tin cup and took it to the room. This was the room me and him slept in, on a straw pallet on the floor, a bare room with nothing but a chest of drawers, a chair with one leg missing, and a hunting rifle. He kept his hickories there too, for to chastise me with.

I should have knocked, because pa warn't expecting me.

He was sitting in the chair with his britches about his ankles. He didn't see me. He was holding in one hand a locket which had a picture of Momma. In the other hand he was holding his bony cocker, and he was strenuously indulging in the vice of Onan.

I was right horrified when I saw this. I was full of shame to see my father unclothed, for was that not the shame of the sons of Noah? And I was angered, because in my mind's eye I seen my momma go down on that bridge, fold up and topple over, something I hadn't thought on for nigh on ten year. I stood there blushing scarlet and full of fury and grieving for my dead mother, and then I heard him a-murmuring, 'Oh, sweet Jehovah, Oh, sweet Lord, I see you, I see the company of the heavenly host, I see you, my sweet Mary, standing on a cloud with your arms stretched out to me, naked as Eve in the Garden of Eden. Oh, oh, oh, I'm a-looking on the face of the Almighty and a-listening to the song of the angels.'

Something broke inside me all at once when I heard him talk that way about Momma. Warn't it enough that she was dead, withouten him blasphemously lusting after her departed soul? I dropped the tin of stew and he saw me and I could see the rage burning in his eyes, and I tried to force myself to obey the Fifth Commandment, but words just came pouring out of me. 'Shame on you, Pa, pounding your cocker for a woman you done gunned down in cold blood. Don't you think I don't remember the way you kilt her, shot her in the back whilst she were crossing that bridge, and the Choctaw watching on t'other side in his top hat and morning dress, with his four slaves behind him, waiting to take her home.'

My pa was silent for a few moments, and the room was filled with the caterwauling of the niggers from the graveyard. We stood there staring each other down. Then he grabbed me by the scruff of the neck and dragged me over to the chair, lurching

and stumbling because he hadn't even bothered to pull his
britches back up, and I could smell the liquor on him; and he
murmured, 'You are right; I have sinned; I have sinned; but it
is for the son to take on the sins of the world: the paschal lamb;
you, Jimmy Lee; oh, God, but you do resemble her; you do
remind me of her; oh, it is a heavy burden for you, my son, to
take on the sins of the world, but I know that you do it for
love,' and suchlike, and he reached for the hickory and stripped
the shirt off of my back and began to lay to with a will, all the
while crying out, 'Oh, Mary, oh, my Mary, I am so sorry that
you left me . . . oh, my son, you shall bear thirty-nine stripes on
your back in memory of our saviour . . . oh, you shall redeem
me . . .' and the hickory sang and I cried out, not so much from
the pain, for that my back was become like leather from long
abuse, and warn't much feeling left in it . . . I gritted my teeth
and try to bear it like I borne it so many times before, but this
time it was not to be borne, and when the thirty-ninth stripe
was inflicted I tore myself loose from the chair and I screamed,
'You ain't hurting me no more, because I ain't no paschal lamb
and your sins is *your* sins, not mine,' and I pushed him aside
with all my strength.

'God, God,' he says in a whisper, 'I see God.' And he rolls his
eyes heavenwards, excepting that heaven were a leaky roof
made from a few planks left over from the slaves' quarters.

Then I took the rifle from the wall and pounded him in the
head with the stock, three, four, five, six times until he done
slumped on to the straw.

Oh, I was raging and afeared, and I run away right then and
there, without even making sure iffen he was kilt or not. I run
right through them darkies, who was a-singing and a-carrying
on to wake the very dead; they did not see a scrawny boy,
small for his age, slip through them and out towards the woods.

I run and run with three dimes in my pocket and a sheaf of
shinplasters that I stole from the chest of drawers, I run and I
don't even recollect iffen I put out the fire on the stove.

And that was how I come to be with the regiment, tramping
through blood and mud and shifting my bowels away with the

flux each day; and that was how I come to be sleeping next to old Joseph, the hoodoo doctor, who become another father to me.

★

I did not confess to old Joseph or even to myself that I had done my father in. Mayhap he was still alive. I tried not to think on him. My old life was dead. Surely I could not go back to the Jackson place, nor the army, nor any other place from which I run. There was just me and the old nigger now, scavengers, carrion birds, eaters of the dead.

Yes, and sure it was human flesh old Joseph fed me that night, and again that morning. He showed me the manner of taking it, for there was certain corpses that cried out to be let be, whilst others craved to be consumed. We followed the army at a safe distance, and when they moved on we took possession of the slain. He could always sniff out where a battle was going to be. He never carried nothing with him excepting a human skull, painted black, that was full of herbs, the same herbs that he always smelled of.

Oh, it was God's country we done passed through, hills, forests, meadows, creeks, and all this beauty marred by the handiwork of men. Old Joseph showed me not to drink from the bloodied streams but to lick the dew from flower petals and cupped leaves of a morning. As his trust of me grew, he became more bold. We went into encampments and sat amongst the soldiers, and they never seen us, not once.

'We is invisible,' old Joseph told me.

And then it struck me, for we stood in broad daylight beside a willow tree, and on the other side of the brook was mayhap fifty tents and behind them a dense wood. The air was moist and thick. I could see members of my old company, with their skull faces too small for their grey coats, barely able to lift their bayonets off the ground, and they was sitting there huddled together waiting for gruel, but there I was, nourished by the dead, my flesh starting to fill out and the redness back in my cheeks; it struck me that they couldn't see me even though I was a jumping up and down on the other side of the stream; and I said to old Joseph, 'I don't think we are invisible. I think ... oh, old Joseph, I think we have been dead ever since the day we met.'

Old Joseph laughed; it were a dry laugh, like the wind stirring the leaves in autumn; and he said, 'You ain't dead yet, honey; feel the flesh on them bones; no, your *beau-père* he nurturing you back to life.'

'Then why don't they see us? Even when we walk amongst them?'

'Because I has cast a cloak of darkness about us. We be wearing the face of a dark god over our own.'

'I don't trust God. Whenever my pa seen God, he hurt me.'

Smiling, he said, 'You daddy warn't a true preacher, honey; he just a *houngan macoute*, a man which *use* the name of God to adorn hisself.'

And taking my hand he led me acrosst that branch and we was right amongst the soldiers, and still they did not see me. We helped ourselves to hardtack and coffee right out of the kettle. In the distance I heard the screams of a man whose leg they was fixing to hack off. Around us men lay moaning. There is a sick-sweet body smell that starving men give off when they are burning up their last shreds of flesh to fuel their final days. That's how I knew they was near death. They was shivering with cold, even though it were broad daylight. Lord, many of them was just children, and some still younger than myself. I knew that the war was lost, or soon would be. I had no country, and no father save for a darkie witch-doctor from Haiti.

There come a bugle call and a few men looked up, though most of them just goes on laying in their misery. Old Joseph and I saw soldiers come into the camp. They had a passel of niggers with them, niggers in blue uniforms, all chained up in a long row behind a wagon that was piled high with confiscated arms. They was as starved and miserable as our own men. They stared ahead as they trudged out of the wood and into the clearing. There was one or two white men with them too, officers I reckoned.

A pause, and the bugle sounded again. Then a captain come out of a tent and addressed the captives. He said, in a lugubrious voice, as though he were weary of making this announcement: 'According to the orders given me by the Congress of the Confederate States of America, all Negroes apprehended while in the uniform of the North are not to be considered prisoners of war, but shall be returned instantly to a condition of slavery or shot. Any white officer arrested while in command of such Negroes shall be considered to be inciting rebellion and also shot.' He turned and went back into his tent, and the convoy moved onwards, past the camp, upstream, towards another part of the woods.

'*Oba kosó!*' the old man whispered. 'They gone kill them.'

'Let's go away,' I said.

'No,' said old Joseph, 'I feels the wind of the gods blowing down upon me. I feels the breath of the loa. I is standing on the coils of Koulèv, the earth-serpent. Oh, no, Marse Jimmy Lee, I don't be going nowhere, but you free to come and go as you pleases of course, being white.'

'You know that ain't so,' I said. 'I'm less free than you. And I know if I leave you I will leave the shelter of your invisibility spell.' For that I gazed right into the eyes of the prisoners, and tasted their rancid breath, and smelled the pus of their wounds, and seen no sign of recognition. There was something to his magic, though I was sure that it come of the dark places, and not of God.

So I followed him alongside the creek as the captives were led into the wood, followed them uphill a ways until we reached the edge of a shallow gully, and there was already niggers there, digging to make it deeper, and I seen what was going to happen and I didn't want to look, because this warn't a battle, this were butchery pure and simple.

Our soldiers didn't mock the prisoners and didn't call them no names. They were too tired and too hungry. The blacks and the whites, they didn't show no passion in their faces. They just wanted it to end. Our men done lined the niggers and their officers up all along the edge of the ditch, and searched through their pockets for any coins or crumbs, and they turned them so they faced the gully and they done shot them in the back, one by one, until the pit was filled; then the Southerners turned and filed back to the camp. Oh, God! As the first shots rung out it put me in mind of my mother Mary, halfway across the bridge, with her old life behind her and her new life ahead of her, dead on her face, and the bloodstain spreading from her back on to the lace and calico.

And old Joseph said, 'Honey, I seen what I must do. And it a dark journey that I must take, and maybe you don't be strong enough to come with me. But I hates to journey alone. Old Joseph afraid too, betimes, spite of his 'leventy-leven years upon this earth. I calls the powers to witness, *ni ayé àti ni òrun.*'

'What does that mean, old Joseph?'

'*In heaven as it is in earth.*'

I saw the way his eye glowed and I was powerful afraid. He had become more than a shrunken old man. Seemed like he drew the sun's light into his face and shone brighter than the summer sky. He set his cauldron-skull down on the ground and said, again and again, '*Koulèv, Koulèv-O! Damballah Wedo, Papa! Koulèv, Koulèv-O! Damballah Wedo, Papa!*'

And then he says, in a raspy voice, 'Watch out, Marse Jimmy Lee, the god gone come down and mount my body now … stand clear less you wants to swept away by the breath of the serpent!' And he mutters to hisself, 'Oh, *dieux puissants*, why you axing me to make biggest magic, me a old magician without no *poudre* and no herbs? Oh, take this cup from me, take, take this bitter poison from he lips, for old Joseph he don't study life and death no more.'

And his old body started to shake, and he ripped off his patch and threw it on to the mud, and I looked into the empty eye-socket and saw an inner eye, blood-red and shiny as a ruby. And he sank down on his knees in front of the pit of dead men and he went on a-mumbling and a-rocking, back and forth, back and forth, and seemed like he was a-speaking in tongues. And his good eye rolled right up into its socket.

'Why, old Joseph,' I says to him, 'what are you fixing to do?'

But he paid me no mind. He just went on a-shimmying and a-shaking, and presently he rose up from where he was and started to dance a curious hopping sort of dance, and with every hop he cried, '*Shangó! Shangó!*' in a voice that was steadily losing its human qualities. And soon his voice was rolling like thunder, and presently it *was* the thunder, for the sky was lowering and lightning was lancing the cloud-peaks.

Oh, the sky became dark. The cauldron seethed and glowed, though he hadn't even touched it. I knew he were sure possessed. The dark angels he done told me of, they was speaking to him out of the mouth of hell.

I reckoned I was not long for this world, for the old man was a-hollering at the top of his lungs and we warn't far from the encampment; but no one came looking for us. Mayhap they was huddled in their tents hiding from the thunder. Presently it began to rain, it pelted us and soaked us, that rain; it were a hot rain, scalding to my skin. And when the lightning flashed I looked into the pit and I thought I saw something moving. Mayhap it were just the rushing waters, throwing the corpses one against t'other. I crept closer to the edge of the gully. I didn't heed old Joseph's warning. I peered over the edge and in the next flash of lightning I saw them a-writhing and a-shaking their arms and legs, and their necks a-craning this way and that, and I thought to myself, old Joseph he is raising the dead.

Old Joseph just went on screaming out those African words and leaping up and waving his arms. The rain battered my body and I was near fainting from it, for the water flooded my nostrils and drenched my lungs and when I gasped for air I swallowed more and more water; I don't know how the old man kept on dancing; in the lightning flashes I saw him, dark and lithe, and the sluicing rain made him glisten and made his chest and arms to look like the scales of a great black serpent; I looked on him and breathed in the burning water, and the pit of dead niggers quook as iffen the very earth were opening up, and there come a blue light from the mass grave, so blinding

that I could see no more; and so, at last, I passed out from the
terror of it.

★

When I done opened my eyes the rain was just a memory; the
sun was rising; the forest was silent and shrouded in mist. And
I thought to myself, I have been dreaming, and I am still beside
the creek where the dead bodies lay, and I never did see no old
Joseph out of my past; but then I saw him frying up a bit of salt
pork he done salvaged from the camp. Warn't no morning
bugle calls, and I reckon the company done up and gone in the
middle of the night, soon as the storm subsided.

Old Joseph, the patch was over his eye again, and he was
singing to hisself, that song I heard as a child. And when he
saw me stir, he said, 'Marse Jimmy Lee, you awake now.'

'What is that song?' I asked him.

'It called *Au Claire de la Lune*, honey; "by the light of the
moon."'

I sat up. 'Joseph?'

'What, Marse Jimmy Lee?'

'Last night I had the strangest dream ... more like a vision. I
dreamed you were possessed, and you pranced about and
waved your arms and sang songs in a African language, and
you raised up nigger soldiers from the grave.'

'Life is a dream, honey,' he says, 'we calls them *les zombis*. It
from a Kikongo word *nzambi* that mean a dead man that walk
the earth.'

The fog began to clear a little and I saw their feet. Black feet,
still shackled, still covered with chafing sores. We was surrounded by them. And as the sunlight began to dissipate the
mist, I could see their faces; it was them which had been kilt
and buried in the pit; I knew some of their faces. For though
they stirred, they moved, they looked about them, there were
no fire in their eyes, and didn't have no breath in their nostrils.
Mayhap they wasn't dead, but they wasn't alive, neither.

They stood there, looming over us. Each one with a wound
clean through him. Each one smelling of old Joseph's herbs.

'The magic still in me,' old Joseph said, 'even without the *coup poudre.*'

I reckon I have never been more scared than I was then. My skin was crawling and my blood was racing.

'I never thought that old magic still in me,' said Joseph again. There was wonderment in his voice. No fear. The dead men surrounded us, waiting; seemed like they had no mind of their own.

'Oh, Joseph, what are we going to do?'

'Don't know, white child. I's still in the dark. The vision don't come as clear to me no more; old Joseph he old, he old.'

He fed me and gave me genuine coffee to drink, for the slain Yankees had carried some with them. I rose and went over to the pit, and it were sure enough empty save for the two white officers. 'Why didn't you raise them too?' I said.

'Warn't no sense in it, Marse Jimmy Lee; for white folks there is a heaven and a hell; there ain't no middle ground; best to forget them.'

So we threw dirt over them and we marched on, and the column of undead darkies followed us. I could not name the places that we passed, but old Joseph knew where he was going. It was towards the rising sun so I guessed it was south.

At nightfall we rested. We found a farmhouse. There warn't no people and the animals was all took away, but I found a ham a-hanging in the larder, and I feasted. In the night I slept in a real bed. Old Joseph sat out on the porch. The *zombis* did not sleep. They stood in a ring outside the house and they swayed softly to the sound of Joseph's singing; as I looked out of the smashed window I could see them in the moonlight, and there was still no fire in their eyes; and I recollected that they hadn't partaken of no victuals. What was it like to be a *zombi*? Iffen that the eyes are the windows of the soul, then surely there warn't no souls inside those fleshy shells.

We found plenty of gold in the abandoned house, they done hid it in a well, which was surrounded by dead Yankees; I reckon they done poisoned it so that the northerners wouldn't be able to drink their water. But poison means naught to the dead.

And we walked on; and the passel of walking dead became a company, for wherever we went we found niggers that had been kilt, not just the ones in Yankee uniform but sometimes a woman lying dead in a ditch, or a young buck chained to a tree that was just abandoned and let starve to death when his masters fled from the enemy, and one time we found seven high-yaller children dead in a cage, with gunshot wounds to their heads; for they was frenzied times, and men were driven to acts not thought upon in times of peace. It was amongst the dead children that I found another cornstalk *poupée* like the one old Joseph gave me ten years before, a-sitting in a vial in the clenched fist of a dead little girl; after we done wakened them, she held it out to me, and I thought there were a glimmer in her eye, but mayhap it were only my imagination.

'Get up and walk,' old Joseph said. And they walked.

And I said over and over to him, 'Old Joseph, where are we going?'

And he said, 'Towards freedom.'

'But freedom is in the north, ain't it?'

'Freedom in the heart, honey.'

We marched. For many days we didn't see no white folks at all. We saw burned hulks of farms, and stray dogs hunting in packs. We passed other great battlefields, and them that was worth reviving, that still had enough flesh on them to be able to march, old Joseph raised up. He was growing in power. It got so he would just wave his hands, and say one or two words, and the dead man would climb right out of the ground. And I took to repeating the words to myself, soundlessly at first, just moving my lips; then softly, then – for when he were a-concentrating on his magic, he couldn't see nothing of the world – I would shout out those words along with him, I would wrap my tongue around them twisted and barbarian sounds, and I would tell myself, 'twas I which raised them, I which reached into the abyss and drawed them out.

Still we encountered no sign of human life. The summer sun

streamed down on us by day and seemed like I sweat blood. It warn't at all certain to me that we was still alive and on this earth, for the land was a waste land, spite of the verdant meadows and the mountains blanketed with purple flowers, spite of the rich-smelling earth and the warm rain. Sometimes I think that the country we was wandering in was an illusion, a false Eden. Or that we was somehow half in, half out of the world.

Though I didn't know where the road was leading, yet I was happy. I trusted old Joseph, and I didn't have no one else left in the world. The only times I become sad was thinking on my pa and Momma's death, and wondering iffen my pa was with God now, for he said he done seen the face of God before I smashed his head. Sometimes I dreamed about coming home to see him well again. But they was only dreams. I knew that I had kilt him.

On the seventh day we come onc't more into the sight of men.

*

The road become wider and we was coming into the vicinity of a town. I knew this was a port, maybe Charleston. There warn't no signs to tell us, but Pa and I had been booted out of Charleston once, I remembered the way the wind smelt, wet and tangy. A few miles outside town our road joined up with a wider road that come in a straight line from due north. On the other road, straggling down to meet us, we saw a company of greycoats.

Not many of them, maybe three dozen. They warn't exactly marching. Some was leaning on each other, some hobbling, and one, a slip of a boy, tapped on the side of a skinless drum. Their clothes was in tatters and most of them didn't have no rifles. They was just old men and boys, for the able-bodied had long since fallen.

They seen us and one of them cried out, 'Nigger soldiers!' They fell into a pathetic semblance of a formation, and them which had rifles aimed them and them which had crutches brandished them at us.

I shouted out, 'Let us pass . . . we don't have no quarrel with you.' For they were wretched creatures, these remnants of the Southern army, and I was sure that the war was already lost, and they was coming back to what was left of their homes.

But one boy, mayhap their leader, screamed at me, 'Nigger lover! Traitor!' I looked in his eyes and saw we were just alike, poor trash fighting a rich man's war, him and me; and I pitied the deluded soul. Because I knew now that there warn't no justice in this war, and that neither side had foughten for God, but only for hisself.

'It's no use!' I shouted at the boy who was so like myself. 'These darkies ain't even alive; they're shadows marching to the sea; they ain't got souls to kill.'

And old Joseph said, 'March on, my children.'

They commenced to fire on us.

This was the terriblest thing which I did witness on that journey. For the nigger soldiers marched and marched, and not a bullet could stop them. The miniés flew and the white boys shrieked out a ghostly echo of a rebel yell, and *les zombis* kept right on coming and coming, and me and old Joseph with them, untouched by the bullets, for his magic still shielded our mortal flesh. The niggers marched. Their faces was ripped asunder and still they marched. Their brains came oozing from their skulls, their guts came writhing from their bellies, and still they marched. They marched until they were too close for bullets. Then the white boys flung themselves at us, and they was ripped to pieces. They was tore limb from limb by dead men which stared with glazed and vacant eyes. It took but a few minutes, this final skirmish of the war. Their yells died in their throats. The *zombis* broke their necks and flung them to the ground. Their strength warn't a human kind of strength. They'd shove their hands into an old man's belly and snap his spine and pull out the intestines like a coil of rope. They'd take a rifle and break the barrel in two.

There was no anger in what the *zombis* done. And they didn't

make no noise whilst they was killing. They done it the way
you might darn a sock or feed the chickens; it were just
something which had to be done.

And we marched onwards, leaving the bodies to rot; it was
getting on towards sunset now.

Oh, I was angry. The boys we kilt warn't no strangers from
the north; they could have been my brothers. Oh, I screamed in
rage at old Joseph; I didn't trust him no more; the happiness
had left me.

'Did you hear what he called me?' I shouted. 'A traitor to my
people. A nigger lover. And it's God's plain truth. If you
wanted freedom why didn't you go north into the arms of the
Yankees? You spoke to me of a big magic, and of the coils of
the serpent Koulèv, and the wind of the gods, and the voices of
darker angels . . . to what end? It were Satan's magic, magic to
give the dead an illusion of life, so you could kill more of my
people!'

'Be still,' he said to me, as the church spires of the port town
rose up in the distance. 'Your war don't be my war. You think
the Yankees got theyselfs kilt to set old Joseph free? You think
the 'mancipation proclamation was wrote to give the nigger
back he soul? I say to you, white child, that a piece of paper
don't make men free. The black man in this land he ain't gone
be free tomorrow nor in a hundred years nor in a thousand. I
didn't bring men back from the outer darkness so they could
shine you shoes and wipe you butts. The army I lead, he
kingdom don't be of this earth.'

'You are mad, old Joseph,' I said, and I wept, for he was no
longer a father to me.

★

We marched into the town. Children peered from behind
empty beer kegs with solemn eyes. Horses reared up and
whinnied. Women stared sullenly at us. The Yankees had
already took the town, and half the houses was smouldering,
and we didn't see no grown men. The stars and stripes flew

over the ruint courthouse. I reckon folks thought we was just another company of the conquering army.

We reached the harbour. There was one or two sailing ships docked there; rickety ships with tattered sails. The army of dead men stood at attention and old Joseph said to me: 'Now I understands why you come with me so far. There a higher purpose to everything, *ni ayé àti ni òrun.*'

I didn't want to stay with him any more. When I seen the way *les zombis* ploughed down my countrymen, I had been moved to a powerful rage, and the rage would not die away. 'What higher purpose?' I said. And the salt wind chafed my lips.

'You think,' said old Joseph, 'that old Joseph done tricked you, he done magicked you with mirrors and smoke; but I never told you we was fighting on the same side. But we come far together, and I wants you to do me one last favour afore we parts for all eternity.'

'And what sort of favour would that be, old sorcerer? I thought you could do anything.'

'Anything. But not this thing. You see, old Joseph a nigger. Nigger he can't go into no portside bar to offer gold for to buy him a ship.'

'You want a ship now? Where are you fixing to go? Back to Haiti, where the white man rules no more?'

Old Joseph said, 'Mayhap it a kind of Haiti where we go.' He laughed. 'Haiti, yes, Haiti! And I gone see my dear *mamman*, though she be cold in her grave sixty year past. Or mayhap it mother Africa herself we go to. *Oba kosó!*'

And I remembered that he had told me: *My kingdom is not of this earth.* He had used the words of our saviour and our Lord. Oh, the ocean wind were warm, and it howled, and the torn sails clattered against the masts. The air fair dripped with moisture. And the niggers stood like statues, all-unseeing.

'I'll do as you ask,' I said, and I took the sack of gold we had gathered from the poisoned well, and I walked along the harbour until I found a bar and ship's captain for hire, which was not hard, for the embargo had starved their business. And presently I come back and told old Joseph everything was ready. And the niggers lined up, ready to embark. Night was falling.

But as they prepared themselves to board that ship, I could hold my tongue no more. 'Old Joseph,' I said, 'your kingdom is founded on a lie. You have waked these bodies from the earth, but where are their souls? You may dream of leading these creatures to a mystic land acrosst the sea, and you may dream of freeing them for ever from the bonds of servitude, but how can you free what can't be freed? How can you free a rock, a tree, a piece of earth? Dust they were and dust they ever shall be, world without end.'

And the *zombi* warriors stood, unmoving and unblinking, and not a breath passed their lips, though that the wind was rising and whipping at our faces.

And old Joseph looked at me long and hard, and I knew that I had said the thing that must be said. He whispered, 'Out of the mouths of babes and sucklings hast thou ordained strength, O Lord.' He fell down on his knees before me and said, 'And all this time I thought that *I* the wise one and you the student! Oh, Marse Jimmy Lee, you done spoke right. There be no life in *les zombis* because I daresn't pay the final price. But now I's *gone* make that sacrifice. Onc't I done gave my eye in exchange for knowledge. But there be *two* trees in Eden, Marse Jimmy Lee; there be the tree of knowledge, and there be the tree of life.'

So saying he covered his face with his hands. He plunged his thumb into the socket of his good eye and he plucked it out, screaming to almighty God with the pain of it. His agony was real. His shrieking curdled my blood. It brought back my pa's chastisements and my momma's dying and the tramping of my bare feet on sharp stones and the sight of all my comrades, pierced through by bayonets, cloven by cannon, their limbs ripped off, their bellies torn asunder, their lives gushing hot and young and crimson into the stream. Oh, but I craved to carry his pain, but he were the one that were chosen to bear it, and I was the one which brung him to the understanding of it.

And now his eye were in his hand, a round, white, glistening pearl, and he cries out in a thunderous voice, 'If thine eye offend thee, pluck it out!' and he takes blind aim and hurls the eye with all his might into the mighty sea.

I clenched the *poupée* in my hand.

Then came lightning, for old Joseph had summoned the power of the serpent Koulèv, whose coils were entwined about the earth. Then did he unleash the rain. Then did he turn to me, with the gore gushing from the yawning socket, and cry to me, a good-for-nothing white trash boy which kilt his own father and stole from the dead, 'Thou hast redeemed me.'

Then, and only then, did I see the *zombis* smile. Then, as the rain softened, as the sky did glow with a cold blue light that didn't come from no sun nor moon, then did I hear the laughter of the dead, and the fire of life begin to flicker in their eyes. But they was already trooping up the gangplank, and presently there was only the old man, purblind now, and like to die I thought.

'Farewell,' he says to me.

And I said, 'No, old Joseph. You are blind now. You need a boy to hold your hand and guide you, to be your eyes against the wild blue sea.'

'Not blind,' he said. 'I *chooses* not to see. I gone evermore be looking inwards, at the glory and the majesty of eternal light.'

'But what have I? Where can I go, excepting that I go with you?'

'Honey, you has lived but fourteen of your threescore and ten. It don't be written that you's to follow a old man acrosst the sea to a land that maybe don't even *be* a land save in that old man's dream. Go now. But first you gone kiss your *beau-père* goodbye, for I loves you.'

My tears were brine and his were blood. As I kissed his cheek the salt did run together with the crimson. I saw him no more; I did not see the ship sail from the port; for my eyes was blinded with weeping.

★

So I walked and walked and walked until I come back to the Jackson place. The mansion were a cinder, and even the fields was all burnt up, and the animals was dead. The place was looted good and thorough; warn't one thing of value in the vicinity, not a gold piece nor a silver spoon nor even the rugs that the Jacksons done bought from a French merchant.

I walked up the low knoll to where the nigger graveyard was and where our shack onc't stood. The wooden markers was all charred, and here and there was a shred of homespun clinging to them; and I thought to myself, mayhap the Yankees come down to the Jackson place not an hour after I done run away, whilst the slaves was still a-singing their spirituals. That cloth was surely torn off some of the slave women, for the Yankees loved to have their way with darkies. And I thought, mayhap my pa is still laying inside that shack, in the inner room, beside the locket with Momma's picture, with his hickory in his fist, with his britches down about his ankles.

And so it was I found him.

He warn't rank no more. It had been many months since I run off. Warn't much left of his face that the worms hadn't ate. At his naked thighs, the bone poked through the papery hide, and there was a swarm of ants. It was a miracle there was this much left of him, for there was wild dogs roaming the fields.

I set down the *poupée* on the chair and got to wondering what I should do. What I wanted most in life were a new beginning. I spoke to that doll, for I knew that old Joseph's spirit was in it somehow, and I said, 'I don't know where you come from, and I don't know where you are. But oh, give me the strength to begin onc't more, oh, carry me back from the land of the dead.'

Without thinking I started to murmur the words of power, the African words I done mimicked when I watched him raise the dead. I knelt down beside the corpse of my pa and waited for the breath of serpent. I whispered them words over and over until my mind emptied itself and was filled with the souls of darker angels.

I reckon I knelt all night long, or mayhap many nights. But when I opened my eyes again there was flesh on my father's bones, and he was beginning to rouse himself; and his eyes had the fire of life, for that old Joseph had sacrificed his second eye.

'You sure have growed, son,' he says softly. 'You ain't a sapling no more; you're a mighty tree.'

'Yes, Pa,' says I.

'Oh, son, you have carried me back from a terrible dream. In that dream I abandoned you, and I practised all manner of cruelty upon you, and a dark angel came to you and became your new pa; and you followed him to the edge of the river that divides the quick from the dead.'

'Yes, Pa. But I stopped at the river bank and watched him sail away. And I come back to you.'

'Oh, Jimmy Lee, my son, I have seen hell. I have been down into the fire of damnation, and I've felt the loneliness of perdition. And the cruellest torture was being cut off from you, my flesh and blood. Oh, sweet Jesus, Jimmy Lee, it were only that you made me think on her so much, she which I killed, she which I never loved more even as I sent the bullet flying into her back.'

And this was strange, for in the old days my pa had only spoke of heaven, and of seeing the face of God, and when he done seen God he would wear me out, calling on His holy name to witness his infamy and my sacrifice. But now he had seen hell and he was full of gentleness.

And then he said to me, 'My son, I craves your forgiveness.'

'Ain't nothing to forgive.'

'Then give me your love,' says he, 'for you are tall and strong, and I have become old; and it is now for you to be the father, and I the child.'

It were time to cross the bridge. It were time to heal the hurting.

'My love you have always had, Pa.'

So saying, I embraced him; and thus it was our war came to an end.

Darker Angels was written in response to a challenge: could I, a person born in Asia and raised in Europe, write a meaningful story about something as American as the War Between the States? Well, Thailand *is* considerably south of the Mason-Dixon line, and I *did* live in Virginia for seven years. But in the end (in this third and last story in this volume to deal with theology and zombies) I found myself using the Civil War to write about families, about reconciliation, and about redemption, which are themes that are common to us all.